NOBODY SAW HIM

BOOKS BY LIZ LAWLER

My Husband's Lies
The Next Wife
The Silent Mother
The Nurse's Secret

I'll Find You
Don't Wake Up

NOBODY SAW HIM

LIZ LAWLER

bookouture

Published by Bookouture in 2025

An imprint of Storyfire Ltd.
Carmelite House
50 Victoria Embankment
London EC4Y 0DZ

www.bookouture.com

The authorised representative in the EEA is Hachette Ireland
8 Castlecourt Centre
Dublin 15 D15 XTP3
Ireland
(email: info@hbgi.ie)

Copyright © Liz Lawler, 2025

Liz Lawler has asserted her right to be identified as the author of this work.

All rights reserved. No part of this publication may be reproduced, stored in any retrieval system, or transmitted, in any form or by any means, electronic, mechanical, photocopying, recording or otherwise, without the prior written permission of the publishers.

ISBN: 978-1-80550-012-4
eBook ISBN: 978-1-80550-011-7

This book is a work of fiction. Names, characters, businesses, organizations, places and events other than those clearly in the public domain, are either the product of the author's imagination or are used fictitiously. Any resemblance to actual persons, living or dead, events or locales is entirely coincidental.

For my parents – my constant inspiration.

ONE

It started to rain as Jo drove into the car park. It was a rough patch of ground with tall weeds growing around the perimeter. It looked busy, but perhaps not all the cars were there for swimming. She wouldn't know until they got inside, so there was no point worrying. The pool building was behind the church and next to a school. It was plain in design – pebble-dash beige walls with high-up frosted windows, held open by latches.

She switched off the engine and checked she had her purse in the outside pocket of the swim bag. She turned in her seat to look at Sam. His light-brown hair, the same colour as hers, fell across his forehead. It was a shame to wake him when he looked so peaceful.

'Hey, sleepyhead, we're here. I'll be the shark first, and you'll have to get away from me. But be warned. I'm very hungry.'

His normal gleeful smile didn't appear, making her heart ache. His happiness was everything. There was nothing she wouldn't do to give him that.

She checked there was room to open her door without hitting the vehicle beside her. Something she had become more conscious of – the Range Rover doors were wider than she was used to. She helped Sam out of his seat, tucking him under her puffer coat to keep him dry, weaving through parked vehicles for the few seconds walk to the glass-door entrance. It was heavy to open and a pity to have it closed. The moisture in the air clung to her scalp and skin within moments. The smell of chlorine was strong even out in reception, so they probably wouldn't be swimming for long, even with goggles.

There was no one at the counter to take their money. The chrome barrier was open. The prices for admission were on a laminated board. *Family Swim: Adult 1 child £6.50.* It was unbelievably cheap, and quite a casual setup. She would pay when she saw someone. Wanting to get out of her clothes before she melted, she led them along a narrow passage to the ladies' changing room.

She opened the toilet door so they could both have a wee before they got changed, but it was tiny, with barely room for one person to get in it. She moved on and found the first empty cubicle and plonked her bag onto the bench.

'I need a wee before we swim. Do you want to have one?'

He shook his head.

'Sure?'

He nodded.

'Okay. Stay on this bench. I'll only be a second.'

The toilet stall was so small she had to angle herself out of the way, knees touching the toilet bowl, to close the door. It was ridiculous. She quickly undid her jeans and was about to pull them down when she saw the wet seat. God's sake, she'd pee herself if she didn't go soon. While she pulled tightly packed toilet paper from the dispenser on the wall to dry the plastic, she noticed the noise of an influx of people using the changing room. Half a minute later, pants up, she was done.

She unlatched the door to see women and children clad in wet swimsuits, waiting for cubicles. Her eyes fixed on the closed door of her cubicle as she made her way towards it. A hand went up in her face before she could touch the door.

'Sorry, love, but I'm next.'

Jo automatically shook her head. 'My son's in there. I was just in the toilet before I got changed.'

The woman frowned, her expression saying Jo was wrong. 'Don't think so, love. My sister's in there.'

Jo tapped on the door. 'You're mistaken. I only just left him there a minute ago. My bag's in there. Sam, can you open the door? It's Mummy.'

'Give us a sec. I'm putting on my knickers,' came an irate voice.

A prickle of fear swept across Jo's chest. Her hand slammed on the door. 'Open it, please. Right now. Or I'll get the manager.'

The door yanked open. A wet round face glared at her. Bare-breasted, wearing just pants, she shoved Jo's bag at her, making Jo grab hold of it. 'There's your bloody bag. You shouldn't have left it in here. You can't reserve it like a towel on a sunbed.'

Jo stared hard at the bench behind the woman to confirm that Sam wasn't there. 'Did you see him?' She held the flat of her hand as a measuring tool at her hip. 'He's about this high, light-brown hair. He's wearing dark-blue joggers.'

The woman was shaking her head.

Jo panicked and turned to ask everyone around her if they'd seen him. 'He's five years old,' she said hurriedly. 'Wearing a dark-green top, with a crocodile on the front. Dark joggers. Spider-Man trainers.' She hollered out his name. 'Sam! Sam! Where are you?'

The woman in the cubicle had thrown on a T-shirt and wrapped a towel around her waist. She caught hold of Jo's forearm. 'Calm down, love, or you'll have a panic attack. We'll help find him.' She addressed the room. 'If some of you check the pool, and some of you go outside, in case he's there. Ladies, in the cubicles, shout out if any of you have seen a small boy on their own. And, please, can everyone just open their cubicles to reassure this mum he's not in one of them?'

Doors clicked open. No one called out to say they'd seen him. Jo made a quick tour along the row of cubicles, hoping every child she saw of a similar height to Sam was him, before spotting a second toilet stall with a baby changing sign. She could hear soft humming coming from inside and banged the door hard. A baby let out a piercing wail, startling her, the crying becoming more intense with every second. Jo was rooted in indecision, standing there waiting for it to open. The piercing cry was suddenly right in her ears with the sound barrier of the door gone. She saw at once a writhing, screaming baby, an engorged breast leaking milk, and a mother jiggling the baby to calm it. Jo held up a hand to say sorry, before the door closed in her face.

She was wasting time. She had to search the rest of the building.

Hurrying toward the swimming pool, she sped past the people telling her the pool was closing, needing to see for herself that he wasn't there. With every step, she could feel the swell of panic pushing its way up into her throat.

A litany of prayers burned themselves into her brain. *Please God, don't let him have drowned, just let me find him, let me see him, let me hear him, please, please, please.*

A lifeguard was trying to fish out a soiled nappy floating in the water, and a lone swimmer was climbing out, shouting his disgust. She dashed back the way she came, grabbing at locked door handles to cupboards or offices, scanning for any potential hiding place.

Maybe he went outside. Maybe because of the noise, maybe to look for her. She could hear his name being called as she ran back through the changing room, along the narrow passage, and out the heavy-glass door. There were too many people obscuring her vision – women in a state of undress, towels around shoulders, bare legs and bare feet. The fear in her chest expanded at the idle way some of them were looking around and under cars, over the stone wall of the church, through railings around the school.

Then giving up, slowing down, showing defeat.

Blood thrummed in her ears as she raced towards her car, pain in her breastbone with every heave of her chest. He would be sitting by the car, waiting for her. Her voice screeched out his name as she ran once, then twice, around the vehicle. Staring wildly around her, she ran back and forth, crossing from one side to the other, looking around every vehicle, searching every inch of ground for clues. The woman with the wet round face and a towel around her waist was standing in front of her, putting her arms out to catch her.

Jo reacted violently and pushed past so fast her foot caught in a pothole and sent her sprawling on the ground. She picked herself up, her palms scraped from the gravel, numb to the pain of her torn skin. She ran through the car park to the road, scanning up and down the pavements on both sides, desperate for a sight of him. Desperate not to give in to panic.

Jo felt a macabre déjà vu. How could it have happened again? She would see him any second now and wake from this nightmare. There weren't that many routes he could take. She stepped out into the middle of the road, and hope beat in her breast at the sight of people standing under the porch of the church, posing for photos. She realised now why the car park was so full. A wedding. She ran towards them, calling out, waving her arms for their attention. 'Has a small boy gone past here? Light-brown hair. Green top?'

Seconds wasted as they conferred with one another, before shaking their heads.

Jo ran to a pub on the corner, pulling at the handle on the

locked door, before darting across the roundabout to the florist, then the bakery, then an estate agent, bursting through their doors to ask if anyone saw him, before tearing back across the road to the swimming pool, leaving in her wake the owners of the shops watching out of their windows. This was taking too long.

She arrived back at the car park entrance and stopped, trying to get her breath, as a white-ribboned wedding car slowly pulled away from the church, the bride and groom waving to the wedding guests and the bride's serene smile showing her intense happiness at the new life in front of her.

Jo shook, violent ripples coursing through her. She mustn't give up. Someone was going to shout at any moment now that they had him, that they had found him. He would appear. It had to be.

A hard raindrop landed on her cheek.

She closed her eyes, summoning every image of God, praying He would help her. Praying that when she opened her eyes, Sam would be standing in front of her.

Rain dropped on her hair, her nose, her hands.

He had no coat on.

She opened her eyes. Everything was the same.

A hand touched her shoulder. The woman with the round wet face shared her worry. 'We've called the police, love. Best thing to do.'

And then it was real. No turning away. She tried to stop the terror from spreading and increasing. But there was no stopping it flooding her being, liquifying her insides, consuming her whole. The pure liquid dread of accepting he was gone.

TWO

At twelve twenty, Moraine Morgan was summoned to DI Stone's office. She knew why before entering the room. A five-year-old boy had been reported missing at ten forty-five a.m., and CID had taken over. An all car respond notice had been sent out. Every available officer had converged on the scene to search the area. Social media was being used to raise public awareness and appeal for witnesses, dashcam footage and doorbell camera recordings. Air support was deployed almost immediately to assist police officers on the ground. One hour and thirty-five minutes had passed with no sightings and no leads. The Golden Hour – where time was of the essence – had come and gone. She had a strong feeling that her plans for the evening – tapas at Pintxo's with singleton friends – were about to be cancelled.

    The SIO's mood was sombre. He was standing up from his desk as if about to leave, a sheaf of paperwork in his hand. 'DC Morgan, I need you with the family. Mother's been taken home. The father can't be contacted by phone. PC Kennedy is there already to lend a hand. Get as much detail as you can about the mother's movements up until the time she lost sight of her son. We'll be going live at one thirty with a public appeal. We need a better photo of the boy asap – the one PC Kennedy sent is blurred. Make it your first job when you get there.'

Moraine gave an affirmative nod. 'Understood, sir.'

'Get a feel for the family as soon as you can. Focus on building a picture of the boy's home life. Background information. Family disputes. If he has any medical conditions.'

'Yes, sir.'

Moraine walked out of the CID office, returning to her desk to collect her workbag and jacket. She'd been in the process of reading a charge file for ABH, going through the victim statement, about to make a referral to Victim Support. The boyfriend was still living at the home. Moraine wanted to make sure the woman felt safe with him being there. Once sorted out with a vehicle, she'd call them from the car before she set off.

Phone call made, she familiarised herself with the Mondeo controls and entered the postcode in the satnav. She could now focus on the task ahead and review the SIO's instructions. *Get a feel for the family.* Vital, in this type of case, to determine if the family was in any way involved. Statistically, twenty-four per cent of child abductions were perpetrated by a parent or other family members. Thirty-six per cent by someone known but not related. Leaving a large percentage perpetrated by a stranger. Equally, the family may not have any involvement and would be in shock. She wasn't jumping ahead. She just had to bear all possibilities in mind.

The rain was easing, but the sky gave no sign of the sun breaking through. The last Saturday of September seemed to herald the forecast for a wet autumn and summer over. The satnav took her past the racecourse, where she had a view across the Somerset countryside, then onto Freezing Hill, one of the highest points between the cities of Bristol and Bath. The village where Sam Jenkins went missing was ten miles away. It seemed a long way to go for a swim when they were much closer to the swimming pool in Bath.

According to the satnav, she should be at the location in six minutes, and she started looking out for signs to Beckley House. In four hundred and forty yards, she had to turn right. She slowed her speed at seeing a cattle grid across the entrance to a private road, and assumed this must be the place. She drove through the open gates passing some magnificent trees, before seeing the house. More like a manor, with multiple-gabled roofs and chimney stacks, surrounded by acres of land. It was not what she was expecting at all, and she set aside her preconceived notion of an ordinary family home.

She brought the car to a standstill in a space marked out for parking at the left side of the house. Plenty of bays, made to look natural, with bushes and slender cypress trees dividing off each parking place. It was cleverly done so as not to distract from the stunning frontage of Beckley House.

Conscious of the time ticking by, she pulled down the sun visor to check her appearance in the small mirror. At thirty-nine she looked her age, which was fine by her. Looking younger might be perceived as lacking experience. Wiping a finger across the sheen on her cheeks and smoothing her short black hair, she collected her thoughts. She had the name and age of the child, and the father and mother's names, and that was about it until she talked to the family.

She'd normally begin by visiting the scene of the incident, gathering information about what had taken place, before making any approach to the family. But because of the urgency of the situation, it was better she start here. Every hour that passed put the child at greater risk. At least her knock at the door would not be to tell a family that their loved one had died. She was there to help reunite them with their son, and every bit of information they could give her could be important to making that happen.

She exited the vehicle, taking a calming breath, and approached a heavy wooden door set in a stone surround. A stone plaque above, cemented into the brickwork, dated the building in faded Roman numerals. She raised the brass knocker and tapped twice. Expecting to be greeted by an adult, she was surprised as a young girl smiled out at her and said hello.

Moraine gave a hello back. 'Can I speak to the policeman who's here, please?'

She needed to know the situation before stepping in – was this a sister or other relative of Sam Jenkins, and, if so, were they aware of what had happened? She didn't want to cause an upset the minute she got here by revealing a brother or cousin was missing.

A moment later, an attractive woman around her own age joined them at the door.

Like the girl, she presented a calm and polite demeanour, but without the bright smile. 'Can I help you?'

Her confident air and flawless appearance made Moraine feel inadequate. The brown suede trousers, cream cashmere top, black patent brogues – her cultured voice *and* the country manor – spoke of considerable wealth. Old money. Someone who had been used to being wealthy for her entire life. Moraine felt suddenly aware of her corduroy jeans and puffer jacket from Topshop.

'I was looking for Beckley House. Have I taken the wrong turn? I was told this was the home of Joanne Jenkins. Sorry, I'm Detective Constable Moraine Morgan.'

The woman frowned, placing a hand on the girl's shoulder to pull her back in. 'Go inside, Lottie, and let me speak to the lady.' She waited until the girl was gone. 'This is Beckley House. I'm the owner. Jo works for us and lives in our annexe, but I don't think she's in. I can't see the car.'

Moraine gave a nod of understanding. 'Would you mind if I check if she's there? A police officer drove her home.'

The woman stepped out of the house, her hazel eyes curious with concern. 'Goodness. Of course. Let me show you the way.'

Moraine walked beside her. 'You have a beautiful place.'

The woman glanced at her sideways. 'Do you mind me asking what this is about? It's just that Pete, her husband, is away.'

The information was already public knowledge. She would need to talk to this woman soon. She might as well mention it now. 'We're trying to contact Sam's father. Sam went missing this morning at around ten forty-five. I've been assigned as family liaison officer, here to see Sam's mother. But I would like as soon as possible to come and talk with you, if that's okay. Once I've spoken to her.'

The woman stopped walking, eyes open wide, a hand over her mouth. Denial in the shake of her head, yet acceptance in her cry. 'No! That can't be right. Are you sure? He might just be... *invisible*? Sam will have wandered off and got interested in something like an ants' nest. He'll be somewhere digging up bugs, hidden by bushes or shrubs, where you can't see him. He does it here, in the garden. Finds a pile of wood or leaves to play in.'

Moraine halted the suggestions. 'He went missing from a village swimming pool. We've been searching for nearly three hours, a helicopter circling the area. Officers on the ground, canvassing neighbours. There's been no sighting of him from anyone in that time. That is why I need to speak urgently to his mum now. She may have seen something important.'

The woman folded her arms as if cold, hurrying now. 'Let's hope she's here then.'

They walked past ground floor mullioned windows, and Moraine could see chandeliers inside the high-ceilinged rooms. They turned at the corner and she took in the depth from the front to the back of the property, the imposing size, before shifting her gaze to a Range Rover parked in front of what once must have been a coach house. The stonework blended with that of the main house, the walls of the two buildings joined by a brick arch, originally to allow carriages to pass through. A sage-green stable door gave it a cottage-like appearance.

'She's home,' the woman confirmed. 'Shall I come in with you? Jo must be frantic.'

'No, that's okay, thank you,' Moraine declined politely. 'There's another police officer inside. I'm sure we'll manage. If I could take your name, though, please? I feel rude for not asking before.'

'Yes, of course. Claire Howell. Call round when you want. I'm home all day. And please let me know if I can do anything.'

Moraine waited until she was alone before knocking on the door. She wanted a first impression of Jo Jenkins while on her own. How she spoke, the tone of her voice, her body language, could tell Moraine a lot about what kind of character she would be dealing with. Judging from the quietness within the home, she wasn't the hysterical type. Something to be grateful for. A calm beginning. At least for now.

THREE

Claire closed her front door and put her hands on her flushed cheeks. She needed a moment to compose herself before letting the staff know what was happening, and to warn them not to let Lottie or Phoebe out in the garden. She wanted them to stay indoors while the police were around. Thankfully, there wasn't a police car outside.

The morning had already been stressful with trying to occupy the children while she ran errands. Bernice had a long face when asked if she could make cakes with them, and Antonio a bitch face when she popped into his salon to cancel her hair appointment. It wasn't like he couldn't fill her space in an instant. He told her often enough the favour he was doing her by squeezing her in ahead of the queue waiting for appointments. She tipped well enough not to deserve any disapproval. She would remember to be less generous next time.

Bernice was in the middle of clearing away the dishes from lunch and in a much better mood, humming a tune as she stacked the dishwasher. Her short curly hair, held back in its customary fashion, with a wide headband. She flashed Claire a smile, pointing at the tray of cupcakes on the island, her deep voice jolly again. 'Phoebe made them all by herself. Didn't need any help. Even remembered to warm the oven before they went in.'

The turquoise frosting was piped in swirls and looked fairly even and edible. She was a clever girl, and Claire was thankful to have Bernice teaching her daughters these skills.

'Where are the girls?'

Bernice raised her ruddy face at the ceiling. 'In their rooms, as far as I know. Playing on their gadgets, I expect.'

'If you see Dougie, can you call him in from the garden? I need a word. Same for Edna. When you see her, come and find me. Something's happened, Bernice, that I don't want the girls to know about. And for the time being, I don't want them to go outside. It concerns Sam. He's gone missing. From a village swimming pool. The police have been searching for three hours. The police are with Jo now. I don't know any further details, but a female officer is going to call here, so we might learn more then.'

Bernice's hand had gone to her chest. Claire watched as she struggled to swallow air, her mouth open wide, and hoped she wasn't about to have a heart attack. Her red face had gone very pale.

A sound behind her had Claire swiftly turning, ready to bar the girls from the kitchen. Instead, she saw James rush into the room and grab a chair from the table for Bernice to sit down. She hadn't heard him arrive home. You couldn't hear a car pull up from this end of the house. From the expression on his face he'd heard what she just told Bernice.

James took a glass from a kitchen cupboard and filled it with tap water. He held it out until Bernice took it from his hand and then stood there, looking like he didn't know what to do. Her heart sank at the pair of them. Sam had worked his way in to all their hearts. Foolishly, she tried to give him something else to think about.

'How did it go?'

The question distracted him momentarily. He looked confused, understandably so, before his attention focused in his protracted stare and he shook his head at her at the absurdity of what she had asked. Claire flushed at the rebuke, at being made to feel callous. All she'd been trying to do was give him some relief from the enormity of what had happened.

Lottie rushed into the kitchen, followed by Phoebe. 'Can we eat one now? You said we could when Daddy was home.'

Phoebe, at nine years old, was more able to read the room and immediately sensed something was amiss. While her seven year old sister was more focused on the cupcakes. 'Why is everyone quiet? Why is Bernice sitting on a chair by the sink, Mummy?'

James took over, calmly explaining the matter. 'Well, it seems that Sam has got a bit lost. But there are people looking for him, so that he doesn't stay lost. So you might see some police officers visiting to keep Jo company until Sam comes home.'

His explanation didn't work on Phoebe. She analysed the meaning accurately. Her face crumpled, her voice almost accusatory. 'You mean he's missing, don't you? It's not the same thing as lost.'

Her crying set Lottie off. James did his best to shush them, putting his arm around Phoebe, while Lottie clutched his leg. They threw questions and statements at their father. 'Why can't we look for him? We can help find him. Why can't all of us go and look for him? Dougie's got a van. Edna's got a car. We can all go. Why are you shaking your head? It's not fair. You don't care.'

The noise was almost intolerable. Claire couldn't feel cross with them. They didn't understand what was happening, or why it wasn't that simple. In their minds, Sam would be easy to find. She wished it were that easy, that a dark feeling in the pit of her stomach wasn't there. Ominously churning. *It's happening again.*

FOUR

Jo gritted her teeth as she held her palms under the kitchen tap. The hot running water brought tears to her eyes. She should have washed them as soon as she got here, instead of waiting until now. But since getting in the Range Rover with a police officer to drive her home, she'd been in a stupefied daze, unable to move from her spot by the window. She shouldn't have allowed the police to bundle her in the car and take her away from where she lost him. She needed to be back there to find him.

PC Kennedy stood by her side, staring at the deep grazes embedded with dirt.

'Do you have a first aid kit anywhere? You need a dressing on them.'

She swallowed down a wave of nausea as she turned her palms under the water to flush the grit out, concentrating on the oddity of his name. John F. Kennedy. Like the president. Only his F stood for Faolan. He had introduced himself with his entire name on the journey home, no doubt trying to distract her. She wondered at the Irish connection, or if he had relatives in America. Was he Catholic, with lots of red-haired sisters? Probably born in England, judging from his neutral English accent. Like her and Pete – people couldn't tell which part of England they were from.

'There's an ice-cream tub on the top shelf in the cupboard beside you. It's got bandages and Savlon in it.'

She was conscious of him searching in the box for dressings. He had already taken the dishes from the sink for her to wash her hands. Sam's full bowl of Coco Pops had melted in the milk. He hadn't eaten any of it, nor the two half slices of toast on a side plate. A rush of guilt swept through her. She had allowed her pain to focus on her needs for these few minutes. But she was here. Home. Without Sam.

Jo turned the tap off and dried her hands on a rough tea towel, deliberately embracing the further pain. She ignored Kennedy's attempt to take hold of them at first, before silently giving in. He was quick and efficient at applying cream and non-adhesive dressings, holding them in place with a wind of bandages.

'You might need to get them checked to make sure all the grit is out so they don't get infected,' he advised, before tidying the box and putting it back in the cupboard. 'Why don't you sit down and I'll make you some tea.'

Jo ignored the suggestion, and instead stared out the window at the bonnet of her car. She never normally parked there, but she hadn't directed PC Kennedy to park it where it normally went. She'd pointed out the building where she lived and let him drive along to it. The Howells might not be aware she was home, and she preferred to keep it that way. She wasn't close enough to them to accept their sympathy. She'd rather be with a complete stranger, so she didn't have to put on a face.

Jo dared a look at the kitchen clock and felt a lurch in her stomach. It was almost two o'clock. Over three hours had passed. She squeezed her eyes shut, willing time to go in reverse so he wouldn't be missing, back to this morning, back to last night, to yesterday when she collected him from school, when nothing had happened except for being handed some wet clothes and having a talk with his teacher. She tried to push down the memory of Sam in the bath last night. One minute happy, the next dissolving in tears – worried about wetting himself again.

She had thought he was upset about wetting himself in the playground, and tried to reassure him it was not the end of the world if he did a wee. Lots of children wee when they're busy playing, she told him, because they were having such a fun time. She bet SpongeBob SquarePants sometimes weed in the sea when playing with his best friend, Patrick Star. And did he know, Mummy nearly wees when she's running to try and catch him. She hoped it would get him to laugh if she said the word out loud enough times.

And then his innocent revelation hit her like a hard blow in the stomach. It was no wonder she couldn't make him laugh. No wonder his sad face reproached her, telling her she wasn't understanding him. If he wet himself again, he would have to wash his pants and trousers like Daddy made him do the last time.

Anxiety twisted her gut as she spotted a figure through the rain-spattered window. Her spine stiffened at the knock on the door, a light tap that she wanted to unhear. It was either going to be to tell her he was found or to tell her he was not. She couldn't bear the suspense.

Her eyes stayed rigidly fixed on the window in front of her, and on the wet leaves of a bush from the earlier rain. She tried to shut out the sound of PC Kennedy opening the front door. She wanted to run away before she could be told, but already a woman had entered her home, had come into her kitchen and seen her. Jo could see the woman's reflection in the glass and had to turn around.

Soft brown eyes, short black hair, a mature face, normal clothes – corduroy jeans, polo-neck jumper, a mid-length puffer jacket a bit like Jo's – she radiated an aura of calm.

The woman read the expression on Jo's face quickly. 'I know the waiting is agony, while we look for him, but you're doing him proud by staying calm. As soon as I have an update, you'll be the first to know.'

The sound of the kettle coming to the boil had her glancing at PC Kennedy. 'If you're making tea, I'd love one. I've got powdered milk in my bag if Jo's low on fresh milk?'

'There's plenty,' Jo volunteered. 'There's coffee as well if you prefer.'

'Why don't we sit down, and then I can introduce myself. PC Kennedy's a dab hand in the kitchen. He used to be a chef.'

The policeman smiled good-naturedly, before turning to make drinks. Jo sat on a dining chair at the table. The woman looked around the room.

'Do you have a clear photo of Sam? My boss wants me to send a good likeness so the public can see what Sam looks like and contact the police if they see him. The one PC Kennedy sent is a little blurred.'

'That was my fault,' Jo admitted. 'I gave it to him off my phone. But behind the bread bin there's some. Safest place to keep them until I get frames.'

The woman went to look for them. They were still in a cellophane envelope, a batch of recent photographs taken at school. Jo watched while she chose a medium-sized image and placed it on the counter, then got out her phone to take a photo. 'I'll just send this to the boss...' She tapped on the phone for a few seconds, then held the physical photograph out for Jo to see. 'May I borrow this one, to take back to the station?'

Jo nodded.

'The police held a press conference at one thirty so Sam's photo will have already been shown. But this one is better if we need to do further appeals.'

Jo stared at her with wide, shocked eyes. 'He was on television and I never saw him.'

'His photo was, yes. Not him. We're still looking for Sam.' Her voice softened. 'Keeping abreast of news or social media is sometimes better handled by someone not as close to Sam. An uncle or an aunt perhaps? But let's take this one step at a time.'

She joined Jo at the table as PC Kennedy placed mugs of tea down. She gently touched one of Jo's bandaged hands. 'What happened? Did you hurt yourself? Do you need to see a doctor?'

Jo shook her head. 'They're bearable. I fell over, searching for Sam. I'll take some paracetamol soon. There's some in the same cupboard as the first aid box.'

PC Kennedy returned to the cupboard and moments later placed a Tesco's own brand box in front of her with a glass of water. Jo popped two from a blister pack and washed them down quickly.

The woman waited and then introduced herself. 'My name's Moraine Morgan. I'm a family liaison officer, and a detective constable. I'm here as a point of contact for you and the investigation team and I'll be asking you for lots of information which will help us find your son. But before I begin, let me know what you prefer to be called. I've just gone ahead and called you Jo.'

'I prefer Jo. My full name's Joanne, but I'm never called that. Just Jo.'

'Jo it is, then. And please feel free to call me Moraine. Or Raine will do. My Welsh father came up with my name and I never know whether it was chosen for the weather or from sedimentary rocks formed from the Ice Age. A few times it's been pronounced "moron", but I can get over that.'

She paused to take a sip of tea, before pulling a leather folder and a pen from her oversized bag. 'I'll be writing it all down, but we can go over it all afterwards to make sure we have everything. I'm going to start by asking for family names, ages, employment, then Sam's full name and date of birth, and any medical history he may have. After that, I'll be asking for a detailed account of what happened today.'

A visceral fear gripped Jo, as she had a vision of Sam's dead body, his skin translucent, his body lifeless in long wet grass. She moaned softly for the images to go. Moraine touched her forearm gently.

'Nice easy breaths. Slowly in, then slowly out. Then drink some tea. You must be thirsty. Have you notified your husband?'

Jo gulped from the mug and felt the hot liquid dribble down her chin. She wiped it with the sleeve of her jumper. She shook her head. 'No. PC Kennedy said the police were going to contact him. He's in Manchester at a conference.'

The policewoman gave her a reassuring nod, and began: Did they have any other children? Any relatives close by? How old were her and Pete? What was Pete's job? And her job? When they got to questions about Sam, her lips quivered.

'He's just turned five. He's at school. He's only just started. His teacher told me yesterday they're concerned about him. He's not interacting with his classmates. They're noticing him pacing by himself in the playground, making repetitive movements with his hands and head, making sounds.

'Yesterday, she hands me a carrier bag with Sam's wet belongings, and said right in front of him that the joggers he was wearing were from lost property. Silly woman didn't need to say anything. She should have just handed me the bag, instead of making Sam think he'd done something wrong.'

Moraine was listening intently, her pen scribbling in her notebook. Jo was relieved she could talk about it to someone. She gave a deep sigh. 'I've been noticing mild traits for over a year. He prefers to be alone, and doesn't like bright lights and noises, and now, with what the teacher is describing, it sounds like stimming.'

Moraine raised her head. 'What's that?'

'Self-stimulation. A way to regulate intense feelings. I studied the subject in my paediatric nursing degree. Sam hasn't been diagnosed with anything, but I'm pretty sure he may have mild autism. If he does, it's not an illness. It just means his brain works differently to other people.'

Moraine looked surprised. 'I didn't realise you were a children's nurse. I put down nanny and housekeeper.'

Jo nodded. 'Well, that's what I am. I look after the Howells' children and help in the house. It's a full-time position. Lottie and Phoebe are lovely girls. Aged seven and nine, they're easy to look after.

'I trained as a paediatric nurse but haven't practiced as one. I was pregnant by the time I took my finals and worked in nurseries instead, for better hours and to have childminding in place once the baby was born. Neither Pete nor I had any close relatives living nearby. I decided it would be better to have a job fitted around bringing up a baby. It's a perk of working in a nursery, so long as you're not their key worker. And I wasn't Sam's.'

'So is that why you are working here?'

'Yes. That and saving for a mortgage. My job comes with this home, plus a car, so we're able to save. We moved in just after Christmas. With Sam starting school this year, it was an ideal situation.'

Moraine jotted down the new information, leaving Jo with a few seconds of silence for her mind to wander. Her eyes were drawn to the clock. Two forty-seven. Another hour had almost passed. In a few hours it would be dusk. How would they find him in the dark?

'Okay, Jo, now take me to this morning. When you and Sam woke up. What did you do first?'

'I played with Sam's toes. They were cold... I was relieved to find his pyjamas dry. Not for me, but for him. He's been toilet trained since he was two. It was horrible yesterday, to see his embarrassment in front of his teacher when she gave me the wet clothes. I got out of bed and decided how we would spend the day. I'd been given the weekend off because Pete's away at a fire conference and I thought we could go to Royal Victoria Park and do a treasure hunt. But it looked like rain, so I opted for swimming instead.'

'Is there any reason you decided on that pool? I mean... when you have Bath on your doorstep, or the one at Culverhay?'

Jo nodded. 'It was a deliberate choice. He gets overwhelmed in crowded places, and Culverhay only has swimming lessons and then adult swimming on Saturday mornings. I wanted to try somewhere smaller and less busy. The website showed a simple rectangular pool, and happy smiling children. I thought the drive would be worth it for Sam to enjoy himself.'

'Okay, so when you arrived, is that what you found? Were there many people about?'

'There were lots of cars parked. I worried they might all be using the pool. I realised afterwards there was a wedding on at the church. But we didn't actually see anyone. There was no one at reception, so we went straight to a cubicle. I was planning to pay when I saw someone. And then I went to the toilet. It was too small to take Sam in with me, so I left him on the bench in the cubicle. I told him to stay there. I'd only be a minute. When I came out, the changing room was crowded. They'd closed the pool to clean it – a soiled nappy was floating in the water. The door to Sam's cubicle was shut. Women were queuing to use it, but I knew he was in there. But when the door opened, he wasn't. He wasn't there.'

A heaving sob rose up from her chest. Tears dripping from

her eyes, mucus running from her nose, she loudly, uncontrollably cried. 'I want Sam. My precious boy. I want him home.'

The sound of a car pulling up outside raises her head. She waited, hearing the slamming of a car door, the banging of the front door, the rush of someone entering the room. She can hear him breathing, heavily, and guards against what she knows is coming. The blame.

FIVE

Pete Jenkins's greeting to his wife was uncomfortable to watch. Not a hug or a kiss, or a how are you, but demands for answers to his rapid-fire questions. Where were you? How did it happen? Why were you there? In his impatience for Jo to speak, he failed to notice his wife was unable to talk, her jaw trembling badly. When Jo suddenly vomited down herself and onto the table, he was more revolted than shocked as he quickly stepped back and checked his smart casual clothes for splashes. Moraine felt sorry for his wife.

Jo Jenkins was not what Moraine had expected. Her light-brown hair with wispy tendrils and her gamine features made her look younger than twenty-seven years. But looking in her eyes revealed the jadedness from experiencing too much of something, so she looked a disillusioned soul, and older.

It was left to Moraine and PC Kennedy to clean up the sick and to help Jo to a sofa in the lounge, while her attractive, fair-haired husband made himself a coffee. Moraine put a throw over Jo and then returned to the kitchen to speak to the husband, where she was less inclined to talk nice.

'Mr Jenkins, I think your wife might need a doctor to give her something to help keep her calm. She's gone through a terrible ordeal and is probably in shock.'

He was leaning back against the counter with his head bowed, breathing harshly. He gave a slight nod to show he heard. His voice croaked when he spoke. 'I'll call our GP. Though she has tablets in the cupboard that might calm her.'

Moraine looked in the cupboard and found a box of Citalopram in the same place as the paracetamol. They were antidepressants, the same as her mum took for her low moods. She wasn't sure this was the right drug for Jo as it was prescribed as one tablet a day only. She closed the cupboard.

'Not sure it would be wise to give her one of these. You'd need to check with her GP. I realise this is a shock to you as well. I'm sorry I've been concentrating only on your wife. My name's Moraine Morgan. I'm a family liaison officer and a detective constable with Avon and Somerset Police. I'm here as a point of contact for you and your wife. Did someone get in touch with you to tell you Sam was missing? I know they've been trying to contact you.'

He shook his head. 'No, one of my colleagues told me. They saw it on Facebook and let me know. I've just driven down from Manchester. I was at a fire conference. I'm a firefighter. I didn't know until then. I haven't actually checked my phone. I was in too much of a rush to get here. I don't know what the current situation is.'

Moraine held back her judgement. She didn't know this man. She was a stranger in his home, and it sounded like he was only just catching up.

'Well, let me bring you up to date then. Sam is still missing. We've had no sightings yet. Child Rescue Alert was activated immediately. It provides the public with a dedicated central telephone number, which passes on any information to the police. A press conference was held at one thirty. It was probably aired on the local news. I take it you didn't hear it on the radio?'

He lifted a hand to his chin, rubbing the stubble along his jawline, before raising his eyes to her. 'No. There was a CD on, and I just kept playing that.' He huffed out a breath. 'So, what now? Sam went missing from a public pool. Someone must have seen something?'

Moraine shook her head. 'Your wife and son never actually got into the pool. Sam went missing from a cubicle in the changing room while Jo was in the toilet.'

'But there must be CCTV. He must be on a camera, surely? You can't go half a mile without being spotted somewhere.'

'You're right, and you'd think so. It should be easy to spot him. Officers have been checking all that. The problem is it's a village—'

'Yes, but not the Stone Age! There has to be cameras somewhere!'

'There are. They're being checked, along with doorbell cameras. There just aren't as many as we'd like.'

Moraine had been checking her work phone for the state of play, and knew the frustration her colleagues were facing. A wedding party had dispersed by the time the police arrived and they had to track down where the wedding reception was being held and get a list of the attendees for photos and footage. It was almost impossible not to pick someone up on a camera. Sam was remaining an elusive anomaly, and the swimming pool building didn't help. Of the two CCTV cameras mounted on the walls, one was at the back of the building, and the other was pointing straight at a church wall. Clearly, no one ever checked them.

He shook his head in angry despair. 'A five-year-old doesn't go wandering off without being noticed. What does Jo say? She must have seen someone nearby for him to go missing that quick. Or have heard something?'

Moraine lowered her voice, hoping he'd do the same. 'Why don't you talk to Jo? I'm sure you both need a moment. Then we can talk. I'd like you to tell me how things were yesterday, before you left.'

He stared at her. '*What?* What do you mean, how things were? Sam was at school when I left, and Jo was here.'

Moraine gave a light shrug. 'I mean, in general, how were things? How was Sam? How was Jo? Anyway, we can discuss that some more after you've had some time with Jo. I do need to let you know we'll need to take something of Sam's. A toothbrush would be best. It's routine in a missing person case to have something we can get DNA from. I hope you understand.'

He gave a terse reply. 'Take what you want. I've no doubt you've already checked to see if he's here. Isn't that the first thing you normally do?'

Moraine didn't deny or confirm that this was something they would do, but it was on her list to check upstairs, in cupboards, under beds, and see if there was access to the loft space. A quick tour of the downstairs showed the home was more than just an annexe; with its own front door it was self-contained. At ground level, a kitchen with dining area, a sitting room, utility and downstairs toilet. Furnished with leather armchairs and sofa, parquet flooring with dark-coloured rugs, a TV on the wall, an aged pine table and chairs.

She noticed the crumbs on the table and floor, and on the ceramic drainer: a plastic Spider-Man bowl full of soggy cereal and a matching plate with uneaten toast. It might be something or nothing, but she would log it in her report. The same for the prescription Citalopram that Jo was taking.

Kennedy came into the kitchen. 'She's asleep, if you want to check on her, Mr Jenkins. Or at least settled.' He wrinkled his nose. 'Could do with some air freshener in here, or the window open. I've thrown away the cloths we used. I hope you don't mind?'

'No, it's fine,' Pete Jenkins answered. 'And call me Pete. Make yourselves at home. I should have offered you a drink when I made mine. Thanks for helping with Jo. I'm just trying to get my head around it. If you don't mind, I'll pop upstairs and have a quick wash, wake myself up a bit.'

'Of course,' Moraine answered. 'And thank you.'

Moraine frowned as he left the room. Kennedy raised his eyebrows at her, possibly thinking the same as her: Pete Jenkins's behaviour was unusual, to say the least. He'd been home for forty-five minutes and he was still here. She had assisted a lot of families in the last ten years, a fair few missing person incidents. In all her recollections of those cases, she'd never known a parent to see to their own comforts first. In slippers or bare feet, they'd be out searching for their child in the rain, the cold, the dark, putting themselves in sometimes severe discomfort. Parents, who felt they needed to punish themselves for whatever their child might be going through. She'd never known a parent to make themselves a coffee, or have a wash, like they had all the time in the world.

She was getting a feel of the family, but not a clear picture. Not by a long shot. Hopefully, the family next door might shed some light – alleviate the niggling sensation that something was off. Who doesn't check their phone or immediately call their wife when they hear their child is missing? Most people would be on their phone the entire drive home, wanting a minute-by-minute update. Could he really have just got in his car and driven two hundred miles without looking at his phone? Surely he'd have wanted confirmation from his wife that it was real. Or confirmation from the police. Hi, I'm Pete Jenkins, father of the missing boy. Can you tell me what's going on?

Strange behaviour. She wondered if it was because he was at odds with his wife. Were there marital issues at play before their son went missing? Moraine found herself hoping so, or that he was just a bit of an aloof character, coming across as unfriendly. She didn't want there to be a darker reason at play. She wanted this little boy home with his mum – for the boy to be found safe and sound. For the day to be forgettable once it had ended.

SIX

The atmosphere in Claire's home was unnaturally quiet, as if any small noise would prevent them hearing a knock at the door. The girls were watching *The Princess Diaries* in the sitting room, with the sound barely up. James had BBC iPlayer on in the kitchen playing the police press conference with subtitles on. The photograph of Sam was grainy, but recognisable to those who knew him. Claire was torn. Someone should be with Jo other than just the police supporting her. She would be with her now if James hadn't advised against it, saying they should wait awhile as the police would need to question Jo about what had happened.

She wondered how long it would be before Moraine Morgan knocked at their door. James had told her what to expect. They would be questioned about the Jenkinses. Claire isn't sure what she will say. She hadn't been able to get to know Jo very well. She was always calm and kind with the children, and capable of any task given her. The other staff liked her well enough, but Claire detected an undercurrent of anxiety in her character sometimes, an inability to relax. Pete, on the other hand, was an open book, and could be a bit of a prat.

She could see the distress on James's face. It was Sam they had all got to know the most. Adorable, introverted, and intelligent. He was a fixture in their garden most days, happily digging up worms and watching insects. For his recent birthday, she had given him a set of children's gardening tools. Bernice had made him a small lemon birthday cake. Dougie had assembled a bug house from left-over wood, layering it with egg cartons, pinecones and bits of bark to attract all the different creepy crawlies. Sam was in his element, and James called him a nature child.

She had worried when she first met him. He looked so much like... *him*. That other child they'd once known. She'd pointed it out to James at the time, but he'd brushed it aside. They hadn't seen Marley and Stuart Lambert in a long time, so it would be unlikely for them ever to meet Sam and be upset by the likeness to their own son.

Now, as if reading her mind, James glanced at her. 'I wouldn't bring up anything about the Lamberts. It won't help find Sam.'

Claire didn't have any intention of mentioning their friends. It was the last thing she wanted the police to know about. But she wondered if he was planning to mention what Sam had recently told him, which had disturbed her as much as James. Or would he keep that back? He didn't have any evidence, which in James's mind would be important. It was hearsay until it could be substantiated. She'd had the feeling he was going to speak to Jo about it over the weekend while Pete was away.

'Are you going to tell them what Sam told you?'

A muscle above his eye was twitching. He pressed his fingers across the eyelid, a sign he was overly tired or stressed. He then winced and pressed his palm against his forehead. She hoped he wasn't getting another migraine. It would be the second one in two weeks, and he normally only had them two or three times a year.

'Why don't you lie down?'

'No, I'll take a couple of Nurofen. That'll settle it. I probably need new reading glasses. I missed my last eye test.'

His face was pale. Claire fetched him the tablets and some water. He swallowed them just as the front door was knocked. He gave her a brief look. 'Don't mention what Sam said. It might do more harm than good. The police will be focused on his parents enough.'

'But Pete's away,' she whispered, even though no one could hear them.

He sat up straighter. 'Trust me. Let them in and don't mention it. We'll talk about it later.'

Claire nodded and glanced around the tidy kitchen. 'I'll bring her in here. Bernice knows not to let the children come in. Do I look all right?'

He stretched his hand out and briefly clasped hers. 'You look fine,' he answered. 'Now hurry before they knock again.'

James was the perfect host as Claire introduced him to Moraine Morgan. He welcomed the detective and asked her to sit at their kitchen table. 'Can we offer you some refreshments? A tea, coffee, or some juice?'

The woman unzipped her jacket as she settled in a chair. 'A coffee would be lovely, if it's not too much trouble.'

James gestured to their coffee machine. 'No trouble at all. It does it all itself.'

'Then coffee with just milk would be great, thanks.'

Claire helped herself to orange juice from the fridge. She'd missed lunch and her blood sugar was low. She should have eaten a sandwich before the police officer arrived, and wondered if she should offer to make some now.

'Can I make you something to eat? We're a long way from the shops, so I'd be happy to make you up some sandwiches to have now or take with you, and we have loads of milk if you run short. Plus, lots of cupcakes our daughter made this morning. We shan't eat them all.'

She gave Claire an appreciative look. 'That's so kind of you. I'm sure we'll be fine, but I'll remember if we run out of milk. It all depends on how the day goes; how successful we are in finding him.'

Claire felt a shiver run through her and sank into a chair instead of making anything to eat. 'How's Jo? Do you think it would be okay to visit? I'd like to help if I can.'

The liaison officer gave a small sigh. 'She was doing well, and then it all became too much. She's lying down, resting on the sofa, and her husband is with her now.'

Claire showed her surprise. His was a car that could usually be heard at the back of the house. It sounded like a motorbike tearing up the drive. James mentioned to him not that long ago that the exhaust might have a crack in it. Maybe he got it fixed, or the girls' crying carried over the noise.

'Well, that's something then. She's not on her own. How's Pete? He must be out of his mind. I won't let my girls know he's back, else they'll be begging to go out searching with him. They wanted us all to get in our cars and look for Sam. Maybe we should. The girls would know the sort of hiding places he could be in.'

James interrupted the conversation by placing some ham and cheese quarter sandwiches on the table, along with side plates and glass mugs of coffee. 'Put that idea out of your head, Claire. A search party is not a place for children. The atmosphere can be very sombre.'

The policewoman agreed with him. 'He's right, Mrs Howell. It can be a very tense time.'

James joined them at the table and offered the sandwiches to their guest. 'Please, take one. And it's Claire and James. We're not formal here.'

She declined the sandwich with a polite smile. 'If it's all

right with you both, I have a few questions. Did you see what time Jo and Sam left the property?'

Claire shook her head. 'None of us saw them leave. I only knew they were out because the Range Rover was gone when I left to run some errands. I've even asked the staff. Dougie, our head gardener, doesn't start work until ten on Saturdays, but he'd have been the most likely to have heard. You don't tend to hear vehicles at this end of the house from indoors. And James was gone at eight this morning. He had a meeting with a client.'

'So none of you saw Jo and Sam leave? When was the last time you saw them?'

'Yesterday, when Jo brought the girls home from school. Normally, she'd come in and help the girls get changed out of their school uniforms and keep them occupied until dinner time. But it was agreed that with Pete away at the conference, and her having the weekend off, she'd finish at four thirty.'

'I see. Do you mind if I ask some general questions about them? How long has Jo worked for you? Do they seem a happy couple?'

James cleared his throat tellingly, expressing disapproval. 'Look, I don't wish to sound unhelpful, but I'm not happy to discuss their personal lives. Jo has been working for us for nine months and has done a commendable job. She's vigilant with the children, and has managed to set boundaries so that all three children know which home is theirs. Sam plays in our gardens, but there it stops. Pete is a likeable enough chap. He went out of his way when I broke down on a country lane in the dead of winter, and he happened upon me. He towed me back home. I learned that he and his wife were trying to save for a mortgage and that Jo was looking for a job, and had no reservations about offering a solution.

'I'm well aware how police investigations go, and that you'll be looking for reasons for Sam's disappearance, but while it remains a missing person incident, I'd rather not have my neighbours looked upon as suspects. I hope you understand. Claire and I are happy to answer any fact-based questions, but that's all.'

A slight flush had appeared in Moraine Morgan's cheeks, and Claire wanted to reassure her, and explain her husband wasn't being rude. It was the job he did that made him so assertive. But she needn't have worried. DC Morgan was already one step ahead.

'Do you work for the police, Mr Howell?'

'No,' he said in a less impassioned voice, lightening the atmosphere a notch. 'I'm a barrister at law. King's Counsel, and still not used to the changed title. QC slipped off the tongue so much better. KC sounds too much like KFC, wouldn't you agree?'

He said it tongue-in-cheek, although Claire could see Moraine Morgan was slightly startled at meeting a barrister at the highest level of the profession. Being appointed King's Counsel by the monarch and recommended by the Lord Chancellor was a great honour and achieved by recognition of excellence. The woman was probably re-evaluating what questions to ask.

James showed his human side. His eyes had misted. 'But none of that counts in this matter. Sam is a child we are very fond of, and, in some respects, I wish I didn't know too much of what is taking place right at this moment. I understand your situation very well and appreciate the difficulties the police have to deal with, especially when you have examples of parents like Shannon Matthews's mother who tethered her child to a bed and said she was kidnapped. While you want only to find a missing child safe and sound, you have to consider vile possibilities. But for now, Claire and I would like to support Jo and Pete in this terrible time, and pray that you find Sam soon. We will help where we can, so please ask any relevant questions.'

She nodded slowly, keeping eye contact with him. 'Thank you. I appreciate that. You've provided them a lovely home, and clearly you care.'

He brushed aside the praise. 'Claire converted it into a workspace for her interior design business, but is taking a break after all the work on this house. It took three or more years to give a facelift to this old girl. So it was going spare, and a family needed a home.'

She sipped her coffee and placed it back down. 'I do have one question that you might be able to help me with. Do you have security cameras on your property?'

James smiled. 'Good question. And yes, we do.'

SEVEN

Moraine put a two-litre carton of organic milk and a Tupperware box of sandwiches and cupcakes on the Jenkinses' kitchen table. 'From next door,' she told Kennedy. 'So help yourself.'

He didn't need any further encouragement and had the lid off and had eaten a sandwich in no time. 'I was starving,' he said, after swallowing a second one. 'Been living off a packet of Polo mints the last few hours.'

Moraine put the kettle on. She had drunk only half the coffee made for her by James Howell, finding it too strong for her taste, and was still thirsty. She reminisced about the house she just visited. The kitchen. Stunning wooden cabinets, wooden beams, wide floorboards and red-brick walls. Rustic opulence. Nothing plastic or shiny or artificial. They were a very wealthy family and she would not be surprised if theirs was an ancestral home. Either his or hers. Everything about them – etiquette, manners, the way they sat at the table, the quality of the classic and quite old-fashioned clothes they wore – defined them as people with an identity they had inherited from birth. They were both attractive, she with her almond-shaped eyes and chocolate-brown hair, him with his light-toned face, rich-auburn hair, and eyes that were deep and expressive. She had to force herself to look away from him because she was staring, and could feel her cheeks warming.

She glanced out the window at the darkening sky and felt a deepening unease. It was taking too long to find Sam if he was simply lost. He could be injured, of course, or unconscious, and some misguided soul may at this very moment be administering to his needs. An old person, perhaps, who didn't have the means to alert the police or phone for an ambulance. She was trying to avoid thinking the worst.

'Did you get anything useful next door?' Kennedy asked.

She shook her head. 'Not really. They have a security camera that shows the Range Rover leaving the property just after nine, but you only see the back of the vehicle. No one next door has seen Jo or Sam since yesterday. How's this family doing?'

He gave a shrug. 'I had to put a stop to her going off out to search for her son. Don't think she can even think straight. She's back on the sofa and he's asleep in a chair. Heard him on his phone talking to someone. Sounded like he was asking why his phone was switched off.' He gave her a long look. 'Don't know how you do this role. The waiting is pretty intense.'

Moraine liked Kennedy. He changed his career in his thirties and was solid and calm. He would be an excellent liaison officer, as he knew how to put people at ease. Plus, he wasn't naïve. He was from a large family and had four kids of his own. He knew how the world worked.

'What's your take on them?'

He brushed breadcrumbs off the table into his palm. 'I don't know. I clocked a couple of things with her. She's not a typical young mum, always on her phone. She's only been on it once, to give me a photo. There's an atmosphere between them, that's for sure. I can't really read him. Might be just a bit of a twat, but I sure as hell wouldn't be sleeping if one of mine was missing. Long drive or no drive, I'd be out there looking.'

Moraine took the opportunity while both parents were sleeping to look upstairs. The height of the roof allowed for a second floor with attic-style bedrooms and bathroom.

In the smaller bedroom there was a damp towel on the bed, and the clothes Pete Jenkins had been wearing lay in a heap on the floor. A child's pencil drawing on the bedside drawers. The wardrobe door was open, plastic storage bags under the bed. In Sam's room, a duvet cover patterned with bright leaves, insects and snails. A child's table and chair. A storage unit tiered with colourful boxes full of drawing materials. Nothing of note in the bathroom. No sign of an attic space anywhere.

She returned to the kitchen to find Kennedy reading the *Mirror* and peered at the front page. 'Is that today's paper?'

He raised his eyes with a guilty look. 'Yeah. Sorry. I was just having a quick read.'

'That's okay. I was just wondering if you brought it with you.'

'No. Mr Jenkins must have left it on the counter when he came in.'

'Oh, he must have taken it from the hotel. It would be a bit odd if he bought it on his journey home, even if he stopped for petrol. Reading the newspaper would be the last thing on his mind.'

'There's a folder on top of the fridge and a calendar on the wall you might want to take a look at. It's Jo's work schedule.'

Moraine went over to scan the calendar and saw the day-to-day of Jo's routine. In neat writing she had marked the days for drop-offs, pickups, tennis, riding, dancing, dental appointments, birthday parties.

'Her employer must be very organised,' Kennedy remarked. 'Look at the folder.'

Moraine brought it over to the table. It was set out like a holiday welcome pack with a history of Beckley House, and was a detailed list of Jo's house duty requirements. By each entry a direction: To assist Edna with laundry Mondays and Thursdays. To assist Edna with bed changing Fridays. To assist cleaners, Meg, Leanne, Danka, with housekeeping Tuesdays and Fridays. On another page a list of products she must use, and a complete list of mustn'ts, like items that shouldn't go in a washing machine, or in a dishwasher.

'I thought linseed oil was used only on horses.'

Kennedy chuckled. 'Nope. Boiled linseed oil is good for wood.'

Moraine calculated it added up to a four-day week until she checked the calendar and saw that horse riding was on Saturdays.

She picked up her workbag. 'I'm just going outside. I want to touch base with DI Stone. You want me to remind him you're still here?'

He shook his head. 'No, you're all right. My wife's taken the kids to Longleat today, so she won't be tearing her hair out for me to get home.'

'Okay, I won't be long. I'll have a quick vape while I'm out there, save me getting cranky.'

'Well, we don't want that. Take all the time you need. What happens later, though? Will someone take over from you if it goes on into the evening?'

'I'll probably be tagged a second FLO if that happens. But let's hope we don't need one.'

A ten-minute update with DI Stone gave her no good news. The whereabouts of the child remained firmly unknown. They didn't have a single lead. Nobody had seen the boy. Plenty of mums had seen the boy's mother frantically looking for him, but not one of them had seen him with her. It was like he was never there.

The camera showing the road to the car park showed Jo driving the Range Rover, but no sign of anyone in the back. It captured her walking between parked cars until she goes out of view, and no way of knowing if she's alone.

Stone's ominous words. He could have said there was no chance of seeing that Sam was with her. Instead, with only Jo seen on CCTV and in-person, he chose to phrase it this way. This might have been their best chance to see him arriving then leaving, either on his own or with someone. But the entrance and exit to the building was not on camera.

The navy-blue Range Rover parked outside the home was barely five years old and a look through the driver's window saw it fitted out with top of the range children's car seats. The tinted side windows would have made it even more difficult to see inside the back.

She didn't envy Stone's responsibility. They had very little to go on. The police tracked down the wedding party to the village cricket club – minus the bride and groom who had departed after a quick celebratory drink for their honeymoon – and were presently gathering photographs and video footage. A mammoth task in itself, encouraging tipsy people to operate their phones while balancing glasses of champagne or beer, interrupting their enjoyment and putting a dampener on a day that should be happy. But so far, nothing had come to light.

Moraine could tell the SIO was worried. He would soon visit Beckley House himself and form his own opinion about the parents. Moraine needed to prepare them for this, so they wouldn't expect him to be bringing good news. Mick Stone would be forthright about the reason for his visit. He'd want to know how it was possible that Sam Jenkins got to where he went, then disappeared, with no one and no camera catching a glimpse of him.

As she headed back inside, she thought she should make a courtesy call on the Howells to let them know they would soon see a police vehicle parked in front of their house, but it wouldn't be Sam being brought home. But first things first, she needed to tell the Jenkinses.

EIGHT

Jo opened her eyes in panic, her heart immediately thumping at instantly recalling Sam was missing. She jumped up in terror, desperate to hear if there was any news.

She was startled to see Pete asleep in the armchair, her breath catching in her throat as she studied him analytically. How could he lie there with their son missing? Until that moment yesterday evening, she'd been trying to hold on to the love she still had for him. But the incident with Sam – the breaking point – turned her heart to stone.

She'd been unable to believe that Pete could humiliate Sam in that way. Sam must have got it wrong. And then Sam further revealed Daddy said he was naughty and only babies wet themselves.

Damn him. The bastard.

Sam was a little boy, and his father shows him this heartless side – coming at him from out of nowhere, from someone he trusted. It would have shocked his mind.

She thought yesterday's accident at school was a one-off and hadn't happened before, until what Sam told her. Pete didn't tell her anything about an accident at home.

His kiss goodbye yesterday hit the side of her cheek, his arms remaining by his sides, in his hurry to get out the door. Duty done and off as fast as he could. She was fully aware of that, and barely been able to stomach hearing his voice on the phone last night. He'd chosen the busiest time of day to call when he knew she'd be getting Sam ready for bed.

The change in him was not attractive. When they moved here he was happy with his life. In fact, he probably thought she had done them a favour by putting them on the breadline. Their new situation was like a lottery win for him at being given a free home, a vehicle for Jo to drive, a fuel card to keep it filled with petrol.

He was a different man to two years ago. Now she no longer recognised him. He'd turned selfish and ignorant and envious. Her fault, no doubt, for upending their lives. She couldn't undo what happened. She couldn't erase that day. For the last nine months she'd been trying to make amends. She had been living with the guilt for two years. But coming to Beckley House, hiding her past, hadn't made things better. It had made life worse.

She swallowed against the ache in her throat. She had never felt so alone in her entire life. He was only feet away, yet she no longer felt she could go to him and fall into his arms. They had been together since she was a student nurse and he was a young fireman, meeting in a fairy tale way – he rescued her from a smoke-filled building wearing full-breathing apparatus like a come-to-life superhero. She described their meeting to Sam in this way – he'd been enthralled by the adventure, seeing his father like Spider-Man. She thought after their first date that she had met the man of her dreams. And he was for a long time, until two years ago when he left her to flounder alone.

Was she unconsciously trying to punish him for not supporting her? Was she making his actions towards Sam into something worse than it was? He hadn't beaten Sam or denied him food. He read him stories at bedtime and made bath times fun, even if he did leave a flood on the floor for her to mop up. He didn't leave Sam in wet trousers and make him wear them. Was making Sam wash his trousers so terrible?

She shook her head and blew out her breath. With another child, maybe not. But with a child like Sam – tender-hearted, sensitive to failure, sensitive to stern looks and tones of voices – most definitely yes. Pete had wounded him deeply.

Her movements must have disturbed him because he opened his eyes. He stared at her without any warmth. He spoke quietly, as if mindful of the police inside their home.

'How did you lose him, Jo?'

Instinct made her change the words she was about to speak. She didn't want him reminded of the past. Her arms waved like butterfly wings as she swayed in front of him. 'I... I'm sorry. I'm sorry, I don't know how it happened.'

His eyes travelled over her. 'You need to get a grip and think about what might have happened. How was he this morning? Did he seem upset? Did something cause him to run off? For fuck sake, Jo, how the hell did you let this happen? How is it that no one saw him? The police haven't had one sighting, and you don't have a clue how it happened!'

She so badly wanted to scream at him, but she couldn't. 'How do you know it's not *your* fault?'

'Me? *Me?*' His face showed shock. 'I wasn't fucking here. *Remember?* He was with *you.* In *your* care!'

She raised her hands to cover her ears. Tears streamed down her face, stinging her salty skin from her previous bout of crying. 'Please stop. Please don't remind me.'

He stood up with his jaw clenched and took a deep breath before saying what he was thinking. 'How can I not? If the police find out, how do you think it's going to look?'

Every inch of her body tightened with those words. A kick to her stomach couldn't have rendered her more rigid. She felt sick, breathless, and dizzy. She'd been hanging on by her fingertips, hoping that he would react differently, that he would show some remorse and think this was his fault, and that when Sam came home, he would want to make his family happy again. Be her hero once more.

Unable to respond, she stood still, looking at him through her tears. He was blaming her because she *was* to blame. Guilt swamped her. And pain, like no other pain she would ever feel, gripped hard. Her heart slammed at the thought of Sam no longer alive, never seeing him, or holding him and loving him again. His arms would never reach for her. His lips never kiss her. And in the dark, she would never again hear him whisper, 'I love you, Mummy.'

She doubled up as she groaned in agony. She retched and choked and retched again, praying for the torture in her mind to end. Dropping to her knees, she curved into a ball, her head on the floor, panting and sweating as sick drooled out of her mouth. And in the darkness behind her tightly shut eyelids, she reached out to her son. Her fingers stretched out to him, desperate for him to see that he was not alone, that she was there with him, that he didn't need to be afraid.

Her chest crushed with pain as she saw him in her mind's eye. He was still, his face turned towards her, his eyes closed and his small fingers just inches away.

'I'm here, baby,' she whispered. 'I'm here now. It's all over, sweetheart. Mummy's here.'

NINE

While Kennedy cleaned the rug where Jo had been sick, Moraine took her upstairs so she could clean her teeth, wash her face, and change her jumper. She was glazed with sweat, while simultaneously shivering. Pete Jenkins was back in the kitchen making them all mugs of tea, away from the sour smell in the sitting room.

Moraine wondered if he had phoned his wife's doctor yet or had let it slide. DI Stone would arrive within the hour and be looking at the state Jo was in to see if he could question her. Moraine needed to log on to her work device and update her report. She wanted the SIO to be aware of certain things before his arrival: the conversation Kennedy overheard of Pete asking why his phone was switched off, his copy of today's newspaper, the meeting with the owners of Beckley House, James Howell's profession. The DI would want to know about those things.

She considered Jo's jumper hanging over the side of the bath, the clothes her husband had left on the bedroom floor, and was tempted to gather the items in evidence bags. It was important to be open and honest with the family, and she had explained to Jo already her reasons for being there. One was to help gather evidence. Her primary role was as an investigator – she was not deployed solely in a support role. This was a critical incident and she already had niggling doubts about the family. This could turn into a criminal investigation, and their involvement had to be considered. Better to have the items bagged and find nothing incriminating than to miss having potential forensic evidence.

Some colour had returned to Jo's face, and she was looking better than she had a short while ago. From her room she had found a cuddly toy to hold. Moraine guided her back down the stairs to sit her at the kitchen table. The chairs were less comfortable but the air more breathable, if a little heavy from pine disinfectant. Pete was on his mobile phone, fast tapping the screen, but as he caught sight of what Jo was carrying his eyes blazed wide.

He started towards her, his voice hard, his tone was accusatory as if she were on trial. 'How come you have his rabbit? He takes it with him everywhere. Never lets it out of his sight.'

Her quivering lips revealed her emotional state.

Moraine watched on in silence as Jo nervously swallowed, sucking in the hollow at the base of her neck. She shut her eyes, head down, shaking.

Her muteness made him shout. 'Answer, will you! We need to know. How do you have it, Jo?'

She let out a strangled sob. 'I found it in our bed just now. He slept with me last night.'

He wiped a hand across his mouth, as if holding in what he wanted to say, his shoulders then sagging. 'He'd never leave it behind... I don't understand.'

Her answer, quietly given, was bleak. 'You never do, Pete.'

Moraine took a moment to let them calm down, then addressed Kennedy in a voice loud enough for the parents to hear.

'I'm just going out to my car to collect some evidence bags. I need them for Sam's toothbrush and some items of clothes. It'll be done then for when the SIO arrives, and he'll be able to take them with him.'

Their faces rose to look at her. Moraine dealt with Jo first, knowing instinctively what she wanted. 'I mentioned it to Pete earlier, Jo. It's quite routine in a missing person situation to have something with their DNA on.'

Kennedy placed a mug of tea in front of Jo with an encouraging smile. 'You'll feel better for drinking that. I've popped some toast on for you as well. You need to line your stomach after being so sick, even if you just nibble at it.'

Moraine was grateful for his timely intervention. They were of the same rank, though she had a decade more experience than him, but you wouldn't know it from watching him. Life experiences had given him the ability to be more than able to understand people's needs.

Pete asked his question. 'Why is the senior investigating officer coming?'

Moraine was not surprised he knew what an SIO was. Apart from being a firefighter and working alongside police, the term was used widely enough on TV for it to become familiar with the public.

'Detective Inspector Stone wishes to meet you both. He would have visited before now if he wasn't so busy. But please don't see this as a sign of bad news. He likes to touch base with the families and let them see who's in charge behind the scenes, and give you the opportunity to ask questions.'

The answer seemed to satisfy him, as he lowered his head back to his phone. Jo simply stared straight ahead with dread in her eyes. Moraine hoped it was because she was simply fearing being asked what she couldn't answer. Or perhaps being visited in her home by the person in charge of the investigation reinforced how serious it was. Moraine hoped this was what made her look so afraid, and not something else. She really didn't want it to turn out that this tiny, terrified young woman had done anything wrong.

Moments later, she let herself out of the front door, relieved to be out of the home and breathing fresh air. She pulled out her phone and saw 17.54 on the screen. It was now seven hours since Sam Jenkins went missing. She swallowed the tension in her throat. That little boy had been gone for far too long. In a little under an hour the sun would set. The search party would continue on foot throughout the night, using flashlights, and the rescue helicopter would use thermal imaging cameras to detect heat. The area would have been separated into grids. But if he was not there, or had been taken, then no amount of searching in that location would find him.

Moraine needed to prepare for the next stage – the more frightening period yet to come. The waiting, and the unknowing, would get much worse if the search continued into the night with no new clues.

She pushed the harsh thought away. With her head in the boot of her car, looking for the evidence bags, she heard footsteps crunching on gravel. She looked around and saw Claire Howell approaching. Moraine was glad to see her. It would save her knocking at the door. She smiled at the woman.

'Hi. I was just about to call on you to let you know my senior officer will arrive soon. He may come in a police vehicle. I just wanted you to know in case you thought it might be Sam being brought home, which, sadly, is not yet the case.'

Claire Howell let go a lengthy sigh. 'Oh God, I was so hoping for better news. None of us can settle until we know what's happened to him. I know it's nothing compared to what Jo and Pete are going through. I don't know how they can bear it.' She pressed her hand against her mouth and briefly shook her head. 'I'll leave you to it. I'm sure you must have lots to do.

If you do get news though, would you please be so kind as to let us know? We're all so very worried.'

Moraine nodded, then waited until the woman walked away before fetching out her police kit bag. She didn't want the Howells guessing at what she was doing, for their sakes as much as the Jenkinses'. Collecting evidence from a person's home tended to label them as a suspect. She closed the boot and locked the car and began the walk back.

A movement at a second-floor window caught her eye. It was Lottie Howell staring out at her. Moraine raised a hand to acknowledge her. She is a lucky little girl to be at home and safe with her parents, Moraine thought, wishing it were that way for every child in the world.

Moraine sighed and trooped on, annoyed with herself for feeling low. She needed to remind herself that only a very small number of homicides happen following an abduction. She needed to focus on that for as long as possible and not give up hope of her colleagues finding the boy alive. They could come upon him somewhere in the dry, fast asleep, unaware that time had passed. He'd blink at them, sleepily, before asking for his mum. It was a warming thought to help her stay strong.

TEN

James looked deep in thought when Claire came to find him in his study. There was a vulnerability about him that took her breath away. Her strong and beautiful husband hadn't looked so sad in a long time. She wanted to reach out and comfort him, but remained standing at the door. He was not a man you could fuss over. He wouldn't welcome her seeing him like this with his guard down. She understood him better than he did himself sometimes, and privacy is what he needed right now. She quietly backed away to leave him in peace.

In the kitchen, she made herself some camomile tea and took it on a tray to the drawing room. She sat by a window in the light from the garden lamps and watched the police car coming towards the house. She'd been expecting its arrival sooner, as it was now ten past seven. When neatly parked, a uniformed officer emerged from the driver's seat. A moment later, the passenger door opened and a dark-suited man climbed out. From a distance, the collar of his shirt looked bright white against his dark skin. He walked under a lamp in the garden and Claire saw his handsome face. His height and build put her in mind of a rugby player. As she watched him, she felt slightly mesmerised, and jumped as a hand landed on her shoulder.

'James,' she gasped. 'Don't do that. You could have burnt me if I'd spilled my tea.'

He gazed out the window. 'I recognise that man. I've come across him before, and I'm trying to recall where. Do we know why he's here?'

Claire nodded. 'I imagine it's to meet Jo and Pete. He's the officer in charge. The liaison officer let me know he was coming, so we wouldn't think it was anything more than just a visit.'

'It will be, though,' he countered. 'He won't have come to just say hello. He's here to vet them.'

Claire stayed silent. It would be unfair to voice what she was thinking. He would see it as a defect in her character, that she was putting herself first. It was not something he needed to hear. The events of today had taken her straight back to that other terrible time that had taken them years to get over. It was the reason she hadn't wanted to agree to the Jenkinses coming to live on their property. Not simply because there was a child with them, but because their child was a living reminder.

Callous as it was, she had drifted from their friends so that she and James could move forward with their lives. Being around them had become deeply affecting when she was trying to bring up a four-year-old and a two-year-old in a lighter and happier atmosphere. She had told herself that by doing so she was freeing her family to have a better life, so they didn't have to sit in other people's pain. Which is why she was now overwhelmed with sadness, a primal awareness that they were about to revisit those dark days.

She stole a glance at James's face and could sense he was retreating inwards. He'd said little at suppertime and had left most of the food on his plate. She was concerned for him – his shoulders held stiffly, a muscle working in his jaw, his mind elsewhere.

James released a heavy breath and gestured out the window. 'I wish we'd had a security camera facing the house.'

'Why?'

His eyes turned to her, and his shoulders slumped. 'Because then we'd have seen Sam get in the car with Jo.'

Claire instantly understood. It was the reason Moraine Morgan had asked about cameras. The police wanted to see if Sam was in the vehicle. She was stunned that they would think that Sam wasn't in the vehicle with Jo when she drove off. She couldn't think it. It was the worst possible idea to imagine Jo would have driven somewhere without her son. To then what? Pretend he just disappeared. Is that what the police thought? She gave a small gasp.

'You must help them, James. If they think Sam wasn't with her...?'

He sighed, and then they heard footsteps coming to the door.

'Mummy?' Lottie's small voice called out as she rushed into the room. 'Do you think the black man has got Sam?'

Claire was startled by her younger daughter's prejudiced opinion and rebuked her firmly. 'You do not say things like that, Lottie. *Ever*. The man you saw is a policeman. He's helping to find Sam. What you said is unkind. Your friend, Latifa, would be very unhappy if she knew you said this.'

'But he is black, Mummy. I saw him in Sam's drawings. He's not a policeman.'

Claire remained firm. 'Did you or did you not see, out of your bedroom window, a man getting out of a police car?'

Lottie shook her head, her eyes round like saucers. 'No, Mummy. Sam draws him in our den. He does drawing when he's scared.'

Claire was perturbed. She didn't know they had a den, or where in the garden they might have built one.

In a calm voice, James commended Lottie. 'That was very

sensible of you to come and tell us. Why don't you pop your coat on so you can show me where this den is?'

She nodded solemnly. 'We need a torch, Daddy. We have to climb over a fence.'

Claire now knew where the den might be: the fenced-off area where all the wild garlic grew, their miniature woodland on the south side of the property.

Lottie's now eager face made Claire want to weep. In her world, she was expecting to find Sam in the den. She wouldn't ask her any further questions. She would wait to see if James discovered anything first. If there was anything concerning, they would have to take it to the police and trust they were doing the right thing.

She watched out the window as James and Lottie held hands and walked toward the woods, before resting her gaze on the police car. She didn't know what the police would do if they couldn't prove Sam was in the car. James would be more familiar with how things might progress. She wouldn't wish this situation on anyone. Losing a child was punishment enough without being treated as a suspect as well.

If only the sunshades had been up. She noticed them down when she saw the Range Rover earlier and briefly wondered why. There'd been no sun all day, only rain. Sam might have been seen inside the vehicle by a camera, or at least a silhouette of him. As it was, Jo might need to prove he was with her. With a shiver, she wondered if the police would think she did it on purpose.

She shuddered silently, feeling dread descending on her. The impotence of being unable to do anything would be with them once more. To her shame, she was thinking more about the past than what was happening to Jo, but she couldn't help it. Any more than she could stem her resentment towards James right now. He'd brought this into their lives by allowing Jo and Pete to live in the annexe when there was no need. She could quite easily have found a childminder elsewhere. Then their paths would never have crossed and she wouldn't be sitting there having to think about another missing child, having to witness another set of parents going through the same pain, having to worry about the police checking historical events at this very house. Theories about her father's death that had long since quietened, and was years since anyone mentioned it. Claire couldn't bear to have it dug up again.

James could have prevented this by turning a deaf ear to the Jenkinses' plight, but he wouldn't have done that. He wasn't the type to turn away from someone in need. It was his way of balancing out all the terrible things that happen in the world, that he had to hear about every day. She loved him for it, but it would be her who had to pick up the pieces and keep them all strong. Just as she had before. Protect them from their imaginations until all the pain was gone.

ELEVEN

Mick Stone's burly frame took up a lot of space in the kitchen. He smiled in a friendly manner as he pulled out a chair from the table and moved another to the side to give him more room.

'I blame my mother. She put me in a grow bag,' he said in a light tone, before clasping hands across his hard stomach and introducing himself.

The Jenkinses would be glad he didn't shake their hands if they knew that behind his back he was known as The Bruiser because of his tight grip. He was an amateur heavyweight boxer and hailed originally from South-East London where he decided on a career in the police instead of turning pro.

Kennedy, continuing to act as stand-in host, took an order for coffees and teas and set about preparing drinks. The uniformed officer who accompanied Stone was standing out of the way, but looking official, even if he was only the chauffeur.

Moraine sat in the chair nearest Jo, quietly wondering which way Stone would proceed. Her reports were up to date, so he would be up to speed. She could see the effect he had on the parents. Pete had his arms folded tightly across his expanded chest, sitting up taller, while Jo was sitting, hunkered down, as if waiting to be attacked.

Surprisingly, she was the first to speak. 'Is there any news?'

Stone glanced at her and slowly shook his head. 'We've had a look at the CCTV showing the road to the car park. I'd like to show you the few seconds of footage we have.'

He took a laptop out of his leather satchel and placed it on the table in a position where everyone could see. A moment later they were watching Jo, clearly visible, driving the Range Rover into the car park. She parks and exits the vehicle, putting a bag over her shoulder, before closing the door. The top half of her visible in a pale puffer coat as she opens the rear door and grabs something from the back seat. She shuts it, then pulls the hood up on her coat. Footage shows the back of her head and shoulders as she threads her way through parked vehicles, before disappearing from view.

Stone paused the video on an image of the car park. 'We've looked at the cameras at the swimming pool, though not very helpful, I might add. We've looked at security cameras from shops, people's homes, a petrol station. The CCTV on the high street. We've looked at dashcam footage. We've not had a single sighting of your son, nor any witnesses who saw him.'

Moraine sensed the tension in the air as Stone laid it out for them. Pete was staring sceptically at his wife. She could understand why – his son was nowhere to be seen.

A panicked look was in Jo's eyes, darting movements signifying her anxiety. She reached out a trembling hand to touch the screen. Disbelief spreading across her face. She shook her head in denial as she gazed in shock at Stone. In a tremulous voice she pleaded, 'How can that be? How is that possible? He was with me the whole time! Right by my side. Tucked under my coat.'

Raw panic filled her cry. 'He was with me! You can see me getting him out of his car seat!'

Stone let out a resigned sigh. 'I wish we could. Your journey. Tinted glass windows and blackout sunshades… Is there a reason why they were pulled down?'

Jo looked cornered, her eyes starting with tears. 'The girls like it dark when I'm driving, if they're on their iPads. The car belongs to their parents. I don't ever touch the blinds.'

Pete was still staring intently at his wife, his eyebrows knitted together in a deep frown. Stone must be aware of it, but didn't comment on it. Instead, he continued speaking to both parents.

'We're using social media, local press, posters of Sam everywhere. The appeal made earlier asking members of the public to come forward with any information has provided no leads. We urgently need to find your son, so I'd like to suggest that together you make a public appeal. Putting the parents on television has proven useful sometimes in locating the missing person. If someone knows his whereabouts or Sam is being held against his will, a parent's plea might give them reason to speak out or let him go. If you agree, we can get that set up asap. It'll mean coming to the station, so we can accommodate reporters. We've missed the local evening news, but it could be aired on the ten o'clock news bulletin.'

Pete uttered his first words since Stone's arrival, standing up from the table as if getting ready to leave. 'I'll do it. I'll do it on my own. Jo's in no fit state.'

Judging from her pale face, he was not wrong. She looked ill. Moraine was surprised by the sudden care, when only minutes ago he had shown no sympathy for her at all, and was glad when Stone asked Jo how she felt about it.

'It's up to you, Mrs Jenkins, whether you feel you can manage it. Sad to say, but the public like to see the parents in cases like this.'

Jo glanced at her husband anxiously, blinking away the

tears, before clutching her stomach to take a deep breath. 'I'll do it with Pete.'

He didn't reply, or look at her. He sat back down instead, reaching for his mug, and drank thirstily.

Stone glanced at Moraine and indicated with a tilt of his head towards the door that he'd like to see her on her own. Standing up, he told the Jenkinses he'd see them soon.

Outside, he wasted little time conveying his concerns.

'My gut is telling me this appeal will be a waste of time. I'd rather be questioning her. But we have to do this on the chance that this is an abduction. We need the bigger picture here, from both him and her. I've read everything she said, and now, having met them, I know it's there. They're hiding something. I can feel it in my bones. Not just her, but him as well. His behaviour doesn't strike me as someone whose son is missing.'

He drew breath, then nodded towards Beckley House. 'Thanks for the tip-off. That's all we need, having a top barrister watch our every move.'

Moraine was glad she'd described James Howell's view of the parents and his support of them in the report. She intended to do everything by the book.

As they neared the police car, Stone stopped and turned to look at the main house. His eyes screwing up in concern, he muttered under his breath, 'Shit. I hope not.'

He turned and gave her a tight grimace. 'I really fucking hope not,' he repeated in a terse whisper. 'I hope some bastard hasn't mistaken this for the child's home.'

Moraine felt her stomach drop. She should have thought of this herself. Surrounded by all this grandeur, and the Range Rover Jo was driving – they were symbols of wealth and success. She should have mentioned right at the start that when she knocked at the door of Beckley House she'd thought it was Jo Jenkins's home. If it was a kidnapping, they were dealing with a serious perpetrator and not an opportunist. Someone who had planned carefully and could have taken a child without being seen.

Stone inhaled deeply. 'Look, I'm aware you'll be needing someone else to take over. Same for PC Kennedy. If I get relief for the pair of you overnight, can you be back here in the morning? The parents are comfortable with you, and Kennedy is doing a great job in there. The two of you work well as a team.'

Moraine's thoughts were going nineteen to the dozen. She didn't want to leave, given that this might now be a kidnapping. She felt responsible for not thinking of the possibility sooner. 'I'm happy to stay all night, sir.'

Stone shook his head. 'No. I need you fresh for tomorrow. Let me sort things out for overnight. I'll need to come back here and talk to the owners to put them in the picture, in case they suddenly get a phone call.'

Moraine was thinking about his opinion earlier and was wondering if that had changed. 'What about the Jenkinses, sir? Are you still of the same mind?'

He looked momentarily taken aback, before a grim look settled in his eyes. 'Hell, yes. Even though she says he was with her, we've hundreds of images from the wedding party, there's not a single one shows him in the background. Not one image to show he was there. So most definitely. Neither one is off the radar.'

When he didn't say more but walked to the car, Moraine took her leave. She needed to get the Jenkinses ready for their plea to the public. She hoped Stone was mistaken, that it wouldn't be a waste of time, that callers would start ringing as soon as the programme aired and that someone knew something. Anything to help find this child.

TWELVE

A raindrop landed on her nose as she stood by the car that would take them to the police station. Moraine was driving, Pete was in the back. She raised her face and stared up at the dark clouds. It was going to lash down very soon. Heavy drops hit her forehead and trickled down her eyelids, soothing the tender skin. She blinked the water away.

'Get in, Jo, you'll get wet,' Pete called from inside the car.

Jo climbed in, wondering if he was even thinking about their son. He seemed more concerned with staying dry.

An image of Sam swam before her eyes. He wasn't wearing a coat. An unbearable guilt swamped her. Her mind tortured her by constantly replaying her futile hunt for him. In her arms, she held his soft blue rabbit and hugged it against her bare neck. Her body felt so tight with pain she could barely breathe. Her mind needed to be focused elsewhere, and she glanced at Pete, hoping for a reprieve from her anguish.

Freshly shaved, wearing a shirt and jacket, he was staring out of the window waiting for the car to start. She wished she hadn't noticed that he had taken the time to change, while she had dragged on her coat and come as she was in an old jumper and jeans.

He was looking at the Howells' home, probably thinking this was the world he wanted for his family. Wine on the table at suppertime, a cook in the kitchen waiting to serve them, to be elegantly groomed and have a child at private school. She remembered the elation in his eyes at seeing inside Beckley House: the furniture, wallpapers, paint colours, artwork, like the pages in the magazines that Claire read – *Architectural Digest*, *Vogue*, *Harper's Bazaar*.

He enjoyed being here. Liked the fact that Sam was brushing shoulders with the children next door, and that he could say that a barrister played the occasional game of golf with him on a Sunday.

It had been *one* Sunday, *one* game of golf, not how he made it sound when on the phone to someone, airily dropping it into the conversation. Like he was best friends with the Howells, and he was well in there.

She shivered in her coat, imagining what the Howells were thinking right now. Probably something along the lines of Jo being an incapable parent and questioning themselves for choosing someone like her to mind their children. Maybe she would lose theirs as well. Her nails dug through the bandages into her palms, bringing a surge of pain. Maybe they thought Sam had run away and were asking themselves what would make a child do that, imagining an abuse of some kind.

Her cry erupted uncontrollably. 'Oh God, what have I done?' Her eyes were wild with anguish.

Pete grabbed her wrist. 'No tears. You don't want Sam to see you crying on the telly.'

A keening sound came from her throat. 'How will he see me? How will he possibly see me, Pete? He's gone.'

He grabbed her other wrist to make her face him. 'Stop it, Jo. We're making this appeal in the hope someone's seen him.

We're making it to get him back. You need to calm down and appear rational.'

She could see he was losing patience when he looked at her. Apart from his outbursts of blaming her, the trauma of the last ten hours didn't seem to have left its mark on him, and she wondered how he was able to manage his emotions. Did his son being missing not terrify him? Was he numb to what she was feeling, or did he simply have no interest?

She pulled her hands away and turned her face to the side window. Her blue eyes, made bluer by the paleness of her skin, stared back at her. She had lost not only her son, but her husband as well. She felt a depression like she had never felt before, a deep dark hole she had fallen in, blacker than black, over her, around her, beneath her. She would stay there and not bother to climb out.

She swallowed against the lump growing in her throat. She was still on the wait-list for the specialist trauma-informed counselling, according to her GP. She couldn't see any point in waiting for it. Therapy wasn't going to change anything. There was nothing more to live for.

The car came to a stop at the back of the building. After Jo was helped out of the car by Moraine, they entered through heavy swing doors. Beige painted walls and an orangey-brown floor led the way down a narrow sloping corridor. It was a dismal introduction to the place, especially with what they were about to do. Halfway along, Moraine opened a door and ushered them through to a grey-carpeted conference room with blue chairs set out in rows in front of laminated tables where they would sit. Water jugs and glasses were set out for them. Microphone cables trailed down to the floor.

Moraine took Jo to a chair while a police officer in a white shirt and tie spoke with Pete. Jo saw the sheet of paper in his hands, which he passed to Pete, and guessed it to be a written statement prepared for him by a press officer.

She took slow breaths and kept her eyes lowered as the room filled. The chairs on either side of her were pulled out and Pete sat down on her right, Moraine on her left. She could hear cameras clicking above the noise of chatter and shuffling chairs. She jolted at the sudden voice coming over a speaker. The detective who came to their home was beginning proceedings. He had a voice that captured attention even when speaking quietly. Heavy sounding. Strong and full of volume, like a storm brewing. She only half listened, keeping her eyes focused on the bandages on her hands, the dirt in her nail beds.

The room silenced. She felt Pete move in his chair beside her. He turned the sheet of paper face down. He wasn't going to read what was provided him, use his own words instead. Maybe he was told he could if confident enough. His voice, unlike the man who had just spoken, was airy, like he was out of breath or nervous. He should take a deep breath, she thought, and start again. Pete cleared his throat as if realising how he was sounding and now made a better job of it. He spoke clearly, using his diaphragm to project his voice.

'Our five-year-old son has gone missing today. His name is Sam. I'm Sam's father, Pete, and this is his mum, Jo. Sam is small for his age and has light-brown hair and blue eyes like his mum. He can be quite shy around grown-ups, but if you talk to him about bugs and insects, he'll come out of himself. Now I don't know if Sam is alone, or with someone, but if you are that someone and you are watching me, please, please let him go. I'm pleading with you: walk away. Make an anonymous call or leave him in a place where he can be found. You can do this. Just walk away from this. It's not too late. No matter what has happened throughout this day, you can walk away.

'You may be frightened and think things have gone too far. Or maybe you're watching this and thinking we should have watched over him more carefully. It's our fault that you've got him. We shouldn't have let him out of our sight. Well, let me tell you, you'd be right. We should have kept our eyes on him. But I'm begging you, for his sake, to let us have our son back. Please do it for Sam. He needs his mum and dad badly. So please, give us another chance. He only has us and we desperately want him home.'

Jo raised her head. She couldn't see the sea of faces in front of her. They were all blurred. She could hear her name being called. Not Pete's, but hers. Jo, look this way. Jo, where did you last see him? Jo, how are you coping? Jo, Jo, Jo…

They had no questions for Pete, just for her. She was the one who was with Sam, the one who was minding him. There was no 'us' in any of what Pete said. There was only *her*. Her fault, her failing, her answerability. She, who let him disappear.

THIRTEEN

A damp cardboard box sat on Claire's kitchen table, full of Sam's drawings. There was no one she could give them to as there was no one at Jo's home. Moraine Morgan's car and the police vehicle were gone from the front of the house unexpectedly. She hadn't heard or seen them leave.

She lifted the lid of the box and leafed through a few of the drawings and understood why Lottie was saying it was a black man. A figure was crayoned jet black, with a hat on its head. There were black skies, black grasses, and black suns. The square shape of a building. Lots of small spiky mounds on the ground, maybe little black hedgehogs. No other colours in the drawings, despite a choice of other crayons in a zipped pencil bag.

She wondered where Pete and Jo had gone. She could only begin to imagine what they were going through. The door behind her opened, and she tensed, but it was only James coming into the kitchen.

He gestured to the television on the wall and picked up the remote to turn it on. 'You didn't see it then,' he said. 'That's why they're not home. They were on the news making a public appeal. I'll put it on for you on iPlayer. You'll be surprised. I didn't know Pete could be so eloquent. It's not scripted, that's for sure.'

As she saw the photo of Sam appear on the television screen, her chest felt heavy. His hair looked shiny and clean for his school photograph, his shirt nice and white with his little stripy tie. The man she saw earlier spoke. His voice suited his appearance. Commanding.

Jo sat beside her husband with her head lowered, wearing her light-grey puffer coat, her hair pushed behind her ears. Pete, in a shirt and jacket, looked far more appealing, yet the camera stayed on her longer. Claire could see fine tremors sweeping along her jawline, and found it uncomfortable to watch. The public could be so cruel and Jo looked bedraggled and at her worst. If she'd gone round to see her, she would have helped tidy her up a bit to make her more like her normal self before letting her go on live television.

Pete's speech, awkward to begin with, was very moving. And then it was over, and Jo's streaming eyes stared out at her. She was caught and held in the lights, which didn't do her pale face any favours, while reporters called out to her. Pete was rising from the table and moving away. The chair where the liaison officer had been sitting was now empty, and for a few moments Jo was on her own at the table until the officer reappeared and steered her away.

She switched off the TV.

James had made her some more tea. 'Thank you, I need that. That was heartbreaking,' she whispered. 'Why didn't Pete hold her hand? He's a blasted buffoon sometimes, with his neat jacket and hair. People will notice that and think he cares more about his appearance than the disappearance of his child. I need to go round and see her and let her know I've been trying all afternoon but couldn't with the police there.'

She glanced at James for confirmation, and instantly quietened her thoughts. He was holding his head in his hands as if in pain, alarming her.

'Do you need me to fetch you some painkillers?'

'No. I'm not in pain. It's just...' He raised his head and stared at her. 'I don't think I can do this again.'

His face looked drained, while painful emotions swam in the depths of his eyes. This was all too much for him. His mind couldn't shut out images like hers could. He had seen too many crime scene photographs in his time. She couldn't take that from his mind. He was too intelligent for her to even try. She could not manipulate him into thinking of something else, either, like she had earlier. All she could do was stay strong for him and recognise the signs when he needed to close off.

He became like this when dealing with a particularly heinous crime, and almost didn't want her and the children to be around him, as if the thoughts in his head might infect them. His knowledge of the worst forms of human behaviour was something he kept to himself and never shared with her. He preferred to keep the horror stories in his head and not put them in anybody else's.

She decided not to state the obvious. That they had no choice. What was happening was already here. Their tenants' son was lost to them. That wouldn't change unless he was found. She didn't like seeing him this low, and wanted to comfort him, but couldn't find the right words.

He glanced up at the ceiling and exhaled wearily, then looked at her with harrowed eyes. 'This is going to bring it all back for Marley and Stuart. They're going to see this on TV and feel it happening all over again.'

Claire felt her heart freeze. It grieved her that James was thinking of the Lamberts now, while he should have thought of them at the very moment when Sam was introduced into their lives. The likeness had no doubted comforted him. She could understand that – it was like looking at Marley and Stuart's son playing in the garden. The same little face.

She felt a surge of resentment that her home was becoming a place of bad memories. It had been her great-grandfather's home and his great-grandparents' heritage long before him. The historic building and surrounding estate would eventually pass down to future generations. The old paintings stored carefully in the attics might one day hang again on the walls if her own children decided against their mother's décor. They would see they were descended from landed gentry with paintings of ancestors mounted on horses with their hounds around their feet, and of ladies in cloth bonnets with embroidery hoops in their laps.

It had taken over three years to change the interior while preserving its original features. She started the project not long after she lost contact with Marley, as it was too painful to be around her and they needed a real change in their lives. The new décor had worked wonderfully well and swept out the ghosts, but they were gradually creeping back because of what was happening now. The only way to make them go again was to find a better resolution.

Only this wasn't the same as before. The parents weren't thought to be involved last time. Jo was being looked at closely because they hadn't seen her little boy with her in the car.

James had brought this on them by wanting to balance out the bad with something good. It was not something she could discuss with him, only what she felt. Her husband had found a coping mechanism that he might not even be aware of. He might refute this irrational feeling, but in her heart she knew this was what had happened. He was seeing Matt in Sam.

She felt her throat closing. Her complicated husband had locked up his traumas after sharing them with her just once. Of the guilt pressing down on him for years. The love for these boys, coupled with the tragedy of Matt, was all tied into that. The shock of Matt suddenly gone had heaped more guilt, that he couldn't prevent it happening.

She had held them safe throughout their marriage, never speaking of them to him. She was there to love him, and protect him from himself sometimes. And now, like before, be strong for him again.

A wave of ill feeling washed over her. What of her traumas? The years of having to protect her family name. They had managed to escape publicity during that whole awful period with Matt. Their home on the outskirts of Bath, they had not been Marley and Stuart's neighbours and had managed to stay in the background as just their friends. But their connection to her and James could become known if knowledge of Sam's address became public.

Her life would be looked at – her father's death remembered – falling from the Juliet balcony in the master bedroom. Was it an accident or suicide? That had been the question in everyone's mind. She had kept the full extent of it secret. Unlike her husband, she never unburdened herself. The sadness, the shame, the turbulent relationship... knowing only tough love.

While she'd do everything she could to help Jo through her predicament, she had to safeguard her own family first. She would do what she could to clear this dreadful suspicion from Jo, as it would be awful if she was found guilty of more than just losing her son.

Claire was well aware what could happen if Jo became a prime suspect. It would mean the end of their privacy – their name and their home would be splashed across tabloids for all to read about. Their judgement would be called into question.

She sighed inwardly and glanced at him wearily, wishing he'd dealt with his demons. Instead of letting them shadow him to affect the rest of his life. He owed it to their daughters and to her to be stronger than this. They had witnessed how horrifyingly fast life got snatched away. There was no benefit to revisiting the past; all it brought was a return of bad memories. Destroying one's sanity. Leaving weakness in the mind and foolish notions. That it was a curse.

FOURTEEN

Moraine was relieved Jo was upstairs, lying on her bed. It would give her quiet time to assess her thoughts. Her initial judgement of the situation on entering the home had undergone a certain amount of readjustment. Like a ping-pong ball getting zapped back and forth across a table, her mind kept changing direction. She had a mother upstairs, clearly distraught, with eyelids swollen from spilled tears, and a father who hadn't shed a drop, yet had managed to deliver that impassioned plea.

She watched Kennedy tuck in to the sandwiches in the Tupperware box provided by the Howells, and didn't blame him. Neither of them had eaten a proper meal since they arrived. Tomorrow, she'd bring provisions, and suggest to DI Stone that Kennedy be allowed to wear civvies. She remembered from her time wearing the uniform that the vest and utility belt weighed you down, and the boots made your feet feel hot.

'I'm just going to check on the husband,' she informed him. 'Make sure he's okay.'

In the short hallway, Moraine could hear Pete talking quietly on his mobile, his words reaching her ears through the open door. She stayed still to listen. It sounded like he was giving someone a mild telling-off.

'Never do that again. No one could get hold of me. I know you didn't think, but it looked bloody bad all the same.'

He stopped speaking and Moraine held her breath, only to relax again as he carried on talking.

'It was bloody hard, I can tell you that, saying all those things with cameras flashing in your face. Jo's a mess and couldn't say a word… Yeah, I know she's in a state, but I am, too. The police are still here now… Yes, I know you do. Thanks. I will. I'll call you tomorrow… Yeah, me too. Night night.'

Moraine hesitated only a second before tapping on the door and entering the room. 'I didn't want to disturb you while you were on the phone. I just wanted to let you know Jo's upstairs on the bed, hopefully sleeping.'

She held his gaze, gauging his reaction. She didn't feel any emotional connection to him yet. It wasn't just his prickly character – he had a right to be himself – it was more his detachment from all that was happening that prevented her feeling empathy towards him.

He stared at her, pulling his hands through his hair. 'Just one of my colleagues. Checking to see how I am.'

'Would that be the same colleague who switched your phone off today? PC Kennedy heard you earlier, sounding a little annoyed. Not surprising really. It stopped us getting a hold of you.'

For a moment, he glared. 'Is there no privacy in my own home? I don't expect to have my conversations listened to.'

She gave him a benign smile. 'It's not deliberate. It's a small building and voices carry. I'm sorry if we've upset you. Perhaps now would be a good time for us to talk. With all that's been happening, I've yet to take a statement from you. Why don't we do that now? Shall we sit in the kitchen where we can write it all down?'

His arms folded tight against his chest as he drew in a long, heavy breath. His condescending tone was as annoying as his remark: 'I see. Are you experienced in handling this type of situation?'

Moraine refrained from jutting out her chin. 'Are you asking if I have experience in taking a statement, Pete?' she said calmly.

His mouth twisted in derision as he loomed closer. '*Oh, please*. You're not here to make us tea and hold our hands. You're here to watch us. Isn't that the way you people set these things up? Get close to the family, find all the skeletons? Get close to the person who you think has done the deed and get all the information you want? But by all means, fire away, jot it all down. Let's not have experience go to waste.'

Moraine wondered if this was manufactured anger – a ploy to avoid their conversation. She was tempted to point out that the F in FLO didn't stand for female, that plenty of male officers also volunteered for this role. But she would prefer his cooperation.

'I can see you're upset, Pete... understandably, but you're not entirely incorrect. While I like to do everything I can to help a family during an unbearable situation, I'm a detective constable and have a duty to investigate. Obtaining a detailed family background history is part of the investigation.'

He brushed past her with a curt reply. 'Fine. Let's get on with it then. I'd like to be with my wife.'

She shook her head behind his back, as so far he'd shown the complete opposite.

In the kitchen, Kennedy set about making Pete a coffee and offering him some sandwiches. His expression seemed to lighten when he found out who had provided them and he gave his first voluntary comment.

'I must thank them. I'll go and see them when this is done and let them know what's happening.'

Kennedy shook his head. 'Might not be the best time to go and visit. The SIO is with them. Maybe better to wait until he's gone.'

Moraine applauded Kennedy in her mind for his timely disclosure. She wanted Pete Jenkins aware of what was going on around him. Knowing that his neighbours were being spoken to might put him off balance.

She pulled out the relevant paperwork from her bag and placed it on the table, together with a pen, then glanced at him to show she was ready.

'Let's start with yesterday morning. How were things before you left to go to Manchester? How was Jo then? Was she all right with you going?'

He gave a slight grimace. 'She was fine. A bit concerned about taking the weekend off because it would mean having to keep Sam with her the whole time. Normally, we juggle minding him around her doing her job. It was today she was more concerned about, as Saturdays she takes Claire's girls for horse riding lessons.

'It was me who suggested she ask for the weekend off, so she didn't have that pressure. She didn't need to take him out to some swimming pool. She gets worried about him wanting to play with them too much. Sees problems where there aren't any. James and Claire are not like that. They don't mind him playing in their garden. They have more than one. Vegetable plots and orchards and whatnot. The household staff have taken to him, and make sure he's fed the same time as them by the resident cook. The gardeners give him sweet treats. They don't mind Sam playing in the garden. It's just Jo who gets anxious about keeping boundaries. Lives on her nerves a bit.'

Moraine was waiting for him to mention again the medication Jo was on. He went one step further and got up from his chair to fetch them out of the cupboard. He placed them on the table and tapped the box with his finger.

'She's been on these for a year. Plus sleeping pills. Not sure if they do any good or not.'

She wouldn't ask him to elaborate on that, not yet anyway. For the time being, she was more interested in hearing about him and his night away.

'So, on the whole, she was fine when you left, just a little concerned about taking time off?'

'Yes.'

'So you travelled to Manchester, driving yourself, for this conference?'

'Yes.'

'Can you give me the name of the hotel where you stayed? We will, of course, need to verify it as I'm sure you can understand.'

'The Marriott,' he replied, before reaching for the mug of coffee and taking a drink.

Moraine made a show of writing it down, while Kennedy made a point of asking which one. 'They've got a few, haven't they? There's one by the airport I stayed at, and one in the city centre, I remember. I think there's a few of them dotted about.'

'The one in the city. It's got a big conference room,' he said in a disinterested tone.

Moraine wondered at his offhand manner. He'd been quick enough to show her Jo's medication. Why wasn't he making the same effort to show her his confirmation email? He must surely have one. Most people, when talking to the police, were eager to show proof of where they had been.

'So, the conference, did it begin yesterday when you arrived?'

'No, they let us settle in. Left us free to do our own thing the first day. I took the opportunity to get plenty of sleep. Not something I get much chance to do at home with a five-year-old.'

'Did you speak to Jo at all yesterday afternoon or evening?'

'Yeah. I gave a quick call around six o'clock.'

'And how was she? Did you speak to Sam?'

'She didn't give me the chance,' he huffed. 'In a rush to get off the phone.'

Moraine was conscious of the multiple slights made against his wife and wanted to turn the spotlight back on him: 'So no other phone calls after that? Were you there at the hotel this morning when you found out Sam was missing?'

'No, we didn't speak again. And, yes. Like I said, a colleague saw it on Facebook. That's why I rushed home.'

'When were you scheduled to check out?'

'Tomorrow. I was meant to be coming back then. But that was out of the question once I knew Sam was missing. I had to come home.'

Moraine asked a few more questions. Nothing to rile him, just some basic facts.

Moraine got him to read the statement before signing his name to it. She'd deliberately not mentioned seeing his newspaper. It would be something to challenge him about later if he was formally questioned. For now, though, she would report what she had so his alibi could be verified.

She put the paperwork away and let him know what was happening. 'PC Kennedy and I will be relieved shortly. Someone else will be with you overnight, and we'll be back in the morning. Is there anything you wish to ask us before we leave?'

He shook his head. 'No. Apart from wondering why someone needs to stay? There's no need for it. You can phone us if you hear anything. I'm sure you've got better things to do than babysitting us.'

Moraine gave a non-committal shrug. 'We'll try not to be in your way. As this is a critical incident, it's best to have someone here in case of fresh developments. Part of our role is to support you. I hope you feel we are giving you this. Your wife is suffering a great deal, and that's a lot to cope with on your own.'

He clasped his hands on top of his head, giving a heavy sigh. 'I'm sure she appreciates all your help. I don't want to think about what she'll be like tomorrow if you haven't found him by then... Just please bring good news.'

She couldn't promise that, and couldn't let him know what she was thinking. Despite reminding herself earlier that only a very small number of homicides happen, she was a trained police officer. The drill on cases like this: think homicide until you are reasonably happy it is not.

It was Jo's eyes... devoid of hope all day long. It worried Moraine that she had none. Hope was the last thing to relinquish, and that usually only happened when it got snatched away by a knock on the door to deliver condolences with a death notification.

It concerned her that Pete didn't get to speak to his son, and that Sam wasn't seen with Jo. Why was that? Did something happen the night before he went missing? Inside this home? Had Jo blocked a traumatic event? Moraine had encountered mothers who had lost a child to sometimes pretend that their child was still alive. Imagining conversations with them, getting out clothes to dress them in, and taking them out in a pram.

Why did Jo have his bunny, if it was something he never let out of his sight? Did Sam forget to take it with him? Was it simply that?

They were unsettling thoughts. And lingering in the back of her mind was an awareness of what was missing from Jo. The constant questions that most people ask and repeat at every passing hour: Any news yet? Any update? Any word? Wanting the constant reassurance of the police finding their child.

FIFTEEN

Jo walked into Sam's room and lay on his bed, wanting to be alone. She didn't want Pete joining her in their bed if he came upstairs. The thought of him lying beside her was too much to bear.

Her clothes were damp from the rain, from where she'd tried to take Pete's car to go out and look for Sam. He'd caught her in the act and taken the keys from her, while their new liaison officer had gently scolded, telling her she was in no fit state to drive and would be better off resting. Her body refused to make that possible. Every muscle and nerve was rigid with fear. No one was believing she had Sam with her.

She pushed her face into Sam's pillow and breathed in the scent of his hair, like sweet biscuits and fresh earth. She hugged his rabbit against her bare neck, wishing it was with him in his arms, knowing how much he loved it. Images of his dead body kept flashing through her mind. She was torturing herself with waiting for the phone to ring or the door to be knocked. The torment wouldn't stop.

The softness beneath her aching body gave no relief. She

may as well be lying on concrete. She didn't know how much longer she could cope with this pain. Her heart felt bruised from beating so hard. She trembled violently. A heavy sob was working its way free. She bit hard on her lower lip, trying to hold it in, and then, unable to control herself, a loud shuddering breath escaped. Her eyes flew open, desperate to escape the dark. Her son was dead and she was not there with him.

She now knew why some people expressed relief at not having children when they heard about parents losing a child. It was to avoid having to feel this unbearable grief. Having that overwhelming love that bound you to them night and day suddenly taken away was something she wouldn't wish on anyone. It was as if a part of her had been ripped out. The thought of never seeing him, holding him and loving him again had plunged her into a constant state of fear. She would surely go insane.

She heard someone on the stairs. Straining to hear something more, only silence reached her ears, until a creak as they went back down them again. She bet it was Pete. He must have sensed she was awake and would not come in and see her. He wasn't checking if she was all right. Today, more than ever, she noticed his complete lack of care.

His unprepared speech had sounded like the words of a loving father desperate to have his son back. Yet he'd shown none of that emotion in their home. Where was his desperation, his crippling fear that he wouldn't see him again? Was his tie to Sam broken as well? Did he not care about either of them? The man she once knew would have been out there tearing down walls to find his boy. He would have had every one of his crew searching alongside him. He wouldn't have been downstairs in a clean shirt, in the warm, drinking mugs of coffee while his son was still missing.

Where had that man disappeared to? The superficial

version of her husband was someone she didn't recognise. His son was missing, and unbelievable as it was, the impact didn't seem to have registered with him. Had he blocked it out? Was he able to do that? Or was guilt eating away at him and he was too cowardly to confide in her?

He didn't know that she already knew about the hurt he had done to their son. Or what Sam's teacher had said.

She couldn't remember the last time he said, 'I love you.' Or 'I miss you'. Or 'Come to bed'. They had drifted so far apart she may as well be invisible.

He showed little interest in what she had to say, unless it was about the Howells. Then he was all ears. He wanted to know every minutia of their lives. What brands they wore, which wines they drank, the food they ate, and betting on it all coming from Fortnum & Mason.

He seemed to forget that they were Jo's employers. Knowing them a little did not make them close friends. Living on the grounds of Beckley House did not give them a higher social standing. The gates he came through, the tree-lined driveway he cruised along to their door, was not their property.

He seemed to forget they were living in accommodation provided to them under false pretences. Or to think about why she might not want a closer relationship with the Howells, or have them become interested in her personal history. He wasn't the one having to hide his past or fool these decent people.

A memory of how they used to be came back to her earlier. She passed a small fire station and drill tower, and thought of the fundraising event he had taken her to on one of their dates. It had been exhilarating seeing him take part in a drill, in a fire suit, with breathing apparatus, an oxygen cylinder on his back, while handling a hose as though it was a garden variety job attached to an outside tap. She had felt in awe of his strength, and utterly feminine and protected in his arms that night. It was a long while since she felt like that.

Tonight, she had felt his accusing stare across the table, in front of the detective in charge. And confirmed what she had been aware of for some time – something she had to accept – he didn't love her.

SIXTEEN

On hearing the front door close firmly behind the police officers, Claire felt a wave of nausea hit her. Clutching a hand to her mouth, she dashed into the bathroom. The sour taste of vomit filled her throat as she retched into the toilet bowl. Several minutes passed before her composure returned. It had been a very unsettling visit.

After handing over the box of drawings, it was decided a visit to the den would happen in the morning, and that a talk with their daughters would be helpful. Poor Lottie and Phoebe. They were gradually being sucked into this nightmare as well.

The video footage of the Range Rover leaving the property was viewed again. A discussion about having their phone tapped was proposed, in the event they received any ransom demands.

Her mind was going round in circles. Did they think Sam had been kidnapped because he was mistaken for a child of the owners? She hadn't once considered the police might think that was the reason for him being gone. She realises then that she's never considered how easily something like this could happen to her daughters.

She sank into a chair and pulled a throw around her, suddenly cold and shivering. She'd been conscious the entire time of DI Stone's presence. Waiting for a comment to pass about the tragic death of her father. She was being obsessively sensitive with the anniversary looming, allowing her mind to fill with turbulent emotions. Feeling forced to remember back and glimpse her ten-year-old self. Adept at hiding her pain, she'd not allowed herself to grieve. It's what had made her a good mother – learning how to stay strong.

James was looking out the window, his jaw set firm, his mouth a thin line, brooding. She glanced at the black-marble mantel clock that kept perfect time, and saw it was twenty minutes to midnight. An overwhelming sadness suffocated her. She wanted to say something to him, tell him he had let her down, but the haunted look in his eyes wouldn't allow her. He was blaming himself already.

She took a deep breath to calm her racing heart. If he was going to be like this, locking her out while he dwelled on the past, she couldn't be with him. She wanted him to help the family next door and make it right for them, to deliberate on the situation and kick down some doors to save them. He had every tool at his disposal – he dealt with cases like this to help others – so why wasn't he looking for a solution for Jo?

She'd learned very little from DI Stone. His eyes told her nothing of his thoughts. But his one comment when watching the Range Rover drive out the gates had sent a shiver through her. *You can't see if the child is in the car.* His voice was deadly serious. He was questioning whether Jo's son was with her in the car when she left the house.

James moved from the window to the fireplace. He pressed his foot against the hearth, his hand against the mantel, and glanced at her with a deep frown between his eyes. 'Tomorrow we're going to have to keep the gates shut. I'll leave word with Dougie. If you can remind the others?'

Claire frowned back at him. 'But the police will be coming.'

'I realise that. Dougie will have to let them in. You can expect reporters at the gate tomorrow. It'll be front-page news.'

His directness was alarming. While she'd assumed his mind was on the past, he was thinking about what was to come. Reporters and cameras, trying to see into their home.

She looked at him, appalled. 'What about the girls? I don't want them being photographed. Maybe I should move them to Mother's?'

He held her gaze for a few seconds, then said, 'Do you think that's wise? Think about the perspective. You'd be moving your children away from a suspect. Is that what you want? To show that you don't trust Jo around your children?'

Her lower lip quivered. Why was he being like this? Was he goading her? 'Of course that's not what I want. I want you to help Jo. I thought you understood that. Obviously, I didn't make myself clear. I can't bear the thought of her being blamed for something she hasn't done.'

'I see.' His eyes bore into her. 'And you're so sure about that, are you? That she's completely innocent?'

Her hands grasped the throw to be free of it. She rose quickly from the chair with a quivering sensation in her chest and had to swallow hard. 'Of course I am. Why wouldn't I be?'

He shifted under her gaze, his face grim. 'I wish I could believe your concern is all for Jo. I'm not comfortable with either parent being a suspect, but I will not run away.'

His words were like a slap across the face. He was saying she was shallow. Trying to be hurtful. Was he hoping to discover great truths with this needling? Resentment shuddered through her body and came out in her voice. 'What are you talking about?'

'Aren't you a little worried how it may come across? That we had a killer in our midst minding our own children?'

She gaped at him, taking a step back. Why on earth would

he say a killer? Surely he didn't think Sam was dead. His eyes pinned her still. This is how he dealt with someone in the witness box. Giving no warning of his attack. She had to stand there and listen to his verdict.

'There are no eyewitnesses who saw Sam with her. Her son has gone missing without a trace. You want me to help her? This is how I help. I look at the facts without getting emotionally involved. At present, they're stacked against her. The husband away, the child disappears, the marriage is not close. Right there, you have opportunity and motive.'

She gave a strangled cry. 'What motive? What makes you say they're not close?'

'Really?' He shook his head slowly and tutted at her. 'I thought it was obvious. I don't see any love between them. And Pete's now an unknown quantity, isn't he, after what Sam confided in me? He may have told his mother that Pete made him wash his trousers. It may be something or nothing, but she may have done something foolish to punish his father. If that was to come out, it gives the police more reason to suspect her. If I'm to help her, I need concrete proof she had Sam in the car. The stack then starts to fall away. Even then, it might not be enough. Sam being seen leaving with Jo in the car will not exonerate her from disappearing him after she left here.'

Claire stared at her husband in dismay. She was exhausted from just a few minutes of verbal combat. This was the side of him that made him such a formidable adversary in a courtroom. What she wanted to see was the human side of him, the man who cared about right and wrong. She wanted to bridge the uncomfortable gap that had suddenly appeared between them.

She needed to get them back to safe shores and protect them as a family. She gave him a sad, weary smile and whispered, 'I'm sorry you're finding this hard. I know how much you care for Sam.'

He returned a similar smile. 'I know you do.'

She didn't wait for him to move. She rushed into his arms and held him close. Her head buried against his chest, she asked what every person wanted to ask of the person defending them.

'Do you think she's guilty?'

His voice rumbled in his chest and against her ear. His answer gave her no comfort.

'It doesn't matter what I believe. It's what I can prove that matters.'

She held him closer so he could feel her heart. 'But you'll help her, won't you?'

She felt his weary sigh push out of his chest as he reassured her. 'I will, Claire. I already am.'

SEVENTEEN

Moraine slept solidly for six hours straight and woke refreshed just before dawn.

Her morning update from Stone apprised her of developments overnight. The police had received a spate of calls with possible sightings of the boy as a result of the television broadcast of the previous evening, some from as far away as the north and east of England. Several other police stations were now involved in checking out each of the calls. None so far had been positive.

She was already tasked with her first job, which was why she was now pulling on wellies after parking her car. Claire Howell was waiting for her outside her house as she arrived, quietly standing by her front door, wearing a black shirt and high-waisted trousers tucked in to calf-length laced-up boots. Her long hair with a centre parting was smoothed back behind her ears in a sleek bun.

She indicated the cup in her hand, offering Moraine a drink. Moraine spoke quietly as she approached her, aware it was only seven thirty and that people might still be sleeping.

'I'm fine, thanks. I had one in the car driving here.'

'I take it there's no news?'

Moraine shook her head.

Claire Howell put her cup on the ground to the side of the doorstep and gestured for Moraine to follow. It was a beautiful morning after yesterday's rain, the sky clear and the sun already shining. It would make for a better day for the search teams after a night of getting wet, and maybe, just maybe, they might find him today.

She followed in the woman's footsteps, along the side of the property and around to the back, placing her rubber soles on the soggy leaves under a tunnel of trees. Wide stretches of lawn broken up with pathways were bordered by shrubs protected by stone walls. Orange-berry pyracanthas, evergreen mahonia and heather, and purple-leaf dogwood covered the foreground, while ground-hugging shrubs with green and golden foliage furnished the fronts. It was a garden rich with colour, and space, and light.

It felt like she was on a tour in *The Secret Garden*, as she spied an arched wooden gate set in the stone wall. They stayed on the paths instead of cutting across the lawn to get to it, which Moraine didn't mind as she was enjoying the moment. Once through the gate, she gasped. She had expected to see a border of scrubland around the property, not acres of land and woods as far as the eye could see. The vastness was staggering, bringing home how wealthy this family was. Theirs was another world.

Claire Howell turned to look at her. 'Not much further now. We need to head to that fence line. There's a dirt track just the other side of it to a small copse of trees. I didn't know they played there, much less built a den. I should have known from their clothes – as you'll see, it's where wild garlic grows.'

Once over the fence, and a few yards in amongst the trees, Moraine smelled the strong oniony scent. She ducked her head to avoid snagging her hair in brambles. Moving a few feet at a time, she saw flattened cardboard boxes on the ground, leading to a crawl space under a curve of dead branches grown over with ivy leaves.

Claire Howell grimaced. 'You probably don't need to go in there. James went in last night and brought out a box of drawings, which we gave to Inspector Stone.'

Taking her phone out of her pocket to use as both a camera and torch, Moraine got down on her knees. She needed to crawl through the dense undergrowth to make sure there was nothing else to find, or that Sam Jenkins wasn't hiding there.

A few crawls in, she could see why the den was so appealing. There was enough room for the children to sit and play. A bit of old carpet had been dragged in, and a mouldy-smelling sleeping bag as well. A couple of damp cardboard boxes had been used as tables, with a bottle of watery-looking squash and two plastic beakers on one of them. Nothing relevant to Sam's disappearance, but she photographed it all nonetheless and would let the SIO decide if he wanted Crime Scene Investigators in there or not.

She hadn't seen the child's drawings in person, only photographs of them. They were all done in black crayon and she couldn't interpret what was being communicated. It would need a child psychologist to understand it and decide if it was something disturbing.

She crawled out backwards and got to her feet, brushing the knees of her trousers and her hands of dirt, and smiled to reassure the mother. 'All very normal and sweet in there. A bottle of squash and some plastic cups, and a bit of old carpet to sit on.'

The woman glanced at her anxiously. 'I feel responsible for not knowing they played here. The girls are older, but Sam's only five. He could have come here on his own, without any of us knowing.'

Moraine gave a small shake of her head. 'You weren't to know. And he might not have. Perhaps after your girls have had breakfast and are awake, I can come and talk to them. I'll be very gentle and careful about what I say. Would that be okay?'

She stared at Moraine in dismay. 'Please, be very careful. Lottie woke in the night crying for him.'

'I'll take it very slow. That, I can promise you. If you see any sign of them getting upset, just give me the nod and I'll stop.'

She inhaled a small breath and nodded hesitantly. 'Well then, around nine would be a good time. If you can come then?'

She glanced about them and pointed out the dense growth of green garlic. 'I should pick some for Bernice. She loves making pesto with it.' Then gave a deeper sigh and turned to leave. 'Not today, though. All our thoughts will be on Sam.'

EIGHTEEN

Bernice was serving James scrambled egg and roasted tomatoes when Claire entered the kitchen. She smiled a good morning and kissed the top of James's head as she passed him to make them coffee.

'Bernice, can I make you one?'

Bernice stared at her blankly before shaking her head. 'No, another cup and it'll give me the jitters. I had one too many in the night, thinking about the lad. It's been a terrible night. All the rain and him still out there. It doesn't bode well. If fright doesn't take him, the weather will.'

Claire tried to remember what time she turned in. It was gone two, and a good while after that before she heard James climb the stairs to his bed. It had taken her a long while to fall asleep and was still dark when she woke, barely rested. Her body felt punished by tiredness. James must be equally shattered, going to bed so late, and she was glad that he was eating breakfast.

She would have to look out for them, him and Bernice, try to lighten the load where she could. They were all affected, but when it came to minding the household, she would be best at managing things. From childhood, she had learned the importance from watching her grandmother of keeping one's head above the parapet. No matter what the unfortunate event – and there had been many in her time running a large estate, raising animals, growing crops, providing for workers and staff, and even when Claire's father died – she mustered the strength to carry on.

That strong influence had passed down to Claire and become her own mantra. She'd put to rest her feelings of the previous evening and wouldn't let her mind dwell on them again. She would banish any ghosts that crossed her path. She had been the last person to see her father alive, and that would remain secret. There were no witnesses as far as anyone was concerned.

Bernice gave a woeful cry. 'It brings back all those memories. Such a sad time then. And both like two peas in a pod. I keep thinking it'll be the same again and they won't find the little lamb. He'll have got drenched to the skin, pneumonia no doubt. My heart weeps at the thought of him.'

James laid down his knife and fork with barely any of the food gone from his plate. From his expression, Bernice was upsetting him. It wasn't her fault. She was reliving a painful time, like they all were. But Claire needed her to stop. It wouldn't do if the girls walked into a strained atmosphere a second time. She couldn't allow this to carry on. They all needed to be mindful of little ears and tender hearts.

'Bernice, why don't you have a rest in your room? I can hold the fort. No one's going to suffer with all the meals you have prepared in the freezer. Take the day off and just rest. We'll cope. And I'll be happier knowing you're not having to look after all of us after such a horrible shock.'

Bernice was firmly shaking her head, her face set in a stubborn expression. 'I wouldn't hear of it. You have your hands full enough with the girls. I need to keep a watch on Edna. She was crying in the linen cupboard yesterday. Leanne and Danka were walking around with dusters and polish, not noticing what they were cleaning. Meg vacuumed the staircase twice. They're all in a tizz. I'll be staying right here, thank you. They can use my shoulders to cry on in private if need be. I'll not have them upsetting your girls.'

James smiled at this, his eyes meeting hers in wry amusement, lifting Claire's spirits. He was thinking the same as her, that if it was anyone it would be Bernice who upset the girls. Especially if they found her sad or crying. They adored her, pestered her day and night to fix something, make something, or sing Tina Turner songs. 'Proud Mary' was their favourite one – dancing the rolling, rolling move with her, getting overexcited and dizzy until Claire had to put a stop and calm them all down.

The best thing she could do was emphasise Bernice's concern. 'You're right. We don't want anyone getting upset. Especially the children. I'll do my part if you keep an eye on poor Edna, Leanne and Danka and Meg.'

It was the right thing to say. It gave Bernice something to focus on. Her strong arms folded across her ample chest, her chin raised determinedly. A much better idea than giving her a bunch of wild garlic.

The sound of running feet, out in the hallway, caught them unawares, and had them scrambling for faces of calm. Phoebe burst into the kitchen, her voice loud with excitement. 'Mummy, Daddy, there's police cars outside. Two of them. And a big police van as well.'

The announcement shocked Claire. Her immediate thought was for Jo. James calmly rose to his feet, while his eyes locked with hers, sending a different message. He was equally alarmed.

'Thank you, Phoebe. We've been expecting them. They're all very excited to see your den. They haven't seen one built in a wood. I think I'll let Sam's mummy and daddy know they might want to talk to them.'

He slid his daughter into his chair and ruffled her hair. 'No slippers. Your feet will get cold.' He gave Claire a pointed stare and a coded instruction. 'Hopefully, it won't take long. Best to stay indoors, though. Maybe make more of those lovely cakes again, in case the police people get hungry.'

He was telling her to keep the children at the back of the house, to save them witnessing anything. It's what she would have done anyway, but it was good they were on the same page and thinking of their protection.

She gave him a grateful smile. He was doing what she asked of him. Going next door to help Jo.

NINETEEN

Moraine didn't know what was going on. There'd been no forewarning of this visit. When the door knocked, her eyes had rounded in surprise at seeing DI Stone and DS Hayden, with uniformed police officers. Her first thought was they were not all going to fit in. Thankfully, it was only the detectives wanting to come inside. A tingle of alarm fluttered in her stomach. This wasn't a courtesy call. Stone had something.

He threw a glance towards the closed doors in the hall. 'Are they awake? If not, wake them, please.'

She had no need to. Pete Jenkins was sprawled in an armchair in the sitting room. Jo was in the shower upstairs.

Moraine quietly told Stone where they both were, and he headed to the kitchen, followed by DS Hayden. His greeting to Kennedy was warm. 'Morning, John. Coffees all round, if you don't mind.'

Kennedy had a tea towel over his shoulder and looked right at home wearing a collared black jumper, black jeans, and lace-up suede boots. He gestured to a Sainsbury's cool bag on the counter. 'Plenty of croissants or sandwiches, if anyone wants them.'

Moraine was beginning to love this guy. She had forgotten to bring supplies, but he hadn't. She was doubly glad to have him here today, especially now they were facing the unknown.

DS Fay Hayden had taken a seat at the table, scrolling her phone. She had a knack for being unnoticeable, merging into the background. It would be a mistake to forget she was there, though, as she was renowned for not missing a thing. Her unassuming appearance, low-profile clothing, and soft-grey hair was in perfect contrast to Mick Stone. While all eyes were on him, she could quietly listen and watch. He was right to bring her along for a second opinion.

His eyes were now on Moraine. 'You okay?'

She nodded.

'Good. Anything to report?'

'I've seen the den. Crawled into it and taken photographs. Just a simple den. I'm talking to the Howells' daughters at nine.'

He gave a slow smile. 'Good work, Raine. That was going to be your next job.'

She heard the soft sounds of movement above the ceiling and focused on the now. 'Do you want to see the Jenkinses separately, sir, or together?'

He glanced towards DS Hayden. 'I think together, don't you, Fay?'

She raised her head and gave a brief nod.

'That's it then. Put them in the sitting room. Tell them I'll be with them in a few minutes.'

Kennedy handed her two full mugs to take with her, nodding at the one in her left hand. 'Tea's for her, coffee's for him.' He then opened the kitchen door for her.

Moraine brought the drinks to the sitting room and was surprised to find Jo there. She must have crept quietly down the stairs. Her hair, darkened from her shower, hung straight and smooth down her slender neck. Her eyes were red and bloodshot in her white face. She wore a navy-blue jumper and clean jeans and smelled nice from the scents of soap and shampoo. She held up her hands to show Moraine the bandages.

'Sorry. They got wet. I didn't want to go in the kitchen because I could hear people in there.'

'Yes, Detective Inspector Stone is here. He wants to talk to you both. I brought you some tea. Why don't you start drinking it while I fetch some clean ones for you?'

Pete looked at her from the armchair, with a surly expression in his face. 'Well, thanks for letting us know we have people in our home. It would have been nice to have been informed.'

Moraine placed his coffee on the side table near him. 'They've only just arrived, Pete. I didn't know they were coming. DI Stone is in the kitchen because he didn't know if you were awake yet. I'll let him know you're both here.'

She exited the room, her stomach feeling cramped from the man's attitude.

Stone waited five more minutes before joining them. His good morning was given in a neutral voice.

While Jo didn't seem affected by the presence of a second detective, the same couldn't be said for the husband. He sat stiffly, holding the arms of the chair like he was at the dentist. Though, to be fair, Jo didn't seem to be reacting to much at all. Her mug of tea was untouched, and the dressings were unused in her lap.

Stone spoke quietly but forcefully. 'Mr and Mrs Jenkins, I have to say that, frankly, I'm becoming very concerned for your son's whereabouts. If either of you have any information that might help, I need it now. Time is of the essence. We can't afford to lose any more.'

Pete pushed himself up from his seat.

'Please sit down, Mr Jenkins,' Stone said firmly.

Pete sank back down and protested. 'What's that meant to mean? We've already told you everything!'

'Everything, Mr Jenkins? As a matter of interest, what time did you get back to the city yesterday?'

His mouth opened and shut before finding his voice and looking at Moraine. 'Well, she was here when I got back. I don't know, what was it... half two?'

Moraine answered his question. 'It was two fifty-four, to be precise.'

Pete turned to Stone. 'There you go, then. Two fifty-four. To be precise.'

'So you got back to the city at that time? Not earlier?'

His eyes blinked fast. He gave a hard nod.

Stone was touching a nerve. Moraine wondered where this was leading.

'Did you stop anywhere en route, for petrol or a coffee? Or a toilet break?'

'No. Straight back. Didn't stop till I got here.'

Stone raised an eyebrow, holding Pete's gaze. 'I see. What about at the hotel? Did you manage to grab anything before you left? Something to eat for the journey. A pain au chocolat or a croissant. They usually serve those things in hotels. Or were you in too much of a rush?'

His voice sounded strangled as he replied. 'Too much of a rush.'

Stone gave a nod of understanding. 'So, you what? Check out and just leave? At what time was that?'

Pete made an impatient gesture, flicking his hand in Moraine's direction. 'I've already told her all this. It's all written down!'

'So, it'll only be a matter of picking up the phone and calling the hotel. Get them to verify it. They'll have your checking-out time logged. What about the newspaper you brought back with you? Was it complimentary, or did you have to buy it from reception?'

Pete visibly swallowed. 'I, um... I must have just grabbed it from a chair or a table.'

There was a long pause while Stone got out his phone and rested it on his knee, the action accompanied by a pleasant smile, a pleasant tone. 'Well, that should be easy to verify. You'll no doubt be seen on camera, dashing through reception, grabbing up a newspaper.'

In some fascination, Moraine watched Pete's throat moving. The man was either going to vomit or cry. She then noticed Jo. She looked lost and confused. Moraine could almost hear the thoughts stumbling through her brain.

Stone put away the phone and smoothly commented on the lack of response to his suggestion. 'I can see you don't want that, Mr Jenkins.' He then gave a weighty sigh. 'Just as well, really. They'll wonder why we're calling again.'

Pete slowly raised his head, his eyes showing fear. He stared at his wife intently, willing her to support him, then covered his face with his hands and cried softly, 'I didn't go.'

Stone didn't have a chance to answer. Someone else was quicker. In a voice equally smooth and commanding, James Howell spoke from the open door. 'Pete, don't say anything more. I strongly advise you not to say another word.'

Stone looked at the barrister appraisingly. 'Good timing, Mr Howell. I'm about to ask Mr Jenkins to accompany us to the police station where we can continue this interview.'

Moraine wondered who let him in, but thankfully Stone didn't seem perturbed. The barrister came further into the room. He placed a hand on his neighbour's shoulder, until the man looked up.

'Stay calm, Pete. The next conversation you have should be with a solicitor. I'll arrange for one to be with you shortly.'

Jenkins's eyes swam with tears. He was shaking his head from side to side, repeating the same words. 'I'm sorry, I'm sorry, I'm so sorry.'

TWENTY

Where had he been? The words beat like hammer blows in her head.

Where did he go after he left her Friday morning?

She closed her eyes and pushed her face into Sam's pillow. He'd lied to her about where he was going. He'd taken his station uniform with him for a conference, made sure she saw it, feeding into the lie. Was there a reasonable explanation for it? Had the car broken down, a hold-up on the motorway, a pile-up maybe? A catastrophic accident where he had to assist? Then couldn't face going.

He had holed up somewhere, in a Travelodge, or in a B&B? He was in different clothes and clean when he arrived back home yesterday. He must have gone *somewhere*.

Or was the real reason clear in front of her, his plan interrupted by Sam going missing and forcing him to come back? Had he been leaving her? With no warning? Had their marriage fallen so far by the wayside, he could just walk away and leave her and Sam behind?

A recent conversation played in her head. She could hear the bite and impatience in his voice. 'Why do you always have to find fault, when you're the one who fucked up? I'm trying to make things work and all I hear is you moan about being found out. Open your eyes... we got a free home, a chance to save. What more do you want? But keep going on like you are, and I'll... I'll...'

His thumb and forefinger uncurled and showed an inch of air. He didn't finish the sentence. Instead, he was showing her he'd reached his limit. He'd had enough of her.

Was he telling her he would walk out?

Had she driven the love out of him with her constant worry about everything? Her monitoring of their spending? Her negative thinking dampening any pleasure? She'd made a fuss about him buying expensive headphones. His justification – best noise-cancelling and a battery-boosting charging case. She'd wanted to bang his head. They were surrounded by quietness. The only noise around them was the sounds of nature.

He must have felt he couldn't do right for doing wrong. She should have just let it go, and not made a fuss, but she couldn't. Every day she was reminding herself why they were there. She'd put them in debt and was trying now to save every penny. She thought they were there to save for a home, but the only way to achieve that was to only spend money on what they needed and could afford.

He may have felt he didn't have to justify buying something for himself. Surrounded by the Howells' wealth was a constant reminder of how little he had. He'd said that to her once, and it made her feel sad for him that he felt that way. Envy had made him a fool. Buying those headphones, Jo knew, was so he had something to show off to the Howells. They were the only ones he would want to impress.

What must he have thought, having to come back? To walk into his home and find his son gone? If he didn't love her before, he would have hated her then. He must have found it unbearable to even look at her, or spare even an ounce of compassion.

Had his resentment for her been so strong he was unable to feel anything for Sam? Surely he didn't hate her that much? His tears, in front of the police, was the first sign she had seen of any genuine emotion. It was as if he'd skipped the last twenty-four hours of pain, somehow avoiding it and able to cope. Or else it was not touching him at all...

She wondered if this was the stark truth. That he had no feelings for either of them.

Tears were blinding her, her thoughts so tangled they were strangling her. She tried to remember the man she loved. His lopsided grin and silly behaviour and impracticable projects. Like the seven-foot bookcase they couldn't get in the room, as it was too wide to go through the door. He couldn't have cared less, then, if they were rich or poor. Or what image he presented. He would quite happily wipe the snot from Sam's nose with the sleeve of his T-shirt if a tissue wasn't handy, and wear it the rest of the day.

Did he realise how fortunate his life had been? Was it beginning to register, now it was gone, that money couldn't bring back his son? All the money in the world couldn't do that. And he hadn't got the chance to say sorry for what he had done.

Where had he been? If not to Manchester, where did he go? Where was he all of Saturday morning that it took until afternoon for him to get home?

She closed her eyes and saw Sam's face. Her beautiful boy had his eyes closed. Guilt as sharp as a knife came at her heart. She clutched his rabbit in her hands and rocked herself in his bed, knowing the pain would never stop. Not while she lived and breathed.

TWENTY-ONE

Claire gasped when she saw Pete climbing into the back of a police car. Even from a distance, she could see the devastation in his face. *Oh God,* she wondered. *Was it possible they had found Sam dead?*

From his expression, it was not good news. He looked stricken. Were they taking him to see... taking him to the mortuary? She shut out the image and came away from the window, shaken. How could it happen again?

She shuddered. Her mind was racing. What was she to do now? How could she help practically? There were no words of comfort she could even begin to give. And how did she tell her own girls? They weren't fickle children. Their affection for Sam was deep.

She wanted them away from the house and protected from what might happen next. She would not allow the girls to see Jo and Pete's grief. It would be too traumatic. The aftermath. Dear Lord, there would be a funeral. Jo and Pete might want a hearse to come to their home. She couldn't bear the thought of them seeing a little coffin, much less her own babies.

Claire heard the front door close and called out for James to come to the drawing room. She needed to know his opinion and what they should do.

He gave a weary sigh. His voice was quiet. 'Christ, that was a debacle. I need to make some calls and get him a good solicitor. Silly, silly man. Telling stupid lies.'

He gestured towards the window. 'Don't, under any circumstances, let the girls see out there. They're going to be searching the home. Forensic van is already here.'

Claire gaped at him, clasping a hand to her chest. 'But I thought... I saw Pete get in a car. I thought...'

'They're taking him in for questioning. He didn't go to Manchester. Or attend any fire conference.'

She was taken aback by the shocking announcement. She felt light-headed and was forced to sit down. She shook her head in confusion. She'd given Jo the weekend off because he would be away, and now she was hearing it was a lie. Why would he do that?

'So Sam's not been—'

He cut her off. 'No. He's not been found.' His voice was thick.

He turned and left the room. His head hunched forward like the weight of the world was on his shoulders. Claire let him go. He had the problem of Pete to sort out. The man was depending on him, though if it was up to her, she'd leave him to get his own solicitor and not make it easy for him. It's what he deserves for lying to Jo. But she knew that James would find the very best to represent him. The man didn't know how lucky he was to have someone like James to help him.

Her pity for Pete was gone in an instant. *Poor Jo.* She would have had a day and night of waiting for Sam to be found, and to now find out Pete had lied to her.

She castigated James in her mind. Why, oh why, had he agreed to their coming here, to put them through all this again?

He would hate that she was thinking these thoughts, but

after everything they had suffered, what they had shared, surely he must know that giving Sam a home would worry her. Replacing one child with another, trying to make up for the past, would only punish him more.

Nothing he did would take away the guilt, until he forgave himself.

Did he not see how his fatherly affection towards Sam, and before him to Matt, could be hard for her – an abiding reminder of her own loss?

Finding their infant son in his crib had never gone from her mind. The doctors said in cases of sudden, unexplained deaths of healthy babies they might never know why. That they shouldn't blame themselves. But it never would. Same as the events around her father's death – it held on to the details, a reminder that life and happiness were fragile.

She rose from the chair. She would not leave Jo defenceless and on her own. She would hold her. There was no need for words.

TWENTY-TWO

Bernice was watching Moraine as she sat at the kitchen table with Phoebe and Lottie. Their mother must have asked the woman to oversee the conversation. Moraine smiled at her briefly, before looking back at the girls. Both were wearing aprons, their hair held back by Alice bands, and something sweet smelling was baking in the oven. Moraine sniffed the air appreciatively.

'Something smells good.'

Phoebe gave a wan smile. 'We're making shortbread for the police, as Daddy said they might get hungry. Mummy said you're a police officer, but you don't wear a uniform. You get to wear your own clothes, because you're a detective.'

'That's right.' Moraine nodded. 'I used to wear a uniform when I was a police constable. I sometimes wear it if I attend an event.'

Lottie looked at her with an inquisitive stare. 'How will people know you're a police person if you don't look like one?'

'Well, I tell them and show them my police badge.'

She pondered this, before fixing Moraine with a little frown. 'I think it's because the baddies won't know. So you can catch them. Like...' She flicked a pink-ribboned wand in the air. 'Magic.'

Phoebe gave a groan. 'Not Cinderella again. *Please.*' She sighed, woefully, as if it was a serious matter, her eyes looking to Moraine for support. 'All she wants to watch every day is *Cinderella.*'

'And all you want is *The Princess Diaries*, so you can be a princess.'

Moraine had to stop herself from laughing. They were like two little mother hens fussing over each other. 'I like both,' she offered, to settle the disagreement.

Then, carefully broaching the subject of the den, she told them she had seen it.

'It's wonderful. You must have worked hard to build it. I love the little carpet and tables. And great idea, building it under the trees. Saves you getting wet.'

'We didn't have to build it. It was already there. We just made it homey,' Lottie explained excitedly.

Moraine knew it was nature that provided the hideaway, but it was nice to give them praise. 'So, you three like to play there?'

Lottie nodded. 'Yes, but we can't 'cos Sam's lost. Sam and I pretend we live there and that we're hiding from the enemy.'

Moraine pulled a mock-scared face. '*Enemy?* You have enemies?'

She nodded solemnly. 'That's why we hide there. So Sam doesn't get caught.'

'Is that what you think happened? Sam was caught?'

Lottie shook her head. 'No.' Her reply was confident. 'I would have heard them coming and we would have run.'

Moraine was alarmed to see Phoebe's chin wobble. Please, no, she wasn't going to cry.

'Stupid place,' she muttered instead. 'We should never have

gone there. Sam's only little. Lottie means he's scared of bees. He gets scared of the noise.'

Lottie leaned closer to her sister, like she was the oldest and not the youngest, to comfort her, placing her small hand in Phoebe's lap. 'He likes it there because it's quiet.'

Moraine imagined it would be quiet, sitting there under the trees. Her mind focused back on the here and now, and oh no, both little girls were now on the brink of crying. She scrabbled for something trivial to say, to stem the imminent tsunami.

Bernice came to the rescue, by drawing their attention to the back door. 'Look what Dougie's brought. The naughty man will have your teeth ruined.' It was said affectionately.

The girls jumped up from their seats and rushed to greet him. Dougie stayed on the doorstep, wearing a wax jacket and wellingtons covered in mud. Not young, but fit looking, with a good head of hair that was mostly grey. He handed them a bag of Haribo, calling it a little treat.

Moraine stood up, thankful to Dougie and Bernice for warding off an upset. She had to hand it to Claire Howell – she chose her staff well. The ones she had met so far seemed loyal and caring, and protective of her children. It would be a good time to leave while they were happy again. And an opportunity to have a chat with Dougie. At some point soon, Stone would want all the staff interviewed, and background checks carried out on them.

She waved a hand at Bernice and quietly let herself out of the house. Outside, she scanned the vast grounds and speculated they were in the middle of nowhere, not just a few miles from a thriving city. A perfect place to bring up children.

Hoping Dougie was still at the kitchen door, she made her way around to the back of the property. He was walking away when she caught up with him, carrying a five-litre drum of liquid by its handle.

'Hi, it's Dougie, isn't it? I wonder if we could have a quick chat? I can walk with you if you need to be somewhere.'

He glanced at her footwear. 'It might be a bit mucky. I'm cleaning out the chicken coop.'

Moraine smiled in delight. 'I didn't know there were chickens.'

He nodded, walking alongside her, leading the way. 'Aye, miss. Got a dozen Rhode Island Reds. Friendly and easy to care for. Lay enough eggs for all Bernice's cooking. Can get a bit smelly, mind, if they're not cleaned out regularly. Vinegar does the job. The hens don't mind it and it helps keep the foxes away.'

Without noticing where they were going, Moraine was surprised to find herself looking back at Beckley House from a new angle, and saw a Juliet balcony she hadn't seen before. A wisteria, covered in green leaves, climbed up the stone wall beside it. She would love to see it in flower, drooping an abundance of purple colour.

The cleaning of the coop had already begun. Heavy-duty garden bags loaded with clumps of damp straw stood beside it. The wire enclosure had an elevated shelter and a corrugated roof. Moraine was enthralled by the rust-coloured birds with their bright orange eyes.

'I bet the children love all this,' she said in a wistful tone.

Dougie chuckled. 'Lottie, maybe. Phoebe runs a mile, scared they'll peck her.'

'What about Sam? Does he like them?'

He heaved a sigh and looked her square in the eye. 'There isn't a creature that boy doesn't love. Don't mean any disrespect, miss, but you being here won't help find him. I wish I could tell you where he was. Put us all out of this misery. That's all we want is for you to bring him home.'

Moraine felt she should leave when he turned and picked up a large yard broom and began sweeping the ground. She'd got nothing useful from talking to him, except that he seemed kind. Before leaving, she said: 'Do you know of any man who visited, possibly black or wearing black clothing, who wore a wide-brimmed hat?'

His eyes fixed on her again and she saw his lashes were wet from when he had his back to her, privately weeping. He raised the broom and pointed the handle at somewhere behind her.

'That's the only one I know who fits that description.'

Moraine turned and looked. Half a field away, she could just make it out. A scarecrow wearing a wide-brim hat.

TWENTY-THREE

Jo stood in a daze while Claire hugged her. She had no idea where Moraine was and the police wouldn't let Claire come in so she was forced to stand at the front door. A team of police officers, covered from head to foot in white paper jumpsuits, trawled through her cupboards and drawers and bins. They had hushed conversations in low voices that she couldn't make out.

'It's just a formality,' John F. Kennedy said in her ear, when he sat her in a chair at the kitchen table.

They asked if they had a computer, a laptop, an iPad. They only had phones. They could have hers if they wanted. There wasn't much on it to look at, only photos and a few numbers. Pete's, the Howells', the doctor, the dentist, the school. Her dad's, even though he was dead – dying from cirrhosis of the liver before Sam was born. Her mum, as Jo was born, in the hospital bed. Blood pressure problem was all she was ever told.

Claire held her closer. 'How are you doing?'

Her concerned eyes skidded over Jo's face. Jo couldn't imagine what she must be thinking. Her skin was prickling with acute embarrassment, turning her more anxious in this woman's capable arms.

'Numb,' Jo finally answered. 'Just thinking about my dad. Deaths and births, he used to say, when in his cups – it's a normal passing. Better than burying your child.'

Claire gently squeezed her. 'Do you want to have a walk outside?'

Jo shook her head, desperate to reassure her employer that Pete was not a bad man. The search was a waste of time. Pete wasn't like that. What he did to Sam was mentally cruel, but he'd never lifted a finger to him.

She couldn't confide in Claire. She'd avoided having any kind of personal conversation the whole time living there. She couldn't now just open up and tell Claire she had deceived her by keeping quiet about her past.

She found it in her to have some sympathy for Pete. He wouldn't be able to cope if the Howells thought him a bad father. She couldn't share any of this with Claire. How Pete left her to flounder – without a lifeline – after one moment of inattention cut the ground from under her, taking all her strength with it. She'd been the strong one in their relationship until that happened.

He hadn't been able to help her up from her devastation. He didn't understand the psychology of mental pain – it wasn't a subject he could deal with. Brought up in a home where men didn't cry – an old-fashioned concept – and a mother who put up with the men without complaining. He never mentioned his family. His two brothers, one in the army, one in the navy, following a military path like his father. A fireman son didn't really cut it – not a real fighter uniform – snippets of a conversation he revealed to her during a maudlin drunken moment. A sad pronouncement on a son.

Deaths and births and wrong parenting. Deaths and births. Better to bury a mother than a child.

She needed Claire to leave. She couldn't handle this kindness. It was not deserved. Claire must have felt her stiffening because she relinquished her hold and stepped back. Jo couldn't meet her eyes, and could only mutter thanks for the visit, before awkwardly closing the door.

She stood silently in the small hallway, crushing Sam's rabbit in her arms, unnoticed by the people in her home. She took Pete's keys from the hook by the front door. The light outside was astonishing, the air cold in her nose after the heat of indoors. She felt deliriously free as she climbed into his car.

Sam's blue rabbit was in the seat beside her. Sam needed her to bring it to him. It was his comforter.

She turned the engine on, released the handbrake, and drove slowly towards the gates. One of the gardeners opened them for her. It was Dougie's grandson, Lewis, who looked a little surprised. He waved to her, like he was trying to tell her something. She waved back. She couldn't stop and talk now. Sam was waiting to be found. Waiting for her to come and bring him home. She would tell Lewis that when she got back later. He was bound to understand why she didn't stop. Sam was waiting for her. She needed to go to her son…

TWENTY-FOUR

Moraine let down her window to poke her head out at the gardener. 'Which way did she go?'

'Left.'

'Did she say where?'

He shook his head. 'No. Just waved at me.'

A wave? Moraine drove through the gates. A wave like how? She should have asked him. A happy wave? A 'see you later' wave? A mind your own business wave? Or the worrying kind? The 'I'm not coming back' kind? She should have kept a closer eye on her. Kennedy was blaming himself, but it was Moraine who should have been paying attention. She'd not had time to spend with her this morning, neither before or after Pete was taken off to be interviewed, and had no clue how she was feeling.

Showering had seemed positive behaviour for Jo, but then Kennedy said she'd not eaten or drunk anything that morning as far as he was aware. He thought maybe two mugs of tea in the whole time he was there yesterday and didn't know about the night. Certainly nothing this morning, unless she drank from the bathroom tap.

She shouldn't have left it to her husband to get a doctor in. The woman was on antidepressants – who knew what her mental state was like now? She could be suicidal. Her child missing, her husband carted off, and the police trampling through her home. No wonder she took off. But to where? Where did you go, Jo? To a clifftop or a bridge to jump off? It's what many would do if they thought they'd never see their child again. Or... if they were to blame for them no longer being there.

British Transport Police had been alerted to be on the lookout at Bath Spa railway station. The registration of her car sent to all response vehicles. Moraine was praying someone would see her before she did anything foolish.

Her phone rang. It was Kennedy. Keeping her hands on the wheel, she pressed the answer button and heard his voice.

'Moraine, she's been located. The police are with her. Do you want them to bring her back?'

'Where is she, John?'

He sighed softly. 'As expected. Where she lost her son.'

Moraine swallowed the knot in her throat. She should have thought of it. For Kennedy, it was the natural place for her to go. He was a father; it's where he would go, back to where he last saw the child.

'Thanks, John. They can bring the car back. I'll go and fetch her. Least I can do for the poor woman.'

Moraine drove the rest of the way pondering the search of the Jenkinses' home. They hadn't found anything incriminating as far as she could tell. It was furnished minimally, with few places to hide things. In the wardrobes, bedroom drawers, and kitchen cupboards, they'd found nothing of luxury. Yellow-labelled Sainsbury's own brand in the cupboards and fridge. Poundland toiletries in the bathroom. The toilet paper was thin. The clothes: Matalan, Peacocks, Primark. The only expensive item she'd seen was a pair of headphones that must have cost them a few hundred pounds.

She hoped they'd be done by the time she brought Jo home, to give her at least some peace while they waited on news about her husband.

Where had the conniver been? His greeting to his wife kept running through her mind. There had been no love from him whatsoever. How long had it been like that between them? Was the marriage already over before their son went missing? He didn't seem to care one way or another. Feeding his face, and not rushing out to search for him, while his wife couldn't eat a thing and throwing up from anxiety.

The ping-pong ball zapped back and forth in her head again.

The whole situation bothered Moraine, and she hoped Stone grilled him thoroughly. He was hiding something – an affair would be her best bet, but was it something more devious than that? Could he have snatched his own kid? Hidden him away to take him from his wife until the search ended and his disappearance was put down to child abduction by a stranger unknown, leaving him clear to make his next move, whatever that was?

The thought left a sour taste in her mouth. He would know how much he had to lose if he admitted committing this crime. He'd be going to prison. Would cowardice keep him quiet, to save his own skin, at the expense of his son's life? Moraine wouldn't like to take a bet on what he would do if cornered. The decent thing might not be in his makeup. She was going to have to talk this through with Stone and see if he was thinking the same way.

It was day two, nearing midday, over twenty-four hours since the boy had gone missing. They still didn't have a clue where Sam Jenkins was. It being a Sunday, she was hoping families out walking would have found him. A dog picking up a scent and barking for its owners to come look.

Moraine pulled into the village pool car park, and saw it mostly filled with police vehicles and officers out on foot. The swimming pool building was closed because of the ongoing investigation, and Jo was standing at the doors with her face pressed against the glass. It was a pitiful sight. She was wearing her slippers and holding her son's bunny in her hand.

Moraine approached calmly and called her name. When she didn't respond, Moraine went to her side. 'Let's go home, Jo. John wants to make you something to eat. He's worried you haven't eaten anything. Let's go home and I'll ring your doctor. You need something to help you cope.'

She inched back from the window and slowly brought her hand up to show Moraine the blue rabbit. 'Shall I leave this here?' she asked.

Moraine shook her head. 'No. Keep it with you.' It would be like saying he had died. People would then start leaving flowers. Jo had been holding on to it since finding it in her bed. Moraine didn't want her to be without it now, when she might need it to comfort her. It might be the only comfort, if the knock came. To have something of his to hold... if she couldn't have him to hold.

TWENTY-FIVE

Claire's stomach somersaulted at the sight of Marley and Stuart on the doorstep. She had a flashback of them, standing in the same spot, raw with grief in the aftermath of Matt going missing. They'd been unable to bear being in their own home, surrounded by memories of him.

Their appearances had changed considerably. Dressed in a careless manner, hair threaded with silver, a vulnerability around them in a way that left her unable to turn away. She stepped back from the door and invited them in.

The last time she'd seen them was in passing at Bath Abbey Christmas carol service. The crowd permitted only a wave, which she was thankful for as she didn't want sadness to mar the Christmas spirit. They moved from Bath to somewhere up north on the third anniversary of Matt's disappearance and Claire had secretly hoped to never see them again. To sever all painful reminders. She hoped they wouldn't stay long and would be gone before James got back. She wanted them gone before anyone knew they were there.

She took them into the kitchen and made a pot of tea and placed some shortbread on a plate before they'd even got comfortable and taken off their coats. Her smiles were as sincere as she could make them. It would be easier if someone else was there, so she wasn't alone with them. Not James, of course, but maybe Dougie. She hated this feeling of weakness and did her best to stay calm. She resented having to be supportive – having to feel their grief all over again. She wished, the same as she wished for James, that time would bring solace to their broken hearts. They were not strong people like her – raised to hide one's grief, to grieve in private and alone, quietly, as she did the loss of her own baby.

How did they know to come here? Was it just a case of seeking them out, the televised appeal bringing it all back to them, and needing comfort from those who knew what they went through?

Marley was holding a newspaper with Sam's face on the front page, her bony fingers a sign of how much she'd aged. The last five years hadn't been kind to either of them. In their mid-forties, they'd fast forwarded to old age, faces lined, lacking the vibrancy they once had. Claire felt deeply guilty at witnessing their decline and had to work past her resentment of them. She would let them talk about Matt if it helped ease their loss.

She remembered Marley saying, about a year after Matt was gone, that the hardest part was people wouldn't talk about him, as if afraid saying his name would bring her more pain. In fact, it did the opposite – she felt a relief when he was remembered.

Once settled at the table with their mugs of tea, Marley laid out the newspaper. Her finger stroked the face of Sam, her own face alight with wonder, her eyes brimming with tears. 'He looks so much like him.'

Stuart reached out to hold her hand, lifting her finger off the photograph. He cleared his throat. 'Marley, we know it's not him.' His voice was soft and kind.

Marley gave him a brief, resentful stare before pinning her

gaze on Claire. 'Why didn't you tell us? I need to see him. I want to look at him and smell his skin and hair.' Her voice went from a plea to an accusatory tone. 'Why didn't you tell us he was here?'

A band of tension tightened around Claire's chest, making it difficult to breathe. *They knew.* They knew this was Sam's home. Somewhere in that newspaper, Beckley House must have been named. It meant other people were now aware of the address, and their lives were exposed to the public. She had to find out if Marley or Stuart had told anyone that the owners of Beckley House were their friends. It only needed one reporter to recognise them and wonder at the connection, to wonder why the parents of Matthew Lambert were visiting the Howells' home. Their names were not mentioned at any time during the investigation.

Rational thinking helped her relax. Marley was in a kind of shock, having a crisis at seeing an image resembling her son. Claire reached across the table to place her hand on top of Stuart's, so that they both held the woman's hand.

'Marley,' she said carefully. 'This boy is five years old. Matt would be eleven now, nearly twelve. This isn't Matt, however much you want it to be. I'm so sorry, darling, for your pain.'

Marley pulled her hand away from both of them and roughly wiped her face of tears. A bitterness came into her eyes. She shook her head in denial. 'You're not sorry. You just want us gone. To leave you in peace with your family.'

'Marley! Stop it. It's not Claire's or James's fault. They had their own lives to lead. They did more than anyone could to help find him. Don't let your mind change that. And don't begrudge them their happiness.'

Claire glanced at him gratefully. Stuart always was a kind man. In that respect, he hadn't changed.

He shuffled in his chair. 'We should go, Marley. Claire and James must deal with a family that is going through hell. It can't be easy for them having to cope with another family in pain.'

'Where is James?' she asked, almost desperately. 'I'd really love to see him.'

Claire was relieved he wasn't there. She didn't want Marley affecting him with this madness and grief. He was already in a vulnerable place. She was glad she could say exactly where he was, to show Stuart was completely correct. James was helping another family.

'He's at the police station, Marley. He's gone to support the boy's father.'

Her small gasp revealed she understood the implications, and Claire instantly regretted saying anything. James would be seriously annoyed, rightly so, for her sharing this.

Marley then gave a different sigh, and Claire was relieved by what she now said. 'They always blame the parents. They did with me and Stuart at first. Separately and together, until we could prove we weren't with him and nowhere near when he was taken.'

Claire didn't know that they had been suspects. Nothing was mentioned in the news. Perhaps it was so brief, they never felt the need to mention it. Or never dared to. Or decided not to air it in case people would think there was a grain of truth.

Marley tried smiling at Claire, returning her sympathy for what she was going through.

'Sorry for being spiteful. I totally understand why we drifted apart. I'd be the same. It's just hard being here, remembering all the happy times. We could never get Matt to want to go home. Following James around like a faithful shadow. James always had so much energy to play with him. I miss both you and him. I miss us.'

Claire felt her eyes smart, and willed her attention to a safer topic. 'What about you, Stuart? Are you working again?'

He gave a vague shake of his head. 'Not for me anymore,

Claire. Can't listen to other people's ruined lives. Too much to take on, I'm afraid. It affects the old mind. James will tell you that. You have to be very disciplined about not letting it in. He can master that, but I can't.'

He was mistaken, but she didn't correct him. James did let it in. All the harmful stuff. All the way in. He would see it as a weakness to see the world through rose-tinted glasses, as a disservice to the victims, and the perpetrators. Highly attuned to people, he could feel at a deep emotional level the feelings and emotions of those around him, to the point of taking on their pain. It wasn't in him to set boundaries. In all likelihood it was the key to his success, giving him the empathy and human connection to see a crime from both sides. All the good and all the wrong inside a person.

She was glad he wasn't here. It was her job to protect him when she could. Encouraging them to leave quickly was how she could make that happen. She didn't want him to walk in unguarded and be an empath for them again. They had their time already. Enough was enough. She would not allow what happened to take anything more from him.

James had loved that child, and his being gone had nearly destroyed him. It had taken her considerable time and effort to put him back together again, and it was not going to be all for nothing. She would not lose him again. Not to the past, or to today. They could both just pack up and leave and take their sadness with them.

She worried about her daughters being exposed to all this grief when they were struggling themselves. She wanted her family happy again. Was that too much to ask for? To be happy? She didn't think so. Like her grandmother, she had to keep her head above the parapet and defend what was hers and not let anyone take it away.

TWENTY-SIX

It was James who brought Pete back, accompanying him inside for support, like an errant husband coming back from a night out on the tiles. He gave Jo a sympathetic look as he handed him over, and took her to one side to explain that Pete had an alibi for the time when Sam went missing. Leaving it at that, he left it to Jo to find out the rest in private with her husband.

Without a word, Jo walked upstairs to their bedroom, not really caring one way or another if Pete followed. Since arriving home with Moraine, she'd been sitting in a trance, ignoring the goings-on of the police, looking out of the window in the sitting room at the clouds in the sky, seeing faces and animals in their shapes – hoping if she kept looking at the clouds she'll see Sam. She doesn't really care where Pete has been, but if he has to tell her, he can tell her on his own, without the support of an audience.

He entered the room quietly and closed the bedroom door. Worry etched his features and his fair hair now stood up on end, as if his hands had continuously pulled or raked through it. Resignation all over his face, he finally spoke. 'It's all sorted. I'm in the clear.'

The words were an offence to her. *It's all sorted!* That was all he cared about – being in the clear. She felt an intense rage, his words bringing her out of her state of not caring, her body feeling an emotion other than pain, firing her nerves with a burning desire to destroy things, break everything apart and smash it to smithereens.

Drawing breath, she felt a molten liquid course through her veins. She wanted the taste of blood in her teeth, to rip his skin open and see if he had a beating heart. The contemptible piece of shit. How dare he say those words, not sparing a thought for his boy, his precious son.

Her attack was fast, her slap aimed as hard as she could make it across his face.

'Get out. Get out of this room and out of this house. You don't give a damn that our son is missing. You don't care a damn that your child is dead!'

He raised shocked eyes. His hand clutching at his stomach as if shot with a bullet, his mouth gaping wide.

She gazed at him coldly, disgusted by his self-serving behaviour. His multiple apologies earlier – because he was caught out in a lie – not because he was repentant.

For two years she'd been paying the price for what she had caused: the mounting debts, the unpaid bills, losing their rented home.

Her penance – to be hidden away in a job, hide what she had done, while reminding her every day that the predicament they were in was all her fault.

He would never let her forget – not that she would be able to. It was imprinted in her memory for all time, and had felt like it was happening all over again when she couldn't find Sam. The same blind panic, gut-wrenching fear, and her heart jumping out of her throat. A mirror image nightmare, just the same, just like before. Not knowing which way to turn, which road to run down, which car to stop or house to knock, for somebody to have seen the missing child. Just wildly begging any passer-by to have seen them?

She flexed her trembling hand, then turned at the sound of the door opening. Moraine quietly came into the room.

'Jo, can you come with me, please?'

A terrible sense of fear walled up around her, that there was something wrong. She forced her legs to move and pushed past Pete to step out onto the landing. Moraine was leading her into Sam's room.

An officer was kneeling at the white drawers. The middle one partly open, with clothes on view. Her eyes widened. She gasped in a lungful of air.

She moved in a trance towards the drawers, the image she was seeing tattooing itself on her brain. Her breath suspended in her throat as she stared at what was found. A dark-green top, with a crocodile on the front...

It was impossible. It couldn't be there, because Sam had been wearing it. How else would she have seen it on him?

She jammed her fist against her mouth to stop her from screaming. How could it be in her home? She wasn't crazy. Her last sighting of her boy, he was wearing it. He was with her, under her coat, at her side.

She turned in bewilderment to seek out Moraine, and saw Moraine was studying her. Jo saw her dismay. The feeling of connection had gone. The unspoken accusation, from Detective Stone, was staring back at her from Moraine's eyes. Her legs buckled and dropped her to the floor.

We've not had a single sighting of your son.

Jo stared up at Moraine beseechingly, trying to find the words to defend herself. But it was impossible. Her brain was giving her no answers. She couldn't understand how this was happening. She could only explain what was obvious.

'I don't understand why it's here.'

TWENTY-SEVEN

Pete came down from the bedroom a changed man. Moraine noticed the deflation in him straight away. He looked shaken, with a sickly pallor in his face, and for the first time he appeared to be in shock from what had happened. As far as she was aware, he didn't know about the green top found upstairs. She hadn't even told Kennedy yet.

He stared at her as if he didn't recognise her, a blank look in his eyes. His voice was hollow. 'You're here to help find him, and I haven't given you any help at all. What can I do now? How can I help get him back?' He glanced across the room at Kennedy. 'What should I do?'

Tears dripped from his eyes. He glanced up at the ceiling. 'I've wasted so much time. I thought... God forgive me... I thought... stupidly thought she had him. Thought she knew about me and... that this was her way of punishing me.'

He grabbed his head, his hands bunched into fists, gripping his hair. 'I've wasted all this time. All this time thinking she had him somewhere, but that he was safe. And all the while he's been lost with me not looking for him. My little boy... he's only just five.'

Kennedy took control of the situation, guiding the man to a chair, his arm around his shoulder as he was now blinded by tears. It was hard to watch. She felt a tightness in her throat. It was seeing him suffer after being so aloof with him. A lesson learned – something to remember – don't judge without knowing the full situation.

Moraine left Pete in Kennedy's capable hands. She needed to relay this new information to Stone and tell him what she had found out. They had been given incorrect information about what the child was wearing. She would need to speak to Jo and see if she could remember correctly the clothes Sam had been wearing. They would start at ground zero again.

She'd felt overwhelmed with confusion in that bedroom upstairs, and slightly sick at not knowing what to believe. How could a mother make such a mistake? Initially, maybe, in all the chaos, you might get it wrong, but afterwards surely, you'd realise you'd pictured them in the wrong clothes? She'd be interested in Kennedy's take, whether he thought her opinion too harsh.

Jo was where she left her, but now sitting on the floor with her back against the white drawers. Her eyelids, nostrils, and the bow of her lip looked red and sore. She was ahead of her husband in who looked worst, bearing the marks of prolonged suffering – cheekbones more prominent, eyes more sunken, hands trembling.

'I can't picture him in anything different,' Jo said in a thick voice. 'I was so sure he was wearing it. I don't how I made that mistake.'

'What about his bottom half?'

'Navy joggers, Spider-Man trainers.'

Moraine gave a small sigh. 'I'll let the SIO know so that we can amend the description.'

She turned to leave, but couldn't without checking Jo was all right. 'Do you want me to bring you a cup of tea?'

She shook her head. 'No. I'm going to have a walk in the garden, if that's okay?'

Moraine had the keys to her husband's car so she couldn't drive off again. The gardeners were also aware to let the police know if they saw her trying to leave. She gave a nod. 'It'll do you good. It's nice out there.'

Moraine stared around the room, finding it hard to know what to say. Her guard was up. Right now, she couldn't get a handle on anything – his revelation that he had misunderstood the situation, her saying she made a mistake – and she needed to step back and get a fresh perspective on what was going on here.

She gave a weighty sigh. 'Well, I need a cuppa, so I'll leave you to it.'

She found Kennedy alone in the kitchen. He'd got Pete to lie down on the sofa, as he was too shaky to stay in the kitchen. She closed the kitchen door, so as not to be overheard while she brought him up to speed.

He raised his eyebrows and gave a low whistle. 'Holy hell… that's going to pee Stone off.'

Moraine eyed him. 'Would you make that kind of mistake, John? Remember your child in the wrong clothes?'

He gave a shrug, his head sinking into his shoulders. 'I'd hope I wouldn't. But it's difficult to know in the moment what you might say. Connie definitely wouldn't. She tells me in detail what clothes to put on them. Hollering up the stairs about the pattern of a dress, the T-shirt with stripes, the one with a collar. She's like an encyclopaedia, knowing every item of clothing in the wardrobes and drawers.'

'What if under stress?'

His expression was less sure. 'Don't know. It might be worth doing a test. On us lot. You know, getting to work and giving a description of what someone at home was wearing when you left. Then check it out. See how accurate we get it.'

She shifted her gaze, saying aloud what she was thinking. 'I can't believe this whole time he's been thinking his wife had Sam. What the fuck...'

Moraine fell silent. She was rattled that she hadn't picked up on these things yesterday. It was her job to watch their behaviour, but she hadn't a clue what was in Pete's mind the whole time. She'd judged him as detached and uncaring – that might be so in some areas – while in fact he'd been thinking his wife had hidden his son somewhere to punish him. It was infuriating that it took his alibi to be checked for him to reveal this.

It took a lot to throw Moraine – she'd been doing this job for a long time – but she'd misjudged his behaviour completely. His standoffish manner had been concealing something she hadn't thought of. And she hadn't given him an opening to share it. She hadn't even talked nicely to him, using a tone of voice that wasn't friendly. Because of her own behaviour, he'd kept this to himself.

Kennedy pressed a mug of coffee into her hand. 'Drink this,' he ordered. 'And stop beating yourself up. He had plenty of opportunity to tell us this. His appeal to the public didn't hint at any of that. The only reason he's telling us now is because he's been found out and realises he's lost us time.'

His presence helped calm her. She suspected there wasn't much that fazed him. She sipped the coffee, and after a moment said, 'Supposing he's right, and she's hidden him somewhere? Maybe the reason no one has seen him is because he was never in the car with her? Perhaps he didn't go with her to the swimming pool.'

Kennedy took a moment to consider the question, before releasing a sigh. 'As a father, I'm hoping he's right. It would be the best chance of finding the boy alive. If she's out only to punish the husband for his sins, she won't have hurt her son. He's the prize that only she gets to keep.'

Moraine pictured Jo upstairs, marked by grief. The mother

on the television with no hope in her eyes. And today, wanting to leave her son his blue rabbit. They were not the behaviours of someone who thought their child was alive.

She gazed at Kennedy. 'What if she decided no one wins?'

Kennedy didn't reply, but his expression darkened, his gaze turning towards the window, looking out at the vast amount of land.

TWENTY-EIGHT

'*An affair?*' Claire's voice couldn't have been more scathing. 'What a cad!'

A perfectly fitting description as far as she was concerned. Yet James seemed to find against her use of the word.

'A cad. How very archaic,' he mocked with a short, derisive laugh.

Her face went crimson with embarrassment. He was mocking the way she talked. She jutted out her chin to prevent it trembling. 'Why are you being so disagreeable? Staring at me like that?'

He dismissed her comment with a shrug, riling her more.

'No, don't turn away. If I'm doing something to annoy you, tell me.'

He gave a hearty sigh. 'Why not just call him a prick? Or a bastard? Like most people would.'

His answer hurt. It was as if he were deliberately trying to find fault with her. Trying to make her feel vulnerable. Since when had he decided to behave like this? In any argument, they both always remained civil, never resorting to belittling the other. Neither of them got to behave like this. It was utterly unkind and unwarranted. If he was in a foul mood, he should keep it to himself. She was fragile enough already with the Lamberts still there. She hadn't even had a chance to tell him about their visitors.

James took a bottle of wine from the fridge and poured himself a glass, and downed it like it was water. He would never normally drink alcohol during the day. He lifted his head and looked at her with apologetic eyes. 'Sorry. It's getting to me. I said I couldn't do this again.'

Claire stopped being mad at him. She was responsible for him getting involved and she should be taking care of him. She'd like to avoid the Lamberts knowing he was back home, if possible. Persuade him to make himself scarce until they were gone. That way, he wouldn't have to face them. At the moment, they were in the morning room, while she was supposed to be making them more tea.

James loosened his tie and shrugged off his jacket, placing it over a chair. Shaking his head in despair, a dullness crept into his voice. 'That poor woman. What she must be going through. Her son missing, her husband playing away.'

'Does Jo know he's having an affair?'

He shrugged. 'I don't know. Maybe.' He glanced at her with a more open look in his eyes. 'I wouldn't say cad. I get a public schoolboy image with that term. Someone who's grown up with a silver spoon, who thinks he doesn't have to be held accountable. Pete doesn't fit that image. I wouldn't even call him a chancer. I see him as someone who's not very strong, who has given in to weakness to prop up his ego. Jo's an intelligent woman. Underneath that nervous demeanour, for whatever reason it's there, she's smart and capable. I think Pete battles against that. Perhaps he tries to ignore it to make himself feel better. He's a fool, Claire. Which, hopefully, he can correct.'

Unexpectedly, she felt her eyes sting as they watered with tears. She loved him so completely that sometimes it hurt. His fairness in all things, not allowing bias to interfere with treating everyone fairly. Recognising value and worth. Discouraging prejudice and from thinking the worst of people. Encouraging one to always treat people equitably.

She eyed the empty glass in his hand. 'Can I have one of those, please? Just a small one.'

While he fixed her a drink, she re-boiled the kettle to fill the teapot. She'd like to deliver it as soon as possible before Marley or Stuart came looking for her.

James placed a glass on the counter beside her, noticing what she was doing. 'Not for me, thanks. I need a coffee.'

She gave a quick smile and told him a lie. 'It's for Bernice. I'm just going to take it to her. I'll come back and drink my wine. Why don't you have a lie down? You've hardly slept and were up before me.'

She heard his bones crack as he stretched his arms above his head, his small groan, and encouraged him some more. 'A couple of hours will do you good.'

'You're right.' He sighed. 'I couldn't sleep. I kept thinking about him... I won't have a coffee now. I'll have a kip on the sofa.'

The suggestion alarmed her and hurried her movements. Throwing tea bags in the pot, quickly pouring hot water, putting the lid on, so she could get to the door before him to herd him upstairs instead.

'You'll get no rest down here. Not with the girls stuck indoors. Go up to bed and have a proper rest.'

She stood in the hall, watching him climb the stairs, waiting for him to disappear out of sight before taking the tray to the morning room. She pushed the door closed with the sole of her shoe before noticing Stuart was alone. Marley was gone from the chair beside him.

Stuart took Marley's newspaper from the table set between the chairs, to make room for her to put down the tray. She made a point of looking at Marley's empty chair, hoping she had gone to the nearest downstairs toilet, and not the one by James's study or by the boot room. She was trying to keep this visit quiet and not have her bump into anyone, particularly Bernice or Edna. Meg wouldn't know her and would just be polite, but the other two would likely dissolve into tears.

Stuart gave a nod at the French doors. His voice was deep with sorrow. 'She's gone for a wander in the garden, Claire. Needed a moment to herself. She had such high hopes coming here today.'

Claire glanced at him in concern, hoping her annoyance with his wife wasn't showing. 'Please say she hasn't gone to look for him?'

He gave her a helpless look, emitting a weary sigh. 'She knows he's not here, Claire. But all the telling in the world doesn't stop the hope. She'll be all right in a little while. She just needs time to process it again.'

Claire would have to go after her. She couldn't have Marley bringing attention to herself and revealing anything about her own missing boy. It would be jumped on if it reached the ear of a reporter – and then it would be them under investigation. She wanted them out of her home before anyone spotted them.

She gave a sigh before glancing at Stuart. 'I'll go and find her. This is all so very difficult, Stuart, as I'm sure you can understand. I can't have Marley seen here... It will bring all kinds of suspicion down on our heads. James's position... We can't have another child going missing with us again knowing the parents. Speculation will become rife...'

His nod of understanding was sincere. 'Hey, I'd be exactly the same if I was in James's position. One has to be unimpeachable at all times, for fear that scandals begin. You were there for us afterwards, helping us search, risking involvement. We can keep it under wraps. You needn't worry. Marley doesn't talk to anybody. Truth be told, she hardly talks to *me*. The news last night floored her. That's all.'

Claire gave a sigh of relief as she headed out of the French doors. She will need to warn Dougie to tell whoever opened the gate to them not to mention the visit, as it will upset James. He, like Bernice, will not have forgotten what it was like to have Marley and Stuart stay there in the aftermath. Unable to bear being in their own home, she and James had taken them in, going out each day with them to somewhere new or returning to a place already searched. Dozens of futile attempts, leaving them broken.

Dougie would understand how upsetting this visit has been, and will see that James doesn't get to hear of it. But right now, she must find this hapless woman and get her out of sight before she talks to anyone. Only then would Claire feel safe to shut the door again on the past.

That was all she wanted. To leave the past alone. To have Sam returned to his parents and the Jenkinses to be gone. Her life back to how it should be before all this ever began. When there was just her and James, and their family and beautiful home. How her life might have been... if they had never lost their beautiful son.

TWENTY-NINE

Jo gazed at the rabbit in her hand, stroking its softness with her thumb. Her other arm tight around her stomach, holding herself while she wandered aimlessly around the garden. She needed to get off the path, to take a different direction away from all the windows of Beckley House, away from prying eyes looking out at her. She didn't want Claire suddenly seeing her and feeling the need to come and talk to her again.

There was nothing she could do or say that would bring any comfort. There were no words to fix this.

All those people who had searched for him in those first minutes had been looking for a boy in a dark-green top. She had told everyone it had a crocodile on the front – not just once, but to the women at the swimming pool, the people in the shops and outside the church, to the police.

It was almost criminal. That's what they would say, and they would be right, because how was it possible that what he was dressed in was in his bedroom drawers?

She went through the gate in the stone wall at the rear of the garden. She'd been the other side of it when they first moved here to see the extensive area of land covered with trees, sloping down a hillside, a vista of lush green fields stretching as far as the eye could see. Straight ahead, a wide spreading oak tree, hiding from view a paddock and empty stables. It hadn't made sense to her to have stables without horses. It seemed a waste when it could be used, especially with the girls taking riding lessons.

She hadn't questioned it. It wasn't her place. Same as it wasn't her business to know what Claire did with her days, or judge the woman's life and relate it to her own. That's what Pete would do – consciously compare himself to others, leaving him dissatisfied – think they lived a pampered life.

She wasn't like that, and thought well of Claire. Beckley House didn't run itself. Someone had to be at the helm, and that someone was obviously Claire. In her bedroom there was a Georgian bureau that was never to have spray polish, only wax, and often looked used with scrunched-up paper in the basket beside it. She may sit there at night, like the mistress of the manor in Jane Austen's day, overseeing the finances, ordering supplies, writing up menus, taking care of staff requirements, as well as safeguarding the estate.

Jo had entered a different world when she arrived here and had learned one thing: the wealthy had a different mindset to those who were just rich. They were the caretakers of a legacy, passed down from generation to generation. The minders of values and traditions.

Claire instilled those values into her children. She saw it in the girls' behaviour. At their appreciation of receiving occasional gifts. They weren't lavished with presents on their birthdays. Phoebe was given a diver's watch and a pair of riding boots. Gifts she could use. The quality of the items was high, and they would have cost a small fortune, which Pete was eager to point out when googling the prices later, but the point, which he'd missed altogether, was that Phoebe wasn't aware of what was spent on her. It could have been a watch from a supermarket or boots from Shoe Zone, she would have appreciated them just the same.

It wasn't about money for the Howells. She'd been in Claire's dressing room. There weren't the rows of clothes she'd been expecting to see, the shelves of footwear. Instead, a moderate amount of classic womenswear, made for quality in fabrics that would last, to which Claire would add a different belt or scarf to give each wearing a fresh look.

What Pete failed to realise was that being wealthy wasn't about how much money they had, but about responsibility to their heritage, to all those who came before and after them. And to every man, woman and child that came under their care.

She pressed her hand against her stomach to relieve the intense feeling. It was the thought of them discovering her past. Would it stop them caring about Sam? Take away any feelings for him in their hearts. Making him just be a child that played in their garden.

Without warning, cramp doubled her over, stopping the breath in her throat. Her hand clutched tighter at her stomach. She should have listened to the warnings about not eating. That, and the constant anxiety, were causing a burning hollowness inside, and cramping from her stomach muscles contracting. She couldn't move until the pain was gone. Putting her hands to the ground, she went down on her knees, arching her back to draw in her stomach, slowly breathing against the pressure.

She closed her eyes and listened to the birds for distraction. She felt the sun on the back of her head, and was grateful it was there, while waiting for her body to untwist, to relax enough for her to move again.

It was easing, enabling her to lower her back and sit on her haunches. She breathed in comfortably and opened her eyes. She was startled to see a woman standing there. Her hand flew to her throat as she gasped.

'Jesus, you scared me!'

Her heart thumping, Jo took in the woman's appearance. She didn't look like a police officer. Her heavy, purple, corduroy skirt was a mismatch in material and colour to the yellow top she was wearing, and hung off her hips. Her dark hair was streaked with grey. She was staring at Jo with an intensity that was unnerving.

The woman raised a thin arm and pointed a bony hand at her. Her voice filled with a strange awe.

'You're the mother,' she softly crooned.

Jo scrambled to her feet, wondering if she should flee. The woman was a stranger and seemed strange. What did she want, and how could she be here? The woman moved towards her and Jo scuttled back, causing the woman to give a small cry and make a bizarre comment.

'I just wanted to see if you look like me.'

Jo moved further away. The woman's behaviour wasn't normal. What did she even mean? She looked nothing like the woman.

'Please, don't go. I want to show you something.'

Jo's eyes pinned on the woman as her hand disappeared in a pocket of her skirt. Barely breathing, she watched for a knife being pulled out, but her hand was holding a photograph. The woman glanced at it before offering it to her.

Jo hung back, wary that the woman might pounce.

'Please, look at it. You'll see what I mean.'

Holding the rabbit under her arm to keep both hands free, Jo quickly snatched the photo and stepped back again. Her gaze dropped to the picture. Her pulse quickening, throat drying, she could not make sense of what she was seeing. A boy... *so like Sam*. A photograph of a boy who could be her own son. She squinted her eyes and saw the image of Sam.

The ground tilted. She needed to lean against something before she fell down. A low-pitched moan forced her to look at the woman. Her hand was reaching out for the photograph. Jo let her take it back. It wasn't a photograph of Sam.

The woman clutched it to her chest. 'That's my son. He's missing too.'

Jo stared at her, aghast. Was this a trick? The photo a fake? Had the woman been there on Saturday, at the swimming pool? Had she seen Jo then? Jo felt the need to appease her. She might be a mother angry with Jo for losing her son, come to do Jo harm.

'I'm sorry. How long's he been missing?'

The woman's face crumpled, making her eyes disappear in a fold of wrinkles. Her voice sounded strained. 'Five years this October. He simply disappeared from the playground. We were in London, my friend minding him and picking him up. But I got a phone call from the headteacher to say he's gone missing, they can't find him.' A sob came from her. 'They can't find him... And they never do.'

Jo realised she was shaking. Her mind was flying, heart pounding at the enormity of what she was being told. How did this woman know to tell her? Had she stalked mothers with sons bearing a strong likeness to the son she had lost? She had to have been following Jo to have seen what Sam looks like. For how long had she been watching her?

In a daze, she walked backwards until she felt the trunk of the tree. Her legs didn't feel like her own. She bent at the waist to get blood to her head, trying, but failing, to understand the connection. Her thoughts were jumbled. She tried to press replay on her memories of Saturday, but nothing would come into sharp focus. Just large groups of people, their faces blurred. Nowhere in the crowd did she see this woman.

A dull ache now across her stomach, she raised her head, ready to ask questions. The woman was gone. Astonished, Jo moved away from the tree to search behind it, gazing left and right, sure she'd catch a glimpse of her, see the yellow top, but she was nowhere to be seen.

Jo couldn't comprehend it. One minute there, the next she was gone, and taking with her an image of a boy who'd been missing for far longer than Sam. Another boy, with a strong likeness to her little boy, who had never been found. Because... *They never do.*

THIRTY

DI Stone made a second unannounced visit to the Jenkinses' home, this time without the company of DS Fay Hayden. But he was not alone. Two uniformed officers stood outside the front door.

He barely glanced at Moraine as he came in and checked in the kitchen to see who was in there, closing the door behind him before speaking to her and Kennedy.

'We're in a shitstorm. Mrs Jenkins is all over the internet. I need her here right now.'

Moraine was startled, and somewhat alarmed for Jo at what might be coming. She hadn't a clue what Stone had seen, but judging by his urgent need to see Jo, it was something serious.

About to fetch her downstairs, she remembered Jo had gone for a walk in the garden. She caught Kennedy's eye, trying to signal the problem. She didn't want Stone to get impatient while she went to fetch the woman.

Kennedy gave a barely perceptible nod to send her on her way, while offering to make Stone a coffee. She hurried out the front door, leaving it ajar, nodding briefly at the two police officers. She made a dash down the side of Beckley House to the rear garden and was thrilled to see Jo walking towards her up the path.

Jo hadn't seen her yet. Her head was down, her arms wrapped around herself as if in discomfort or cold. She raised her face, and Moraine saw she was as white as a sheet.

They stared at each other. Jo's eyes looked deeply troubled. Moraine wished she didn't need to rush her, but was conscious of Stone waiting inside.

'The inspector's here, Jo. He wants to talk to you.'

It didn't seem to register. Jo had come to a standstill and was now twisting the toy rabbit in her hands, twirling the ears together.

Moraine tried to get her to move. 'Come on. We don't want to keep him waiting.'

Jo's response was to take a step backwards, followed by a frantic cry. 'I have to go back and find her. She's lost her child too. She was there and then disappeared. I opened my eyes and she was gone. *Just gone!*'

Fuck! Moraine was concerned for Jo. She wasn't sure what was happening, but was thinking along the lines of a psychotic episode. She'd witnessed it before when dealing with mental trauma. The person would lose contact with reality. A thought flashed through her mind. Had Jo taken her medication? Was this some sort of withdrawal?

Shit sake! She should have got a doctor in. Had her checked over. She was mentally and physically failing before Moraine's eyes. The dressings on her hands looked like she'd been crawling in the dirt and she'd smudged some on her face. She should have gone with her and not let her go out alone, as she was clearly in need of minding.

'Jo?'

Jo lifted her head at the sound of her name and gave a tired smile. 'Hello, John F. Kennedy.'

Moraine gave a sigh of relief, glad to have some help. They needed to get her home, and for Moraine to call a doctor.

Kennedy was warm and friendly. 'Hi, Jo. Just coming to check what's keeping you both.'

Moraine wondered if he was going to take Jo's hand and lead her back to the annexe, but there was no need. She was moving her feet, apparently happy to accompany him.

Surprisingly, she seemed back to normal: 'I hope I haven't kept him waiting. Is it just me he wants to see, or both of us?'

'You, I believe,' Kennedy replied.

She gave a slight nod. 'Just as well. I'm not in the mood to see Pete.'

Moraine was confused as she walked behind them. It was good that Jo had back mental capacity, but a couple of minutes ago she'd been talking gaga. She'd have to explain that episode to Stone, and document the behaviour. And it was still a good idea to call a doctor.

They entered Jo's home and found Stone making her a mug of tea in the kitchen. He gave her a brief, polite smile. 'PC Kennedy said you prefer tea to coffee. Hope I've made it as good as his.'

He placed the drink on the table and hovered his arm over a chair like a waiter, showing her where to sit. Moraine watched from the sidelines, standing by the sink next to Kennedy. Something about the situation called for them to wait, quietly inconspicuous. Stone's manner, mainly. He was shepherding the woman into a comfortable place.

Moraine thought about the two police officers outside and Jo's reaction to being told it was only her Stone wanted to see. Jo should be desperate for it to be both of them, regardless of any hostility. Their son had been missing for twenty-nine hours, and the SIO was there to give them news – good or bad, it would be something.

Stone positioned the furniture like he had the evening

before, to give him more room at the table. The chair he sat on looked too small. The mug in his large hand was like a child's mug. Moraine was getting an image of Daddy Bear in the *Goldilocks* story, and wondered if it wasn't just his formidable size making her visualise this, but knowing he could also roar enough to bleed ears if something annoyed him.

He settled the mug on the table and clasped his hands, giving his full attention to Jo. 'I'd like to have a catch-up with you before I go on to another matter. Where we stand, at the moment, so to speak. There's been zero sightings of Sam. Every doorbell camera in the village has now been checked. Dashcams on the local buses, taxis, cars and vans – not a single sighting of him.'

He paused a couple of seconds to let that sink in, acknowledging it with a remark. 'I know, a lot to take in. Something else I'd like to briefly mention, as I know you're not aware of it yet – a collection of Sam's drawings were found in a den on Mr and Mrs Howell's property where their children and Sam have played. We're having them looked at by a psychoanalyst to help interpret them.'

He opened a folder that lay on the table and handed a copy of a black-crayoned drawing to Jo.

'I'm not an expert. I leave that to those who are. The analyst thinks it might be a real place. The spiky blobs on the ground might be spiders. Is the place in the drawing somewhere you might know?'

The paper was shaking as she held the picture in her hands. Her eyes teared over as she breathlessly answered, 'No.'

She let the drawing fall from her hands to rest on the table, her eyes darting anxiously to him and around the room. 'I didn't hurt him.' She shook her head hard, her hands showing white knuckles as they twisted together.

She may have said something more, but wasn't given much of a chance. Stone was nodding at her, already speaking. 'I know, a lot to take in. All of it. Your husband...' He gave a heavy sigh. 'Not the best time for that to come out, I have to say. Hardly time to acknowledge it, or did you have an inkling already? Or did it come as a complete shock? A shame he didn't speak out sooner, save us all a lot of time. Hiding it made him look suspicious.' He tutted. 'He'll feel it now... The guilt of thinking his son was safe.'

At this, Jo's mouth gaped. Stone honed in on it straight away, his black silky eyebrows rising. 'You didn't know. All yesterday and throughout the night, he was thinking you took Sam and put him somewhere to punish him for his affair. He thought you knew about it, and were getting your own back, so to speak.'

Her gasp came from deep inside. She shook her head firmly in denial. Her eyes stretched wide as she put her anger into words. 'I would never do such a thing. I lost him. Just that. Nothing more...'

Stone's hands unclasped, and he held out his large palms, his focus first on Jo, then around the room at Kennedy and Moraine as if his thoughts were jumbled. Moraine knew it was a ploy to get Jo to further drop her guard. Giving the woman a sense of quiet confusion, with him trying to catch up with what she had just said.

'I'm aware there was a mistake in the description of the clothing you gave. We've amended that to the police and the public. I have to say, though, in looking for a child of Sam's age, we would be interested in every child seen on camera of a similar age, regardless of the colour of clothing.'

Stone gave her a look of pity. 'Why do you think you made that mistake? Was the top we found a favourite of his?' he asked softy, wonderingly. 'Is that what happened? You loved him so much you wanted him to be wearing it? Did your husband's behaviour cause you to do something? Was it easier to make yourself believe Sam was missing or ran away?'

Her eyes wide, she stared at him in disbelief. 'I didn't make a mistake. You're trying to confuse me. Sam went missing. Wearing his green top.'

Moraine felt the kitchen counter digging into her back, her chest feeling heavy as she waited for Stone's reveal. Jo's face was filled with anguish. Tears pooled in her eyes as Stone stared fixedly at her. 'The thing is, it's not the first time, is it, Mrs Jenkins, that you've lost a child? And that child was wearing a green top.'

Jo gasped loudly – covering the sound of Moraine's own intake of breath – like she was being strangled. She struggled to speak, but Stone carried on.

'It must have been a tough time. I'm sorry to say that it's now on the internet. You were recognised on the television. Is that why your husband wanted to do the appeal alone, so that you wouldn't be seen? It must have been of great concern if your current employers were unaware. Unless, of course, you told them. Did you, Mrs Jenkins? Did you disclose the reason you were sacked from your previous employment?'

'Jo, don't answer that.'

Moraine swivelled her head to see James Howell standing at the open door. His unannounced appearance, following in Stone's footsteps, caught them off guard. James Howell and DI Stone stared at each other, their faces both unreadable.

Stone arched an eyebrow and slowly smiled at Howell. 'I must say, you do arrive at the most opportune moments.'

The barrister moved forward a pace, his voice mildly surprised. 'Opportune for whom? If you wish to continue questioning Mrs Jenkins, it might be an idea to caution her.'

Moraine held her breath. She could imagine several evaluations going on in Mick Stone's head. The barrister was right. Any evidence gained from this interview would be inadmissible as it was unlawfully obtained. Stone needed to decide his next move.

He pulled his shoulders back and glanced at Jo calmly. 'Mr Howell is quite correct, Mrs Jenkins.'

Moraine shut her eyes, overwhelmed by what was about to be said. She was riven with emotion – sickness, impotency, despair – and could feel Jo's helplessness. She had so not wanted it to be her. The words were already being said aloud. She wanted to open her mouth to protest. But at what? What could she protest? No eyewitness reports. No surveillance evidence. Nothing and no one spotted this one small boy in all this time.

The only shot they had right now was to question the mother. She may be the only one who knew where her son was. Dead or alive. She may have been the last person to have seen him. Moraine didn't hope for that. She hoped only to find him.

THIRTY-ONE

Claire ended the phone call from a busybody acquaintance, alarmed by the woman's questions. Had she known about Jo Jenkins's past? Had she looked at Facebook? Did she know what they were calling Jo? That it was all over the internet? Claire ended the call quickly, claiming she had a pan on the stove about to overboil. Her phone rang again. She ignored it. She didn't want to hear again that it was *everywhere*.

Probably Facebook counted as everywhere for some, for those with vacuous lives who posted and photographed their every movement as if it were vital to let the entire world know what they were doing every minute of the day. It was not for her. She didn't understand why people felt the need to post everything they did online. She valued her privacy and couldn't abide the thought of being exposed. Her staff had never mentioned where they worked on social media, which she was grateful for, but they knew she wouldn't tolerate it. That now seemed immaterial. The whole blasted country probably now knew of Beckley House. People would be looking at its history.

Now more than ever she wanted the Lamberts gone from her home before the police came knocking again. Despite her chat with Stuart, they seemed in no hurry to leave. After finding Marley wandering around the garden, she thought they'd go, and they would, they assured her, after one more cup of tea.

She slammed the teapot on the counter, debating whether to use the same teabags left in the bottom. Give them weak tea so they didn't ask for another. Keeping them contained in the morning room was testing her limits. She was trying to keep it quiet downstairs so as not to disturb James. But soon he would come down to see them still there and all she would have done was waste her energy.

She grabbed up her phone. She had no choice but to look into Jo's history, before she got any more calls about it, or Marley or Stuart discovered it and came bouncing into the kitchen to exclaim the frightful description she had already heard: Jo had been branded *A dangerous mother*. What a dreadful label.

Her hands shaking, she tapped out 'Joanne Jenkins'. Her stomach dropped. The school mum acquaintance was right. It was everywhere. *BBC News*. The *Mirror*. The *Sun*. YouTube. Facebook. Twitter. All with today's date. On Facebook she saw something most alarming: A dangerous mother loses a second child...

She tapped open a *Metro* article from two years ago:

Joanne Jenkins, 25, has been dismissed from her job as a nursery assistant due to negligence following an incident at Whitebells Nursery in Bath.

A two-year-old girl in her charge was lost while out visiting a local garden. The party of ten toddlers, including Ruby Ashman, were headcounted after the visit was over and before setting back to the nursery. At that time the alarm was raised that Ruby was missing.

The child remained missing for a further ninety minutes. The toddler was discovered by a postal worker on Newton

Road, one of the city's busiest thoroughfares, who quickly realised the child was injured. The police and an ambulance were called, and the toddler was taken to the hospital. Her identity was discovered by a name label in her dark-green polo top. An X-ray showed Ruby had a broken left arm and grazes to her knee.

Her parents report that since the ordeal their daughter has anxiety at being separated from them.

Police have made a safeguarding referral to Bath and North East Somerset Council. Whitebells Nursery have issued a full apology and conducted their own internal investigation. Mary Davis, owner of Whitebells Nursery, said in a statement that 'no such event has occurred here before. We have put changes in place to ensure it can never happen again'.

Joanne Jenkins declined to comment.

Claire's insides squeezed with anxiety. Her employee was being labelled a dangerous mother. How was she going to quieten this down? Prevent further busybodies from digging up the past? How was she meant to rescue Jo with all this coming out?

She didn't want to question the reason Jo never told them – it probably wasn't her decision. It explained a lot, though – the undercurrent of anxiety, Claire detected in her character. An inability to relax. Hiding the truth put a great deal of pressure on one's shoulders.

If anyone was to blame it was James for failing to do due diligence. For allowing himself to be hoodwinked by Pete, with his simple explanation that his wife needed a job.

The subject of her thoughts casually strolled into the kitchen, eyes bright and alert. Claire had to look away as she felt the urge to do some physical damage to her husband. It was all his fault. Damn him.

He stood by her side. 'Making more tea, I see.'

She glared at him. 'Yes. More tea. For Marley and Stuart Lambert. Blasted more tea before I can get rid of them.'

Her voice broke, causing James to put his hand on her shoulder. 'Hey, what's wrong? I didn't know they were here. I would have come and said hello.'

She bit her lip to stop herself from shouting. 'Don't! Stay out of the way so I can get rid of them.'

His eyes creased with confusion. 'Why? I told you this might happen. They were bound to visit.'

Her mouth trembled and wetness filled her nose. 'James, we don't want them here, talking about the past. You've got no idea what's been happening. It's in the news that Sam lived here. Out there for anyone to read. And Jo… my God, James, Jo's name is all over the internet. She lost her job at a nursery for losing a child on an outing. A two-year-old who broke her arm. I've already been informed by one person asking me if I knew what she had done, knew about her past. My phone has just rung again with someone else probably wanting to tell me.'

'Ignore it.'

Her head swivelled to look at him. '*Ignore it!*'

He nodded firmly. 'Yes, Claire. Ignore it. It's more important that you support Jo. Forget what people are thinking and saying. If you condone it, you'll come across as heartless. And if you think sacking her is the answer, in light of her terrible ordeal, I'll think you heartless.'

She stepped back so she could look at him properly. She hadn't meant what she said to come across as care for her own welfare. Yet he saw it that way. She hadn't denounced Jo, merely relaying what she read. She didn't deserve this judgement. All she had ever done was try and protect her family. It didn't occur to him, she was protecting his name as much as anything.

Her eyes fixed on the Wedgwood teapot. More than a hundred years old. She picked it up and slammed it down a second time, startling them both as they heard it crack. They looked and saw a white line in the blue glaze across the wing of a bird, a figure on a bridge, a weeping willow.

Claire stood there, stunned. Shocked tears coming into her eyes. She felt him release her grip from the handle and take her hand in his, inspecting it for any damage before folding her fingers gently. 'We'll use it for decoration,' he said softly. 'No need to throw it away.'

He tugged her towards him and let her rest her head on his shoulder, holding her still while he spoke in her ear, quietly and gently. 'I should never have brought him here. I'm sorry I did that. I can't bear the thought of the same thing happening again, a child never returning to his parents.'

He felt her stiffen and held her firmly, keeping her there. 'We must do everything we can to help Jo. She's been arrested. It's no longer a missing person. It's a criminal investigation. Everything is stacked against her, Claire. They're looking at Jo as a firm suspect. No one saw Sam with her. She's being treated for depression after what happened in her last job. As I predicted, the police are thinking she has made her own son disappear. Out of revenge, because she discovered Pete was having an affair. Sam has been missing for thirty-three hours. Tomorrow the police are going to search here.'

Claire pulled back in shock, wondering how he knew all this. He'd only just come down the stairs. 'How do you know this? Did the police phone you?'

He shook his head. 'No. I saw the SIO arrive out the bedroom window, accompanied by uniformed officers. I recalled where I knew him from. London. He was working there at the time and appeared in court to give evidence. The child that was found in the freezer. A difficult case. Thought to be a murder. A tragic accident, as it turned out. The curious child managed to get in there. He was gunning for the parents.

Hazard of the job, I suppose, when you see something like that. You want to blame someone for letting it happen.

'I went over to the Jenkinses and found Jo being questioned. A moment later, she was arrested. I managed to get in a few words with the liaison officer. She's very compassionate. Gave me some insight into how Jo's coping. Something I can pass on to her solicitor. I've managed to get her Anthony Clark. She was hoping I'd accompany her and represent her at the police station. I couldn't, of course. It wouldn't work out at all well if she later needs me to represent her in court. I didn't tell her that. She was shaken enough, without worrying about what comes next. So you'll help her, won't you, Claire?'

Claire nodded, moving her head against his chest. He had finally acknowledged that bringing Sam into their lives had been wrong. He was sorry he'd done that. Now wasn't the time to tell him his sorry should be as much for Matt's parents as it was to her. Jo's son was missing. All that mattered now was getting him home to his mother.

She couldn't convey her other worry – that all the while this was happening it left the door open to reporters to dig up anything they could in search of a story – even one from thirty years ago, they would write about it. She would give anything to turn back time, to step into that bedroom and not see her father standing by the Juliet balcony. To be the only witness to what happened next.

'Are you okay?'

She looked up into his gazing eyes and wondered if he would be shocked if she told him. He had told her everything about his past, and she had kept it safe. Would he do the same for her? She opened her mouth to speak, but no words would come.

'I'm fine. It was just a shock,' she replied, hoping her tone didn't sound forced.

James's sudden intake of breath and the weight of his arms

heavy on her shoulders had her quickly supporting him. His face had glazed with sweat as it screwed up in pain, and his hands reached up to hold his head while he groaned.

She grabbed a kitchen chair for him to sit on, and guided him into it, before hurrying away to fetch paracetamol and Nurofen from a cabinet and fill a glass with water. She popped two tablets from each foil container and watched his shaking fingers feed them into his mouth. He guzzled the water, dripping it on his shirt.

He reached out a shaky hand to take hold of hers, trying to reassure her, his voice tight with pain. 'It's okay. I'm fine now.'

Claire closed her eyes and gently kissed the top of his head. He was anything but fine. These headaches were coming one after the other. It filled her with a terrible sadness to see him suffer like this. He needed these dark days to be gone. This part of their life had to end, before they both believed Beckley House was cursed.

THIRTY-TWO

Jo, strangely, felt at peace while sitting in the cell. Everything around her was still and quiet, the colours of the walls and floor muted, the rubber mattress beneath her fingertips cool and smooth to the touch. It was all soothing. Something she badly needed after hearing those words that brought her here: *You do not have to say anything...*

Phrases so familiar from every police drama she'd watched on television, said *to her*. It had been a surreal moment. She felt a strong relief hearing such powerful words. The taking of her arm to guide her to a police car assured her the situation was real. Yet her uncuffed hands lay in her lap, making her uncertain if it was an actual arrest.

Snapshots of everything that followed – getting out of the car, a hand on her arm guiding her inside the police station, standing at a high counter, a glass screen separating her from the custody officer, being informed she had the right to free legal advice, to tell someone where she was, to have medical help if feeling unwell. A notice being shown to her, telling her of her rights to regular meal breaks, and use of the toilet. Handing over her wedding ring, the only piece of jewellery she was wearing, and in return given a property sheet to check and sign. All so vividly real, it held her under a spell.

It was all strangely soothing – everything was taken out of her hands, and she was no longer responsible for any decisions. She could stay here and just rest. She looked at the white ring mark around her finger and felt free of entrapment, and decided she wouldn't put it on again. Pete had thrown her to the wolves. She had to hand it to him, by saying he thought she took Sam and put him somewhere to punish him for his affair, he couldn't have made it any worse if he tried. DI Stone's comment seemed to excuse Pete's behaviour, but it was too lenient considering how he lied to hide where he'd been.

He'll feel it now... The guilt of thinking his son was safe.

His question to her – did she sense it? Have an inkling it was happening?

No one had mentioned the woman's name; it didn't matter if they did. The image of her would be just the same. Jo had met her – in her firefighter uniform and wearing pink gloss – and knew it could only be her.

Had she sensed it? She had felt it in her bones the moment she met her. Did it come as a complete shock? She'd being praying she was wrong, that he would never have an affair.

She had so wanted to keep on loving him – he'd always been there, almost from when she began adulthood. From her student days as a nurse, when both young and fresh. Her fast forward into motherhood – when both were new parents. Making a life together, a history to look back on, full of busyness, full of good times, and bad times, and okay times. He was always there, until he wasn't.

The loud noise of the cell door being unlocked made her look up. A police officer beckoned her out. 'Your solicitor is here.'

Once more, she found herself in the realm of the surreal.

He ushered her through a doorway marked 'Interview

Room 2'. The décor was exactly as she imagined it would be. The man waiting inside was sitting at the only table. He rose to his feet to shake her hand.

He smiled. 'Anthony Clark. Let's have a chat, shall we?'

She took in his immaculate presentation: the sharp suit, the meticulously styled brown hair, and the calmness of his voice. It was all soothing. She didn't mind that he was there. He sat down after she took a seat, and put on a pair of brown-framed glasses. He clasped his hands loosely on the table.

'You're in custody, but you haven't been charged. Shortly, two officers will interview you under caution. We have about twenty minutes, so let's use that time wisely. Let me ask you a question, which should speed things up. Why do you think you're here?'

Jo told him. 'They think I've hurt my child. They no longer think he's been kidnapped or taken by a random stranger. They think I made him go missing, that I've hidden him because my husband's having an affair. They think it's some sort of habit, that I lose children in my care, because I lost a child once on a nursery outing. Little Ruby, in a green top, who was eventually found with a broken arm and cut little knees.

'They think I deliberately imagined Sam wearing his green top to make it easier for me to believe in a lie. That Sam was with me and then he went missing... They think Sam wasn't seen because he was never there. And after this afternoon, they think I'm delusional because I said I saw a woman who was there one second and gone the next.'

He inhaled a deep breath, as if it was him who'd done all the talking. 'That was certainly efficient. Well done for getting all of that out.' He gave her a long sympathetic look. 'The top the police found – how do we explain that?'

Jo gave a helpless shrug. 'I see him wearing it. But how's that possible when found in my home?'

He gave a pondering look before responding. 'When you

left him in the cubicle, could he have started to undress while waiting for you to return? And you somehow brought the top back home with you?'

A memory of bright pink knickers on a bare-breasted woman flashed through Jo's mind.

There's your bloody bag. You can't reserve it like a towel on a sunbed.

Uncertainty crossed her face. 'The cubicle was in use when I came back to it. The woman inside opened the door to hand me my bag. I never thought of Sam's top being in it. I never saw it. But if so, I now have to wonder how it got in Sam's drawers. I don't remember putting it there.'

He gave a satisfied nod. 'Let's not worry about that for now. It's enough to show how it could have returned to your home. One thing is confusing me. The woman who disappeared. Was she really there?'

Jo found herself able to smile, and gently touched her lips to feel the curve. It felt so long since she'd moved those tiny muscles, she'd forgotten the sensation. 'She was real. Dark hair, streaked with grey. A little taller than me. Maybe early forties, but with the frailty of someone much older, or who'd been ill. Dark purple, heavy corduroy skirt, summery, bright-yellow blouse.'

'And what's the significance of her? Why is it important that she suddenly disappeared?'

Jo felt a sharp pang in her stomach. Thinking about the woman was hard. She could relate to the same suffering, the same madness, the same fear.

'Because of what she told me. What she showed me. A photograph of a little boy with an incredible likeness to my son. He was *her* son, and he's been missing for five years this October.'

His eyes behind the lenses opened wide. 'Did you get her name?'

'No. I thought at first she was a mother who might have seen me at the swimming pool, coming to tell me I was irresponsible. Or something like that.'

'I've googled Beckley House. There don't seem to be any neighbours close by.'

'There aren't. The Howells own a great deal of land.'

'Entrance?'

'Through the main gate, which is mostly open. But there are probably other ways in.'

He nodded thoughtfully. 'So it's possible she was visiting?'

'She wasn't police, so possibly she was there to see the Howells.'

He sat back, wearing a calm expression. 'One more thing. Were you questioned on all the matters we've discussed?'

She gave a slight nod. 'Mostly. Some of it I've interpreted from the questions they asked.'

'And were you questioned under caution?'

'No. I wasn't cautioned until I was arrested.'

'I believe James Howell's timely interruption has benefited you. Especially given his credentials. I'm going to give you one piece of advice. You have the right to silence and to provide a "no comment" response to the questions put to you by the police. It isn't an admission of guilt. That's my legal advice to you.'

Jo had the disquieting feeling that things were being made too easy for her, when they shouldn't be. Why could she not remember how his top appeared in his drawers? Why couldn't she remember her strange and quiet little boy saying a single word after his tears, after what he told her. She couldn't recall any conversation with him, couldn't hear the sound of him in her memory. Not a laugh or a giggle.

Her memory of his bath time with tears. *Daddy*, the bastard, hadn't told her. She bet SpongeBob SquarePants sometimes weed in the sea when playing with his best friend, Patrick Star.

Then Saturday morning, Sam lying beside her in the bed, feeling his cold toes... his dry pyjamas. She wondered if she imagined his snuffly breathing, his pencil scratching against paper – if she had really heard it like that.

Then the frantic panic that followed.

She couldn't have run any quicker. Blood was thrumming in her ears, raw panic pushing its way up into her throat. Echoes of his name called again and again, with every heave of her chest. Flashing images. A mother's wet face. A crying, red-faced baby when a door opened. Memories of voices.

We've called the police, love. Best thing to do.

An empty bench, confirming his absence. Her own frantic cries.

Did you see him? About this high. Wearing a dark-green top, with a crocodile on the front.

Why could she remember these things and not have a single memory of hearing his voice? Instead, silence the whole time. Not a whisper. Just a silence.

THIRTY-THREE

Claire swung round and told Bernice to keep the noise down. Not everyone wanted to hear the racket. The television was far too loud, not that she could make out the words above the banging of pots and plates. Even with the door closed the sound would reach James's office, where she hoped he was at least resting, if not trying to sleep.

Everyone else did not need to hear her pain. Because that's what she was hearing. Bernice was stomping around like a wounded animal. Claire hadn't been able to prevent her from seeing Marley. She'd clung to Marley's slight frame until Claire had to rescue her from being bear-hugged to the floor. By then, emotions had dissolved into a river of tears, from both women, while Claire did what she did best – found another teapot and made endless cups of tea.

It had been horrible seeing her still in so much pain. It hadn't lessened one iota in all this time.

Dougie tapped at the back door and Bernice ushered him in. Claire envied him being out in the fresh air. They were all cooped up inside after the parade of police cars and van this morning, and after that, being stuck with visitors that didn't seem to know when to go home. A short while ago, a Police Search Adviser in a hi-vis jacket had knocked at the door and told her they would make an early start in the morning, but while daylight was still good, he was getting the lie of the land and having detection equipment delivered.

They would do a grid search in specified areas initially. He asked if she had any plans for the outside of the property, and whether there were any septic tanks, drain covers, or wells. The only pleasure in her day so far was that she could hand him detailed drawings of every structure and square foot of land.

He said he would lead the search and hoped to keep disruption to a minimum. She needn't concern herself that they'd be traipsing in and out of her home. They were bringing a Major Incident vehicle as a command centre, along with portable loos and a refreshment van. Dougie would be their point of contact if they required any information. So, he told her, they should, please, just go about their normal lives and ignore their presence.

As if that was possible, she thought.

She threw Dougie a grateful look for taking care of things, keeping her informed, especially about the onlookers at the gate, the reporters and the TV vans out on the narrow road. Long-lens cameras pointed at the house, every activity being watched and recorded.

For once she wished it would rain heavily and soak the lot of them – instead, it was dry and balmy weather. The only good thing to happen was Marley and Stuart finally leaving, taking the weight off her shoulders so she could breathe again. They didn't get to see James, which was another blessing, as he wasn't in a fit state to talk to them.

She blamed his glasses, as he was squinting in his present pair. Clearly, the current prescription wasn't strong enough anymore. She made a note on the calendar to phone the opticians tomorrow and get him an eye test.

Her to-do list was never-ending. Keeping the household running was a constant job. Most of her time was spent telling people what to do: okaying repairs, saying yes to replacements, and giving the go-ahead for new purchases. The estate didn't run itself, and she was always on duty. First thing in the morning, she would call the girls' school. She was not driving them anywhere until this circus had gone. Edna had drawn the curtains across every window facing the front and, in the girls' bedrooms, moved furniture in front of them as a barrier to their trying to open them. She had told them to stay away from the windows and have the lights on all day if necessary. They were good children and would obey Edna unless they thought they might see Sam.

Dougie indicated he'd like a word. She passed Bernice and stepped out of the back door with him.

He kept his voice low. 'Just to let you know, the police officer in the Jenkinses' home gave me a tip-off. Jo will be back in about an hour. I'll make sure I'm there to get her through the gates quickly and with no trouble. I was thinking those gates actually need a hose down.'

She smiled at him, grateful for the brief humour. 'Don't you dare, Dougie. Not while I'm around. And then only so long as it looks like an accident. A sprinkling maybe, while you water the trees.'

His chuckle accompanied her as she went back indoors, warming her momentarily, until the images on the flat screen on the wall chilled her blood. *Her home.* Aerial footage showed her entire property. She hadn't seen a helicopter in the sky or heard one. Reporters probably didn't need to use them anymore, not when there were drones that could fly over trees and walls to breach barriers and pry into private lives.

Her first instinct was to tell James. He'd know if it was against the law to film private property. But she stopped herself. The BBC wouldn't be airing it if it was breaking rules, if public interest didn't outweigh their privacy. She lowered the volume. Bernice was watching the news. Her expression a mixture of awe and fear. She, like the rest of the staff, was aware the police were about to search the area for Sam, leaving them all in a state of confusion – why here, when they all thought he'd gone missing from a swimming pool?

Claire set about fixing James something to eat. Thin slices of turkey on wholegrain bread. If she found him asleep, she'd put it in the fridge for later. She took a Bud Light from the cooler, not bothering with a glass. He preferred drinking it out of the bottle and would probably welcome it over a hot drink.

Taking a moment to settle her nerves, she added a second bottle. She would sit with him and enjoy ten minutes of peace. Never in her life had two days seemed so long. The weekends normally went by in a flash. These last two days felt like they'd been going on forever. A nightmare. It was the endless waiting for news. Never could she have imagined the police thinking Jo a suspect. She'd heard nothing more in regards to their phones being tapped – this being a possible kidnapping. The idea of that seemed to have gone quiet. She had absolutely no idea how Lottie and Phoebe were doing, her time taken up with so much else happening. Edna was keeping an eye, but it was not the same as having their mother there for them. Tonight she'd read them a bedtime story, let them curl up on her bed for some close time, just her and her girls.

James was behind his desk, his chair at an angle, with legs crossed and feet up on the corner of the walnut wood, his eyes closed. He must have felt her presence, because he stirred, and lifted his head.

'Nice nap,' he mumbled.

'I'll leave,' she said gently. 'Go back to sleep.'

He gave her a warm smile, becoming more awake. 'Stay. And yes, please, to what you're carrying.'

She placed the tray on his desk, and saw a small picture

frame he'd had resting on his chest fall into his lap as he sat up. She didn't comment. Instead, she watched him place the photograph back on the desk where it normally sat with other small frames. It was a photograph of James and his brother when they were children. It went with his collection of family pictures of her, him, and the girls.

She uncapped the bottles of beer and handed him one. 'You look more rested. Is the headache gone?'

He stretched his shoulders back. 'Yes. Feeling much better.' And gave a little shake of his head to prove it.

Claire sat in the leather wingback chair beside the desk and took a swig of beer, feeling the fizz and coldness soothing her throat, realising she'd been parched.

'Jo will be back soon. I don't know any further details, but Dougie's going to make sure she's not hassled by reporters. You were right. They've descended, unfortunately.'

He drank half the Bud Light, and reached for the sandwich. 'Anthony Clark is bringing her back, so at least it won't be a police car. She's been released under investigation.'

Which meant she hadn't been charged. And was probably why James looked more relaxed.

'It seems unfair then, doesn't it? They're making her look guilty by searching here. Everyone is going to think that.'

It was hard seeing her in a state of anticipatory grief. She was worried for Jo. None of this would be happening if Sam had been visible. The police wouldn't be searching the property. The Range Rover was still being forensically examined, but she couldn't imagine how they would prove he wasn't there.

James ate some of the sandwich, while her eyes roamed over his face, his torso and broad shoulders. She forgot sometimes how attractive he was. His bearing could easily hold a room. His ability to hide what he was thinking was powerful – it made him a mystery man.

He sighed, his face turned to the window. 'I keep wondering,' he said softly.

'What?' she asked, wanting to feel a closeness to him.

He slowly shook his head.

'What? Tell me.'

He gestured to the panes of glass. 'I keep wondering... What if they found him?'

Claire sat in stunned silence, knowing instinctively who he was talking about. Horror grew at the back of her mind. It was completely illogical. Was he losing his mind? They were not searching for *Matt*!

She managed to breathe, and gripped the arms of the chair to pull herself forward. 'What on earth do you mean?' she asked urgently, in a forced whisper, casting her eyes at the open door.

Slowly, she rose to her feet, her eyes glued on him. 'Why on earth would he be on our land?' she said in a biting, low voice.

He turned his head and peered at her. His voice was strained. His eyes searching for answers.

'He wouldn't be. But it's how I vanquish the fear in my soul – for someone to find the place where he's buried.'

THIRTY-FOUR

Moraine strode back and forth in the kitchen. Endless thoughts banked one on top of the other in her mind. She had read what was on the internet and seen how the story had snowballed. Someone copied and pasted an article from the *Metro* and put it on Facebook. Jo didn't have a criminal record, and she didn't do social media. The only reason it came to light was because she was recognised by someone who knew about her past.

Since Jo's return, she hadn't been able to settle. She couldn't passively accept a woman just appearing in front of her. The solicitor who accompanied her had been frank with his request. He'd like the police to enquire about a woman seen earlier by Jo who might be visiting the Howells.

It seemed presumptuous to knock on their door just because Jo said she saw someone. And not just anyone, but a mother who had a son who went missing five years ago. She was waiting on a callback from the SIO, as she'd rather run it by him first.

Kennedy interrupted her pacing to place a croissant in her hand. 'Coffee's on the counter when you're done with the marching. You must have done at least two miles.'

She stopped still and pulled a goofy face, before taking a

bite of the pastry, then trying to chew and swallow it quickly so she could talk. 'It helps me to think. I'm at a loss. I don't know whether to believe her or not. And the annoying thing is, I like her.' Impatience clouded her eyes. 'I think I'm going a bit stir-crazy.'

He nodded vigorously in agreement, with a twinkle in his eyes.

She gave him another face. 'Stone wants my take on her and I can't get a handle on either of them.'

Kennedy looked her in the eyes. 'Then I'd stop trying. Don't overthink it. Give yourself some leeway.'

She lifted the mug off the counter, hiding her slightly warm face. She never usually revealed her inner thoughts, especially ones that showed her uncertainties. It was his calm, almost fatherly, manner that lowered her guard. She gave him an appreciative nod. 'You'd make a good counsellor.'

He shook his head with a small laugh. 'Comes from growing up in a large family. Bouncing from one drama to the next. There's always some sort of shenanigans going on.'

Moraine smiled. It sounded like fun. Hearing him talk helped clear her mind and make a decision. She would speak to the Howells. Think of it as a welfare check for Jo. Better to know for sure if she was suffering from hallucinations.

Using her phone as a mirror, she checked for food in her teeth. 'Won't be long,' she said. 'Going to find out about this mysterious woman.'

He rubbed his hands together. 'And I'm going to make them some food. Bring them together out here. Might learn something.'

Moraine scrunched her way across the gravel, noticing the sharp drop in temperature, shaking off her nerves as she rehearsed what she would say. She knocked and was happy and surprised to see the lovely Lottie opening the front door. It was a quarter to nine and she was still up, wearing pink flowery pyjamas. The door opened wider and James Howell stared out at her, his eyes asking if she was there with news.

She discreetly shook her head and saw him relax. 'Just a quick visit, Mr Howell. Bit of a strange one, I might add.'

He held the door as she stepped inside, where she was then greeted immediately by his wife.

'No news, darling,' he quietly murmured. 'Why don't you take care of DC Morgan while I pop the rugrats up to bed?'

The woman turned to her daughter. 'Clean your teeth. Then you can both get on my bed and I'll come up and read you a story.'

Lottie whooped as she raced ahead of her father, calling for her sister.

Claire Howell smiled pleasantly. She brought Moraine into a sitting room and invited her to sit. The décor was in keeping with a period home. Beautifully elegant with timeless furniture.

Moraine perched on a deep-navy velvet sofa, cupping her hands over her knees to hold herself upright. 'I won't be here long. Just a quick query, if I may? Something Jo's solicitor asked to be checked.'

'Anthony?' Her voice was surprised. 'Lovely man. I didn't see him. James said he was going to represent Jo.'

'He didn't stay long. Just a few minutes.'

'And he wants you to check something with us? How strange. He could have just asked himself.'

Moraine had thought the same, but now suspected his reasons were down to some protocol in how he obtained the information. He hadn't requested she call him, but asked for the police to check it out.

'It's regarding what Jo said she saw when out walking in the grounds, by a paddock and stables. A woman. She didn't get a name but is positive she spoke to her.'

A deep frown appeared on Claire Howell's face. 'Is she talking about one of the staff? No, that doesn't make sense – she knows all their names.' She spread her arms out to the sides with her palms facing up, accompanied by a shrug of the shoulders. 'I'm at a loss. I have absolutely no idea. Dougie's been manning the gates, so I can't imagine a stranger would have snuck in. Unless...' She paused and shook her head, as if vexed. 'Unless some blasted reporter found a way.'

'So, no visitor?'

'No.'

'Oh dear.' Moraine sighed. 'So hard to know if it was just in Jo's mind. Wouldn't be surprising, given the mental turmoil she's going through, to imagine meeting another mother who's lost a son.'

She rose wearily to her feet. 'Thanks so much for your time. I think the best thing I can do is give Jo's doctor a call. Something I should have done already.'

The woman nodded. 'It's been a horrible day for her. Maybe tomorrow things will be clearer.'

Moraine puffed out her cheeks, releasing the air on a sigh. 'Oh well, once more unto the breach, as they say.'

Back out in the brisk air, she regretted quoting Shakespeare. It wasn't the right thing to have said. It made it sound like she was going into battle, not carrying out her duty as a police officer.

She returned to the annexe and found the atmosphere in the kitchen was thick with tension. Kennedy had managed, in the brief time she was away, to get both parents at the table with bowls of tomato soup and buttered brown bread in front of them. The smell was divine and her mouth watered.

She ignored the tense pair as she took off her jacket. Best not to say anything to either of them. From the corner of her eye, she saw Pete using his spoon, and thought at least one of them was eating and not allowing Kennedy's culinary skills to go to waste. She kept her back to them, feeling the tension of silence behind her, and pretended to be busy with her work phone. Kennedy was being equally unobtrusive, very quietly wiping the surfaces.

Jo's voice broke the silence. Soft, but clear. 'How could you do that to him, Pete?'

Moraine froze, hardly daring to breathe. Jo was revealing something that might be important.

He made Jo wait, his spoon clinking against the bowl. In a hostile tone, he said, 'Do what, Jo?'

Her words came out shaky, like her mouth was trembling. 'Humiliate him. Degrade him for wetting his trousers. Making him wash them. Do you have any idea how much you damaged him by doing that? Have you any idea what that would do to the mind of a child who already finds it hard to deal with everyday little changes? Who finds it hard to understand what others are thinking? Who finds it hard to make friends? Have you any idea how your disgusting, brutish behaviour would have hurt his innocent mind?'

A spoon clattered to the floor. Chair legs scraped back. Moraine waited for him to kick off. She could see in the window's reflection that he was still sitting, and held off from intervening.

There was a defensive shock in his voice. A harsh breath as he breathed in. 'It wasn't like that! Not the way you make it sound!'

A sceptical huff escaped her lips. 'Wasn't it? Sam told me. Friday night, when I was bathing him. He was worried about having another accident. He'd had one that day at school. I thought this was what he meant, but it wasn't. He told me if he wet himself he would have to wash his pants and trousers again, as Daddy made him do it the last time.'

His breathing was more intense. 'Why are you doing this, Jo?' His tone was challenging. 'Is it for their benefit? So they can hear?'

'I just want to know why you would do something like that.

Sam didn't have his rabbit with him, and I bet you I know why – trying to be a big boy after his father taunted him for being a baby.'

'Oh, fuck off, Jo. It wasn't like that. He was pacing up and down. I kept telling him to go to the toilet. Next minute, he's wet himself. I didn't make him wash his trousers in a sink, just shove 'em in the washing machine. Better than letting him think it was all right, like you would.'

'He was stimming, you ignorant man. Something you wouldn't bother to educate yourself about.'

He snarled. 'Yeah, that's right. I'm the thicko you married. Well, don't worry, Jo. It won't be for much longer.'

There was a pregnant pause. Moraine waited to hear what she would say, wondering if she was crying. Her voice, when it came, was surprisingly calm. And strong.

'Were you going to leave me?' She inhaled a small breath. 'I can see by your face I'm right. You were with her Friday and all Saturday morning. Why did it take you so long to get home?'

His chair scraped the floor some more. 'Give it a rest, will you? Your audience isn't paying attention.'

'Was it just me, or Sam as well you were leaving?'

Moraine watched his reflection stand up and lean on the table with rigid arms. His head turned to the side. She could feel his eyes on her back. He faced his wife again and gave a disdainful snort.

'I would have gone a long time ago if I could have. I had no choice but to stick it out until I cleared our debts. And, Jo... be careful what you say. I'm in the clear. Are you?'

Another scrape of a chair. This time Jo's. There was no fight in her voice. No anger or bitterness. More of a calm acceptance. 'Well, your alibi can have you. Our debts are cleared, so there's nothing to stop you. You don't have to worry about a wife or a son anymore. You're free to do what you want.'

At the sound of a chair being pushed fully back, Moraine

turned. Jo's slight form was ramrod straight. She didn't glance in Moraine's direction, only at Kennedy.

'Thank you, John. I'm sorry I didn't eat it.'

Kennedy moved across the room. 'Let me walk you upstairs. Been a bit of a shitty night. You can try to eat again later.'

Moraine was left with Pete. She didn't want to look at the man. Kennedy had brought them to the kitchen to learn something. And now they had. Lack of money had stopped him from leaving his wife. She was relieved when she saw him walking to the door. She needed the room to herself. So she could pace... and think.

THIRTY-FIVE

Jo couldn't wake herself up from the dream. She could hear the panic in her voice as she called out to him: *Sam!* She couldn't get the door of the cubicle to open.

Flattening herself down on the wet floor, squashing her breasts against the hard tiles, she slithered under the gap, scraping her back against the sharp wood, raising her head to see.

The bench wasn't there. The walls of the cubicle weren't there. Instead, an open gate. Ahead, a forest of trees. She got back on her feet, and ran towards them, when a forceful grip on her shoulder dragged her back. She twisted and turned and saw Pete holding the back of her jumper.

He brought his face close to hers, and snarled, *What did you do with him, Jo?*

She shoved him away and ran to hide in the trees and could hear his angry shouts following.

How did she break her arm, Jo?

There was a figure in black moving up ahead and she crouched down to follow. Then, a high wall was in front of her with a tunnel dug underneath it. She could hear Sam in there crying.

She went down on her knees to crawl through. Dirt fell at her face. She could see Sam on his knees, trying to hide. His body was soaking wet, and he had a towel over his head.

The walls of dirt clamped her shoulders. His breathing sounded wrong, like the air in his throat was trapped. She tried making grooves in the dirt with her shoulders to push herself forwards. The rocks were tearing at her skin. Pete's voice echoed behind her.

You put him here. And now you can't get him out.

Her body could not move. She was stuck. Sam became agitated. The wet towel was too heavy around his face. He was breathing in water.

A sob was trying to come out of her throat, but earth had filled her mouth. Soil was clogging her nostrils, packing the small hollows. The dirt was falling in her ears. Heavy on her eyelashes, she couldn't blink it off. Every part of her was petrified in place and she couldn't move. Suffocating silence surrounding her as she strained to hear him.

Then something tugged at her feet. A vice around her ankles, pulling her legs straight, preventing her from getting to her knees. She gripped the ground with her hands, digging fingers in deep, and felt searing pain as her palms dragged along razor-sharp grit. She was being pulled feet first out of the tunnel while Sam was still in there.

She spluttered. Fresh air filled her nose. She turned to attack whoever had pulled her out, but they were gone. Relieved she could try again, she hurried to crawl back in, hands feeling for the opening, head lowered, eyes searching frantically. *It wasn't possible. It was just here...* She wildly swung around... feeling, searching, staring, the air squeezing from her lungs. *The tunnel was gone.*

A piercing scream tore out of her.

THIRTY-SIX

Claire took refuge in her bedroom to clear her head and wait for her heart to stop pounding. Edna had already drawn the curtains across the Juliet balcony to prevent any invasion of their privacy. She'd known the minute she'd told the lie that it couldn't be undone. It had taken her back to when she was ten years old, to that intense fear when she looked down and saw her father dead.

The riding crop had fallen from her hand onto the floor. She'd kicked it under the bed out of sight, where it was never discovered and only retrieved long after the funeral. Her beloved horse's death – same day as her father's – a rifle shot to the head after the leg was broken in a fall. Why couldn't her father have offered her comfort – instead choosing to ignore her grief, her weeping having no effect on him. She tried in vain to make him see her pain. His voice was firm so she was made to hear:

Your carelessness killed your horse.

She put flowers on her father's grave. The visits from the police, the questioning of the circumstances – why a man in his prime loses his balance and falls from a balcony – ending with a coroner's findings. An accidental death.

Tears brushed against her cheeks and she swiped them away angrily. She had her grandmother's willpower and would not allow such weakness.

She survived it, the same as she would do now. She was putting loyalty before the truth. That's what mattered.

It was inevitable, a miscommunication, considering the circumstances. With so many people coming and going, she couldn't be expected to keep track of every visitor that day. Her day was so busy, she hardly had time to see her own children. DC Morgan had spoken about a woman walking in the grounds, out by the stables. It hadn't registered with her that Marley could be this woman, as she'd been constantly making her guests refreshments. How could Marley have wandered into the grounds, her entire visit was spent drinking tea.

She stared around the room, guilty that she hadn't kept her promise and read her daughters a bedtime story, leaving it to James. They had spent the first night of their marriage here, before taking a honeymoon in Paris. His father, a property and land solicitor, an expert in all rural affairs, had been her grandmother's solicitor, and then her mother's, for many years, acting for her family in looking after their interests along with half the county's other landowners of farms and estates. She'd not known he had a son until she met him one day driving with his father.

It had most definitely been love at first sight. The moment he stepped into her home, she'd seen he was a perfect fit for her. The right man to have by her side at Beckley House. With his help, the guardianship of her birthright would be in safe hands. There was nothing they couldn't achieve together.

How foolish she was to think it would be as simple as that. How foolish that she didn't foresee that her perfect, faultless husband was harbouring a secret. She hadn't accounted for him telling her it on their honeymoon – changing the dynamics of their marriage in an instant – that forever she would have to keep it safe. Which she could only do so long as James kept it between them.

Hearing him speak like that earlier had made her fear for his mind. She sometimes wished he would ask her what image she held of him, and that he would realise the load she carried. She sometimes wanted him to know that at every visit from Marley and Stuart, she had been scared that Matt's presence would make him vulnerable. Stir up his memories and make him impetuous.

Why had he said that about their land? What possible reason could he have for wanting to keep the police at their home? Did he imagine a search of their land would miraculously bring Matt back?

While she was trying to safeguard their lives, he was a loose cannon, wanting to throw open the doors to Marley and Stuart again. Causing her to make rash mistakes. Telling that foolish lie.

Anthony Clark had an excellent reputation. It would only take Jo's insistence that the woman she spoke of was real for Anthony to keep digging. With a little research, he would discover the name of the boy who went missing five years ago, and remember the high-profile investigation. It would be a small step to realising that Stuart Lambert was a barrister and the woman was his wife. With minimal effort, he would discover Stuart and James shared the same chambers.

She held her head in her hands. *What the fuck had she done?*

She relished saying the word in her head, liking the blunt impact of its sound. Like a sharp crack.

FUCK. Said out loud, it wouldn't have the same impact in her voice. It would come out unliberated and create embarrassment instead, and regarded as crude from someone so well-spoken, trifling with language that didn't suit her.

James had taunted her earlier for not using profanity to describe Pete but calling him a cad instead. She resented his hectoring, and wished she'd argued back in Latin to show she wasn't a dullard. His love of the recondite language stemmed from his love of the law. He'd have been surprised to hear a phrase she understood and learned from him. *Mens rea* – the guilty mind.

It captures perfectly what must be on his mind. Regrettable deeds. Always there... leaving him no peace.

Was he willing to tear down the fabric of their lives? She couldn't allow him to offer himself up in order to atone.

How did she dampen down this torment in his mind, so he didn't do anything foolish? They didn't have to speak about it – it would remain as it was, there between them, secret. She just wanted to find a way to reassure him that she understood, and that she always had. And it had never stopped her loving him.

THIRTY-SEVEN

Jo's scream had Kennedy up the stairs to Sam's room before Moraine. The scream was bloodcurdling, alarming them both. Moraine recovered her breath at finding Jo unharmed, with no sign of blood, and was relieved it had only been a nightmare.

Jo lay tangled in the bedclothes, with vomit on one side of her face and in her hair. No food particles, just yellow fluid. Her stomach was so empty it was all she could bring up.

Moraine was firm but kind. 'Jo, I'm going to help you have a wash and put you in something clean, while John makes you something light to eat. You need some food, Jo, else you're going to be ill. Will you do that for us?'

Her voice was shallow and shaky. 'I'll try.'

Kennedy helped her out of bed, then Moraine took over to lead her to the bathroom. The second bedroom door was closed. She would need to check if Pete was in there, as ten minutes ago he'd been in the sitting room.

Jo was steady enough to wash by herself and said she'd take a shower. Moraine turned the water on for her before giving her some privacy. A quick glance at the bed showed it didn't need changing, just the sheet and duvet straightening, and the pillow picked up off the floor. She did it briskly, then left the room and tapped on the adjacent door.

The mumbled response allowed her to enter. Pete was lying on the bed, stretched out on his back with his arm across his face.

'Sorry to disturb you. Just need to fetch Jo some clean clothes.'

He lay still and didn't reply. She was already familiar with which drawers were Jo's and quietly retrieved pants, a T-shirt, and cotton pyjama bottoms. Leaving quickly, she closed the door behind her.

She held the clothes in her arms and wandered back to Sam's room, sitting down on the bed feeling slightly wired. It was ten forty with no sign of a relief arriving. As soon as Jo was sorted, she'd tell Kennedy to go home and then make a call to see if someone was coming. There was no point in them both staying here when one of them could get some sleep.

This was the second night, and morning was a long way off. Not that she thought she would sleep. Her mind was too active. She'd logged in on her work tablet and brought her report up to date, and wondered what Stone would make of it. He'd not returned her call, but by now would be aware she'd gone ahead with a visit to the Howells.

Moraine felt in her bones that something was seriously amiss in this home, but couldn't tell if it was from a fractured marriage or something darker. She struggled to see either of them clearly, and felt an emotional entanglement that shouldn't be there. She was breaking all the rules of her training, something she'd never done before.

She'd gone from disliking Pete to feeling empathy towards him, and was now bordering on loathing him. With Jo, she'd felt protective the entire time until finding the clothing in her child's room.

She'd lost trust in Jo in an instant, and hadn't found it again until hearing what she said to Pete downstairs.

Questions buzzed through her mind. Was Pete involved? Had they let him off the hook too quickly? The possibility of him getting rid of his child for financial reasons chilled her. Like Jo said, it would free him up, with no child maintenance for the next thirteen years. It would be a lot of money to not have to spend if there wasn't a child around to pay for.

She took a ragged breath. She chased phantom leads, conjuring scenarios that existed only in her imagination. Stone was intuitive. He must have thought of all this himself. She was tempted to call him again, to settle her mind. He'd probably think her erratic.

Or else, tell her to get her head out of her arse. It was a favourite expression of his when dealing with stupidity. Not that he'd ever said it to her, but that didn't mean he never would. She needed to settle down and do her job professionally and, most definitely, not start picking sides.

Another hour rolled by before everything was calm again. Kennedy managed to get Jo to drink a hot chocolate and eat two slices of bread. Both parents were now upstairs in separate beds, hopefully sleeping.

She dried the few dishes on the draining board and put them away in a cupboard. And froze, staring at the child's plastic bowl on the shelf, remembering the uneaten cereal, the uneaten toast by the sink when she'd first arrived. The child had eaten nothing that morning. She blinked in dismay as the pendulum of doubt swung again.

She jumped when her phone rang loudly, and answered quickly before the noise reached upstairs. She was breathless in her hello.

'Raine, I've got news. Anyone in earshot?'

Stone's voice sounded heavy, making her stomach turn to liquid. 'Just PC Kennedy.'

She wished she didn't have to hear what came next, or have to prepare for what followed. She was giving off tension, and Kennedy moved quickly to her side.

Then Stone said it. 'He's been found.'

She gave a small gasp. Then felt her knees wobble at what Stone said next.

'He's alive.'

Moraine stood there in a daze. She had been sure they would find a body. Her harsh breathing must have sounded in his ear, from the impatient tone he was now using.

'Moraine! Get a grip, because I need your full attention. The boy's condition is still to be determined. It's going to be a long night. I'm sending relief for both you and John, because I'll want you back bright and early. This is a possible attempted murder, following abduction.

'You can let the parents know he's been found alive, but no details yet about his condition. They'll have to be patient and wait for us to contact them, but assure them I will as soon as possible. Understood?'

Kennedy was leaning over the sink, taking deep breaths, as deeply affected as she was. He gave a nod that she copied, even though Stone couldn't see it.

Her mind level again, she said, 'Yes, sir. Understood.'

THIRTY-EIGHT

Immersed in a waking dream, wondering if sleep deprivation was making her imagine him, Jo watched as the nurse inserted a thermometer into Sam's ear. She'd been waiting since midnight, nearly five hours, to be with him, while a forensic medical examination was carried out, and now was unable to take her eyes off him. She'd not been given the details of the police findings, only his medical condition and what treatment they were prescribing.

There was a soft beep. She saw the nurse check the inflation of the Bair Hugger. Resembling an inflated lilo, and made of the thinnest of thin plastic, the cells were pumped up with warm air to treat hypothermia. Her glance at Jo was reassuring.

'He's gone up a degree. Warming up.'

Continuing with her observations, the nurse attached a padded grip onto one of Sam's fingers. The monitor immediately beeped louder than previously. Short red lines lit up, building a slim column on the monitor. Numbers beside the lines also appeared in red: ninety-one, ninety-two, ninety-three, finally staying and settling at ninety-three.

'He'll need to stay on the oxygen,' she remarked. Slightly

adjusting the green tubing that encircled Sam's face, she eased the nasal prongs back into each nostril until satisfied with how it looked. 'There, that's better; don't want his little face marking.'

She smiled at Jo. 'Now, is there anything I can do for you, Mrs Jenkins? I'll stay with Sam if you want to stretch your legs or get something to eat. You've got to keep your strength up as well.'

Jo knew nothing would entice her to leave her son's side. She had sat quietly beside him for the last hour – still not believing he was there.

'It will have to be a vending machine, though,' she added. 'Canteen doesn't open until eight a.m., so not for another two hours.'

Jo needed nothing except to be with him, and to see him, and touch him, and place her face against his and feel him breathing. There was nothing more she would ever want after being given this second chance.

'No, thanks.'

'Well, I'll pop you along a fresh cup of tea. I can see that you didn't touch the last one, and it looks like it's gone cold.'

The cubicle door opened and Chelsea Turnbull, the liaison officer who had accompanied Jo, entered. Smiling pleasantly at them, she addressed Jo. 'No sign of Pete anywhere. I'll check again in a while. Probably finding this hard.'

Jo swallowed down the resentment in her throat. He wasn't finding it hard. He'd been ready to ditch them. She didn't want him near Sam. She wanted hers to be the first face Sam saw when he woke. She wanted him to see in her eyes how sorry she was, and that he would never be left on his own again. It was going to be hard to convince him, given the trauma he'd been through, but she'd be a brilliant nurse given the chance, and the best mother he would ever have. She'd smother him in love when he woke up.

She'd trained to be a paediatric nurse and her own son

would be her very first patient. The decision to put that career on hold had probably been the worst mistake of her life. It would have been better to have taken maternity leave, then taken up her first post as a staff nurse. She could have put Sam in the nursery here at the hospital. She would have made it work. Then everything that followed would never have happened.

The assassination of her character had all but destroyed her options. She could never get back what she lost. One moment of inattention, a bad decision, was all it had taken to crumble what she and Pete had built. Ruby Ashman, in her little green top, the sweetest little girl imaginable, would be forever in her thoughts. She'd kept Jo company through so many nights, through so many nightmares, while Jo tried to find her. In a dark-green top – that's all Jo ever looked for.

She had mixed feelings about Moraine not being there. She sensed Moraine's feelings towards her changing back and forth over the last two days. A distancing for sure after she saw Sam's top in his drawers. The clothes he'd been wearing must be with the police as she'd checked the locker and saw nothing in there, except a hospital towel, a small washing-up bowl, a sachet of liquid soap, and a pink J-Cloth. None of it had yet been used.

She would have liked to have seen the clothes he was wearing – to know for sure in her mind if she'd made a mistake and put him in something else.

Sam's hair and face, and what she had seen of the one hand she held, needed washing. Dirt was ingrained in the nail beds. His skin looked like it had been lightly painted with very diluted brown earth. His hair was a greasy texture, the way it sometimes got if his scalp got sticky running around in hot weather. She wanted to wash him, but it was more important to get him warm first.

The 500ml of normal saline was warmed fluid to avoid a further drop in body temperature. Antibiotics, to treat infection, were fed from a second, smaller bag of fluid. Normally the body temperature rises as it tries to fight off a bug, but Sam's was low and could be a sign of sepsis.

It was a miracle he wasn't dead. Thirty-seven hours. Dehydrated. Any longer and his organs would have started to shut down.

She wondered if she'd ever see Moraine or John again. Was this the end of it, their services taken away now Sam was found? The liaison officer with her now seemed only to be there to hear updates of Sam's condition and report back to DI Stone.

Stone hadn't spoken to her or Pete yet. At some point he would give them an update, but she'd been told he was very busy. Maybe that's where Pete was now. Trying to find out information. Maybe at the police station, demanding some answers. As long as he stayed out of her way, she couldn't care less where he was. What he did was no longer her concern. What she did now, none of his business. From now on, it would be just Sam and her.

Somehow, God had given her a second chance and would not punish her for wanting to punish her husband. For that, she was eternally grateful. He had given Sam back to her.

The woman she met yesterday came to her mind. She hadn't been as fortunate. Or as blessed. She was still looking for her missing child. Her little boy was still out there because they couldn't find him. *Because they never do...*

THIRTY-NINE

Claire stared out of the bedroom window, stunned by what James had told her. Sam had been found. 'I cannot believe it,' he whispered, an air of awe imbuing his voice.

He stood behind her, holding her against him while he buried his face in her neck, while she remained dazed. Sam was coming back. She'd been positive he'd be dead. There was no second tragedy to have to carry.

This intense affection felt difficult to take, and she tried to relax into it. He needed this explosion of warmth to drive the darkness away. His manner was almost giddy.

'I had to wake you as soon as I was sure. I saw Pete and Jo leave around five. A policewoman drove them. Then Anthony called. He's alive, Claire. In the hospital, but alive.'

'So now they won't be searching here,' she managed to say.

His grip slightly tightened. 'I wonder where he was found. Maybe they could search the same place for Matt.'

Claire tried not to stiffen, and forced a no-nonsense tone into her voice. 'You need to put those demons from your head. You carry on like this and you'll end up like Marley, going slowly mad.'

He cleared his throat and set her free, stepping back from her. 'You're right, of course. Just wistful thinking.' She could hear him standing close behind her, breathing softly.

'Can I say something?' he then asked.

She kept her eyes focused out through the window, staring at the scatter of violet and pink clouds on the horizon, wondering if he was going to speak more about Matt. 'Of course.'

'I know it's hard to talk about certain things, but for years I've felt you've kept a secret. Nothing about that, but something else. The paddock and the stables. You've never kept horses here. The girls have been riding since they were three. The obvious thing would have been to use what we have and have an instructor come here.'

Claire turned in surprise. 'Why have you never asked this before? What on earth have you been thinking? There's no mystery to it. It's not just a case of plonking a couple of horses up there. There's daily stable care. Feeding, watering, cleaning stalls, and exercising. Making sure they don't get injuries or diseases. The girls learn to ride just as well elsewhere, without time being taken away from their schooling. Because, if you have a horse, James, you should be the person who looks after it, not just ride it and leave it for someone else to mind.'

He held his hand up placatingly. 'Sorry. I should have known there'd be a valid reason. I should have asked you about it years ago.'

She eyed him coolly. 'Instead, you've been thinking I've got someone buried there? Do feel free to dig it up any time you like. You might even find your beloved Matt there.'

He looked shocked, like she'd slapped him. She'd never seen him so off guard. Making him feel vulnerable was not her intention at all. She wanted to end his emotional crisis, not stir it up more.

Softening her tone, she met his eyes. 'I'm sorry, I shouldn't have said that. I'll never speak like that again. Look, it's hardly morning. We should try to get back to sleep. And stop this foolish talk. It's not helping either of us. We can't change what happened.'

She saw the torment in his eyes, before closing off his feelings.

'You're quite right,' he said easily, playing his part and being strong. It was all she ever wanted him to be. 'We can't change any of it, we can only choose how we redeem ourselves.'

It was more than she'd expected him to say. It was better that he was acknowledging... there was choice.

She stepped forward and hugged him, feeling the tension in his strong back, smoothing her hands over his shoulders. She'd geared herself up all these years for warning signs. If only he could see all the good he did, all the care he bestowed on others, that it outweighed any wrongs he did, it would give him some peace. It's what she prayed for... his beautiful mind to be set free.

FORTY

At 6.30 a.m. in a house nearly three miles away, Elsbeth Crosby stepped into her oversize wellingtons. Putting on a thick winter coat to ward off the sharp cold air from the early morning frost, she buttoned it up to the top. She placed a felt hat over her thinning hair and tied it securely with a woollen scarf. Lifting the metal latch on the heavy wooden door, she bade the old dog to stay, and beckoned Stone and Moraine to follow.

Stone's early phone call didn't include Kennedy – he was letting the man sleep. He wanted Moraine with him for this visit, though. Normally, she would visit the area where a person went missing, instead of visiting the scene where they were found. Maybe Stone thought she might have some insights, some kind of telepathic feeling that would channel information to her mind. In fact, her eyes were pinned open from double-strength coffee, and her limbs moved less nimbly than the small, wiry figure in front of them, leading them briskly a good way away from the stone-built farmhouse with an agility that belied her age.

Her robust voice calling out to them to be careful. 'Mind

where you put your feet, the ground's very uneven. I don't venture up here anymore. Don't want to be falling at my age.'

Stone had mentioned she would soon be eighty-three and so far had outlived her husband by twenty years.

In the distance, Moraine saw felled trees and orange diggers in the morning light. The wooded area across the property was being levelled. The diggers would remain stationary, the work stopped for the time being. Entry to the farm was limited while scene of crime investigators did their jobs. The police vehicle they passed at the top of the lane would stay put until a forensic team arrived to carry out a fuller investigation.

They ventured along a dirt track, staying in the middle of deep parallel ruts, to an old barn and dilapidated outhouse, both in disrepair and in danger of falling down. Pulling open the loose-hanging door of the outhouse, their guide stepped gingerly inside, followed by Moraine and Stone. Accumulated rubbish filled most of the space. Some of it was years old. Rusty pieces of machinery had weeds and grass growing through, binding them to the ground as redundant machines, no longer of use. A wheelbarrow turned upside down had rusted away so much its centre was now gone.

Elsbeth Crosby stopped just inside the door and pointed towards the left corner. 'He was over there. I was looking for Tommy and thought he might be hiding in here. Something shiny caught my eye. A big bundle of tinfoil, it looked like. I wondered how it got there. But I had to check Tommy wasn't in it. The shy little fellow's not used to us yet.'

She gulped a breath and Moraine wondered if they should be doing this. Grappling to undo the buttons of her heavy coat, Elsbeth got her hand into her cardigan pocket to pull out an inhaler. Jamming it into her mouth, she pressed down hard on the plastic plunger and inhaled. Giving it a quick shake, she repeated the process before putting it away again.

'There, that's better. The chilly air does it,' she explained, fastening her coat again. 'It was a foil blanket, wrapped around a child. The shock nearly stopped my heart... seeing him there. Thankfully, it carried on pumping, so I could help the poor mite.

'I saw how small he was. Bless his little heart. I kissed his cold cheek, and told him I wouldn't be long, and couldn't believe I felt his breath against my own. As white and as cold as he was, he was still alive.'

They had a quick look around the area, then accompanied her back indoors, where she removed her coat and quietened the dog. 'Shush now. No need to bark at them again.'

She set about making tea, her felt hat still perched on her head.

Moraine thought how remarkable Elsbeth Crosby was. She had dealt with a shocking event, had probably been up all night, and was still managing to be a gracious host. Moraine went to her side to help set out the cups and saucers, while Stone sat in a chunky wooden chair at a solid wooden table.

'Does he always bark when you have visitors?' he asked.

She glanced at the black collie fondly. 'Only if he doesn't know you. He's a good watchdog.'

His face in thought, he continued with a previous conversation that Moraine hadn't been privy to.

'It must be hard to let it go.'

Her slight frame turned to him. 'No point in holding onto it anymore. Without a brick in sight yet, it'll be years before completion. God willing, I'll still be alive when it's done and have tackled most problems by then. Mainly somewhere to live, where all these lasses and fellas won't mind too much. They're used to these surroundings, and prone to sulk if out of sorts.'

Stone was nodding in response, while Moraine was baffled. She understood the bit about letting the farm go, but not the rest. Were they talking about cows, or maybe about goats, or possibly chickens?

She scanned the room, seeing the very lived-in home. Armchairs used over decades, clay tiles scattered with mats, the furnishings and cups and saucers probably used since she'd been married. The coal fire burning in the same hearth, with a dog always lying there beside it.

She hadn't noticed the small mound on the bookcase at first, the one on a footstool, another on the windowsill, hidden behind a curtain. Not until Elsbeth opened the fridge, when they all came running. Others arrived, one by one, through an open door that must lead upstairs. Lots of furry creatures, some with smooth coats, some with long, spiky hair, weaving in and out around Elsbeth's legs, meowing and wanting food. Cats, a dozen or more.

Moraine shook her head in wonder as it dawned on her, and thanked God for these cats. Without them, Elsbeth would have had no need to look in the outhouse and Sam might not have been found in time.

As they left the farm, Moraine puzzled over the insulation blanket wrapped around the child. Was it to keep him alive or something the perpetrator just had with them? He had to have been taken there by a vehicle that could get up the track, or else carried there by someone strong. She wouldn't attempt it in her own car. The base was too wide, the wheels would be in the ruts, the chassis touching the ground.

Who had brought him there? Who left him in that derelict outhouse, and drove away? Because that was a person who seriously needed capturing.

FORTY-ONE

Jo saw a police officer stationed outside Sam's room. He'd arrived just after nine. It wasn't enough, apparently, to have him outside in the corridor, outside the unit's doors, where every visitor was screened before being allowed entrance. He'd been ordered to station himself where he could keep a close watch.

Did DI Stone think the abductor would just walk right in and snatch Sam out of the room with no one noticing? It seemed extreme. The security on the children's ward was constantly monitored. To gain entry, a person had to use the intercom and identify themselves and the name of the patient they were visiting. It must be off-putting for the staff and for children's parents, as well as scary for the children themselves, to see a policeman outside a door guarding someone.

She switched her gaze back to Sam and anxiously pondered his condition. She could tell by the doctor's visits and the frequent observations taken by the nurses that they were quietly worried. While his eyes had briefly opened once, he remained mute and appeared to be in a catatonic state. He hadn't opened them since. A child psychiatrist would visit shortly to assess him.

The consultant paediatrician speculated it could be Flop Trauma Response, the human equivalent of an animal playing dead. It was a way to reduce the mental impact of the experience. Similar to a freeze response, when flight or fight are not options, the mind will surrender to a shutdown.

Jo was trying to suppress her fear and the overwhelming guilt consuming her. A social worker would pay a visit later, too. Memories of the previous evening haunted her. She shouldn't have revealed what Pete had done. It would be documented now and a source of concern for a social worker to pick over. It may be decided that Sam wasn't safe with either of them, that their childcare was inadequate.

She and Pete had both been questioned and were still under investigation. That, in itself, was bound to be of concern. Safeguarding was a hot topic in the news lately. Every time she turned on the radio, there seemed to be a discussion going on about it. It was becoming a common phrase, and one she'd already been familiar with from her time at Whitebells Nursery.

The social worker would certainly consider the events of two years ago. A woman who loses a child on two separate occasions and had been labelled a dangerous mother. She googled her name and found herself surprisingly liberated by what she found. Her history was no longer brushed under the carpet, and Pete couldn't hide it anymore. Maybe he wasn't showing his face because he was too embarrassed to be seen in public.

He would have to face James Howell, and Claire, at some point, and give some sort of explanation. He couldn't blame the deception entirely on her. They weren't fools. They would know they'd been deceived by him as well as her, and now knew he could lie. Four months of lying to his wife showed him more than capable of deceit. That's how long he'd been having an affair. He spat out the information during their ride to the hospital.

When the time was right, hopefully in the next few days, she would go and see them and apologise for causing them distress. Their kindness had been abused. She would move out immediately and contact the council for emergency housing for her and Sam. That needed to be in place as soon as possible, to show she could give Sam a safe home.

Behind her, the liaison officer had nodded off and was snoring quietly. She was much younger than Moraine, and maybe didn't have as much stamina. She was probably younger than Jo, so maybe had a busy social life.

Her mind returned to her worry that someone unknown had power over what happened next. The power to have Sam taken from her and prevent her from seeing her child. The thought of Sam being on his own, after promising to never leave him alone again, brought a fresh ache to her throat.

A tapping on the cubicle window had her turn, and roused the liaison officer from her sleep. The uniformed officer was staring through the glass, wagging a finger at his colleague.

Chelsea muttered under her breath. Jo turned to look at her, raising her eyebrows in question, making light of the mild admonishment.

'Oh dear. Do you think he wants a cup of tea? He must be bored silly out there. He doesn't even need to be there while you're in here. Sam's completely safe.'

An awkward expression crossed Chelsea's face, a look of regret and embarrassment. It took Jo a few seconds to realise the cause. Her breath stopped... An immense self-awareness scalded her all over. She could feel the pounding of her heart.

The only reason a police officer was there was because *she* was in the room. The only reason for him being there was to see Sam didn't come to harm... *From her*...

FORTY-TWO

The front door to the annexe was wide open. Claire stepped in and called out, 'Hello?'

She expected it to be empty. A sound above made her look up and see Pete at the top of the stairs.

He seemed reluctant to come down. Claire closed the front door behind her, giving him a moment to decide.

Breathing out a heavy sigh, he descended the stairs slowly, stopping at the bottom step, a sullen look on his face.

Claire hid her steadily growing distaste for him. 'I thought you were at the hospital.'

He snorted contemptuously. 'I was. Jo doesn't want me there. Not that it's any of your business.'

She didn't take offence. She would rather see him in his true form. His child was in hospital and he was skulking here, feeling sorry for himself.

'How is Sam?' she asked, to remind him of this.

He shrugged. 'Physically, okay. Mentally, not good. He's always been oversensitive. Probably affected him more than it might another kid. A nurse I spoke to said he was in some sort of daze. Might be a while till he's back in the real world.'

His take on his son's development was appalling. Sam exhibited different behavioural patterns. The first time she noticed was seeing Sam line up a bucketful of stones in meticulous order on the step by the kitchen door. They'd all been careful to step over them so as not to disturb his peace.

Her hand gripped the envelope in her pocket. She wouldn't be giving it to him. He wouldn't be getting a penny. He didn't deserve the same help. Jo would be better off without him. Have a fresh start. A new place to live. Somewhere with a back garden, close to Sam's school.

Claire would help her find somewhere, pay a year's rent upfront so Jo didn't have to worry, and throw in furniture as well. Jo could have what she liked from the annexe, the entire contents. It wouldn't be used as a home for anyone again. They would take in no more lookalike boys. Those days were over.

'Are you going back to the hospital?'

He shrugged dismissively. 'None of your business, Claire. How come you're here? Come to check we haven't done a runner? Stolen all the teaspoons?'

God, he was rude. She didn't let it affect her. 'If you do decide to do a runner, best you let someone know. I think the police might like to know your change of address,' she said back in a dry tone.

His lip curled. 'Don't worry. I'd let that solicitor bloke know.'

'You mean Anthony Clark?'

'No. Amir something. An Indian bloke. Wears a turban.'

He was meaning Amir Khan, another excellent lawyer, another associate of James, called upon to represent this man. James shouldn't have wasted Amir's time and expertise on someone so ungrateful. He shouldn't have lifted a finger to help him. He didn't deserve to breathe the same air as Amir Khan. *Indian bloke. Turban.*

She cast him a disdainful glance, and was pleased to see it register on his aggrieved face.

'James will be disappointed. He was hoping you could correct your behaviour. Hoping you'd become a better man.'

His hand balled into a fist at his side. Resentment simmered in him, which showed in the curl of his lip and the stare he levelled at her. 'Easy for him to think that. He's not got the same ball and chain around his neck. He got you. Class and money. Easy to have principles when you've got all that,' he added with a sneer.

His envy was an ugly thing to see, his simplification of James's life an insult. She wanted him to suffer. She wouldn't put it past him to think he was entitled to have what James had, or to be of a mind to act on it. If someone had made contact to demand a ransom, his was the voice she would imagine hearing on the other end of the phone. If he could abandon a child who was ill in hospital, he could use one for gain.

It was more than an interesting theory. It was believable. And gave her the urge to goad him.

'Was this how you saw us from the very beginning? A rich, privileged family, while you had to scrape a living? Wasn't it enough to have a free home for you and your family to live in? Were we meant to have given you more? Maybe another car for you alone to drive?'

He laughed, a not very nice sound. 'I don't give a tuppence for what you think, with your posh voice, your fuck-off mansion, your flash cars, kids in private schools—'

'But you'd like to have all that,' she cut in nastily, in her poshest voice ever, to get a rise out of him.

With a shrug, he expressed his indifference before staring down his nose at her. He gestured around them, his voice matter-of-fact.

'You know why the rich stay rich? They give chump money, which they can easily afford. If James had really wanted to do us a good turn, he could have forked out for a mortgage, and not noticed the cost. There's never something for nothing. You people always want something in return. Us, here? Probably some kind of comfort to his conscience for having so much.'

He turned, carried on up the stairs and didn't look back, leaving her standing there thinking. James was right about one thing. Pete could be eloquent at times.

If she didn't know better, he almost made her believe this *was* the reason James invited them there. The real reason, the only one that brought them there, was Sam. She knew it with every fibre of her being. She knew her husband that well…

FORTY-THREE

Moraine had been closeted with Kennedy and Stone in the SIO's office for the last hour, while they discussed how to move matters forwards. After this, they were heading back to Beckley House to check if Pete was there, as Chelsea Turnbull couldn't see him anywhere in the hospital.

Stone was up to date with everything that had transpired since yesterday evening, including the suspect actions of Pete Jenkins.

In the meantime, Elsbeth Crosby was compiling a list of every visitor who had been to the farm. The hope was that someone on it was the perpetrator of this horrific crime.

Stone's large barrel chest expanded as he breathed in hard.

'The finding of the child's top in his home is not evidence of a crime. Anthony Clark has put forward a plausible reason for why it was found there. His client was not in possession of her bag the entire time and was unable to know if her child removed his top while left alone. It could have been spotted by the woman in the changing cubicle and put in his client's bag, where Mrs Jenkins inadvertently carried it back to her home...

'What I'd like to know is how it transported itself to the child's drawers. It didn't put itself there.'

Kennedy offered an opinion: 'She might have done it while in shock.'

Stone briskly shook his head. 'I'm not buying it. The shock of seeing it would make her realise her son was out there in only a vest top. We haven't disclosed that this is how he was found.'

Moraine wanted an opinion on Pete. 'Sir, Pete Jenkins was planning to leave his wife. The only thing stopping him was lack of money.'

'He's still on my radar, Moraine. The woman he's having an affair with is going to be asked about their time together in minute detail, especially during the hours of Saturday morning. At what time did Jenkins go out to buy a newspaper, and for how long was he gone?'

His answer reassured her. Though, none of this would be enough to refer a case to the CPS. They didn't have the evidence to make one yet, which was why Stone had Moraine and Kennedy with him. He wanted them to find a connection to Elsbeth Crosby's farm.

They shared the pool vehicle, Moraine in the driver's seat, parking at the Co-op on Julian Road so Kennedy could run in for more provisions before leaving the city.

Getting back in the car, Kennedy opened a bag of jelly snakes and handed her one, then posed a question.

'Anything in particular you think we should ask Pete?'

Moraine swallowed the sweet jelly. 'Get him talking about his relationship with Chrissy Banner. See if there were plans for the future. Don't be too sympathetic or he'll immediately know we're trying to soften him up.'

He held out another snake to her, holding on one end so she had to pull it from his grip. He laughed. 'Don't worry, I have thumbscrews for that part.'

'You think it's him?'

He shrugged, raising his shoulders right up around his ears. 'Honestly haven't got a Scooby Doo. What I do know is, Chrissy Banner hasn't got a pot to pee in. She rents a one-bedroom flat on the Wells Road. Been there three or four years. A member of PureGym. Has dated more than a few of her colleagues. Pete is about number seven.'

Moraine's eyes widened at him. 'How on earth do you know all this?'

He quirked an eyebrow, grinning. 'Comes from being from a large family. One of my brothers-in-law is a fire officer.'

She gazed ahead, sighing with mild exasperation. 'So what's the appeal? It won't make his situation any better. If anything, it'll make it worse if she's in the same boat as him – both without money. He'd still have to support his child.'

'I dare say sex is the appeal,' Kennedy replied in a nonchalant tone. 'She's twenty-four and a bit of a stunner, by all accounts.'

'Your brother-in-law say any more?'

'Oh yes,' Kennedy confirmed in a voice that suggested a great deal more. 'She's been regaling everybody about her good fortune. It seems like Pete was the one she was holding out for, because he lived at a mansion. Good friends with the owner. He was going to be rewarded for a good deed, had already been given a coach house to do with as he wanted. And a Range Rover, which he was letting his wife drive.'

Moraine's foot hit the brake pedal, then the clutch to lower the gears and bring them to a quick stop on the side of a country road. Her head swivelled to gape at him.

'Why haven't you let Stone know this?'

He released his grip on the dashboard. 'Because I only just found out while I was in the shop. I got a phone call from my brother-in-law. I wanted to tell you first so you could ring Stone. He's more your boss than mine. I'm only the support.'

Moraine released a deep breath. 'Jesus, John. You were only in there five minutes.'

He grinned.

She grabbed a snake from the bag of sweets and shoved it in her mouth, speaking while she set the car in motion again. 'Let's go see Pete and see what he's got to say. Then you get to tell Stone. Not me. Your find. Not mine.'

A moment later, she quietly chuckled. 'I didn't know until yesterday, when Jo said your name, your initials were JFK... I can just hear it. They'll all be calling on you for a visit to the White House.'

Her teasing brought a non-committal grunt in reply. Then, as the windscreen wipers came on, he lamented the weather. '*More rain.* Never knows when to stop.'

FORTY-FOUR

Bernice was clearly trying to make herself invisible by standing completely still at the stove with her back to them. She'd become like a statue during Claire's outburst at James.

Claire wanted to send her out of the room. She shouldn't have to hear them arguing. There was a time and a place, and they should have saved this for when they were on their own. But his obtuseness was driving her insane and making her fly at him.

She put her head down and carried on preparing the runner beans, removing the strings from the sides, hoping he would leave.

His sigh carried across the room. 'Tell me what I don't understand. You shouting it doesn't help. All I said was there must be some reason.'

She raised her head in resignation. 'Phoebe's play date for this coming Friday has been cancelled. Isobel's mother has never cancelled her coming to play here, *ever*. The woman would rather cut off her ear than risk Isobel not having this friendship. She's been fawning shamelessly, doing everything in her power to make them best friends – something I've been well aware of for a long time.'

'Don't be a snob, Claire. She's an excellent teacher and doesn't strike me as fawning at all. An awful description, I might add.'

She gritted her teeth, no longer caring if Bernice was present, to let him have it. 'You can add what you like. This won't be the first time this has happened. Do you not realise that parents might not let their children play here anymore? That they'll think our home is unsafe. You don't have to think about any of this. But it's thanks to you we're in this mess.'

He gazed at her in astonishment. 'Well, thank you for sharing that. What would you suggest we do? Throw them out on the street? Carry out a public flogging? Would that be enough?'

He was standing almost next to her, his face only inches away, and she could see the vein in his temple pulsing.

She lowered her voice: 'You could leak it to the press? What he did to his son?'

The rigidity of him showed his shock. A quick glance at Bernice reassured her she'd said it quietly enough to reach only James's ears. It was up to him whether he wanted to denounce her in front of the help, or cast aspersions on someone who deserves no mercy to help free Jo. A father who cares more for his own needs than for his ill son.

He gripped his head, a groan erupting from deep within. As she watched the pain stretch his mouth in a sudden grimace, she felt guilty and selfish for wanting to take it out on him. For wanting him to fix it with her vile suggestion.

Bernice quickly brought tablets and water and offered advice while Claire just stood there. 'You need to lie down in a dark room until it passes.'

Claire wasn't surprised he'd got a headache. He probably

hadn't gone back to bed like her, standing at the window long before he woke her, waiting for Jo and Pete to appear.

She was startled when his legs went from under him and he reached for the counter to stop himself from falling. In a second, Bernice shoved a chair beneath him, like he had done for Bernice when she felt faint after hearing Sam was missing.

It was becoming a familiar theme, Claire thought distractedly.

His face looked grey while he continued to groan, making her reach for her phone.

'I'm calling the doctor. You're ill.'

He grasped her forearm, stopping her. 'No. I need a cold compress on the back of my neck. That will get rid of it.'

From a first aid cabinet, Bernice, a dab hand with sprains, twisted and squeezed an ice pack to activate it and placed a thin cloth under the bag of ice on James's neck.

They watched his shoulders gradually relax, his forearm fold under his forehead for a pillow, his breathing slow down and fall silent. Feeling relief. Until he pretended to snore.

Claire wanted to kill him. It was not in the least funny. He'd been in agony.

'I'm fine,' he said, raising his head slowly, his face less grey. 'Sorry for the drama, and for the one before,' he said, smiling lightly at Bernice. He patted Claire's hand. 'And sorry for not understanding. Can't do what you suggest, but I'll think of something.'

When he was ready, Claire walked with him up the stairs, taking him to her bedroom and the bed they shared when they made love. He had his own quarters, his own bedroom, a necessity for his restless nights, which went along with a job where one's mind couldn't easily switch off. She didn't want him there while he recovered. She wanted him lying on her pillow so he would feel her close to him.

Her suggestion had crossed a line and made him ill. It

shouldn't be his responsibility to put everything right. There were things she could do which didn't require an anonymous phone call, or even much imagination.

It only required the right opportunity to present itself. And it already had. Pete's car was gone.

She glanced at James in repose, his face relaxed, eyelids closed.

He would never forgive this meddling, which is why he would never know about it. There were some things that didn't need to be known by anyone else. Things that were done for the greater good, like deciding who was expendable.

It was all about the balance between right and wrong. No one could dispute that. Not even James.

FORTY-FIVE

Jo was in a state of shock at the speed the social worker delivered her decision. Speaking politely, professionally, and in a sympathetic voice, she said they would look for a place for Sam when he was well again. He would go into temporary foster care while all this was going on. It would be better for Sam to not be with his parents until it was all figured out.

The social worker's eyes had glanced away from her when she looked through the glass partition at the police officer stationed outside, and her acknowledgement of Chelsea in the room told Jo she was only permitted to be with Sam because of their presence.

Unable to bear the social worker being near her, Jo couldn't breathe until she left the cubicle. Her physical presence terrified her. She could hardly grasp what had just happened.

A glass of water was held out to her. She barely registered Chelsea's concern. Jo took it from her hand in a daze.

'I really wasn't expecting that,' Chelsea said in a tone of awe. 'So quickly. All so matter-of-fact.'

Jo gaped, but she couldn't find the words. How thick could this policewoman be? She was sitting in the room with Jo, with another police officer outside the door, watching her every move. Their presence would have been a red flag to the social worker.

Chelsea gave a long, drawn-out breath, before offering some dumb-arsed opinion: 'I'm sorry that had to happen. As painful as it is, we have to think those that love him are just as suspect as a stranger.'

Jo pinched the bridge of her nose to stem the tears. She didn't want to be hearing this. Chelsea needed to work on how she approached matters like this. She was no Moraine Morgan, that was for sure, and didn't seem to have much experience either.

Jo lowered her head into her hands, needing some space, wishing she could be on her own with Sam. Hearing he was alive had been like a miracle. That she could lose him again so soon was like the worst punishment. She couldn't imagine how the woman she met had coped for five years not knowing where her son was. How could she carry on living with that much pain?

She put a hand to her throat to ease the tightness, lifting her head, needing to ask Chelsea about that. Anthony Clark said he was going to mention it to the police.

'Did anyone find the woman I spoke to?'

Chelsea glanced at her. 'The one your solicitor mentioned? No, I'm afraid we didn't. I know Moraine spoke to Claire Howell. She wondered if it might have been a reporter who got in somehow.'

Jo's steady gaze conveyed her determination to be heard. 'One who just happened to have a photograph of a boy who looked almost identical to my son? They could be twins. I doubt very much she was a reporter.'

Chelsea looked cornered. She was gripping her phone like it would save her, probably hoping it would ring so she could escape to answer it.

Jo laughed harshly, shaking her head at Chelsea. 'She's not someone I imagined or made up. She was as real as you are. She told me her son had been missing for five years. Do you know if anyone else was asked if they saw her?'

Chelsea blinked, not able to maintain eye contact, her answer reluctant. 'No. I don't think anyone was.'

Jo's throat swelled again. Her voice pushed through painfully. 'Don't you think someone should?'

Chelsea raised her shoulders and then lowered them, signalling she didn't know.

Jo drank some water, moving muscles that had constricted from not being able to swallow the lump lodged there.

It hit her then.

Finding Sam's top had made it hard for people to believe what she was telling them. It was in print that she was a dangerous mother. Who's to say she wasn't a fantasist as well?

She slumped in the chair. They had no confidence in her. It didn't matter if she was innocent or not. The damage was already done. They didn't believe she had Sam in the car with her. They didn't believe he was with her when she arrived at the village swimming pool.

It wouldn't matter what she said. They had already made up their minds. It was only a matter of time before they put the cuffs on her.

FORTY-SIX

Moraine and Kennedy looked in each room twice, before meeting back at the kitchen.

'Unbelievable,' Moraine said for the umpteenth time, as if her disbelief could somehow bring Pete back.

Clothes, toiletries and other items were gone from drawers and shelves and wardrobe, leaving vacant spaces.

Moraine dumped her bag and jacket on the table, frustrated and angry. He had come and gone unnoticed like a thief in the night. And there was little anyone could do about it.

There were no restrictions on what he could do following his release. He was free to carry on life as normal. Which was just plain unfair and chafed at her sense of justice. While he swanned off, his wife was dealing with everything alone.

She pulled out her phone. Jo needed to be informed that her husband was gone.

A catch-up with Chelsea let her know about the awful morning Jo had had. The social worker had told her Sam would be placed in foster care once they released him from hospital. The boy was still not talking. Chelsea wanted out as she was feeling unable to cope.

Moraine told her to take a deep breath and tried to instil some confidence. 'I'm sure you're doing better than you think.'

'I'm not,' Chelsea replied. 'It's my first solo. I don't have enough experience to deal with this. And now you want me to tell her that her husband's scarpered.'

Moraine held her patience. 'Chelsea, I understand. But you need to let Jo know about her husband. You might find she's not that surprised.'

'Fine,' Chelsea said with a small huff. 'But you need to update her about what's happening with finding the woman she said she saw, because she's asking if anyone else was questioned about her.'

Moraine sighed as the conversation ended, thoughts flitting through her head. Jo's solicitor must have told her they were checking out her story. Damn Pete for leaving his wife alone.

'Are you practising the art of speaking in silence?' Kennedy asked, putting a mug of coffee in front her. 'Your lips have been moving in a very intense conversation. Would I be right in thinking it was a seething diatribe against Pete?'

She'd look up diatribe, but nodded. 'Yeah. That, plus Chelsea wants to bail.'

When Kennedy walked towards the table, she thought he was pulling out a chair to sit on, but he picked up an envelope from the seat with Jo's name on it.

Moraine hadn't noticed it. She was glad Kennedy was there and more observant. Out of habit, she grabbed a pair of gloves from the side pocket of her bag, pulling them on quickly so she could take it from Kennedy. The envelope had been opened, a sticky residue still on the flap. A single sheet of paper was still inside. She teased it out and put the envelope aside, then unfolded the note on the table so they could both see it. Kennedy read aloud, starting at the top, which was underlined.

An emergency fund to tide you over.

Hi Jo,

I can only imagine the relief you're feeling at Sam being found. James has kept me up to date. I'm sorry for everything that has happened to you. Shock after shock, you poor, poor thing. Please don't feel anyone is judging you. We certainly are not. We want only to support you.

I'm enclosing ten thousand pounds. It's a gift, Jo, to tide you over. To allow you to stay in a hotel if you want, to save being hounded by the press. To give you privacy, away from all this, to process all these horrible shocks.

Everyone is rooting for you, and for darling Sam. You're in our thoughts and prayers, which I hope will help keep you strong.

Claire

Kennedy drew breath, and then stooped to look under the table, then around at the floor, lifting the rug. He walked the entire room, eyes to the floor then to surfaces, opening cabinets and drawers, even lifting the bin off the floor after checking inside it.

Moraine watched, waiting for him to finish. When he did, she shook her head.

'It's gone, John. He's taken the money.'

FORTY-SEVEN

Claire answered the door and was startled to see Moraine and an auburn-haired man standing there. She gave a breathy laugh, gesturing at the butcher's apron she was wearing. 'You've caught me doing kitchen duties. Please say this is an agreeable visit so I can take a break.'

The auburn-haired man smiled amiably. 'I sympathise. It's the hardest part of a house to clean.'

Moraine introduced him. 'This is PC Kennedy. He's been keeping Jo's home in order and making sure we all eat.'

'Whoever made the cupcakes knows how to bake. They were delicious.'

Claire beamed at him. 'My daughter, Phoebe, made them. She'll be so pleased.' She opened the door fully. 'What am I doing keeping you on the doorstep? Please come in.'

Her mind was whirling as she showed them to the sitting room, wondering why they were visiting. 'Make yourselves comfortable. I just need to let Bernice know I'm not skiving. Can I fetch either of you something to drink?'

They shook their heads.

'Well, I won't be a moment then.'

She quickly nipped back to the kitchen, ditching the apron and grabbing a small glass of white wine, and telling Bernice she wouldn't be long.

Moraine was perched on the same sofa as the evening before, while PC Kennedy stood by the window, looking around the room. 'It's as beautiful inside as out,' he commented.

He was charming, Claire decided, and had the same lovely colour hair as James.

She held aloft the small glass in her hand. 'I know it's barely lunchtime, but I've been up since the crack of dawn. Bernice's way of expressing happiness – about Sam, of course – is to get knee-deep in scrubbing, and she feels it only fair that I join in.'

She invited the man to sit down. 'You must be on your feet most of the time. It must get exhausting having to stand.'

She turned to Moraine. 'So what brings you here? Hopefully, nothing bad with there being the two of you? It gave me a start seeing two officers at the door. Not to put you down in the slightest,' she added, glancing at PC Kennedy. 'I'm well aware you're both of the same rank. I just thought you were the same as DC Morgan, a detective.'

'Hopefully, one day.' He smiled. 'When I'm as experienced as her. Not been on the force that long. Took a change of career in my thirties.'

'Good for you,' she acknowledged. 'You're clearly a people person.'

She sat back then, allowing a lull for Moraine to speak. She looked tired and tense, cupping her hands tightly over her knees, making Claire slightly apprehensive.

'Did you go into Jo's home today?' Her tone was tentative, as if finding this awkward.

Claire frowned. The question made it sound like she'd been snooping. Her expression must have conveyed her displeasure, because Moraine held up her hands placatingly.

'Sorry. That came out wrong. I should have explained why

I'm asking. You see, Pete has packed all his things and has left without letting Jo know. He did it while she was at the hospital, leaving her completely unaware until we arrived a short while ago and discovered he was gone.'

The glass shook in Claire's hand, forcing her to place it on the table beside her. Her voice lowered in shock. 'What! That can't be. I thought he'd gone back to the hospital.'

'You saw him then?'

'Yes! I didn't realise anyone was there. I was just leaving something for Jo. Then I heard a noise upstairs.'

She inhaled deeply, pulling herself together. Pete was a devious coward. She genuinely thought he had gone to the hospital and would be back later. It was the only reason she went back to the annexe after his car was gone. To set him up by leaving the envelope open with only the note and no money, so that when it was discovered, it would look like he had taken the ten thousand pounds. She had taken the money out and had it safe upstairs to give to Jo. Only he wasn't coming back and her ruse had failed. They hadn't noticed it sitting there, while checking around Jo's home.

Making her voice strong, she put the matter aside, as there was nothing to be done about it now.

'I cannot believe he came here and then just went. When I saw the car gone, I thought he'd gone back to see Sam. He said Jo didn't want him there, but I thought he might try to make amends.'

Her stomach turned at his lack of morals. She gave a scathing look. 'Well, good riddance to bad rubbish. She won't have to cope alone. We'll support her.'

'Do you mind if I ask something?' PC Kennedy said with a frank expression on his face.

She shrugged her shoulders automatically. 'Of course. Ask what you like. I don't mind admitting I'm frankly appalled right now. So if it helps, please feel free.'

He sat forward in the chair and laced his hands loosely together. 'With everything that's happened and with certain things coming to light that, as Jo's employer, you were unaware of, and her still being under investigation, has there been any moment of doubt? Have you ever once thought her guilty?'

Claire raised her eyes to the ceiling, slowly shaking her head. The police were still gunning for Jo, even with her husband just deserting her. She sighed heavily.

'I really wish your SIO was here right now. Someone needs to talk some sense into him. If it wasn't so serious, I'd think it was a joke. What they've put her through is a travesty. Shameful treatment, which they were willing to continue by searching this property. Rather than a proper investigation, you've gone for the easy way out. You've targeted a mother who can't defend herself against impossible odds by trying to prove Sam wasn't in the car with her.

'Has anyone tried putting a child his size in the back of a Range Rover to see if he can be seen through the windows, even without the sunshades? I'd be surprised if you could see the top of his head. Has anyone looked at the child seat in the Range Rover? They're designed with wide shoulder protectors and low seats. They're not like the ones that sit them a mile up in the air, looking over the heads of the driver and front passenger.

'I'm sorry to be harsh, but I have zero confidence right now in the police establishment. Not when you can believe a woman like Jo could ever harm any child, let alone her son.'

She breathed in deeply. 'We've never doubted her innocence. Never for a single moment could we think her guilty. I hope that answers your question.'

Silence from both of them. Claire could feel the tension she had created in the room. She lifted her eyes and saw them both gazing at her. It wasn't fair to them. They were both excellent. She placed her palm against her forehead, to show her regret, and gave a rueful smile.

'I'm sorry to both of you. I didn't mean to go off on a diatribe against the whole of the British police force. Not warranted, and most definitely not polite. I have better manners normally, so I hope you'll forgive me my improvident speech.'

Moraine gave a light shake of her head. 'Second time I've heard that word today. Diatribe. John used it with me earlier. Wasn't sure what it meant, but now I know. You have nothing to be sorry for. It is right to let fly about something you feel is wrong. I know I will be thinking about what you said.'

Claire gave an appreciative look. She picked up the glass of wine and took a sip. 'I feel guilty drinking this in front of you. Are you sure I can't offer you something?'

Moraine answered for them both. 'Honestly, we're fine. John has the kettle going all day.'

Claire smiled at this and rose from her chair. 'Well, then, thank you for letting me know about Pete. Do I need to lock up or anything?'

She caught the look on Moraine's face, and sat back down. 'Did I miss something? I thought we were done.'

'Nearly,' she answered. 'There's just one more thing. We found an envelope addressed to Jo with a note inside from you. It was open.'

Claire's eyes fixed on a spot somewhere over Moraine's head, as she went perfectly still. Her voice was almost monotone. 'You're about to tell me the money is gone.'

'Yes,' Moraine confirmed in a soft voice, possibly hoping to take some of the sting out.

Claire was picturing the scene they walked in to. His car and all his clothes gone, an open envelope on the table. It couldn't have played out any better. He could deny ever seeing it, which of course was the case, as only put there after he was gone. It didn't matter either way. The focus would switch to him and less on his poor wife.

'I left it on the kitchen table.'

'We found it on a chair.'

She shook her head from side to side and looked at Moraine. 'I don't want Jo to know. I don't want her hurt any more by this. She doesn't need to know what's transpired here today. I hope you support that.'

When she showed them out and closed the front door, she leaned her back against it. She hadn't lied. She left it on the kitchen table. The wind coming through the front door must have blown it onto the chair. But they still found it.

Clearly, it was meant to happen as it did.

FORTY-EIGHT

The psychiatrist wore a colourful scarf around her head and shoulders, and a red dot between her eyebrows. The nurse introduced her as Dr Devi.

She moved Sam's head from side to side, and his gaze remained fixed like a doll's. She asked the nurse to turn off the lights in the cubicle so she could examine his eyes with an ophthalmoscope, then asked for them to be turned back on.

He had his blue rabbit tucked into the bed with him. Jo was hoping he'd reach for it, but he didn't. The only change was his thumb, which he had put in his mouth when she wasn't looking. The paediatrician had asked if this was his normal habit. It wasn't. She'd only seen him with his thumb in his mouth once, and that was on a sonograph image when she was carrying him.

Dr Devi remarked on it, speaking softly, while she moved his limbs. 'Thumb sucking can be caused by PTSD. Developmental regression can happen after trauma.'

Jo hadn't really considered children getting PTSD, though why wouldn't they if exposed to traumatic events?

She saw his little legs and arms as he was examined, relieved to see not a mark on him.

Dr Devi completed the examination, before addressing Jo. 'I'd like to consult with the paediatrician before deciding treatment, then come back to you with what we decide.'

Before she could leave, Jo asked if she'd seen this before.

A tiny frown accompanied her nod. 'Yes. In this country and in my own.'

She would have left then, but Jo pressed for details of cases. 'Are there any you remember where a child stayed this way? Or did all of them get better?'

An expression of regret came over her face. 'Only one stayed like this. A boy of seven. After seeing his brother swallowed whole by a python.'

Jo immediately swayed, causing Dr Devi to place a hand against Jo's face, and rebuking herself instantly. 'Forgive me for putting that in your head. What is commonplace to one who has grown up with animal dangers is a horrific happening to one who hasn't. I speak of them without thinking.'

Jo took some more steadying breaths and forgave her, relieved to have such an experienced doctor looking after Sam, someone who had dealt with unimaginable horror.

Dr Devi patted her shoulder, seeing her lips tremble. 'Let's not worry. He needs Mum to be strong.'

The moment she departed, Chelsea came back in the room, having stepped outside to take a phone call. Her expression revealed she had some bad news.

'I'm so sorry, Jo. It looks like Pete got a taxi back to your home so he could clear out his things. His car has gone.'

Jo listened numbly while she was told about Pete. She now understood why he'd been absent all this time. He went to pack his belongings while she was with their son. That way, he could leave without being seen, without saying goodbye. As far as she was concerned, the only generous thing he'd done so far was to remove himself from her and Sam's lives.

'I'm getting some books,' she said, passing Chelsea to let herself out of the room.

The officer outside the door gave her a brief look. Not unpleasant, but not engaging enough for her to say anything. She drifted down the corridor to the playroom and saw it occupied with mums and dads with their children, keeping them entertained while they got better.

The bookcase was packed with lovely stories, her fingers pulling out a few before spotting some old Ladybird books. She picked one she knew Sam would enjoy: *Insects and Small Animals*. She could remember reading the same book as a child, borrowing it from the library and learning about butterflies.

As she turned to leave, she saw she was being scrutinised, phones in the parents' hands, looks being shared. Her skin prickled, heat flooding her, anxiety overcoming her. She couldn't move, rooted to the spot so they could watch. She couldn't see through the opaque film of her mortified tears. The book slid from her hand, making a small slap on the floor.

Her name was being called. She turned her head to see a tall, dark shape. The police officer was standing in the open door. He walked into the room, bent down and picked up the book. He looked at it and put it back in her hand. 'Good choice. I said you'd find something here.'

Her legs like jelly, she followed him back to the room. Trying to swallow the massive lump in her throat, she said, 'Thank you.'

He popped his head in the door as she sank back in her chair and spoke to his colleague. 'Might be an idea if you get Mrs Jenkins something to eat. Maybe a nice cold drink, a bar of chocolate?' He pulled the door closed.

Chelsea didn't flounce, but the small huff she gave showed she wasn't pleased. When she was gone, Jo let the tears come, discreetly turning her back so he wouldn't see. His act of kindness was her undoing. She couldn't hold back the sobs.

That he might think her guilty of doing harm to her son, and still show her kindness, said more about him than her. He was a decent human being, but she hadn't made a friend. He'd go back to his job now the moment was gone – watching her.

Like the people beyond the walls of this room, conscious of her here, all on alert because a dangerous mother was near. Wondering, thinking, speculating – was her child safe?

FORTY-NINE

Moraine paced agitatedly around the kitchen. Presenting a ramrod back to Kennedy, her voice like ice, she said, 'So now he's resorted to theft. He should be charged.'

'It's not that simple.'

Kennedy's remark made her turn swiftly to face him. 'Why not? He's stolen ten thousand pounds from Claire Howell.'

He gave her a look. 'You know that's not true. Anything acquired by a husband or wife belongs to both of them. What's hers is his. The money was given to Jo. If it had been taken from Claire Howell's home before it reached theirs, then it would be a crime. Technically, it would still belong to Claire Howell.

'As it stands, the money was here in his home. Opening an envelope, with no instructions that it was private, left on the family table. It's hardly a crime. It could have been a get-well card. He could claim he took the money to keep it safe.'

'All right! I hear you. I'm just so bloody angry.'

'And tired,' he added calmly. 'But we can't circumvent the law to get him.'

'I am exhausted,' she admitted. 'It wasn't exactly easy in there. She certainly speaks her mind, and is clearly not a fan.

Full marks to her, though. She's not afraid to stand up for justice.'

Moraine mulled over the last hour, trying to shake off the gloom.

She needed a release from the focus on one situation then another since early morning. Seven hours ago, with Elsbeth Crosby. So much had happened since, it didn't seem like the same day. Hard even to remember it was Monday. Harder still to realise the child had been found. He was in hospital. They were not looking for him anymore. They were just...

And that, she realised, was what was wrong with her. All this irritability – because of drifting along and not getting closer to uncovering the truth. They needed to know who had done this to Sam.

Her phone rang on the table beside her. She grabbed it and looked at the screen. It was Stone.

'Raine, I just got a call from Elsbeth Crosby. Can you go and check out the problem? She's talking about some logs. I tried to get more information from her, but she seems a bit distressed. I just hope that outhouse hasn't fallen in on her. You're the nearest, otherwise I'd send an area car.'

She chewed her lip in irritation and hauled herself to her feet humourlessly. Of course she could. She wasn't busy with much else. It wasn't like she should be checking on Jo, to see how she was faring after her wonderful day with the not-coping-very-well-Chelsea for support. 'Will do, sir. I'm on it.'

'And while you're at it, check if she's done making that list. We need it asap.'

She put her phone away and glanced at Kennedy. 'We've got a job. A visit to a farm.'

FIFTY

Claire was packing when James found her upstairs. He eyed the children's clothes on the bed. 'What are you doing?'

Her frustration with him caused her to speak through gritted teeth. 'Taking the girls on a short holiday. That's what I'm doing.'

'To where?'

'Where do you think? To France, of course. Unless you're going to tell me we have another home somewhere else. I've already rung Pierre. He's meeting me at the port.'

He looked astounded. 'You're going to St Malo now!'

'Yes! On the evening ferry from Portsmouth.'

'Why, for God's sake? Would you mind telling me what's the rush?'

'I'll tell you what the rush is, James. They're back by the gates. In droves. I can't let the children outside for fear of a drone flying overhead. Something's happening that we're not aware of. I just had a phone call from another so-called well-meaning friend, who tells me I need to be careful. I have two daughters who could potentially be living next door to someone dangerous. I am not subjecting them to this circus.'

'Think what you're doing!' he cut in sharply. 'You're proclaiming her guilty!'

She turned her back, continuing with her packing. 'Well, I can't help that. I've done what I could. I now need to think of the children.'

'Claire, stop! I'd know if something was happening. You're being rash. They're probably there because they know Pete has scarpered. That's what they do. They're looking for the next story. Please, just calm down and think.'

Claire felt the breath drain out of her. She turned and slumped on Lottie's bed. Something was dying in her – the will to keep pushing through. She was running from shadows. She couldn't punch away what was buried in her mind, that he put there. She couldn't push away the growing fear chipping away at her from inside. It would consume her if she let it, which is why she was making practical preparations instead. Taking her daughters away, at least until she felt calm again. With her gone, James might consider the value of what he had and stood to lose.

She registered what he said to her this morning, just a short while ago, while staring out of her bedroom window. A flashback of the torment in his eyes, before closing off his feelings. His words on going forwards... *We can only choose how we redeem ourselves.*

She lifted her head and met his eyes, knowing he would speak the truth if she asked him.

Fear punctured the temptation.

No one wanted known the deepest part of their soul. Once revealed, it could never be hidden again.

She needed to change her plans, and stay. He was too vulnerable to be left alone. She rose from the bed. 'I'm going to take a bath. Could you kindly cancel my arrangement with Pierre?'

She moved to the door and his voice followed her.

'If I could turn back time, and undo what I did, I would. You know what I'm talking about, Claire. I should pay for these sins. There are some things that can never be forgiven, no matter how much you might hope for it.'

She didn't bend. His words were pressing on her heart. She didn't hesitate in her light footsteps to the bathroom. In the mirror, she saw her grandmother's eyes, hazel, with hues of gold and brown and green. A pigment of blue in a different light. Same shape, same look staring back at her. Resolute, as ever.

She stared firmly back, remaining steadfast. She couldn't allow him to give in. It was inconceivable – the ripping up of their lives, shredded beyond repair. There was too much at stake for her to weaken. She didn't bend. Or ever would.

FIFTY-ONE

Elsbeth Crosby wasn't in the farmhouse.

Moraine and Kennedy searched to make sure. Upstairs, a double bed showed the room where she slept, a knitted bedjacket on the pillow. A dressing table with a rectangular lace doily to protect the wood, with a brush and comb set and tiny bottles of perfume.

In a smaller room, a made-up bed, a set of drawers and a wardrobe with a few items of clothing: a long cotton coat with a wide collar, yellowed with age, some heavy wool jumpers that looked handknitted. On a shelf above the clothes rail, an old-fashioned beekeeper's hat.

A lean-to off to one side of the kitchen housed a stone-floored scullery. On one wall, held up by a large iron nail, was an old-fashioned tin bath, which presumably the old lady used to wash.

In the kitchen-cum-sitting-room, where Moraine had had a cup of tea that morning, the dog was also gone but cats were everywhere. Having already checked the outhouse and barn, they headed back outside.

On the horizon, Moraine spotted Elsbeth's tiny figure standing still by the diggers, which were flattening the land near a small island of trees that hadn't been cut down yet. At first light that morning, the diggers that had looked like Dinky Toys were now given scale next to Elsbeth. Giant excavators.

Glancing at her footwear and Kennedy's suede shoes, she led the way across the overgrown grassland. Kennedy keeping up with her in quiet conversation.

'I wonder if she wandered off in shock.'

'Maybe,' Moraine acknowledged, thinking more about what Stone asked earlier – if the dog barks at visitors. She said only at strangers. She found Sam Jenkins because she was looking for one of her cats, not because the dog alerted her. Maybe it was deaf and getting old, or the child didn't cry out in the time he was there.

As they got closer, they saw boulders and rocks buried deep for millennia that had been dug up and moved to form a small hill. Tree stumps, a chain still around one of them, dragged from the ground by a tractor to form another hill.

Moraine saw the black collie straining at a leash held in Elsbeth's hand, as she stayed in her position with her back to them. Possibilities traipsed through her mind: one of the cats had died, delayed shock from finding Sam, or shock from seeing her excavated land and registering that it would soon all be gone.

Her head turned at their approach. The movement slow, just an acknowledgement, as she faced forward again.

Moraine and Kennedy walked up to her side and looked around for what they were supposed to be seeing.

Large boulders, half covered by black clay. Severed roots and shrubs in a deep cavity. Churned up grass, leaf mulch, and silver birch twigs in the soil. Rotten wood poking out of the undergrowth. Tree logs and branches entwined with bindweed.

Then she saw it and her chest clenched with shock, her insides shivering deep in her belly.

A child's shoe, the lace still tied, was attached to one of those rotten logs.

FIFTY-TWO

A nurse delivered the gift box for Sam to his room. Jo untied the ribbons and saw a soft, fluffy elephant inside, and recognised it as a Jellycat toy, the same as his blue rabbit. A small card had a typewritten message, which she read to him:

To Sam.

Hurry up and get better. We all miss you. Dougie's looking after your bug hotel, but could do with your expert help.

Love from Lottie, Phoebe, and all of us.

She would let Sam take it out of the box when he was ready. It was thoughtful of Claire. It would have been she who organised it and wrote the message. Her kindness lifted Jo's spirits. By now Claire would know of her past. She was glad she had been wrong to think it would stop them caring about Sam. The gift showed they still had him in their hearts.

She wished she'd opened up to Claire, been honest from the start, and not been so weak. She had made herself look untrustworthy – and now a version of the truth was out there in the world.

She caught hold of Sam's hand and kissed his fingertips. She held his palm against her cheek, kissing it before laying his hand back on the sheet.

Fear and shock shook her as the reality of the day impeded on her senses. Her mind could no longer block out what was going to happen. She was going to lose her son. They were going to take him away from her. As much as she wanted him to get better quickly, it would mean her not being able to see him anymore. They were going to give him to a family of strangers who wouldn't understand his ways, who would try to shush him if he hummed, and try to still him if he moved around in circles waving his fingertips in the air.

They wouldn't understand that he didn't like labels on his collars. That he didn't like showers, only bubbly baths. They wouldn't understand that he enjoyed doing things on his own. That he didn't notice the time it took for him to dress himself, put on his socks and shoes, do the zip or buttons up on his clothes. They wouldn't know that he liked his hot milk to be in a blue cup, that he liked being stroked behind his ears, not over his forehead or hair, but on the skin behind each lobe. They wouldn't know his sweet, sensitive little soul like she did.

They wouldn't care if he missed her. They would try to blot out the memory of her from his head. See it as a breakthrough if he stopped crying for her. See it as the best thing for him, while they sorted the situation and decided if his mummy was dangerous. It would be better for him not to be with his parents for the time being.

Fear of what he would go through was destroying her mind. It was saying she wasn't fit to be his mother. They wouldn't allow her to make decisions regarding his welfare. When he was ready to leave hospital, others would take charge of her child's care. She would only be the biological mother of the child in care. She wouldn't even know where he lived.

Suddenly, she couldn't breathe. The room was closing in on her. She needed to find a place where no one could scrutinise her, somewhere to be alone for a few minutes.

In a dash, she left the room, stumbling into the nearest bathroom. With trembling arms, she leaned on the hand basin. In her grey, sickly face, the agony in her eyes stared back at her from the mirror.

On shaking legs, she turned to the shower and stepped into the cubicle. As hot water drenched through her clothes to her shivering body and her cheek pressed against the tiles, a frenzy of cries broke free. Feelings she'd bottled up tightly burst forth like molten lava. Mucus and tears streamed from her eyes, nose, and mouth, washing down her face.

The miracle of her second chance at having Sam back had been a fool's dream. God had not given Sam back to her, but taken him further away. Perhaps it was a warning to other mothers to keep what they had safe. God was watching and could take their children from them.

Sinking down onto the shower tray, she curled in a ball, rocking to ease the unbearable pain.

FIFTY-THREE

Claire pulled the gown over Jo's head and tied the strings at the back before combing her damp hair. The state of her bloodshot eyes had shocked her, staring up at her like a drowned cat.

It was a good job she came, otherwise Jo would still be sat in a shower. She gave the excuse of needing a change of scenery, to get out of the house for a while. She couldn't let the day go by and not visit. She wished now she'd brought some provisions, as seeing only a plastic jug of water to drink.

The officer outside Sam's room helped Claire by fetching a towel and something dry for Jo to wear. The young officer sitting in the room, in her trendy trousers and jacket, fiddling with her damn phone, had scarpered. Jo looked like a patient in the gown, which was easy to believe with how ill she looked.

Claire found it astonishing that in the hospital, with so many doctors and nurses around, no one had noticed how weak she was, hardly able to stay on her feet. They were either blind or too busy to notice she was ready to collapse.

She asked the officer to find an armchair to replace the hard chair Jo had been sitting on, and found a blanket on a trolley in the corridor to wrap around her bare feet and legs.

And all the while, Jo told her of the tremendous difficulties she'd had to deal with that day.

Not done, she requested some hot tea and something substantial for Jo to eat. The nurses looked at her as if she were asking for the moon until she spelled out the state Jo was in.

'I might not be medically trained, but I can recognise shock when it's staring me in the face. My goodness, surely one of you understands the basic concepts of psychology. Her child might be the one in the bed, but his mother is equally traumatised. She's under enormous distress from everything that's happening. So much so, she's gone into one of your showers fully dressed. Does that sound like a person who's coping? Her life has been shattered like none of you can imagine.'

She walked away from the dozen pairs of eyes watching her, already penning a letter to her MP in her mind, and another one to the Commissioner of Police. It was outrageous to have a uniformed police officer right outside the door. It was giving credence to the idea of Jo being guilty of a crime with an officer there to guard her, when she hadn't even been charged.

The food was some sort of chicken casserole. It smelled better than it looked. She wheeled a table in front of Jo's chair, ordering her to eat.

'I want every bite gone. It's not a big serving, a toddler could eat it. No wonder people lose weight in these places.'

She placed the mug of hot tea, handed to her at the door, next to Jo's plate, then sat down in a chair and looked at Sam.

Her heart shot into her throat at seeing his eyes open. She stayed perfectly still, waiting for him to see her. The blue eyes continued looking straight ahead.

'That's the sixth time,' Jo said, beside her. 'He opens them and stares without seeing you.'

Claire was aghast. 'How long will he stay like this?'

'They don't know. He could come out of it any moment or stay like it for a while. The psychiatrist and doctor are thinking of giving him lorazepam, as a sedative, to slow down his brain. I suppose they mean thoughts, so he can better handle them. They're holding off for now, hoping he'll come out of it gradually by himself.

'I think he knows I'm here, because his heart rate and breathing stay normal and steady. Earlier, when I popped out to the loo, the nurse said his heart rate went up and his breathing got faster as soon as I stepped out of the room. I think they're holding off with medication because of this response. It's his way of letting me know he's there.'

Claire eyed the monitor. The heart rate was the same as thirty seconds ago. And now his eyes were closed.

She turned to Jo, pleased to see her eating some of the food. A bit of colour in her cheeks. 'Jo, you should speak to Anthony Clark. Tell him what's happening. Get him on the case as soon as possible. He might be able to appeal this decision.'

She responded with a tearful expression. 'I didn't think of that. Thank you for suggesting it.'

Claire gave a shake of her head. 'No, no. No more tears. Your poor eyes can't take it. I'm just so sorry that this is happening. We're on your side, Jo. Please know that.'

She gave a small sniff. Then took the tissue Claire handed her. 'Even with what you know about me? What we kept hidden? It was wrong, and for that I'm truly sorry.'

Claire gave her a no-nonsense look. 'Hush now. We're not judging you. We know you're a good person and are wonderful with children. What I'd like to say is, when this is over, I want to help find you and Sam a new home. Give you a fresh start. A two bed with a garden, near to Sam's school. And if you're worried about affording it, please don't. We'll cover the rent until you're on your feet again. Whether that takes a year, or more, we'll cover it.'

Jo's eyes rounded like pennies, disbelief on her face.

To halt Jo's rising emotions, Claire pushed up from her

chair. 'They need to bring one of those bed cots in here for you to sleep on. That's what they normally provide for parents staying with their child. I'll have a little word on the way out, see if I can't chivvy them along.'

Jo reached out a hand, then gestured to the white box on the bedside locker. 'Thank you so much for Sam's gift. It was really thoughtful. He'll love it.'

Claire waved the thanks away. She was not comfortable receiving compliments. She was glad she had come, and just at the right time. This good deed made her feel better. She would now sort out a home for Jo. She was not rushing her out of the door. But soon, when this terrible time was over, she was shutting all of it out. James needed solitude, and time to make peace with himself, and with their home. It was not under a curse. She and James were not broken.

If they could master that – let everything from the past scatter in the wind – it might one day feel like none of it happened. None of it will need thinking about ever again. Erased from their minds for good.

FIFTY-FOUR

Moraine and Kennedy stood in silence in Elsbeth's kitchen, processing the magnitude of the discovery. It was barely credible. The remains of a child found on the same property where the missing child was found, and only a day apart. Fate had struck a blow on poor Elsbeth and decided that she would be the one to find them.

Moraine wasn't drawn to the supernatural, but in this she couldn't help but consider the existence of some external force. Coincidence sounded too benign. Like a soft explanation. Stone would probably scoff at the notion and point out the obvious, that it was the diggers that unearthed the body, and the remains were bound to be revealed eventually.

Stone and a team of officers were on their way and would arrive without the rest of the world knowing anything about it, because of Elsbeth's only phone call.

She had walked more than a mile to make that call. Her ramble with the dog led to her discovery, followed by her hasty walk back to her house to pick up the old-fashioned landline. Another journey back, with the dog on a lead, to await someone's arrival, before Moraine and Kennedy led her home again.

The kettle whistled. Kennedy roused himself to make them all tea. He put sugar in all three and brought Elsbeth's to the table where she sat upright and strong. Stronger than either of them, and shaming a strength back into Moraine. Soon to be eighty-three, twice her age, and twice making horrific discoveries, all on her own. A child near dead, another dead and buried.

Kennedy patted her shoulder as he returned to pick up his cup, and spoke softly in her ear. 'Sorry for the weak knees. I never knew I could be so shocked.'

Moraine let him see the strain in her own eyes. They might be coppers, and more used to dealing with death, but that didn't make them immune from experiences like this. The little leather shoe, the lace coated in mud, still attached to the remains.

It was hard to equate what had been found in these surroundings with the home of this gracious old lady. Someone had buried a child on her land, and hid another in a place where he might never have been found.

She couldn't imagine the fear he must have experienced at being left there. At night-time, being alone in the dark.

Kennedy sliced off a piece of fruit cake, buttered it, maybe because it was stale, and brought it on a plate to Elsbeth. 'A little sustenance is in order.'

She patted his hand. 'I made it a week ago. I would have put a bit of custard with it later. Nice to have it with butter.'

She set about munching, and Kennedy sat with her at the table, leaving Moraine to find a loo. She needed a moment alone, to get over seeing those remains.

Returning a few minutes later from the perfectly adequate and clean washroom with a good-size sink, she was in time to catch Elsbeth's question to Kennedy.

'How is the dear boy? Is he going to be all right?'

'He's on a children's ward. His mum's with him, and the doctors and nurses are looking after him.'

Her eyes opened wide with regret. 'Poor little thing probably has pneumonia, but don't you go worrying now. He's young and they do wonderful things in hospitals these days. When I was a child, catching something like that might have finished you off, but not today. So don't you go worrying. He'll pull through, you'll see.'

Moraine saw her hand on Kennedy's and felt deeply moved. This incredible old woman was comforting him, and this excellent policeman needed comforting.

FIFTY-FIVE

Her joy was so great, Jo didn't even mind that Pete had turned up. So happy to see Sam making actual eye contact, she'd grabbed hold of his arm to bring him close to the bed so that he could see the improvement himself. If his reaction was tame, it was because he hadn't been there for thirteen hours with only the fixed look in Sam's eyes.

For an hour he'd been looking at her, blinking when she came close to kiss his face. It was incredible. She sent Claire a message – the only other person she wanted to tell about the good news. The police officer outside gave her a thumbs up at seeing her exuberance.

She glanced at Pete and saw him sitting tensely. They were alone in the room. Chelsea had departed at some point during Claire's visit, with no explanation, not even a goodbye.

'You don't have to stay,' she said quietly, conscious that Sam might hear. 'If you want to go, I'm not stopping you, Pete.'

He shook his head, avoiding her eyes. 'It would be best if I leave. You don't want me here.'

Jo heard the self-pitying tone. She wouldn't get angry, but neither would she appease him. 'I'd like you here for Sam.'

He nodded, slowly. 'I see. But not for you?'

She was a different person from the one she was four days ago. She no longer saw him as part of her future. Their marriage was irretrievably damaged. He surely must realise that.

'No. Not for me. You don't love me. And as hard as it was for me to let go, I don't love you. For the last two years, I've been trying to hold on to what I thought we had. But it's all gone, Pete. I now want to focus on trying to find myself again. The person I was, before that all happened. I lost my confidence, my self-esteem, my self-belief. I blamed myself and let you hide me away. But the worst of it is – you no longer made me feel safe.

'I haven't felt protected in a very long time. I don't want to be like that anymore. I want to feel strong. Raise our son. I'd like you to be the best father you can be for Sam. But only you can decide that. Only you can decide what's important to you.'

He was chewing gum, his jaw pressing firmly, muscles pounding away.

Her heart fluttered, waiting for his reaction.

He shifted his chair around until he was in front her, and looked into her eyes. He flicked his gaze then at Sam, heaving a small sigh, keeping his voice low. 'Yeah, well, it's all fucked up now anyway. I met Miss Beaky Nose on the way in. Like a rash all over me when I said my name. Getting ready to justify her decision for Sam to go into care. I soon put her right. Sam will be coming home with me.'

'What!'

He looked at her and gave a helpless shrug. 'Good bloke, my solicitor. Knows all the right lingo. It seems I'm now NFA. No further action. File closed. I just let that social worker know Sam still has one parent he can live with. So she can fuck off.'

He was watching the shock in her eyes. He was telling her he was free. He would get Sam. She didn't have a say in the matter. But he had plenty to say.

'I've had a right busy last hour. Getting through to the

council was a joke, but I think I managed to jump the queue with all this being on the news. They'll have a place sorted by tomorrow. Temporary housing until they find us somewhere permanent.'

He shifted his chair back to where it was before this conversation, leaving her feeling as if the life had been sucked from her. She couldn't even speak. Her brain couldn't think. She was stuck on what she just heard.

He gave a weighty sigh. 'Fuck sake. What did you expect? For them to hand him back to you? You could plead temporary fucking insanity. Or blame the antidepressants for loss of fucking memory.'

It was like hearing a bomb go off. The shock rang in her ears, spinning her in the air. Careening her past flickering footage of her life. Gone before it was barely seen.

Her jaw was like a trap. She couldn't force it open, her teeth clamped together. She peeled her fingernails away from her palm, the lines of new scabs marked with fresh spots of blood. She dug her thumb deeply into the centre of her palm, opening the skin up, forcing her mouth to react and croak out a cry.

'I didn't do it!'

His voice cut through the air. 'Didn't you! You didn't take him to where you took him and leave him there! Of course you fucking didn't! He just happens to be found in a place you once took him to. How could you? He loved those cats. And you put him there! Fucking shame on you.'

He stood up. 'I'm going to get a sandwich. Do you want one?'

She looked up at him, unable to respond.

He then put his hand in his pocket and brought out the car keys, putting them in her hand. 'You probably need to go home. Get some clothes. You look like a patient otherwise. I'll stay till you get back. No need to worry. He's in safe hands.'

FIFTY-SIX

Claire put her phone down, her eyebrows drawn together.

The expression didn't go unnoticed by James. 'What is it?'

She vaguely shook her head. She'd only just come from there. He was totally unresponsive. And now he was awake.

It was on the tip of her tongue to tell him. But then he'd go rushing over there to see the boy. The best thing would be not to say anything.

Slowly, she breathed in and out, deciding to be calm.

Out of the corner of her eye she saw him looking at her, waiting for her to respond. He could be so irritating – being so exceptionally observant he picked up on every little thing. She should have closed the bedroom door so he didn't just wander in.

She raised her head to give him a quick smile. 'Need to get an eye test. My eyes are getting as bad as yours. I can hardly read my phone.'

Then she put a hand to her mouth and gave a genuine gasp. 'Blast, I meant to make you an eye appointment. I completely forgot.'

'Not to worry. I can make one myself.' He returned a brief smile, then rubbed at his temple.

It looked like he was getting another headache. Her mother got them all her life. She liked to let people know hers were rare, plaguing only one per cent of the population. Cluster migraines. Debilitating her. Claire put it down to her living off her nerves. Resilience, passed down through the generations, skipped by her. She had spent half her life in bed. It was left to Claire's grandmother to stand by her side at her father's grave and keep her strong. Something she appreciated. There was no display of sentiment to confuse her young heart.

'Let me do it tomorrow. I promise I won't forget. Having the children home is making me think it's a Sunday. *And* having you at home. I thought you had a new case.'

'I did. I let my clerk know I wouldn't be attending. The judge has been notified. Another barrister has been appointed to deal with it.'

Claire was astonished, and consciously stopped her mouth from falling open. Not once in fifteen years had she known him to withdraw from a case. This was exactly what she'd been worried about – him going off at the deep end. Abandoning his responsibilities. For what?

Why couldn't he make the same effort for her as she was making for him? Turn back time. Pretend it never happened. Forgive himself for her sake.

She lifted her chin off the floor, gathering her wits to think calmly. It was difficult, with this just sprung upon her. She drank a sip of water from the glass on the table by her bed.

Carefully modulating her voice to express her concern, she said, 'I think you made a wise decision. You've had too many headaches from all the stress. I know how hard this has been. You need to recharge your batteries, James. Sam is safe in the hospital. He'll get better and live with his mother. She will get free of this. She will never be charged for any crime. I'm certain of that. If necessary, I'll lie. I'll swear under oath I saw him get in the car.'

The intensity of his gaze was difficult to withstand. She could feel his eyes burning into her.

Didn't he believe her? She was telling the truth. She would do that. She would lie for Jo and for him. If it gave him peace, that's all that mattered.

He had to believe they could put this behind them.

He searched her eyes, studying her every miniscule expression until he was satisfied with what her eyes were telling him.

'You'd do that?'

'Yes.' She nodded affirmatively and slowly. 'If it stops me from seeing this sadness in your eyes, I'll do anything. But, James, I have to know that we can move forwards and not revisit this again. It's not only you that carries these painful secrets. We've lost so much already – our darling little boy – I can't lose you as well.'

Tears escaped his eyes. It broke her heart to witness this. In all the years she'd seen him cry a handful of times.

His voice was choked. 'I can try... Maybe it will stop anything bad ever happening again.'

Burning hope showed in her eyes. 'I promise you it will stop everything.'

He breathed out explosively, finally letting go. His eyes glimmered with tears. He tried smiling, making her heart ache from knowing how difficult this had been for him. He had made a choice to be happy, to choose *them*.

She reached out and placed her hands against his face, pulling him close, while looking in his eyes as she kissed him. She felt his hands slide across her back, and the kiss building with more passion. Walking her slowly backwards, keeping hold of her, he closed and locked the door.

He wanted her, and was letting her know he couldn't wait. He didn't care that it was barely evening, or that the children were downstairs. He cared only about this time being theirs alone, and being on this bed with her. Nothing could be more perfect than this.

FIFTY-SEVEN

Stone sat in one of the faded gold-velvet vintage armchairs, sharing a small table with Elsbeth. He pushed her tea closer in case she'd forgotten about it.

She gave him a wan smile.

Moraine thought how very tired she must be. The wait for Stone was longer than expected. She'd encouraged Elsbeth to have a nap, but she declined, saying she was used to long hours from the days when she had a milking shed. She had learned to do without sleep.

When this case was over, Moraine would take time to visit her, and let her talk about the better times of running a farm.

'How long do you think he was there?'

He leaned forward, shuffling a little closer, as if to make it more private and intimate. Moraine sat on a kitchen chair, keeping quiet, while a cat sniffed at her shoes.

'He went missing Saturday morning and wasn't seen until you found him at nearly midnight on Sunday.'

Her wrinkled cheeks quivered. 'Oh my word! All that time out in that awful, damp cold. How in God's name did he survive?'

'I'm told from talking to one of the doctors that the foil blanket is probably what saved him. Acted as insulation, keeping out some of the cold.'

'I see.' Her voice was bleak as she added, 'Imagine if I hadn't gone there. He would have eventually...' Her voice trailed off, leaving a silence in the room, which Stone gently addressed.

'I think he had a guardian angel looking after him. Probably enticed your Tommy to go wandering off so you had to go look for him.'

The image he portrayed brought a smile to her face. 'I think you're right, Inspector. I acquired Tommy from a church. The vicar said he was making a nuisance of himself.'

Stone gave a quiet chuckle. 'Well done, Tommy. He got you to go in the outhouse. When you found him, did you realise he was the boy we were looking for?'

She shook her head. 'No. I didn't know a child was missing. I never had the radio on, I suppose. I usually get a *Bath Chronicle* when I go into Weston Village to give the van a run once a week, to keep it ticking over. On Saturday morning when I went to post a letter to my solicitor, the queue was so long, I forgot.'

Stone gave an understanding nod. 'Did you recognise him at all? Had you ever seen him before?'

Moraine could see she was disturbed by the question. Her eyes were full of worry. 'I only had a torch with me. I can see his face, but I can't say I recognised him. Children used to come more often. Sometimes with parents delivering stuff. We kept Friesians back then. They would watch Harry milk them. Now, it's just the occasional parent who might wander in with their children hoping to see livestock. I can't say if this little lad was ever one of them.'

He glanced at the dog, sleeping on the floor at her feet. 'Did he go with you? To the post office?'

She shook her head. 'No. Bert's place is here. No point in having a watchdog otherwise. They're a good breed, ranked the most intelligent. He's getting on, but still lets me know if someone's coming.'

'The list I asked you to make—'

'It's done. Every name I can think of.'

'And if Bert doesn't know someone?'

'He'll bark the place down. Like he did with you this morning.'

Stone waited quietly while she picked up her cup to drink the tea. Moraine took the opportunity to gently shoo the cat from clawing her trousers.

'And no one else lives here with you?'

She shook her head. 'No, not for a long time. In all the years, I've never had a problem, never had a break-in or trespassers.'

It must have dawned on her, the reality, that her home had very much been trespassed against. Her voice quavered with emotion. 'Such a wicked thing to do. To bury a child where no one can find them. And I never knew it was done.'

Stone picked up her hand, calloused from hard work, and held it in both of his. 'You have nothing to reproach yourself for. There was nothing to tell you it was there.'

With a gentle smile, he released her hand. 'In the meantime, you mustn't worry. You stay strong. As my old mum would say, him up there will never give you anything you can't handle. And you are proof of that, if there was any needed.'

'Harry used to tell me I had an iron backbone. Mostly when he wanted me to dig.'

Moraine was relieved to hear a little humour in her voice. This must be horrendous for her, discovering her home had been used to commit these crimes. Moraine hoped she could recover from this and was able to stay strong. It had been a shocking turn of events to deal with. Especially for someone her age.

Stone called her name. 'Moraine. Walk me out.'

Moraine reluctantly left the home – leaving Elsbeth sat in

her chair – and joined him on a short walk, to stare in the twilight across the field, to the white forensic tent, already up and busy.

He didn't waste time, but went straight in with instructions. 'The woman Jo Jenkins claims to have seen – I want a name. You asked only Mrs Howell if she saw her. Maybe she didn't, but someone else might have.'

Moraine felt her stomach twist, feeling this was a dig at her. He hadn't pressed for further investigation, leading her to think he agreed the mystery woman didn't exist.

He glanced at her, then looked to where the remains were found. 'Find her. Before this hits the news. My gut is telling me that what's buried over there is that woman's missing son.'

FIFTY-EIGHT

Jo tried to call Anthony Clark, but he wasn't answering. He was probably finished for the day. Her phone had rung while driving, but she couldn't answer it. Their car wasn't kitted out with Bluetooth.

She didn't know what he was calling about, but she should have contacted him when Claire suggested it, when he might have been in his office to take her call. Now, she had lost the opportunity, right when she desperately needed advice.

She needed him to tell her, in his honest opinion, what he thought the chances were of her being charged. She had to know. After what just happened – she didn't even know what to call it. A torturous revelation to blame her for something she didn't know she had done?

He just happens to be found in a place you once took him to.

To make her face the truth? To crack open her mind and force her to remember?

She put her phone in her coat pocket and went up the stairs to Sam's bedroom. Turning on the light, she stared at the rumpled bed and the duvet cover, patterned with bright-green leaves and colourful bugs.

She shivered violently. Sam would never sleep in it again. The last time he slept here was in her bed. And in the morning, the nightmare began.

She cried, and sank to her knees. Was Pete just trying to make her think she had lost her mind? That she'd gone through some sort of psychosis and left her son at the place where he was found? Was he being vindictive, or truly believed this of her?

Time stopped as she knelt there. Then Sam's sweet voice echoed in her head.

I love the cats, Mummy. They're so soft and fluffy. Like branch's hair.

She climbed slowly to her feet, using Sam's bed for support, and looked down at what she was wearing. A hospital gown under her coat. It forced her to move. Forced her to accept, to realise. She was running out of time. The cuffs were coming for her. She needed to act fast.

Every word Pete said – a death knell for her. They were coming. People with the power to take her away and take Sam from her. Forever.

And with this thought, a surge of nervous energy galvanised her into action. Undressing, she threw on clean clothes. Racing from room to room, grabbing warm wear, jumpers, jackets, shoes. Toys, books, phone charger, passports. Leaving even bigger gaps than those already left by Pete in cupboards, drawers, on shelves – the contents now loaded into a large IKEA bag.

She would change their names, change the colour of her hair, grow fat, go skinny, wear glasses, wear shoes that made her taller. Clothes that made her broader. Walk with a limp if need be. Cut off a limb if she had to. She would do anything and everything to keep her son.

Her name, her face, would be plastered everywhere. So where she decided to go would have to be as remote as possible. It must be far away where no one would find them. The moment she ran, they would come looking for her. A criminal on the run.

They would see it as their mission to not let her get away with it. They would have all available surveillance in place to capture her. It would become national news. Every single report claiming her culpable.

She had nothing to lose. Nothing to stay for. No other option.

They already thought her guilty of the crime she would commit – abducting her child.

FIFTY-NINE

Moraine stood by Kennedy's side for the briefing. The team was gathered together now that Stone had been updated with fresh and accurate intel. They were waiting for the SIO to appear.

Moraine felt sick. She had given Stone a child's name after searching the Police National Computer database, and it was highly likely the woman Jo met was the mother of this child.

Kennedy elbowed her gently, nudging the top of her arm. 'You're doing it again. Stone's looking at you. Your lips are moving like a pair of castanets.'

She giggled. Immediately covering her mouth, she felt mildly hysterical. Her head swam with emotions – discomfort, insecurity – and like a terrible failure who hadn't done her job right. It took the remains of a child to be found, one desperate mother talking to another desperate mother, before she did her job properly. She should not have been so quick to believe Jo was delusional. She had been telling the truth.

She thought maybe she shouldn't be there, as she'd be of no help with her mind like this. She'd been awake since five thirty. It was now nine o'clock at night. She was drained. She thought of Elsbeth, with her iron backbone, years of doing without sleep, *her day*. Moraine's day was nothing compared to what she'd had to endure.

She focused. Giving her full attention to the tough part: nailing someone.

Stone summarised the day's incidents and outcomes. One, which she hadn't known, was that Pete Jenkins was now in the clear, NFA. One, which she was aware of – the discovery of a child's remains, still unknown to the press. Elsbeth Crosby had helped keep it under wraps because the only phone call she made on discovering the burial site was to Stone.

His eyes found Moraine. 'Raine, if you're too tired, I'll get someone else. Totally understand. Been a long day. But for more reasons than one, I still want eyes on Jo Jenkins. Would you be up for it?' His eyes turned to Kennedy. 'The two of you, in fact, would be better. I'm arranging with the hospital's chief executive for a room on the children's ward where you can be out of sight. If all stays quiet, you can take turns getting a kip.'

Moraine nodded, even though she didn't understand the purpose of this clandestine approach. They wouldn't be able to keep eyes on Jo through a wall.

'The officer outside Sam's room has been removed,' he then announced. 'Instead, a surveillance team will be set up at every access point to the paediatric ward, and we'll see what comes out of the woodwork.'

Kennedy spoke up. 'What are you expecting to happen, sir?'

Stone shrugged his large shoulders. 'Maybe something. Maybe nothing. Maybe none of the dots will join. But there are a few loose connections: Matthew Lambert, at age six, disappeared from his school in Bath. I'm predicting those remains are his. Five years ago this October, that's how long he's been there. Stuart Lambert, the father of Matthew, was a barrister and friend or associate of James Howell. Rupert Howell, father of

James, was Elsbeth Crosby's long-standing solicitor who, incidentally, was also the long-standing solicitor for Elenor Beckley, mother-in-law to James Howell.

'Sam Jenkins lives on the grounds of Beckley House. He was taken, and left in an outhouse on the property of Elsbeth Crosby, with an insulation blanket wrapped around him. We can't know what the perpetrator intended – to keep him alive for another purpose, or the intention of leaving him there to die.'

He spread his arms out to encompass the entire room, staring around at all the officers present.

Moraine was stunned. His research went a lot deeper than hers. From giving him the name Matthew Lambert, he'd made a connection to James Howell. His voice boomed out.

'By some miracle, Sam Jenkins was found. Against all odds, he was discovered. He survived. That will beat in this miscreant's heart. He's conscious, barely, and hasn't spoken a word. But that could change.

'A lot of you standing here probably wonder how any of this helps to identify the perpetrator. You're thinking, why the change of focus on the mother? Has The Bruiser...' He gave a rumbling laugh. 'Love that title. Has The Bruiser forgotten that not one shred of evidence has been found to show the child was with her, in that car, on that journey to the swimming pool? Has he lost his grip? Maybe one too many knocks to the head?'

He shook his head at them. 'I'll tell you why. I don't believe in coincidences. I don't believe two children found in the same location, five years apart, can be a fluke.'

An arm shot up. Karen Lester, a seasoned DS, on the force for over twenty years. Stone nodded for her to talk.

'Sir. Just an idea to throw in here. As there is five years between the disappearances, and the incident with Ruby Ashman, the two-year-old who went missing on a nursery outing, happened right in the middle of those two incidents, might Joanne Jenkins be suspected of trying and failing to disappear Ruby as well? It's just a thought, but is it possible she could have done all three? Another Myra Hindley, or a Beverley Allitt. *She* was a children's nurse. Joanne Jenkins qualified as a paediatric nurse.

'She would have been training to be a paediatric nurse, six, seven years ago, when Matthew Lambert was still alive. He could have been a patient at some point and she could have met him.'

Moraine felt the hairs go up on her neck and down her arms. She protested. 'Jo isn't—' Then stopped.

Stone was shaking his head at the DS, his voice mellow. 'I appreciate the input, Karen. Even considered it myself. But the maths doesn't work. Mrs Jenkins gave birth to her son ninth of September. Matthew Lambert went missing third of October. I don't see how, a little over three weeks later, she would abduct a boy out of the playground of his school, take him and bury him on Elsbeth Crosby's farm. I think it's unlikely, if I'm being honest.'

Karen nodded amiably and gave a light shrug. 'Back to you then, guv.'

He glanced around the room at the waiting expressions on the officers' faces. 'The person responsible is probably kicking themselves for not moving the child sooner, or ensuring the child was dead, because now they're worried about a witness. Are they going to run? Or plan their next move?'

Moraine felt her spine tingle at his closing words. She was worried that Stone was using the child as bait. She'd rather be in the room with the boy and not take the chance of something happening to him. Because assuming Stone was right, Sam was a sitting target, with no protection from whoever might come for him.

It sounded too dangerous. The risks were too high. She

didn't want to sit in another room, unable to see what was going on. If a threat came, she needed to be there to stop it.

She'd think of something. Assess the layout when they got there. Pretend to be a parent if necessary. One thing was for sure, she would not leave it to providence to keep him safe. Her eyes would be on him.

SIXTY

Claire came awake as she noticed the absence in the bed. James was gone. She slid her watch off the bedside table to check the time. Quarter past nine. The evening had gone. Bernice would be wondering why they hadn't made an appearance at supper. She sank her head back on the pillow, feeling the languidness of her limbs, and smiled contentedly. She wanted him to sleep with her tonight. To curl into his strong back and feel him next to her.

Maybe she could persuade him to come away with her for a few days so they could both take time to de-stress. Unwind in Paris. Take leisurely walks along the banks of the Seine. Dine at Le Vent d'Armor on oysters and soft-shell crab. Sip Veuve Clicquot champagne with perfect chocolate mousse. Spend their nights at Maison Souquet with its dark, seductive décor.

She stretched her limbs to her toes, before climbing out of the bed. Naked, she walked to her bathroom and stepped in to the instantly warm shower, soaping herself, then rinsing, before folding herself in a soft white towel.

She dried and dressed slowly, brushing her hair, putting gloss on her clean lips and perfume behind her earlobes. Her casual wear of soft linen trousers, cashmere sweater, leather slip-ons, felt superbly comfortable against her skin. Putting her watch back on, her phone in her pocket, she left the bedroom looking for James.

She checked in the kitchen first, then in his study, before wandering through the downstairs rooms. Returning upstairs, she checked all the bedrooms and bathrooms. James's sitting room, his dressing room. Everywhere was quiet, the girls fast asleep in their beds.

She descended the staircase again, looking in the utility areas and storage rooms, before heading down to the lower floor and opening the heavy door leading along a stone passageway to the wine cellar and cold cellar. He was nowhere to be seen.

Returning to the door, she closed it firmly to keep Bernice's quarters warm. Walking through a modernised passageway to Bernice's rooms, she tapped lightly at the door, hearing the television on, and waited to be allowed in.

Bernice stared at her, surprised, as it was unusual for Claire to venture into her domain.

'What is it? Do you need me for something?'

Claire waved her to stay seated, noticing her trying to put on her slippers. She was one of the first of James's many 'help out' decisions. One of his best decisions, bringing her into his fold. Bernice gave back in spades. Way beyond what they had given her.

She was thirty-one when her husband went to prison. She had been a witness at his trial and shunned by his and her own family for speaking the truth. James had found her on the court steps after the trial was over, completely alone without a friend in the world, and brought her home.

In all the time she'd been with them, she had never mentioned her husband, or what he had done. Claire, of course, knew. He had killed a schoolteacher. A twenty-three-year-old woman. Stabbed her in the heart as she tried to stop him fleeing with a handful of money from a corner shop. Bernice had seen it all while waiting in the car, thinking he was buying cigarettes and not in there to rob and kill.

Claire was never tempted to pry, believing that people managed difficult secrets best by themselves.

She smiled and shook her head. 'Absolutely not, and nothing is wrong. Just wondering if you have seen my darling husband anywhere. I've searched the house and can't find him.'

Bernice blinked, before gazing up at the ceiling. 'He was in the kitchen last time I saw him. Maybe he's chatting with Dougie. He's still here to deal with all the nuisances at the gates.'

The reminder that there were reporters still watching their home dampened Claire's spirits. They definitely needed to get away from all of this.

Claire arched an eyebrow. 'Of course. That's where he'll be. Nighty night, Bernice. Go back to what you were watching before I disturbed you.'

She gave a bashful look. '*The Sixth Sense*. Doubt it would be your cup of tea. It's too spooky. About a child who can communicate with the dead.'

Claire grimaced, put a hand up to shield her eyes, exaggerating a little. 'No. Definitely not. I can't do horror. I'll leave you to it.'

She returned to the kitchen to look for signs of any food left out, crumbs on a plate, dishes in the sink. Everywhere was spotless.

Taking the hallway to the front door, she went outside and walked to the designated parking area, the spaces marked out by topiary bushes that Dougie didn't allow to get too ornamental. James's car, the most easily hidden – ludicrously small for someone his height but which he insisted was comfortable and perfect for driving in London and major cities – was not in any of the parking slots. The Mini Hatch was gone.

She pulled out her phone from her trouser pocket and stared at the bright screen, felt her stomach drop. A missed call from Marley. She'd had it on silent without realising. Irritated at being bothered this way, she swiped at the screen, sending the message away. Why couldn't she just leave them in peace?

Calming herself, she rang James.

His 'hello' sounded breathy, like he was walking fast.

'Where are you? I was hoping to have a glass of wine with you.'

'Why didn't you tell me?' he answered.

Claire was trying to decipher his tone. It sounded guarded. She stood completely still, gripping the phone tightly.

'Tell you what?'

'That he's awake.'

Her eyes stretched wide. She must have left her phone unlocked and he saw Jo's message. Moisture gathered under her arms.

'I would hav—'

He interrupted her. 'I have to go. I'll see you later.'

She blinked in shock. Shivered in reaction. Why did he have to go tearing off now? Jo may be trying to sleep. Was it to remind himself he didn't deserve to be happy? That he needed a glimpse of Sam's face to destroy any chance of that?

He had so much love surrounding him. Their bright, beautiful daughters, who filled them to the brim with love every single day – why couldn't that be enough to take away what he carried inside him? She pleaded for him to hear her voice in his head.

Please, think about that. Of how much we love you. Please, just come home to us...

SIXTY-ONE

While she had been gone, someone had placed a narrow fold-up bed in the room, and Pete was now stretched out on it asleep, using Sam's gift from Claire as a pillow, the gift box discarded on the floor.

Walking to the side of Sam's bed, she quietly tucked the IKEA bag behind the bedside locker, laying her coat across it to hide the contents. She then retrieved the car keys from her pocket and laid them on the table where Pete would see them when he woke.

She stroked the skin behind Sam's ear before lowering herself onto the chair. Sliding the carrier bag handles off her wrist, she reached inside for his storybook about little trolls. She left the cartons of juice and snacks in the bag for when he could enjoy them.

It was when she reached the bottom of the stairs, almost about to leave, that it clicked what Sam meant about branch's hair. It wasn't hair on a branch on a tree, as she bizarrely imagined, but hair on a troll, a cartoon character named Branch that was in his storybook. He had the plastic toy of Branch, with its blue-black fluffy hair, that he liked to carry in his pocket and stroke.

Behind her, she heard the metal frame creak as Pete's weight came off the mattress. He yawned noisily, before dragging the car keys off the table.

'I'll be off then.'

Jo turned to acknowledge him. 'You might need coffee. There was just enough for one cup when I checked.'

'I won't be needing it. I'm not staying there.'

'Right, then. I just thought I'd let you know.'

She saw no point in saying she already knew he'd packed his things.

He shrugged, as if it didn't matter. 'Wouldn't be allowed back anyway. I burned my bridges with Claire. Told her what I thought of her snooty life.'

Jo said nothing and tried not to react. After all their generosity, he ended it with them with rudeness, and Claire hadn't mentioned it.

She kept eye contact until he left the room. He didn't kiss or say goodnight to his son, or even look at him. About to turn back to Sam, she saw there was no police officer outside the door. She hadn't noticed he was gone when she arrived, but he couldn't have been there, otherwise she'd have been self-conscious about carrying the large IKEA bag.

She looked back at Sam and saw his blue eyes open. She smiled at him and spoke softly. 'Hello, beautiful boy. I've been home to fetch one of your storybooks, the one where Branch has a birthday and doesn't want a party.'

She lifted the book from her lap, showing the cover. Pointing at the characters. 'There's Poppy with her pink hair, and Branch with his purple hair.'

His eyes followed her finger, and she wanted to kiss his little face. Fear of alarming him kept her movements gentle and slow.

She turned sideways in her chair so he could see the pages while she read him the story. It didn't take long to read, just a few minutes, but his eyes moved across each page every time she turned to a new one. She looked into his eyes and let him see the love in hers.

'I'm here, Sam, when you're ready to say hello.'

He held her gaze and sleepily let his eyelids lower.

She watched him sleep.

A light tap on the viewing window made her turn. She was startled, never expecting James Howell would visit. Easing the chair back from Sam's bed as he entered the room, she tried not to show she was nervous, conscious that he knew everything about her now.

He greeted her in a quiet voice. 'Hi. I waited until you finished. I could see him drifting off and didn't want to disturb him. Pete let me in on his way out.'

Her face felt stiff with embarrassment. She began to stand. 'I, um...'

He waved a hand lightly. 'Don't get up. I'll find somewhere to sit.'

He sat on the cot bed carefully, choosing to sit in the middle, and grinned ruefully. 'I hope it doesn't collapse.'

In black trousers and pale-blue shirt, he looked casual. She was more used to seeing him in suits and ties. The clothing didn't change him. He could be dressed in anything and still have a strong presence in a room. A combination of intellect, sophistication, quiet charm. It was his eyes – extraordinarily direct, yet patient, like he had a complete understanding of the person he was looking at.

She lowered her gaze, not wanting him to see inside her.

'Jo, you have nothing to explain. Nothing to feel guilty about. I just wanted to see how you're both doing. I don't want my coming here to make you uncomfortable.'

She gave a small shake of her head. 'It doesn't, and thank

you.' She breathed in and, surprisingly, felt herself relax. Relieved now that he had come and spoken so openly. She didn't feel she had to hide in shame now.

'He's not talking yet,' she said, keeping her voice low. 'But he's aware of what is happening around him. Before, he just stared forwards with a fixed look, not moving his eyes.'

'That sounds positive. He's reaching out. Just keep talking to him, so he knows you're here.'

His hands lay loosely in his lap, his fingertips pressing together. 'I'm sorry about what happened to you. In your last job. It must have affected you a great deal.'

She gave a short laugh. 'It changed everything. One moment I felt the outing had gone well with no mishaps, the next an avalanche of fear at realising Ruby was missing. I can't describe the terror that came over me so suddenly. I took off, running back the route we came, knocking on doors, stopping any passer-by to have seen her, not knowing where she had gone. Sam shouldn't have been with me. I rang to tell them he wasn't well, but we had a new intake that morning, so it was all hands on deck and I couldn't get the time off.'

'So you went in because it was busy, and took him with you because he was unwell.'

There was no judgement in his voice.

She nodded miserably. 'He was never normally in my charge at the nursery. One of the rules. If you had your own child there, another staff member minded them. But his key worker wasn't keen for me to leave him. She had a new toddler starting. She suggested fresh air might do Sam good. So he came with us on the outing and was fine until we started back. He started lagging and his face felt warm. I took my eyes off the group while I gave him Calpol. It must have been then that Ruby wandered off.'

'So you stopped,' he commented.

'Just for a moment. To give him medicine.'

'And how many staff were on the outing?'

'Three of us.'

'Were the other two members aware Sam was unwell?'

'Well, yes. They had to know why we were taking him. He wouldn't normally be with us.'

'What about headcounts? Was one done before you continued?'

'Yes. By my colleagues. But they included Sam in the count, so thought they had all ten children.'

'Did you mention all of this afterwards?'

'Initially, no. I was too distraught about Ruby breaking her arm. Poor thing fell over while all on her own. The next day, the manager called me to the office, said it was a serious incident and had been reported as a safeguarding issue to the police. I said I'd write it all down, say exactly what happened. She then looked at me like she didn't want to tell me something. I'm thinking the worst. Maybe Ruby was seriously ill, hit her head or something. I was terrified.

'But that wasn't it. Ruby was at home with her mum, safe and sound, with a plaster cast on her arm. No, the thing she seemed reluctant to say was to do with me. She wanted to know why I took Sam on the outing. Why I broke policy. Why I thought that was all right to do.

'I explained what happened. Every detail. When I got to the end, she asked me what exactly Sam's key worker said. I answered truthfully: fresh air might do Sam good.

'From there, everything snowballed. I was dismissed with immediate effect for gross negligence, for failing to follow policy, for a disregard of the consequences that resulted in a child getting injured after going missing from my care.'

Jo breathed in deeply, shaking her head. 'There was nothing I could have done or said after that.'

A silence fell, giving Jo time to calm her nerves. It was the first time she'd ever spoken to someone other than Pete about what happened. Even after all this time, it was hard to relive it.

'Pete and I ended up broke. It was several weeks before I could even force myself to enquire about Universal Credit or Jobseeker's Allowance. They apply a sanction if you're sacked, and it was months before I could claim any benefits. I couldn't even look for a job, as losing my job meant also losing free child-minding at the nursery for Sam. Plus, who would give me a reference? The shame was unbearable.

'I budgeted where I could, but with only Pete's salary coming in those first several months, we went into the red. Our rent was twelve hundred a month, then on top of that we had gas, electricity, insurance, tax for Pete's car, phones – the bills didn't stop. It broke us. In more ways than one, as you can see.

'Last November, before Pete met you, we'd been given notice to vacate our home by the landlord for being in arrears with the rent. When we moved into the home you gave us, we paid what we owed before the landlord could put it in the hands of debt collectors. For Pete, your offer was a dream come true. You saved us from being out on the streets.

'I didn't think beyond that, or how long we would stay, but I can't lie. The hope of one day getting a reference from someone like Claire... it would open the door to being employable again. It would allow us to start over. Pete let me think you knew, and this was the reason for not having to give a reference. Then that first day I met you, I just knew you weren't aware of my past. He denied it at first, then admitted I was right. Whatever cover-up story you were given, it wasn't the truth. But I should never have just gone along with it.'

His attentive silence made her conscious of how long she'd been talking. She forced a light laugh. 'Anyway, enough of that. Can't keep living in the past. I've seen what doing that has done. I'm now a suspect without credibility.'

His gaze was steady. Jo hoped she hadn't bored him with her sob story.

Then he spoke. 'The night I met your husband, he showed me a photograph of his family. I sensed you were a good mother. Do you remember that first day when I met you and Sam? His eyes were like saucers as he gazed in awe at the surrounding land and proclaimed it the most beautiful place in the world. Better even than Butlin's, which he said Mummy and Daddy liked, but he didn't want to go to ever again. Too noisy, he said. Adorable child. That comment – so honest and innocent.'

He paused, remembering the moment, before speaking again. 'Your diligence was compromised by having charge of Sam. When you're able, and feeling stronger, you should claim for wrongful dismissal in a civil court. Anthony Clark would agree with me, I think. You have a strong case.'

What he was saying was clearly meant to be kind, but it was also pointless. Who would believe her after all of this? She was about to suggest it was a pipe dream when she saw him hold his head, pressing his palm to his forehead, his eyes screwed shut.

'James, are you all right?'

He breathed in and out through his mouth, slowly.

'I've got some paracetamol if you'd like some?'

He sat still for several more seconds, then opened his eyes. 'I've got migraine tablets in the car. I'll take them. But thank you.'

He used the edge of the bed to help himself up, before smiling reassuringly. 'Home to my own bed, I think. Before I get too comfortable here.'

'Thank you for coming,' she answered back.

'My pleasure. And, Jo, I want to thank you for the care you've given my children.'

As the door closed behind him, she sighed heavily, feeling out of sorts. In the longest conversation she'd ever had with him, she revealed her innermost thoughts. She wished there had been a way to have had this talk long before now, or someone like him had been around when it happened. People like him saved people like her from drowning, and let them carry on with their lives, instead of hiding away in shame.

It had come too late to save her. The wheels were already in motion. Sam would be given to his father, while she...

There was only one option left to her. She had to run.

SIXTY-TWO

The hours ticked by. Claire expected the phone to ring, but prayed it wouldn't and the front door would open instead and James would come home.

She hadn't been able to contact him since the call he abruptly ended. Several times she was tempted to ring the ward and see if he was there, but had been too afraid to follow through as she dreaded hearing something had happened. Something involving her husband and the police.

She'd been equally tempted to phone Jo, but again was too afraid in case she heard the worst. That James had told her everything. She was fixated on the idea that this is what he had done – erased their future together on this very night.

She couldn't help but note the bitter irony: exactly thirty years after losing her father, she now faced the loss of the only other man she had ever loved. Losing control lost her father to her. When she rushed at him she never expected him to turn his back, but instead take her in his arms and tell her he was sorry for what she was going through. Instead he left her alone – her ten-year-old mind in shock staring at the Juliet balcony – her father no longer there.

There was control in what James was doing. He was choosing his conscience over their unity – something far more persuasive than she could ever be. She'd been battling his conscience for years, hoping it never came to him settling it at the expense of her peace.

She wanted to run before the news broke. Take Phoebe and Lottie away from all the unpleasantness. Their lives would never be the same. They could never be carefree children anymore. Everything they knew would change. They would no longer go to the same school, or keep the same friends, or live in this home. All of it would have to go if they were to ever find peace again. It was not a future she cared to dwell on.

Her birthright, her name, would be immortalised as a time of unsavoury history. Her ancestral home, Beckley House, forever tainted. Her children would never want to be associated with its name. It would no longer be a place of beauty, but a place to avoid, relegated to a distant memory and no longer important, until it was little more than the name of a place they once knew.

That's what he had chosen for their future. She didn't know if she could ever forgive him. She had loved him through thick and thin, and loved him more in those hours they shared this evening than she ever thought possible. All doubt transcended, they were stronger than they had ever been. But he had taken that strength to the opposite extreme, and she could not stop him.

With a sickening shudder, she heard the front doorbell ring. It would be the police. She wouldn't think beyond this or prepare for any outcome. She didn't want to remember anything other than how she remembered seeing him in her bed. His eyes, so direct, looking in hers, while he made love to her.

She gripped her hands together and twisted the wedding ring on her finger, searching for the strength to open the door.

Channelling the strength of her grandmother, she masked the fear on her face. She was a Beckley. From a strong bloodline. She would hold her head high and not bend.

The most senior police officer had come to give her the news, perhaps to afford some dignity and privacy for what he was about to tell her. DI Stone stood at the door alone.

SIXTY-THREE

Moraine could see Jo was unsettled by her visit, which was understandable. Apart from it being very late, Moraine's distrust and holding back had caused Jo to be reserved. She was avoiding conversation and keeping quiet. Her welcoming smile was only for John, her greeting a connection to him. 'Hi, John F. Kennedy.'

She felt guilty about failing her. Jo's face bore witness to all the trauma of the last few days. The stress had taken youthful fat from her cheeks and drooped the corners of her mouth.

Moraine couldn't even tell her in what direction the investigation was now going. She had already ignored the task Stone had given her, as had Kennedy, both agreeing they were not comfortable having Sam out of sight. It was not enough that the ward had entrance doors that automatically locked and a camera outside the unit. If someone wanted in, they'd find a way in. They were not taking the chance of that happening.

The suspect was a watcher and would look for an opportunity. They'd managed once to snatch him without being seen. They could do so again.

Moraine didn't know how Kennedy coped with having four

children. All the normal everyday worry of keeping them safe. It was no longer enough to say, 'don't talk to strangers,' 'mind the roads.' The dangers could be right in the home.

Children could be targeted by phone, or sitting in front of a computer. Paedophiles, pretending to be children, used chat rooms to make contact, establish trust and then sit back and wait for the right piece of information to lead them to their victims.

Stone was leading them towards the possibility of James Howell being a person of interest. He'd mentioned the man's name a number of times. His father's name, friend's, mother-in-law's, the name of his home.

She knew no one was exempt, but she struggled to see how it could be him. She wanted to believe, needed to believe, that someone in his position is someone good and trustworthy She wasn't convinced. And thought that if anyone was guilty, it was more likely to be someone like Pete Jenkins. She wouldn't put it past him to have meddled in some way, seen an opportunity to make Jo look guilty. He'd not once defended her. But according to Stone, he was NFA. It must mean he was in the clear for the hours of Saturday morning. It might not have been him to leave the love nest, to go out to buy a newspaper, but Chrissy Banner.

She looked at Jo. Her focus was on Sam, stroking his hand. His eyes were open, light blue like his mum's. He could so easily have met with the same fate as the buried child. They were yet to determine if the child was male or female, but Stone seemed sure it was Matthew Lambert.

The encounter between Jo and his mother seemed like a hallucination. Appearing out of nowhere, then disappearing just as quick. Why had Marley Lambert gone to Beckley House? To commiserate with Jo on her loss? Moraine had seen the photographs of her son, and the likeness between him and Sam was remarkable. It must have been a shock to see Sam's image on the news. It must have felt as if she was looking at her son.

She checked the time. Eleven forty. This time yesterday, she was about to get the call from Stone to tell her Sam had been found. And now there was another mother, unaware still, that they might have found *her* son.

Five years. How can any parent live through that? It could send them insane. They could never forget. Never give up. No respite. They'd look and look, searching every boy's face, seeing their son everywhere and nowhere, and then they'd—

A sudden realisation gripped hold of her mind, leaving her cold. She could see it... oh so clearly. The years of searching, never finding, then one day Marley Lambert sees a child that looks just like her son, despite knowing her son would now be eleven, not five. Living at Beckley House. She thinks the family who has him had taken him from her. Then she comes to Beckley House to show a photograph to this false mother to prove it is her son, and to justify what she has done – taken her child back.

She looked dazedly at Kennedy, wanting to share the staggering idea with him.

Her phone rang silently, on vibrate, suspending the thought. She whipped it out, saw it was Stone and made her way out of the room to answer the call.

She listened to her new orders, shaken by what she heard.

SIXTY-FOUR

As soon as PC Kennedy and Moraine left, Jo got her purse out. She would need money. There was a cash machine in the hospital by the café. If she was quick, she could draw three hundred out just before midnight, then wait a few minutes and draw out the same amount again after midnight.

She was confident Pete wouldn't notice. He was great at zapping his card at a till, but ask him his pin number and he didn't have a clue. He wouldn't know the money had gone until he got a statement, and by then it wouldn't matter. She'd be gone.

It wasn't enough, but it would get them to Fishguard by coach, then a ferry to Dublin. She wouldn't need to show passports, as long as she had a photo ID. From there, flee to somewhere remote until she could decide their next move.

Northwest Mayo. She'd been there as a child with her father, in search of her mother's remaining relatives. All except a distant cousin were gone. She remembered the wilderness at the edge of the ocean, and not seeing any people.

About to leave the room, she heard Sam's voice. 'Mummy.'

A lump swelled immediately in her throat. Her little lamb.

Returning to his bed, she went to him. Smoothing his face with gentle fingers, she spoke softly to him. 'Hello, my beautiful boy. I've been waiting to hear your lovely voice.'

'Mummy.'

He sounded croaky. His throat must be dry, being hydrated only with fluids through his veins. Now he was responsive, she'd give him sips of water. Pouring some into a beaker, she held it to his lips, and felt his soft hand grasp around hers to steady it. His stomach made gurgling noises as it was so empty.

She sat back in the chair. The money would have to wait. Sam getting well was far more urgent. They couldn't go anywhere unless he was well enough to travel. If he tolerated the water, she'd let the nurses know and see if they suggested something to eat. She was hoping so, feeling how weak he was while supporting his head.

She hoped by tomorrow he'd be much stronger. As for the psychological healing, she didn't know what the plan would be. Most likely therapy with a child psychologist as an outpatient over a period of time. But they couldn't stay for that. She'd have to get Sam well by herself. She would research treatment for child trauma, a traumatic event, emotional abandonment from being left on his own. She would do everything possible to get him better.

What she couldn't do was lose her window of opportunity. The route out of the ward and through the corridors to the exit was going to be nerve-racking. She would have to plan it for a period when nobody would notice him gone immediately.

That window could close soon, because at any moment they could come and arrest her. At the sight of Moraine and PC Kennedy, she'd thought that's what they were there to do. She'd sat rigid the whole time they were in the room, waiting for Moraine to say the word, for the handcuffs to go on, taking away her chance to run.

She felt Sam's fingers touching her palm. Her eyes hadn't

come off him the whole while she was thinking. He looked increasingly awake.

'How are you feeling?' she asked softly.

He moved his hand to his face and touched his cheek and nose, and gave a heart-rending answer. 'With my hand... I can see them.'

She dared to ask, 'Can you remember anything, Sam?'

She waited, anxiously, fearing the question could trigger memories he was trying to block out. It was foolish and far too soon to ask anything like that. Thankfully, his eyes looked calm.

He looked up at the ceiling, pointing at some stuck-on stars. 'You were cross with Daddy when I was in the bath.'

Jo was shocked. She was positive she'd hidden her real feelings, because she hadn't wanted him to see how angry she was with Pete. She remembered thinking Sam needed to see her calmness, but her anger had shown through.

She felt shameful. If Sam had died, this would have been the last thing he remembered of her. His remembering it meant it affected him.

She was too afraid to ask him if he remembered anything else. She couldn't recall showing her anger, but it was possible, with her mind filled with the voices of her and Pete in imaginary arguments, that she didn't hide her facial expressions. Perhaps that was why she also couldn't recall hearing Sam's voice after his bath. Her anger towards Pete drowning out every word Sam said, overwhelming any memory of what he said when she woke Saturday morning.

Logic was telling her he must have spoken. A memory of the untouched cereal and toast in his favourite dishes... did he say he wasn't hungry, and she let it go? He was always fussy in the mornings if offered food too early. He liked to be awake for ages before eating anything. She couldn't recall the details.

Sam in the bath Friday evening, and then waking with him beside her on Saturday morning, finding his toes cold and gently squeezing, was crystal clear in her mind. Moving her hand up his leg, she let her palm rest on the curve of his bottom and was relieved to find dry pyjamas. Not for herself, but for his sake.

Driving to the swimming pool – in the rear-view mirror she saw him asleep. He looked peaceful. The sunshades over the tinted glass made it dark in the back.

Maybe she had zoned out to everything else. Was it so implausible? Given the accumulation of two years of anxiety? What Sam told her about Pete making him wash his trousers, possibly closed her mind down.

Fear wormed into her belly. The blanks worried her. She couldn't recall him at the kitchen table, or squeezing toothpaste onto his toothbrush and combing his hair.

She gulped, trying to quell her alarm.

Had hearing what Sam said tipped her over? After the trauma of losing her job, carrying the guilt, the feeling of worthlessness, the hiding away, the feeling everything was her fault. Had she gone temporarily insane? Was Pete right? He didn't think Sam should be in her care.

Was she blind to reality?

How could she ever know if she was not sound of mind? She needed a professional to tell her. The specialist trauma-informed counselling she was still waiting to have. Maybe her mind had been waiting too long for this help. Maybe the police and the social worker were right to watch her.

Maybe Sam wasn't in safe hands.

SIXTY-FIVE

Claire had to disturb Bernice again and ask her to mind the children while she was gone. She told her James's car had broken down and that he needed her to fetch him. She gave her the audio monitor so she wouldn't have to get up, just listen out for either of them getting out of bed.

She'd put on something more formal after DI Stone departed, to present an outwardly confident image, and styled her hair into a sleek low bun, wearing her Cartier earrings. As the wife of James Howell, she was not to be trifled with. She was there to support her husband and preserve the dignity of his name.

With the keys to the Mercedes in her hand, she was ready to leave.

At one in the morning, the country lanes were empty. She drove in silence, just noting the landmarks as she passed, her mind otherwise blank. Bath came into view with lights twinkling across the city, she drove down the steep, winding hill to her destination.

She parked in an outside car park and checked the board by the payment machine. It was pay on exit, accepting both card and cash. She headed to the entrance, swishing through the automatic door. Adjusting her eyes to the bright interior, she made her way to the reception window. A woman in a uniform blouse looked up from a monitor with an enquiring look.

Claire spoke immediately. 'I believe my husband, James Howell, is here. Can you take me to him, please?'

The woman's eyebrows rose slightly at the blunt request, her stare considering if Claire was a problem customer. She picked up a phone and spoke to someone. 'Mr Howell's wife is here.'

Her eyes returned to Claire. 'They're with your husband at the moment. Shouldn't be long, if you care to take a seat while you wait.'

Claire opened her mouth, but no words would come out. She looked around the waiting room for a seat. Packed, even at this time of night. It was no wonder the NHS was at breaking point. Half the people looked like there was nothing wrong with them, certainly nothing that needed urgent attention. Probably using the place instead of going to their GP. Or to a chemist.

She found a seat opposite a man working to dig out a splinter from his finger. A woman two seats from him was showing her giggling companion the graze on her knee and demonstrating she had full movement of her leg. She'd probably fallen over from walking in a pair of what looked like platform slippers.

What was wrong with these people, that they couldn't put a plaster on, or learn basic first aid? They would rather abuse overstretched resources. She couldn't abide the waste, the lack of common sense, the expectations of all these people sitting in this waiting room while ambulances were queuing outside to bring in those that needed emergency help.

She turned her gaze away to keep hold of her composure. She had more important things to worry about, like what she might find out soon. DI Stone told her very little: James had been found in his car and taken to the hospital. What did that even mean?

The fact the inspector came to tell her James was in hospital had to mean he knew or thought James was guilty of a crime. He wouldn't involve himself otherwise. High-up police officers didn't visit homes to tell a wife her husband was in hospital. He must have had a reason, and James must have given him one.

She clasped her hands to hide the slight tremor and took steadying breaths. What did he tell them? she wondered. She loved him dearly. But if he'd confessed, she really wasn't sure she'd be able to forgive him. Maybe he didn't want forgiveness – it was less important to him than his need to right wrongs. He couldn't change who he was any more than he could change the past. She just wished he loved his life with her more.

SIXTY-SIX

For someone on the brink of death only a short while ago, James Howell made a quick recovery. This was primarily because of where he was found, in his car in the hospital car park, and by whom he was found, a paramedic who instigated immediate help and administered naloxone, the reversal drug for an opioid overdose.

Bare chested and propped against a pillow, his eyes acknowledged their presence. Leads attached him to an ECG to monitor his heart. An intravenous needle in the crook of his elbow gave him fluids. The doctor Stone had spoken to said it was all right to talk to him – his condition was now stable. Curtains around his bed provided privacy, and the bay beside him was empty so there was no one to overhear.

Moraine felt deep disillusionment. There could be no other reason than guilt for James Howell trying to end his own life. Her gaze fixed on the machines around him, because she couldn't look him in the eye. Maybe he was sorry he survived. Stone would get the truth out of him now.

Stone was rubbing the back of his neck as if unsure how to

begin. Placing his large hand on the bedside rail, he inhaled softly.

'How are you feeling?'

Moraine stole a look at James Howell. He gave a light shake of his head.

'I had hoped to slip away,' he replied in a frank tone. 'I got tired of life, Inspector.'

Stone gave another sigh. 'I'm sorry to hear you felt there was no other option.' His concern sounded genuine.

'Why are you here, Inspector?'

Stone ignored the question. 'There was no other reason, then, for taking this path?'

Howell gave him a direct look. 'Such as?'

Stone tapped his fingers on the bedrail, holding the look with one of his own. 'I don't know. Any number of reasons. Perhaps with all that's happened, it became too much. Sam Jenkins, a child you know, residing on your property, disappears when in the care of his mother. And today, the remains of another child were found on the property of someone else you know, Elsbeth Crosby.

'I believe your father was her solicitor for many years. Sam was found in Mrs Crosby's outhouse. It's derelict. A dumping ground for rubbish. Someone thought it was okay to dump a child there. It was only by sheer luck that Mrs Crosby went in the outhouse late Sunday night and discovered him.'

Howell gazed at him wordlessly. Moraine detected no change in his demeanour when he heard about the discovery of a child's remains. Not even a faster heart rate on the monitor.

'Mm-hmm, no answer then,' Stone commented, before raising eyebrows to emphasise his surprise. 'How well would you say you know the Crosbys' farm? Do you know the outhouse I'm referring to?'

Howell treated the question with a grim look. 'I know the

building you're referring to. It went to ruin a decade ago. I advised Elsbeth to stop using it for storage.'

'So you know the farm well. You visit there often.'

'Often? No, Inspector. Possibly once or twice a year.'

Stone tapped his fingernails on the metal rail. 'Can you think of anyone who might know the farm well enough to do this?'

'You mean the outhouse,' Howell contradicted. 'Not the farm.'

'Let's not be pedantic, Mr Howell.'

'I agree, Inspector, but let's at least be accurate when discussing the location where the child was discovered. One doesn't have to know the entire farm to choose a building, only the means to access the place.'

Stone gave a nod of acknowledgement. 'They would indeed. They'd need to know it was in a remote area, and no longer in use. They'd need a four-wheel drive to make it up that track, or a vehicle narrow enough to stay centre of the deep tracks made by tractors in years gone by. Not nice for Mrs Crosby, finding him there. She thought the boy was dead. Then discovering a second child had been buried on the land. It seems strange, don't you think, the same location used to commit a second crime?'

Moraine was becoming concerned that Stone would carry on questioning Howell without him being cautioned. Howell drove a Mini Hatch, with a front-wheel drive. With the engine located over the driving wheels, the extra weight offered good traction. Hinting at what vehicle may have been used was failing to elicit any sign of a confession.

She tried to signal her worry to Stone. Stone blanked her, continuing the conversation.

'You can see why I might wonder if there's another reason for you taking the path you took. A lot of connections. The remains have yet to be identified. Curiously, though, Jo Jenkins might have met the child's mother on Sunday. Marley Lambert. On your property. We're presently using DNA to determine if the remains belong to Matthew Lambert. A shock for them, if so. Five years is a long time for them to have waited for him to be found.'

James Howell shook his head, an unreadable expression on his face.

Stone fell silent. There was a lot riding on what Howell said next.

'I have a grade four brain tumour.'

Stone looked genuinely shocked. His *'Really?'* in no way intended as sarcasm but spoken in genuine surprise. 'You don't look like a man who is ill.'

Moraine was equally taken aback. James Howell looked like a man who had many years ahead of him.

Howell raised his shoulders in a shrug. 'I know. But this clever cancer can only arrive as grade four. When it presents – no matter what the treatment – it's terminal. I was given six months, and that was in July. I didn't want my family to witness all that. So please don't mention my medical condition to my wife. It's my business alone. It would have been kinder for me to just slip away.'

Stone raised his gaze to Moraine, his voice low, as if saying this only to her. 'Seems I was mistaken.'

He stood still, his expression drawn, digesting this new information. Tucking his hands in his pockets, he rocked back on his heels as if unsure which way to turn. He took a deep breath and held it, his strong white teeth biting down on his lower lip.

Lowering his gaze to Howell with a confused expression on his face, he shrugged as if to say *help me out here*, before expelling his held breath. 'I was sure there'd been another reason.'

Howell looked back at him, saying nothing.

Moraine was reeling. After Stone expressed his sympathy, they left the man to rest. She followed Stone outside the building and gulped some fresh air. Stone studied her face intently, his typical self-assurance giving way to concern.

'Fuck sake,' he said under his breath. 'What the fuck now?'

Moraine didn't know. From his words, it sounded like he still thought Howell was their suspect.

He wrapped his large hands around the back of his neck, staring intently at the doors they'd come out of.

'He's one clever man,' he shared with her. 'There isn't a better reason for ending your life. Some might even think it noble. He's never going to admit to another reason. What he said in there, about not wanting his family to have to witness all that? He's going to take what he did to the grave.'

Moraine cast about for a better answer. She couldn't be as certain as Stone. She had to ask him. 'How can you be so sure it's him, sir?'

A resigned look spread across his face. 'Because, Raine, he's not denying that there's another reason for trying to end his life.'

Moraine didn't say anything. Her concern now was for Jo again. Would she become the sacrificial lamb if they couldn't get Howell? Because, at the moment, the police, the press and the public all thought her guilty. She didn't say any of this to Stone. It would be easy to go with that. Stop all other avenues of enquiry and settle for it being Jo. Case solved. Pats on the back all round.

She hoped not. She hoped Stone had enough integrity to keep going after what he believed, and not just settle for a convenient result.

SIXTY-SEVEN

Sam ate a thin piece of bread and chocolate spread, and a strawberry yogurt. The nurses were pleased with him. They'd helped sit him over the side of the bed so he could wee in a cardboard bottle, and now his temperature was normal, earning him more pleased looks.

'Clever boy, Sam,' one of them said as they straightened his covers before leaving them alone again.

Her own significance seemed to be diminishing. He hadn't spoken to her again since telling her about the bath incident. He drank from the beaker she held to his lips, but didn't make eye contact. And he didn't look at the pages of the Ladybird storybook, instead keeping his gaze on the ceiling. It was like she wasn't there. As if he had tuned her out.

She wanted to touch his soft skin, but feared he'd pull away. She felt he would reject her urge to comfort him and hold his hand in hers. His silence told her he didn't want to engage with her. She no longer knew how to get him to trust her again.

She sat very still, giving him space, hoping he could relax. James had said to keep talking to him to let him know she was there, but what if he didn't want her there?

She reached for a drawing pad and pencil that she had taken out of the carrier bag earlier, and set it on her lap, turning to a clean page. She started by drawing a bird and talking quietly.

'I'm drawing all the things you love. I'm good at birds, they're easy. Then I'll draw woodlice, and some ants. A spider's web with lots of small spiders. Maybe a worm, and a snail. You do snails better than me, though. And some leaves for them to sit on. And some water for them to drink. Maybe I can draw an insect farm, where they can all live.'

He softly spoke. 'They like bricks with holes in, and pine cones.'

Jo pressed her lips together as they trembled, keeping her eyes wide to stop them from filling with tears. 'That's right. They like places where they can hide.'

'And straw to keep them warm,' he added.

'That's right. It will help to keep them dry. They should have lots of little places they can play in.'

'And play with their friends and be with their mummies.'

Jo swallowed the heaviness from her throat. 'Well, yes, that's very important, playing with their friends and being with their mummies.'

'And if they don't see their mummies, their friends can help them find them.'

'That's right, Sam.'

'They won't lose them then,' he said in a tearful voice.

'That's right, Sam. Then they won't lose them.'

In a sudden movement he turned in the bed and climbed onto her lap, his head finding her breast to rest against as he clung to her, sobbing. She gathered him in, as close as she could, and smoothed his hot wet cheek, telling him over and over she was there... 'I'm here... I'm here... I'm here...'

The cry from her throat was blessedly silent. He needed her to be so strong. This time together was to fill him up with all her love, so that afterwards he would remember her this way.

There were so many things she wanted to tell him she was sorry for, but none of that was as important as him feeling her love. She tucked her head close to his so she could draw in every scent of him. She would hold him like this for as long as she could. It didn't matter if her love for him would also break her heart, so long as he could feel in this moment she was with him, and have this memory for when she was not. He could look back on this and know she never wanted to leave him. Never wanted to be without him. Never wanted to say goodbye.

SIXTY-EIGHT

Claire stared at her husband with guilt in her eyes, his unadorned explanation of what he had done filling her with remorse. That he would choose this way to be best for his family showed how much he loved them. He hadn't unravelled, but had chosen instead not to live.

Why couldn't he have believed her when she said she could stop everything? That she would set Jo free, and they would never revisit anything like this again. She had thought he had finally let go and was choosing *them*.

She moved closer to bring his hand to her face. 'Why, my darling, did you have to do this?'

His eyes glimmered with tears. 'I thought he would be safer with me gone.'

His words shook her to the bone. His concern was for Sam. It was his only reason for leaving his life. His honesty wouldn't allow him to console her. He wasn't even trying to make it look accidental, to soften the blow. What had he feared? The same ending as what happened to Matt? He would have atoned for his sins. Leaving her with the fallout – every newspaper would show his image and speculate on the cause of an eminent barrister taking his own life. No thought for his own children, how they would suffer when they heard their father had taken his own life.

Mens rea – the guilty mind.

She took his hand off her face and laid it down by his side, moving her chair further away so she wasn't so close to him. She could feel him looking at her, pondering her reaction.

How could she control the situation? How could she keep what happened out of the papers and prevent it becoming public knowledge?

She resented him for putting her in this position, but had to force the negativity away. She couldn't let her disappointment spiral out of control but needed to recover her strength and move forwards. She could only look towards the future when this situation was behind them. And if James ever decided to do something like this again, he better well do it right and make certain it looked like an accident. If his intent was to leave his life, let him do so with minimal fuss.

He caught hold of her hand. She fought the urge to pull it away. His expression was grave, sending a chill down her spine. What else could he say that she hadn't already heard?

He cleared his throat. 'They've found the remains of a child on Elsbeth Crosby's farm.'

Her attempt to hide her shock was futile. She couldn't move her limbs to back away from what he was telling her. Her mind was spinning. Her gut instinct told her she needed to get her children and run. After all this time, they had finally found Matt. It could only be him, or James wouldn't be telling her.

She rose stiffly from her chair, ready to come apart in a thousand pieces if she didn't cling to her inner strength. His words fell like a blow on her head as she reached the door.

'Claire, think about Marley. She can now put her son to rest.'

Outraged by the one-sidedness – of protecting him for years – she spun to confront him.

'Damn you, James. Damn you for saying that. You should never have told me. You should have just been the husband I loved. All I ever wanted was to be your wife and have you by my side. You should have walked away from the beginning, not let me first fall in love with you and then put that in my head. You killed a child, James. I forgave you that. But to then surround yourself with the constant reminder was so self-indulgent of you.

'When our son was born, I thought it would give you the strength to live with what you had done. Instead, after our precious boy died, I knew you blamed yourself, that it brought up all the guilt you had about your brother. But it was a tragedy, we didn't do anything wrong; we didn't fail our little boy. But you kept finding ways to punish yourself. Matt. Sam… You'd go to your office and sit with that photograph.

'You say it's hard to talk about certain things – well, think long and hard about the circumstances when Matt disappeared. He would have stayed with us while Marley and Stuart were away. I would have fetched him from school, instead of saying we were busy. But I was too afraid it would make you vulnerable seeing him, and make you do something foolish. Having that constant fear that you would reveal what you did.

'You did that to me, James. That's why Matt is dead. You wouldn't let go of the past.'

SIXTY-NINE

Late Tuesday morning, Stone informed the team that the remains of the child were identified as Matthew Lambert. However, the forensic autopsy could not determine the cause of death. The parents had been informed, and a press conference would be held at noon.

Fingerprints matching those of Elsbeth Crosby had been found on the foil blanket that was wrapped around Sam Jenkins. Fingerprints, found on the Spider-man shoes, were a match for Joanne Jenkins.

An update on Sam informed them he was fully awake, and an officer was in place outside the boy's room. The psychiatrist in charge of his care was saying there was some indication of amnesia. The memory of what happened can be wholly or temporarily lost. There was evidence of benzodiazepines showing in a urine test, which may be the cause of it. As so far, with baby steps questioning, the only reference Sam made to his abduction was Mummy was gone. From the child's point of view it was a blessing, but not so much for the investigation.

Moraine had been waiting for Stone to say that Jo was no longer a suspect, but was disappointed when the briefing ended with no mention of it. Stone must surely realise the torment she was going through while waiting for the moment her son was taken into care? This wasn't fair, and she couldn't leave it like this.

Kennedy put a hand on her arm as she started to follow Stone, concern on his face. 'You are scowling.'

'I am angry,' she flashed back. 'He's just leaving Jo to sit there without her knowing what's going on. He already decided she's not our suspect, so what's he playing at?'

'Don't go in guns blazing. Lose the anger first.'

Moraine huffed petulantly, but knew he was right. She hadn't shared with him what James Howell revealed, or Stone's conclusion afterwards. She couldn't talk about it unless Stone revealed it, and he was respecting Howell's wishes.

Calmer, she gave him a thumbs up, and made her way to the SIO's office.

She tapped on the door before entering. From his comment, he didn't seem surprised to see her.

'I wondered how long it would take for you to find your way here. There's no need to fret, Raine. I can see it on your face. I'm leaving to see Mrs Jenkins shortly, let her know we're exploring other leads, and you can tag along if you like.'

Moraine breathed a sigh of relief, which Stone shook his head at. Then he spoiled the moment by adding, 'I'll be honest. I'm up a creek with this one. I'm a hundred per cent convinced Mr Howell is guilty in some large measure, but I haven't quite managed to convince myself Mrs Jenkins is completely innocent. That's what a lack of evidence does for you. Keeps you twisting in the wind, looking for answers.'

Moraine could see this was difficult for him. It would be on his head if he got it wrong. That and having an unsolved case. Two unsolved cases, if no evidence was found that led them to who buried Matthew Lambert. It could be a tough time ahead for him, answering to his superiors for his decisions. Including this next one. Moraine hoped he didn't change his mind.

He was pulling his coat on when the phone on his desk rang. Moraine waited as she watched him shrug it back off and drop it on his chair, hoping it would be a short delay.

He answered, listened, and hung up, then gave a breathy, low whistle before raising his eyebrows at her.

'Well, that's a turn-up for the books. James Howell wants to give a statement. He's waiting in reception. Mrs Jenkins, I'm afraid, will have to wait.'

Moraine stood like a statue, wondering how Stone could be so calm.

'Raine.' Stone was watching her from the door. He gave a small shake of his head. 'Don't get your hopes up. He's probably here to ensure his medical records are protected. He knows we can't share his data for non-law enforcement purposes and is probably here to make it official.'

She breathed out her disappointment, following Stone out of the door, hoping the man wasn't wasting their time.

SEVENTY

Jo thought back and forth the entire morning, frightened to make a decision. After holding Sam all night, she resigned herself to letting him go until she saw how much better he was, having the doctor confirm it, and realising how close it might be to his discharge.

He wasn't ready for this parting. He was only just beginning to feel safe. They would reverse every bit of healing unless she could prevent it.

She could smell the lunch trolley on the ward. It was always busier when they were giving out the food. And Sam could do with a bath. It was the only idea she could come up with to get him out of the room. She wouldn't be able to take the IKEA bag under the watchful eye of the police officer outside, but she could wrap some of Sam's clothes in a towel and take that with her instead.

Quietly, while Sam was looking at a book, she went to the back of the locker and pulled the items she needed out of the bag, grabbing her coat as well. Crouching down in front of the locker, she used the space inside the cupboard to hide Sam's clothes in the towel. She stuffed the puffer jacket in her shoulder bag as well. Standing, she checked around the room as if looking for something, but actually making sure her purse, phone and charger were in the bag and not left lying around.

Finally, with nothing more to do but take this chance, she breezed out of the room, calling over her shoulder to Sam that she was running him a bath. She stopped at the food trolley and was pleased to see they hadn't even started. She stopped a nurse rushing by.

'I'm just giving Sam a bath. But anything with chips is good.'

The nurse nodded and gave a harried smile. 'Be another ten minutes, but sausages and chips then.'

Jo ducked into a bathroom, put the plug in the bath and turned on the tap, letting the water run over her forearm. She returned to Sam, making a show of drying her arm, leaving the door open for the officer to hear.

'Right, Sunshine. A bath before sausages and chips.'

Sam, thankfully, didn't protest and hopped off the bed to follow her. Jo kept her eyes averted and her fingers crossed, praying the officer would stay put, and feeling cautious relief as she saw his reflection in another cubicle window still in place.

In the bathroom, she shut the door and explained to Sam that she had to get him dressed. They must hurry because they only had a little while to sneak outside and play before someone came looking for them for lunch.

He was five, and the thought of playing was enough to make him compliant. Yet, while relieved, it felt wrong to be tricking him after what he'd been through. She was tricking him into being abducted again, which felt so morally wrong.

His innocent face showed his trust in her, and she couldn't consider stopping now. He needed her. With a renewed sense of purpose, she dressed him quickly in plain joggers and top, a zip-up blue anorak, trainers and a plain cap on his head.

Panting with fear, she pulled a woollen hat over her hair

and turned her grey puffer jacket inside out, turning it black. Hanging her bag over her shoulder, she led Sam by his hand out of the bathroom door, keeping herself between him and the rest of the ward. Nurses were milling around the food trolley, parents standing close to choose dinner for their child. Jo kept her head lowered and hugged the other side of the corridor to pass them.

As she turned into the next corridor, she realised she and Sam could be mistaken for visitors who were leaving. Her heart pounding in her chest, she reached the exit door and tapped the release button on the wall. The doors opened onto a busy main corridor with people walking on both sides in opposite directions. She turned and picked Sam up in her arms, burying her face in his neck for a few precious seconds to feel him. His arm went around her shoulder. She kissed the top of his head before moving her legs in purposeful strides.

'Mrs Jenkins.'

Her insides froze with fear. Air caught in her lungs. Her legs moved faster, trainers slapping the floor, panting breaths wheezing out of her chest.

'Mrs Jenkins!'

The shock forced her to stop. Her body was trembling all over. Sam was clinging to her like a koala bear, whimpering in distress.

'Mrs Jenkins.' The voice was now right behind her.

Tears squeezed out of Jo's eyes. They had so nearly made it. She kissed Sam on his forehead, gently rocking him. 'It's okay, it's okay,' she whispered.

Then, summoning the courage, she turned and faced the social worker, her head high, not giving the woman the chance to speak. She gave her a steely glare. 'Did you really need to shout like that? Anyone would think it was a crime to take your child out for some fresh air. You frightened Sam with all your shouting.'

It was a performance she could be proud of, but it didn't work on the woman in front of her.

Her voice was flat and uncaring. 'Take Sam back to the ward, please, so I don't have to call security.'

Jo made her way slowly back to the ward, using every second to reassure Sam and telling him the sausages and chips were too yummy to wait, and the nurses wanted him to eat them all up. Mummy was hungry, too, so maybe she should get something to eat as well. And after lunch, he should draw lots of pictures so they could hang them up in the ward. All his favourite animals and insects. Daddy would want to see them as he would be coming soon. Then Mummy might have a little rest and Daddy could read to him.

She talked softly in his ear the whole way back, passing other children's rooms, seeing the censorial looks cast her way from the nurses and the parents standing around, watching. A nurse waited in Sam's cubicle for Jo to hand him over. Jo set him down on his bed, taking his shoes and coat off, lifting the cap from his head, retrieving his blue rabbit from her bag.

She snuggled it in to Sam's arm, before brushing her lips on the skin behind his ear.

'It's lunchtime now, beautiful boy. Eat it all up.'

She pulled a funny face at him as she backed out the door, and got a small giggle in exchange, taking the sound with her like a precious gift. Her brave and quiet little boy – he was the best thing to happen in her life. Awash with love, she moved out of sight away from the window, so Sam wouldn't see the police officer waiting for her, and wouldn't see the price of loving him buckle the legs from under her.

SEVENTY-ONE

Claire drank a shot of brandy, needing a stiff drink to recover from the uncomfortable phone conversation she'd just had with Anthony Clark. He'd been curious to know why she hadn't mentioned Marley Lambert's recent visit, when asked by the police about the woman Jo Jenkins said she saw. He wanted as much clarity as she could give him, in light of Jo being arrested a second time. Anything she thought worth mentioning that might help his client.

She put her lapse of memory down to the extraordinary circumstances, the constant flow of police officers coming and going, and the worry of all the reporters at the gates. She would, of course, correct the misunderstanding at once, and let the police know her brain that day had been like a sieve. The bizarre thing, she told him, was that Marley's brief visit hadn't registered with her as a lone woman, because she'd come with her husband, Stuart.

She rambled just enough to get him to soften his tone, and tell her why Jo was arrested again, but maybe not explain the cogs turning in his brain.

'It must be quite a shock that something similar happened

before, especially with you knowing both sets of parents. It must have reminded you immensely of the Lambert child's disappearance. Not to mention the worry of speculation.'

Her murmur of agreement brought the conversation to an end.

Her hands were shaking. Lying to DC Morgan had been a huge mistake. How could she now swear under oath that she saw Sam in the car with Jo? Disputing the theory that no one saw Sam with Jo was the largest hurdle to overcome, as far as she was concerned. That was the idea, and it would have worked if she'd done it sooner and not already told a stupid lie. She couldn't think of a way out of this for Jo – unless someone like Bernice or Dougie came forward and declared a sudden memory of Sam getting in the Range Rover.

She put her empty glass in the dishwasher, and the brandy back in the cupboard before Bernice noticed it was out. But she'd be surprised if Bernice noticed anything today. All morning she'd been half asleep, after staying awake to keep an ear out for the girls until Claire got home. Claire's explanation about James's car was swallowed whole. The Mini was at a garage. And James's whereabouts – sorting it out – giving credence to the story Claire told her last night. In reality, it was still with James.

Claire didn't know if he was still in hospital, or had been discharged or admitted to a psychiatric unit. She couldn't think about his personal welfare right now. The finding of Matt's body had been aired on the news when, thankfully, Bernice was out of the kitchen. Claire immediately switched the television off, hiding the remote in a drawer. It was hard enough to concentrate on even simple matters like slicing a loaf of bread, without having Bernice fall apart. She was hacking instead of sawing, making a mess of it. Bernice was equally clumsy, fumbling dishes and dropping both a plate and a cup on the floor.

She sighed wearily, getting herself ready to test Jo's get out of jail free card. She brought Bernice's attention to the breadboard. 'I've ruined your lovely loaf. I can't think straight after what I've just heard from Anthony Clark. Jo's been arrested again. I don't know how to help her, Bernice. I'm so tempted to lie and say I saw Sam with her, getting in the car. That's all the police have got. No one saw Sam with her. And now Jo has done something rash. She tried taking Sam off the ward without anyone knowing. She was caught by the social worker. Of all the people to be caught by, it had to be the one who's taking Sam away from her.'

Thankfully, Bernice's reaction was not to burst into tears or clasp her chest in panic. She was breathing steadily, moving Claire to one side so she could salvage the bread. Her face was as serious as Claire had ever seen it. Her voice was quiet, almost too difficult to hear, making Claire stand still to listen.

'When my husband was sent down for murder, there wasn't a person in the world could tell me it was wrong. He deserved it. He took the life of an innocent woman for the sake of getting away with a few pounds. Bad blood was in him. Then your husband showed me a way out of the shame. He must have sensed that was the biggest emotion I was feeling. Pure shame. Like a by-product of my husband, and all that entailed.

'It's a damn pity James didn't leave the same time as Jo that day. If he'd stayed and had breakfast like I urged him to, he might have seen Sam and Jo leaving. Who better for a witness?'

She wiped breadcrumbs from her hands onto her apron, then looked steadfastly at Claire. 'I'll say I saw the little lamb. I confused Saturday with Friday, as Jo usually works Saturdays.'

Claire's palms were clammy, her body trembling.

Bernice opened the cupboard beside her and pulled out the brandy, taking a clean glass from the cabinet above to pour a hefty measure and shaking her head in bemusement. 'You shouldn't have put it away. You need another one, the number of shocks you've had. Being a little numb won't hurt you.'

Claire was glad she was there. Her grandmother would have approved. She believed hardship was a necessary lesson – no better teacher to test your strengths. Bernice's had come to the fore. Her character suited this house – as she showed by how she dealt with her past.

Withstand the tests of time – never giving in.

SEVENTY-TWO

Stone and an interview specialist sat opposite James Howell, who had requested for Stone to be present and had declined a solicitor. Given that the evening before he was admitted to hospital after a suicide attempt, Stone was concerned that the interview could be excluded on the basis of unreliability if Howell was mentally unfit.

Howell produced his medical discharge summary, including a psychiatric evaluation, which carried out a Suicide Risk Assessment, putting him at low risk of further attempts.

He was cautioned, and all PACE safeguards were in place. Howell reassured the two officers that he was there of his own free will, without coercion or oppression, to confess to the crimes he had committed.

Moraine observed on a monitor. She had never witnessed anything like it. The barrister was ensuring that the police didn't fail in their job, going so far as to check with them that the recording equipment was working.

Without preamble, he admitted to the unlawful burial of Matthew Lambert on 4 October 2019. He took the body from a milking shed that used to be there in the north field on the Crosbys' farm. It was gone now. The child died on the second night after being taken from his school. He had stopped breathing, and no amount of trying to revive him could bring him back to life.

Stone's reaction was masked due to his experience of dealing with serious crime, but Moraine was betting his stomach was churning. It was the candour of Howell that shocked her the most. She couldn't reconcile the idea of a person who presents evidence of a crime to a jury, to the person who committed the crime. Both in the same room and both the same person. The prosecutor facing himself, the accused – bringing justice to himself.

Her mouth was bone dry as he provided details. He gave a description of the clothing the deceased was wearing and the exact location of the burial site. He described the preparations he carried out before burial – waiting for nightfall, before digging a grave in among a thicket of trees, a place that wouldn't be disturbed.

Then, as if none of that had been said, and with barely a pause, he admitted to the abduction of Sam Jenkins on 28 September this year, and of taking him to the same location as where Matthew Lambert was buried.

Moraine felt physically sick and would have used the plastic bin if not for the assistant chief sat next to her. His lips pressed firmly together – a sign he was moved as well. She jumped when he spoke to her, and was surprised by his comment.

'DI Stone will need more detail than this summary.'

As if hearing his superior's voice, Stone asked the question. 'Why?'

Moraine hunched forward, wanting to see how Howell responded.

His face was composed. Moraine's heart was racing,

expecting some dramatic explanation, but instead she heard a firm, polite, non-explanation.

'I don't have the answer to your question.'

The assistant chief slapped his hands against his thighs and stood up in a huff. 'Knew it! Not going to reveal the sordid details. The gall of him!'

With that, he departed, not waiting to see Howell being arrested. Moraine had the weird sensation she was about to cry. The closest she could come to understanding it was like feeling an idol had fallen. Howell represented virtue – he was a symbol of moral goodness and justice, and the values that represented. He had destroyed all that goodness and decency, making a mockery of what he stood for. He left those that served the law, like her, struggling to understand how he could be this way.

SEVENTY-THREE

Jo didn't think her legs would hold her.

'You can go.'

Stupefied, she couldn't move a muscle. Staring from DI Stone to Moraine, she couldn't believe it.

Moraine flashed her a smile. 'It's true. You're free. No further action.'

She felt she was emerging from quicksand, only half out, waiting to be pulled back in. Her lips stuck to her gums, her mouth was so dry. Her voice was wracked with emotion.

'You mean I can see Sam? They'll let me?'

Moraine took hold of her hands to guide her back into the chair she'd been sitting in when they entered the room. Hunching down in front of her, she gently squeezed Jo's hands, while watching her face.

Jo was surprised to see Moraine blink back tears. She shook her head sadly before giving a determined smile. 'No one is going to stop you, Jo. Social services have been informed, the ward has been informed, Pete has been informed. Everybody knows that you're innocent, and not guilty of any crime. And when you're ready, I'll drive you back to the hospital.'

Jo glanced at the man in charge. He nodded kindly at her and repeated it. 'You're free to go, Mrs Jenkins.'

Tears slid down her face. The words should have set her free, but she couldn't feel them. From thinking her life was over to this sudden release had numbed her.

'Jo.' Moraine was nodding her head as if understanding. 'I wouldn't be surprised if you need some counselling after this. You have been through a great deal of trauma. And now this – it probably doesn't feel real. It's going to take a while to adjust back to your life.'

The memory of leaving Sam on his bed, his small giggle, flashed through her mind. All the moments of fear, the aloneness, the invisibility – conscious all the time that she might never hold him again, then the fear of losing him again. All of it now welled up inside.

She barely registered reaching out, and didn't care anyway as she clung to Moraine and sobbed. She needed to be held while she shed this pain. It was the only way to make room for any joy.

SEVENTY-FOUR

Bernice took the call on the landline. James was in the Emergency Department, having had a seizure. She relayed the information to Claire in a daze.

A dozen thoughts flitted through Claire's mind. It must be from what he took last night. Causing a fit. He'd been in hospital all day, and she hadn't known. She hadn't rung. Or called anyone to see how he was. And now they were calling to say this had happened.

Her heart drumming in her chest, she threw on a coat and put on shoes. Letting Bernice take charge of the house and children, she was out of the door and in the car, driving to the hospital again, but this time in daylight, in heavy traffic, and with rain battering the windshield.

At the hospital she picked the same parking area and whipped through the automatic door, this time not needing her eyes to adjust to the bright lights.

She stopped. Near the reception desk she saw two people she recognised: DI Stone and DC Morgan. Telling herself they shouldn't be there – James's every medical crisis didn't need a police presence – she walked up next to them and gave her name to the receptionist. A light tap on her shoulder brought her around to face DI Stone.

'Mrs Howell, may I have a quick word?'

He gestured to a passageway that looked quiet. She followed him and DC Morgan, giving her permission for him to begin.

'I would have called but it happened so quickly. I was about to when a nurse let me know you'd been informed. We've been waiting for you to arrive.'

Claire tried not to react, taking a moment to decipher what was being communicated. Was he saying he was here when it happened? If so, why? Had James been speaking to him today? She needed DI Stone to explain. It would be quicker.

'What are you saying? Were you here with James when he had a seizure?'

His eyes flashed open in surprise, then he shook his head. 'No. It wasn't here that it happened. I believe your husband was discharged from the hospital this morning. It happened at the police station.'

Bernice's words rang in her ears. The things she called out while Claire was hurrying out the door.

Don't worry, don't drive too fast, don't forget to let them know his condition.

Her gaze turned to Moraine and she remembered their brief time looking at the wild garlic. She could see in the woman's eyes a sympathetic pity. *She knew.* They both knew. James had confessed. Her harsh words to him last night had made him talk. She had wanted to wound him, not have him ruin their lives. His leaving her to deal with the collateral damage: the pain that would be inflicted on their innocent children and the emotional harm done to all those who loved him. The aftershocks to everyone in their circle. All this suffering to come – all to salve his conscience.

She didn't want to see him. She didn't want to hear what he

had told them. Or have him repeat that she should think about Marley.

She made an attempt at being polite, forcing a strained smile at Moraine. 'Have you seen James? How is he?'

'He's lucid, but tired, and they're keeping him in for observation.'

She looked away. She didn't want this life. *This*, what he had done, binding them to this moment, *forever*.

She straightened her back and raised her head, surveying them for a few moments. People she hardly knew would now think they had the right to pick apart her life, examining it for everything bad or wrong.

Fastening a button on her coat that she had missed, she delivered a parting request.

'Please let him know I won't be visiting.'

SEVENTY-FIVE

Moraine was counting the hours until her shift ended, feeling exhausted by the lack of new developments in the investigations. The last three days had given them a big fat nothing. They had James Howell's confession, but it didn't seem nearly enough to explain these crimes.

She needed the weekend off, to have some time to set aside all the difficult emotions she was carrying around. Feelings of failure and worry and hurt. Thoughts she was suppressing. A boy buried, unearthed, and no explanation about why or how he died. It seemed inconceivable that all they could tell the parents was that he had been found.

Examination of the crime scene, often the best place to gather evidence, was ongoing. Soil was being sifted, layer by layer, for insects living where the corpse was found, feeding off decaying flesh, studying mating habits, life cycles, looking for everything that had leaked from the body into the earth. It could yield no end of scientific information, but it would not determine the cause of death.

It was hard to believe it was only seven days ago that Sam

went missing. A week when so much had happened. The week before was a doddle. Into bed, up for work, home to watch TV. She needed to decompress. Block the memories of broken people, broken marriages, an old lady serving tea in a cup and saucer, a small boy crying at seeing his mum.

It had been heartbreaking to witness. Taking Jo back to her son and seeing the stark relief on the child's face. The damage inflicted in just a few hours of her being taken from him was colossal. She had left the hospital hating her job, hating the police, hating social services, and hating Pete Jenkins. Sat there like he was in charge, telling Jo she was too late, and he was applying for full custody. She wanted to claw his face.

At least now Jo could be with her son without fear of him being taken from her, sitting by his bed like any other parent whose child was in hospital.

She jumped in her chair and nearly fell off it as a hand landed on her shoulder. Kennedy's laughing apology had her glare at him. Settling himself, he perched on her desk, back in his uniform. From his pocket he produced a bag of jelly snakes for her, with a flourish. It made her realise something nice: they had become friends.

He cast his eyes around at her colleagues on computers and phones, and lowered his head to tell her something quietly. 'They found something at the scene. A forensics mate of mine discovered it. Only just gone to the lab. That's all I know.'

Moraine's mouth opened wide. A tingle travelled down her spine. 'Please let it be something helpful,' she whispered back.

He stood up and sauntered his way through the CID department to the exit, leaving Moraine waiting in anticipation.

By four o'clock, she hadn't heard a thing. Not a single jungle drum. Either it was still being analysed or it wasn't an important find. She jumped for the second time when a heavier hand tapped her shoulder. It was Stone.

He gave her that look of his, then glanced at the bag of sweets. 'Too much sugar, Raine. Makes you hyper.' He then helped himself to the colourful jellies, chewing quickly before getting to the reason for his visit. 'If you're not busy, you might want to come along for this.'

She was off her chair in a flash and following his long strides, past his office and down the stairs to the ground floor. He stopped at an interview room with the door closed, and gave a brief explanation.

'A couple in there just got back from their honeymoon. They think they have a photograph of Sam Jenkins.'

Before she could react, he'd opened the door and was greeting the lightly suntanned pair. Moraine's first impression was that they looked too young to be married – barely out of their teens. They sat close together, holding hands.

The young man introduced them. 'I'm Luke, and this is my wife, Sadie. We just got back from Malta. We could only do six nights, as I'm about to be deployed to Cyprus.'

Moraine took a closer look at him. He hardly looked old enough to be in the army.

He caught her examining him and grinned. 'I'm twenty-eight, and still asked for ID.' He then got out his mobile phone, showing it to them. 'Anyway, the reason we're here: my mate who did the photos for our wedding emailed them to me this morning. Sadie and I looked at them on the plane. Then Sadie caught up with all her social media, and she saw on Facebook the police alerts for the missing boy. Well, we were both surprised, because it happened just as we were getting married, right next to the church.'

Sadie gave a soft sigh and a sad smile. 'We didn't know about the child's abduction. We didn't stay for the party as we could only have a quick honeymoon. No one let us know, probably didn't want to spoil our time away.'

'I can understand that,' Stone replied. 'And your friends were all very helpful. Taking the time to stop the celebrations to show us all the photographs they took with their phones. Your friend, the photographer, emailed us every image. But, regrettably, we didn't find a single image of the missing boy.'

'Nor did we,' Luke answered. 'But then Sadie remembered as we were leaving the church that I took photographs from the rear window of the wedding car of everyone cheering us off. So we looked through the photos, and you could have knocked our socks off, as we're suddenly looking at him in one of them.'

Stone gestured to the phone. 'Can you show me?'

Moraine felt a nervous tightening in her stomach as she watched Luke tap and slide his finger on the screen. He then turned the phone sideways, holding it with a finger and thumb, to pass to Stone.

Stone held the phone steady, not saying anything, as they stared at the image. His only reaction, heard by Moraine, was an intake of breath. He handed the phone back and reached in his jacket to take out a small wallet of business cards. He handed one to Luke.

'Can you email that to me, please? And when you get home, send me all the photographs that you took from the car.'

Luke placed the card on the table, concentrating while he emailed Stone the photograph of Sam, taking only a moment to raise his head and say, 'Done.'

Stone thanked the couple. 'We're very grateful to you for coming in. I hope you get to enjoy the weekend, before Luke's deployment.'

After showing them out, he told Moraine he'd be back. She sat quietly, almost numb. This was a week she would never forget. She felt like going home, having a good cry, and shutting out all the bloody horribleness.

His little green top had a crocodile on it.

Stone returned to the room in a sombre mood. He looked at the clock on the wall – quarter to five – then at Moraine. 'Do you want to finish on time?'

She shook her head.

'Okay, let's grab our coats, then. Gone cold out there.'

SEVENTY-SIX

Moraine drove, which allowed Stone to catch up with work on his phone. She parked and was about to get out of the car when Stone's phone rang. For most of the short call he just listened, then at the end he said thanks and put the phone in his pocket. Shaking his head, he said, 'It's a win-win today.'

They climbed out of the car and Moraine locked it, wondering what Stone meant.

At reception they were directed to a medical ward, then at the nurses' station they were directed to the patient's room. They entered quietly.

James Howell no longer looked a well man, his vitality gone. Stone quickly hid his look of dismay. He took off his jacket, loosened his tie, and carried a chair to sit by the side of the bed.

Howell smiled in amusement. 'This actually feels like a visit.'

'Sorry, no grapes.' Stone smiled back.

Moraine was happy to blend into the background, and found a windowsill to lean on.

Stone pulled out his phone and glanced at Howell. 'I'd like to show you something. Do you need glasses?'

Howell inclined his head to the bedside cabinet. 'On there somewhere. If you get a moment, could you wheel it around to my right side.' He nodded at his left arm, propped up on a pillow. 'The tumour gave me a stroke. The CT shows it's grown bigger.'

'That's a bummer,' Stone remarked, while moving the furniture. 'Should be a law against that.'

Howell gave a dry laugh. 'Hardly. It's only just beginning to flex its muscles.'

Moraine had to look away. Having this cruel cancer would be hard on anyone. It just seemed extra wicked to be destroying a brain like Howell's.

The cabinet now in easy reach, Stone sorted his phone and passed it to him.

The screen lit Howell's face as he studied the photograph that Luke sent. He handed the phone back and looked at Stone.

'A wedding at the church,' Stone said. 'The groom didn't even realise he'd captured it. The newlyweds got back from honeymoon today and brought it in.'

Howell dipped his head in acknowledgement. 'I'd say that was a fortuitous find... As a parent, I see a sad and desperate measure to protect one's own.'

He removed his glasses and set them on the bed, then glanced over at Moraine. 'You might want to record this conversation. I probably won't get the chance to retell it.'

In her workbag she had a digital voice recorder. Taking a minute, she set it up on the overbed table and waited for his signal. He nodded at her to start recording. Then, like earlier, he gave his name, the date, where he was, and who he was with, which Stone and Moraine confirmed, stating their names and ranks.

He let his head rest back against the pillow. Then, in a voice that was made for recording, he began. 'You asked me why, and I told you I don't have the answer, but that was to evade telling you the truth. To something I did, the guilt of which I have carried for thirty-one years.

'I was twelve. Robin and I were on holiday with our parents. They'd hired a cottage close to the beach, and Robin and I would spend our days there throwing stones into the North Sea. This one particular day, I was trying to improve my skill and skim flat stones across the water. Robin was spoiling the fun, darting in front of my view every time I prepared to throw. I warned him he'd get hit if he kept doing it. He didn't take heed and kept deliberately blocking me. I had a flat, heavy pebble in my hand, one that would make better leaps out of the water. I pulled back my arm and threw it at him.

'He cried out in shock, and clutched the side of his temple, he was going to tell on me. I persuaded him to say he fell over instead with the promise of giving him my dragon Lego. His favourite game was "let's play hunt the dragons".

'When we got home, he fell asleep on the sofa. He vomited when Dad tried to wake him. Within minutes we were all in the car, heading to the hospital. Neither of our parents were aware at this point that he'd fallen and hit his head. They heard me tell this to the doctor when he asked if they'd been any injury.

'He died a few hours later from bleeding on the brain. He was five years old, and I killed him. Our parents lived the rest of their lives mourning him, not knowing his death was caused by their elder son.'

He closed his eyes tight, before continuing. 'Until now, the only other person I told this secret was to my wife. I told her on our honeymoon, along the banks of the Seine. She couldn't hide her disillusionment, even as she forgave me. I regretted it instantly. I had burdened her with this immoral version of me, forcing her to spend a life of worry, that one day I would weaken and confess to the killing of my brother, then five years ago to a second deplorable crime – burying a child to hide his body.

'I reasoned I was doing this to save his parents from knowing their son was dead – to give them false hope that he was out there somewhere alive.

'Over the last five years, I've been praying for Matt to be found. I wanted it despite the consequences to my children's lives and knowing how much it would hurt them.' His voice choked with emotion. 'I buried Matthew Lambert, knowing it was a heinous crime. I went with his parents, searching for him, hiding from them what I'd done, Knowing their complete devastation. Their perpetual hope. Knowing—'

Stone's startled voice alerted Moraine to a problem.

'Mr Howell, are you okay? James!'

Howell's limbs were jerking repeatedly, his eyes rolling back in his head. Stone hit the emergency call bell on the wall behind the bed, and moved out of the way as a nurse entered the room.

Within moments, more staff arrived. Moraine picked up the voice recorder, wondering if she held the last words James Howell would ever speak, as she and Stone left the room.

It was a harrowing story. The man was critically ill, and he had confessed to something he did as a child. The age of criminal responsibility is ten years old. At the time he was twelve. It hadn't been accidental to throw that rock. He had aimed for it to hit his brother. The intentions would not have been to kill him, but his actions caused his death.

He had allowed a mother and father to suffer for years while knowing the whereabouts of their missing child. They only had his word that the boy died on the second night after his abduction. That he simply stopped breathing. It wasn't proof that he didn't kill Matthew Lambert.

Moraine looked to Stone for direction. 'So, what now?'

Stone gave the smallest shake of his head. 'Now, we talk to his wife.'

SEVENTY-SEVEN

Moraine sat alone, watching the proceedings on a monitor.

In the interview room, Claire Howell sat mutely after hearing the recording of her husband's voice. Like him, she waived her right to a solicitor. DS Fay Hayden had taken a seat at the table, but a few inches away to help her merge into the background, her soft and bland appearance a contrast to DI Stone's physically large and strong presence. Claire Howell's eyes were on Stone.

'Do you wish to comment on what you have just heard?' he asked.

She breathed deeply, taking her time to respond.

'Do you have any idea, Inspector, what it's like to be married to someone you have to protect? To constantly have the worry that they might do something foolish? To be forever questioning their behaviour? It was not only the fact that Sam was a reincarnation of Matt, it was that the boys bore a resemblance to James's dead brother. That is what the last fifteen years of my life has been about. Protecting James from himself.'

Stone made a gesture at the portable recorder. 'Did he ever tell you he buried Matthew Lambert?'

She shook her head at him. 'No. Never.'

'Did he ever speak of the burial site where the child's remains were found?'

'No. Apart from mentioning it during my visit to him in hospital, that the remains of a child had been found on Elsbeth Crosby's farm.'

'Did you ever think the events might be related when Sam Jenkins went missing?'

An attentiveness flickered in her eyes, her brow furrowed. She took a moment to alter her expression, before composedly answering. 'When I first met Sam, I was alarmed at his likeness to Matt. I had to wonder if James found this a comfort and was the reason for taking this family in, and giving them a home.'

'And did this cause you to worry for Sam?'

'No. It caused me to worry for James. Matt was gone, and now Sam was there, as if he felt the only way to atone was to have a reminder of his brother.'

'So you never wondered at the similarity of the same thing happening again?'

'Similarity? Yes. Related? No,' she said with a light shake of her head. The diamonds in her ears dazzling. 'Looking for a connection, doesn't mean there's one there, Inspector.'

Stone stared at her for a second, his manner unhurried. He idly tapped his pen on the desk with a patient look in his eyes. His steady intake of breath, prolonging his response. 'You see,' he said softly, 'I think it is there. I think both boys went missing for the same reason. I think what your husband told you, you had to keep from coming out. It would mean the end of his career, his reputation ruined, the life you built together gone. And the only way to lessen this happening was to remove what reminded him most – Matt, then Sam. Isn't that right?' he stated.

She pressed back against the chair, turning her head from side to side.

Stone acknowledged the reaction. 'Mrs Howell is shaking her head in denial.'

She then sat still with her back straight, her head held high.

Stone took a moment to drink some water from a paper cup. Placing it to one side, he continued. 'Your husband found Matthew Lambert too late and buried him. He found the child had stopped breathing, and tried to revive him. You see, we now know that it couldn't have been your husband who took Matthew from his school on the third of October 2019 – it was a simple matter of checking criminal court cases to know where your husband was that day.

'He was Queen's Counsel for the case against Robert Williams, a man charged with the brutal murder of his wife and child. He was in court that day to hear the guilty verdict delivered by the jury.'

Her expression didn't alter.

Unfazed, Stone continued: 'Maybe he buried the child to protect you, or because he didn't want to believe it. What he didn't know was that he buried a piece of evidence along with the child. Something that belonged to you, given to you by Marley Lambert – as a gift for the birth of your firstborn, a son you named Philip. You told her it meant lover of horses. She said it was a terrible time, when at only a few weeks old, your son died from sudden infant death syndrome. That you and your husband never spoke about him afterwards – not even telling your future children that they once had a brother. It may have been this that triggered your husband's behaviour – to carry out this unlawful act – maybe he convinced himself the Lamberts were better off not knowing that their child was gone forever. Mrs Lambert has confirmed the validity of this finding.'

DS Hayden handed Stone an envelope, and Moraine realised this was the evidence Kennedy told her was found at the scene. The phone call Stone received in the car on the way to the hospital to see James Howell – was the win-win today.

Stone took out a set of photographs and laid them out so Claire Howell could see. 'I am showing Mrs Howell items numbered one-six-three to one-six-eight. Item one-six-three was found close to the remains of Matthew Lambert. It is a silver locket in the shape of a heart. Items one-six-four and one-six-five show water-damaged photographs of Claire Howell and an infant inside the locket. Item one-six-six to one-six-eight show where the links in the chain are broken, and the clasp still fastened. Mrs Howell, do you recognise this locket?'

She stared at the photographs for a long minute without commenting.

Stone prompted: 'Do you remember the swab that was taken?' Moraine imagined the tiny scrape of skin cells buried in the links of the chain as it was pulled from her neck.

She raised her eyes and stared at him. 'Finding my locket has no bearing on where it was found. Matt might have played with it. James could have had it. It's circumstantial evidence.'

Moraine wanted to find her repulsive, but couldn't. In that moment, her haughty beauty was compelling.

Stone didn't allow himself to be drawn. He continued as if nothing surprising had been said. 'Your husband must have known that it was you who had taken Matthew for him to go looking? You must have known the body was gone – that *somebody* had moved it – for the Mrs Crosby never to discover it? Was the farm a deliberate choice? Your modus operandi. Your behavioural pattern. To use the same location for Sam.

'You were a frequent visitor there, and would know where was best to hide someone. You couldn't use the milking shed again. It's gone now. So you had to choose somewhere different, and not easy to get to.'

She gave a shrug of her shoulders. 'As could any other visitor who went there. And I'd hardly call birthdays, Easter, Christmas frequent visits, but a normal amount of times to visit someone.'

Her answer brought a curious, almost sad, expression to his face. 'It's hard to imagine the life you had together. Your husband must have been in purgatory the whole time. To have on his conscience another child dead. Did you make a pact never to speak of it, to forget it ever happened and just leave it all behind...?'

'If you're referring to what is on that tape, Inspector, please don't imagine it was easy. I had to come to terms with what I knew. I have loved James through our entire marriage, despite his flaws...'

'His flaws...' he pondered aloud. 'Did his flaws lead him to returning Sam's top to the child's bedroom drawers?'

DS Hayden had the image ready and handed it to him. He placed the photograph on the table in front of her. 'This was taken by a newly married couple from their wedding car. He's wearing his top in this photograph.'

It had been this that had Moraine wanting to shut out all the bloody horribleness. How she had let Jo down so badly – thinking her unhinged, having auditory, visual hallucinations – when her son had been wearing exactly what she said.

She rejected the idea with a flick of the wrist. 'What a preposterous notion. I have no idea what you're talking about, or understand the relevance of Sam's top.'

'The relevance: Sam is wearing it in this photograph moments before he was taken. It was then found in the child's bedroom drawers. *Someone* put it there.'

'And you think it could be James?' She scoffed at the thought. 'It's absurd. If it was found in his home, why aren't you looking at his father instead? Maybe he put it there for to make Jo look guilty. James wanted her free of suspicion. The same as he knew how important it was to me that he help Jo, that I would find it impossible to bear if she wasn't set free, knowing she was innocent.'

'Is that why you chose to take Matthew Lambert when his

parents were away in London, so that suspicion didn't fall on their shoulders?'

'I have no comment, Inspector.'

Stone signalled to DS Hayden to hand him a second photograph. He placed it on the table. It was different to the one shown to her a moment ago. Sam on his own – by a low wall in the car park. This one told a different story.

Her mouth partly open, she went instantly still. The soft expulsion of air from her throat almost went unnoticed beneath the sound of Stone's voice.

'It was taken at the same time as Sam went missing. Look at the photograph, Mrs Howell. Can you identify the person in this photograph with Sam Jenkins?'

Moraine waited with bated breath. Something translated itself across her face. Fleeting expressions of an internal struggle. An intimate witness to her thoughts. There was dead silence in the room.

Then it came… A defeated cry of capitulation… released in a quivering sigh. She touched a trembling finger to the image, at a loss to dissemble the evidence in front of her, barely breathing her admission of guilt. 'It's me.'

She bowed her head.

Stone quietly acknowledged her plight. 'The hard part is over, Mrs Howell. Now we need the truth.'

Her eyes flew open, the expression on her face seeming almost affronted by the request. 'Sam was never going to be hurt! Whatever else you might think. He was outside by the entrance door. He was looking for his mummy. He let me help him over a wall, and he came with me happily.'

Stone's face was solemn, his mouth set firm. 'Did you follow them? Plan out this day? We didn't pick you up on CCTV.'

'A GPS tracker led me to where he'd be. I took a different route and used the gardener's jeep. I was parked in a lane that ran parallel to a school. I didn't want him to be afraid… I added a crushed sleeping tablet to some apple juice and gave it to him, ones my mother takes that makes her forget things. He took his top off in the car, he said he was hot.

'When we arrived he was sleeping. I didn't want to disturb him to put it back on him. I looked for something to keep him warm until I could come back for him.

'Only things started to go wrong. I didn't count on Sam not being seen by anyone. He was only meant to be there overnight, to have his parents think he was abducted, so that when he was found and I brought him back home, they'd want to leave Beckley House and start somewhere new, somewhere safe.

'I put his top in a drawer the night his drawings were found in the den. I was wanting to hand them over, only there was no one home. Jo and Pete were with you, making a public appeal. You must understand. I had to keep James safe. But Sam was never going to be hurt.'

'Can you hear yourself?' Stone asked, but didn't wait for an answer. He tapped the photograph hard with his finger. 'You took a child to keep your husband safe. There was *never* going to be a good time to bring him back.'

'No! It was just for one night. I was going to bring him back.'

'The same as you intended to do for Matthew, no doubt. When did you remove the tracker?'

The tip of her tongue appeared and moistened her lips. In her face a hint of defensiveness. 'When I showed DC Morgan to Jo's home, the Range Rover was parked outside. I waited until she was inside and then removed it.'

'And then what? You told your family that Sam was missing. You pretended to be shocked. Were you there when Matthew died?'

She visibly startled. Shock projecting her voice. 'It wasn't intended. Everything was fine. We left his school without anyone seeing. He was laughing that we were on an adventure.

He was asleep, the same as Sam was, when we arrived. I was checking the shed for a place where I could lay him down. I was gone only minutes... When I returned, he had stopped breathing in his sleep.'

Stone shook his head in disbelief. 'What made you this way? What led you so far from the moral compass?'

His words sparked an anger in her. 'Don't judge me, Inspector. I had to put loyalty before sentiment. Protect what James would have destroyed. Protect one's heritage above all else. My ancestors and the future ancestors of Beckley House deserve no less.

'Elsbeth's farm was a place that children loved. I never thought further than that. I wondered if it was then that I lost the locket... I couldn't go back to look. I couldn't bear to see him there.'

Stone's expression was strained. She had got to him with the unashamed, stark truth. She had put bricks and mortar over value of life.

'No. You just left him there for your husband to bury.' His voice was drained. 'I visited your mother before this interview began. She told me that as soon as you were of age, she moved out of Beckley House. Retiring to her childhood home. She found it had too many painful memories. She never understood how her husband fell to his death. Happening only hours after your horse was shot. Her health, she said, was never the same.'

For a moment it appeared she wouldn't respond. Then she lifted her chin and met his gaze defiantly. 'When my horse fell, I thought my father was running for the vet. I knelt weeping and praying for it to be all right. In minutes he returned – in a second Blu was gone – I never even got to say goodbye to her.'

The interview was ending. All that remained was to charge her.

Stone was jotting something down in a notepad. DS Hayden was putting photographs back into the envelope. Claire

Howell leaned across the table and tapped his forearm. He raised his head and met her eyes. Moraine could feel the intensity of her gaze even through the screen.

Her voice was soft, almost witchery, as she spoke to him. 'Think of me as you will. But when you have a responsibility that goes beyond your own existence, you do anything to keep hold of it. I held on. I didn't bend. Not even in the face of the end of my freedom.'

Moraine wondered how she managed to stay so poised. She considered for a moment whether Claire Howell was aware she would go to prison and be parted from her children. If she was aware her childhood paralleled that of her husband. Her every instinct was telling her that Claire had a hand in her father's death. It made sense of this fatal flaw in her character.

Stone stared back. He shook his head in dismay, sadness deep in his eyes and in his voice, as he said, 'I hope you take away with you, Mrs Howell, a regret for everything you have done. You took innocent children and made them suffer. Premeditated, so you could hold on to some grandiose beliefs that your existence to the world was important. That your mission was one of impunity for the sake of your ancestors and those that come after.'

He drew breath, and gazed at her. 'I almost pity you. You haven't realised yet that your good name no longer exists. You acted without integrity. And without it, your other values don't matter. You profess a love for your husband, yet your actions caused him to try to take his own life, to keep a child safe. If he'd succeeded, Sam would no longer be a concern. That's the reality, Mrs Howell... Nothing so fanciful as your spin. An inflated belief that you are special...

'You brought shame on your family name – to the history of Beckley House. That's what people will say about you when this day is done. There was nothing noble in what you did. It was all a sham.'

Under his pronouncement she was disintegrating slowly. Her eyes guarded so she couldn't give away her dismay. Moraine could see the energy going out of her. It would have poured out freely, had her social restraints taught her to express her feelings as well as it had accustomed her to hide them. It was hard to feel pity for someone who willing chose such methods for the sake of preserving one's name.

Then a habit of lifetime straightened her shoulders, lifted her head, eyes with hues of gold and a pigment of blue in the light, resplendent in her purple heather suit and diamonds in her ears, she didn't bend or give in. 'What's done is done, Inspector. The history of Beckley House will continue long after I am gone.'

Moraine took a last look on the screen at Claire Beckley-Howell and knew weeping inside her, making its claim, was an acceptance of Stone's truth. The good name of Beckley House was gone.

EPILOGUE

A fall of snow had changed the landscape from the one Jo remembered. In the summer it was green fields with grass up to her knees, fences marking out boundaries, and in the distance a woodland of trees. Where they once grew, bright orange diggers now stood, the only colour in the blanket of white.

It had been a glorious day – marred only and briefly by Sam's fear of the bees. The farm housed two wooden beehives over by a hedge, and Sam had been terrified by the intensity of buzzing as thousands of bees overlaid on top of each other.

She had not come to see where Sam had been found, preferring not to, though she was aware it was in the falling-down building along the track from the farmhouse. She hadn't wanted to spoil the one and only memory she had of being here, although that had to be compartmentalised into the parts she wanted to remember and the parts she wanted to forget.

She had visited the Crosby farm with Claire and Phoebe and Lottie. Sam played with all the cats, while she and Claire had tea with the lovely owner of the farm. And now she was here with Sam again – an outing suggested by Sam's psychologist, the visit arranged by Moraine, as a way to find out how much or how little he could remember.

She cast a look over at him and was reassured by his gleeful face as he scooped snow up in his hands, squeezing it through his woollen gloves. The scenery would look different to him, too. For him it was like a winter snowland, everywhere bright and beautiful.

The psychologist, over the course of the weekly sessions, had gained an insight into Sam's mental condition and identified that most of the trauma lay with the period he was separated from her, conscious of that fact for possibly hours at a time. Jo could testify to that, as he would call out for her in his sleep, thrashing the covers until she came to him and stroked the skin behind his ears till he settled.

When recalling the past, he spoke about Phoebe, Lottie and Dougie, and he also said Claire's name a few times, showing no sign of fear. It could be that he didn't remember her with fear, because, as she learned when Sam was discharged from hospital, his blood and urine samples taken on admission showed the presence of benzodiazepine.

The sessions would resume again after Christmas, which Jo didn't mind. She wanted their first Christmas in their new home to be a time when they could both completely relax. The two-up two-down, now permanent accommodation, was a stone's throw from Sam's school, and within walking distance of the hospital.

She wasn't ready yet, but when she felt mentally stronger, she would write to the head of HR and be upfront about her circumstances and her hope of starting a career. But for now, she was happy to watch the pennies, and just be there for whenever Sam needed her. His wellbeing was her therapy.

She had said this to the therapist she eventually saw, in their one and only long-awaited appointment. She'd already turned the corner by the time the help came, largely because of James and his counselling of her while he sat with her in Sam's room. He'd given her the courage to believe in herself again.

She struggled to equate the compassion he'd shown her to the inhumanity shown another mother. How can a man who spent his life following the law abandon his principles and become someone else? At a crossroads, he made a decision to save his wife by burying a child. Did he make that choice because it was too awful to face – the prospect of his children losing their mother? Stone said he was a man of contradictions. That she may hear things about him during the court case that wouldn't sit well. The media proclaimed him a man with two sides. His duplicity, unforgiveable.

When Moraine told her he had died, she felt a loss, and a sadness for Phoebe and Lottie. They'd moved in with their grandma, along with Bernice. With their mother set to face a long sentence, and with both parents gone from their lives, she frequently wondered how they would fare – hoping they were watching their favourite films and playing their favourite games together, and helping each other to overcome their grief.

During the last three months it was her awareness of others sadness that kept her from sinking into depression. Mrs Crosby, who she was seeing today, learning her home had been used to hide two little boys. The suffering of the other mothers and the heartaches that they faced. Marley Lambert's search for her son had finally ended, because sometimes they do find those who go missing. And Claire – Jo had seen the love she had for her daughters – no longer allowed to have the feel of them in her arms. When she thought about those mothers, she counted her blessings that she was still standing. And more than that, she was learning that every day was a fresh start. Sometimes a challenge, but more often giving something good.

Yesterday, the last day of term before the Christmas break, Sam's teacher let her know he was playing less by himself, and could make other children laugh by telling jokes. Jo had walked away on cloud nine, hugging the total feeling of happiness. She messaged Pete to let him know, and in return received a thumbs up.

Pete was the only person Sam didn't mention. It worried her that he didn't ask for him. Pete was getting on with his own life. Again through Moraine, she heard he had moved in with Chrissy Banner. Jo wished him well. She didn't love him, but neither did she hate him. And if it was in him to want to be a good father, she'd support it all the way. Her eyes were wide open now. Nothing would get past her to hurt Sam again.

'Jo!'

Her name was hollered from the open door of the farmhouse. Moraine was beckoning and shouting. 'Hurry up. They're all awake!'

She'd come to like Moraine, but knew they could never become friends. Once the court case was over, Moraine would make an exit strategy from their lives. Part of the role was knowing when the case closed, it was time to say goodbye. Her support had made Jo feel like she was ready to get back in the world and make new friends.

Without Sam being aware, Jo guided him towards the farmhouse door. Mrs Crosby was waiting there, wearing the same felt hat over her wispy hair as last time. She called out hello. Sam raised his head in surprise and recognition, his feet suddenly still in the snow. Jo held her breath, waiting for his reaction, praying this moment didn't go wrong.

From inside the house came the sound of a meow.

A wide grin appeared across Sam's face as he hurried into the house. Jo followed him in, stopping inside the door to give Mrs Crosby a small hug. On the wall behind her, Jo saw a small snapshot of history of her as a young woman. In a wide beekeeper's hat and long cloth coat, a leather belt tied around the waist and netting covering her face and shoulders. It was something to appreciate, before crossing the room to where Moraine was filling a teapot with boiling water.

She remembered something DI Stone said when showing the black crayon picture Sam had drawn. The analyst thought it might be a real place. The spiky blobs on the ground might be spiders.

They had never got to understanding any deeper meaning. Sam's psychologist didn't find it necessarily alarming. For some children, using dark colours is a form of stress relief. Given that Sam was in a den, playing 'hiding games', getting rid of feelings of fear can come through in artwork.

Jo wondered if it could be more than this. A mixture of the two opinions. And maybe the analyst was only right about it being somewhere real. Maybe he'd drawn a happy memory of his day at this farm. The shapes in the drawings, the ones thought to be spiders, weren't spiders at all. The little spiky black blobs were cats. And the figure standing with a hat on its head was Mrs Crosby.

A person to be unafraid of...

Moraine winked at her and Jo felt a sting of tears. Both Moraine and Mrs Crosby were in on it, and Jo could hardly contain the emotions she was feeling. Moraine elbowed her gently in the side and whispered a warning. 'They better be happy tears.'

Jo nodded that they were. How could they not be at seeing Sam so contented?

She couldn't wait to see his expression when he realised this wasn't just a visit. That somewhere in a box an eight-week-old kitten was waiting to be chosen to go home with a little boy.

A LETTER FROM LIZ

Dear reader,

I want to say a huge thank you for choosing to read *Nobody Saw Him*. If you did enjoy it, and want to keep up to date with all my latest releases, just sign up at the following link. Your email address will never be shared and you can unsubscribe at any time.

www.bookouture.com/liz-lawler

I hope you loved *Nobody Saw Him* and if you did I would be very grateful if you could write a review. I'd love to hear what you think. I was inspired to write this story after experiencing what can only be described a truly terrifying experience that happened one afternoon while visiting Covent Garden.

The area was packed with tourists crowding around stalls. I was holding my four-year-old daughter's hand and let go of her to get out my purse. It took only seconds to pay for the item. I put my purse away, and then I suddenly realised I couldn't see her by my side. In an instant every imaginable fear gripped hold of me. I started shouting out her name. People around me stood still. Like a Chinese whisper the information passed from one person to the next, and people began shaking their heads – nobody could see her. The fear bursting out of my chest lasted about three minutes, but in that time I convinced myself I would not find her. A woman's voice shouted out that a little girl was standing at a jewellery stall, and seemed on her own. It is a moment I will never forget – the sick fear if something had happened to her.

It is an experience that many parents face when their child wanders out of sight, the horrendous panic, until they see them again…

I love hearing from my readers – you can get in touch with me through social media. If I'm late in responding please never think it's because I don't care or that I've ignored your name. it's only because I'm absent for a little while writing.

Thanks,

Liz Lawler

facebook.com/liz.lawler.90
x.com/authorlizlawler
instagram.com/lizlawlerauthor

ACKNOWLEDGEMENTS

All the characters in *Nobody Saw Him* are fictional, as is the home Beckley House, though life events have influenced my writing. When I read this story back I see all the special inputs suggested by those who have helped. My deepest gratitude to all of you!

My editors, past and present, Cara Chimirri, Natasha Harding, Jayne Osborne, Ruth Jones, Jennifer Hunt, for teaching me along the way, and for squeezing out every last drop of each story with your gentle, guiding hands; the brilliant Bookouture publishing team who are a joy to work with.

Thank you for everything!

To Rory Scarfe, to Hattie Grunwald, and everybody else at The Blair Partnership always there to root me on so that I continue to grow.

Research is always a worry should I get it wrong. I am therefore deeply indebted to the experts for helping me get it right.

To Dr Peter Forster MBBS FRCA. My endless gratitude for giving your time once again! Once more you make it all better!

To Detective Inspector Kurt Swallow. I'm indebted to you for reading this through a policeman's eyes! I hope you'll be with me for the next one!

My thanks to Martyn Folkes, my brother-in-law Kevin Stephenson, and sister Bee Mundy for reading first draft! As ever, I owe a debt of gratitude to my husband, family and friends for waiting patiently in the wings for me to finish and press send.

To the loves and lights of my life: Lorcs, Katie, Alex, Harriet, Bradley, Darcie, Dolly, Arthur, Nathaniel. It's going to be a busy, wonderful time ahead with two more grandchildren coming along. I can't wait to be with you, and just be Mum again...

Finally, to you, my reader – THANK YOU for picking up my book! I hope you enjoy *Nobody Saw Him*.

PUBLISHING TEAM

Turning a manuscript into a book requires the efforts of many people. The publishing team at Bookouture would like to acknowledge everyone who contributed to this publication.

Audio
Alba Proko
Sinead O'Connor
Melissa Tran

Commercial
Lauren Morrissette
Hannah Richmond
Imogen Allport

Contracts
Peta Nightingale

Cover design
Eileen Carey

Data and analysis
Mark Alder
Mohamed Bussuri

Editorial
Jennifer Hunt
Charlotte Hegley

Copyeditor
Jane Eastgate

Proofreader
Jon Appleton

Marketing
Alex Crow
Melanie Price
Occy Carr
Cíara Rosney
Martyna Młynarska

Operations and distribution
Marina Valles
Stephanie Straub
Joe Morris

Production
Hannah Snetsinger
Mandy Kullar
Ria Clare
Nadia Michael

Publicity
Kim Nash
Noelle Holten
Jess Readett
Sarah Hardy

Printed in Dunstable, United Kingdom